D1599190

POSTCOLONIAL DURAS

POSTCOLONIAL DURAS

CULTURAL MEMORY IN
POSTWAR FRANCE

JANE BRADLEY WINSTON

First published 2001 by
PALGRAVE™
175 Fifth Avenue, New York, N.Y. 10010 and
Houndmills, Basingstoke, Hampshire, England RG21 6XS.
Companies and representatives throughout the world.

PALGRAVE is the new global publishing imprint of St. Martin's Press LLC Scholarly and Reference Division and Palgrave Publishers Ltd. (formerly Macmillan Press Ltd.).

ISBN 0-312-24000-7

Library of Congress Cataloging-in-Publication Data

Winston, Jane Bradley.
    Postcolonial Duras : cultural memory in postwar France / Jane Bradley Winston.
    p. cm.
    Includes bibliographical references and index.
    ISBN 0-312-24000-7
    1. Duras, Marguerite—Political and social views. 2. Duras, Marguerite—Criticism and Interpretation. 3.Colonies in literature. I. Title.

PQ2607.U8245 Z95 2001
843'.912—dc21

                                                                              2001021792

A catalogue record for this book is available from the British Library.

Design by autobookcomp

First edition: December 2001
10 9 8 7 6 5 4 3 2 1

Printed in the United States of America.

FOR ERIK, PETER, SHANNON, AND ERIN

CONTENTS

Acknowledgements   ix

Abbreviations   xiii

Introduction   1

1. The Rise of the Spectacle: Critical Practice in
   a Modern Age, 1950-1958   9

2. Going International: *Créoles,* Criticism, and
   the French Colonial Subject, 1960-1996   53

3. Rationalizing Empire: Scientific Management,
   Colonial Education, and Cultural Placing   93

4. Holocaust and Revolution: Communist
   Ethics, Lol V. Stein, and *La Douleur*   123

5. Transatlantic Connections: Wright's *Black Boy*
   and Duras's *Colon* Girl   151

6. Diaspora and Cultural Displacement: Linda
   Lê and Tran Anh Hung   183

Notes   213

Works Cited   225

Index   245

ACKNOWLEDGMENTS

This book was long in the making. In its course, many colleagues and friends lent me their support. I owe a special debt to two exceptional women: Toril Moi and Françoise Lionnet. Toril Moi, my most generous and demanding dissertation director, taught me the virtues of intellectual rigor and lucid writing. She believed in this project from the beginning and taught me to believe in myself. She is my first intellectual guide and professional example; for her, my respect and gratitude are boundless. Françoise Lionnet, my former colleague and my mentor throughout the period of this project's revision, gave generously of her friendship, read this book in all its versions, and proffered her advice. With her I have sustained my most consistent dialogues on its subject: to her I offer my deepest thanks.

I thank Fredric Jameson for telling me to take my time on this book, Alice Yeager Kaplan for inviting me to find my own style, V. Y. Mudimbe for his intellectual guidance, and Michèle Longino for her careful reading. I am grateful to have had the consistent support and counsel of my colleagues, past and present, in the Department of French and Italian at Northwestern University. I thank Scott Durham for believing it this project and giving it a thorough critical reading, Bernadette Fort for her steady encouragement, Michal Ginsburg, for her steadfast dedication, Jean Mainil for his infusions of humor, Jerry Mead for his understanding and support, Bill Paden for his careful copyediting, Alessia Ricciardi for her salutary laughter, Sylvie Romanowski for her useful comments, Mireille Rosello for her enthusiasm, Tilde Sankovitch for her remarkable grace, good cheer, and smart counsel, and Davide Stimilli for his kind words. Over the years, many others have read sections of this book. I extend a particular thanks to John McCumber for reading its philosophical sections.

Much of my thinking on this book developed in the contexts of seminars, colloquia, and conferences. I am thankful to Françoise Lionnet for selecting me to participate in the NEH summer institute that she directed at Northwestern in 1995, "Identities, Communities, and Cultural Practices," which provided an ideal forum for rethinking my project in the frame of postcolonial and Francophone studies. I also extend my thanks to all of the panel organizers who have given me the opportunity to present my work over the years and to the audiences whose questions helped clarify my thought. I thank especially Lynn Higgins for having me on her panel, "Colonial Hexagon: Remembering Empire and Decolonization" at the Twentieth-Century French Studies Colloquium in Amherst, to audience members Mary Jean Greene and Alice Yeager Kaplan, whose positive reactions to my paper invigorated my research, to Stella Harvey and Kate Ince for allowing me to share my work with a European audience at the Duras Society in London, to Walter Putnam for permitting me talk about Duras's cat at the 1999 French Studies Colloquium at the University of Pennsylvania, to Panivong Norindr for his supportive and challenging remarks, and to Jack Yeager, for inviting me to participate on his panel on Indochina at the 2000 meeting of the Conseil International d'études francophones in Tunisia, thus giving me an opportunity to benefit form the feedback of Francophone scholars from around the world.

This book has benefited from several women's reading groups. I am particularly grateful to Karen Pinkus and Sharon Achinstein for our tiny reading group, it intense discussions, and their gargantuan effect on my thinking. And I thank Betsy Erkkila, Hollis Clayson, Françoise Lionnet, Susan Manning, and Sandra Richards for their close readings and useful advice. I offer heartfelt gratitude to my students as well, especially those in courses on Duras and on Indochina, for their keen interest in these subject matters, their challenging interrogations, and their many insightful remarks.

Over the years, I have benefited from funding from several institutions and fellowships. In 1991, travel grants from the Graduate Program in Literature and the Graduate School at Duke University funded my research stay in Paris. In summer 1994, a Northwestern University Research Grant funded my return to Paris to continue that work. Both trips were crucial to my project: during the first, Edgar Morin gave me an interview and put me into communication with the late philosopher Dionys Mascolo, who had a profound and lasting impact on me, my way of thinking, and this book. Thanks to him, I was able to interview the poet Claude Roy and historian Jacques-Francis Rolland and, on my return, to meet Marguerite Duras. In 1996-1997, a fellowship at Northwestern's Alice Berlin Kaplan Humanities Center gave me the time to complete research into areas the previous summer's NEH Institute had opened up for me and complete the writing of significant sections of this book.

I extend my thanks to my editor, Kristi Long, for her confidence and intelligence, Roee Raz for his efficiency and congeniality, Karin Bolender for her great copyediting, and Donna Cherry, for her smart, speedy and surprisingly good-humored production editing. I am indebted to North-western University's Interlibrary Loan's Cheryl Anderson, Liz Fraser, and

Victoria Zahrobsky, who got rare books to me in record times, and to the
reference department's William A. McHugh for teaching me internet
routes to cinematic information that greatly expanded the richness of this
study. I also thank the office administration staff in the Department of
French and Italian at Northwestern, Jolie Cordero and Tom Sweda, for
their crucial support.

Others have offered other forms of support in the years of this book's
production. I am grateful to M. Roger Casey for lending me calm quarters
outside of Paris that provided eminently conducive to reflection and for
sharing his memories of Paris under the Occupation. I thank Toril Moi for
introducing me to Michèle Le Doeuff and Marcelle Marini over dinner
one Paris evening. I thank Dominique Drapier for her help in transcribing,
from nearly inaudible tapes, my interviews with the rue Saint-Benoît
intellectuals. I thank Margaret Sinclair for her excellent help in translating
those interviews. Finally, I offer my deepest appreciation to my family, my
mother, my brothers, and especially my children, who had the unenviable
task of growing up with this project, but who managed, even in its most
challenging moments, to give me the gift of their unconditional and loving
support.

A very early version of chapters 1 and 2 appeared as "Forever Feminine:
Marguerite Duras and Her French Critics," in *New Literary History* 24. 2
(May 1993): 467-82. I gratefully acknowledge permission from the follow-
ing to reprint excerpts from the works indicated:

Editions Gallimard for Marguerite Duras, *Un Barrage contre le Pacifique*,
copyright © Editions Gallimard, 1950, and Dionys Mascolo, *Le
Communisme*, copyright © Editions Gallimard, 1950; Editions Bernard
Grasset for Jean-Jacques Annaud, *L'Amant*, copyright © Editions Bernard
Grasset, 1992; Editions de Minuit for Michèle Porte and Marguerite
Duras, *Les Lieux de Marguerite Duras*, copyright © Les Editions de Minuit,
1977; Pascal-Emmanuel Gallet and the Ministère des Affaires étrangères
for *L'Œuvre cinématographique de Marguerite Duras*, © Ministère des
relations extérieures, 1984; Le Monde for "A propos de la conférence de
Hot Springs," *Le Monde* (1 February 1945); Lire for Pierre Assouline, "La
vraie vie de Marguerite Duras," *Lire*, October 1991, 49-59 copyright ©
Lire; Le Nouvel Observateur for Frédérique Lebellay, "Marguerite retrouvée,"
Le Nouvel Observateur, 24-30 May 1990, 59-63, © Le Nouvel Observateur;
Time, Inc., for three entire pages; pages 118 and 119 from their 16 March
1953 issue and page 110 from 23 February 1953 © 1953 Time Inc,
Editions Julliard for Linda Lê, *Les Evangiles du crime*, copyright ©
Editions Julliard, 1992. Photographic reproductions of the three review
pages from *Time* magazine courtesy of the Newberry Library, Chicago, the

photograph of Marguerite Duras in 1955 courtesy of Roget-Viollet, the photograph of "Riga and her son Nirgat" courtesy of Astrid Bergman Sucksdorff, two photographs of Jane March courtesy of Jean-Jacques Annaud, the photograph of Alain Vircondelet, copyright © F. Ferranti/ Agence Opale, the photograph of Ho Chi Minh courtesy of Keystone Pressedienst, and the photograph of Linda Lê courtesy of Les Publications CondéNast, S.A., Kate Barry, and Vogue Magazine.

ABBREVIATIONS

Page references appear parenthetically preceded by author name and shortened or abbreviated source titles, as needed. Those that are cited especially frequently, or that might cause confusion, are preceded by the abbreviations listed below. For Duras, I give reference to the French source first, followed, without source abbreviation, by the English translation. Readers will find the English translation listed after the French source in Works Cited. When I have amended a translation, I have added the abbreviation "mod." (modified) after the English source page reference. References to other French texts are either to the original, in which case the translation is mine, or to the published translation. In the first case, Works Cited lists only the French text used; in the second case, it lists first the English translation used and then the original publishing information.

A2	Annaud, *L'Amant*
A	Duras, *L'Amant*
ACN	*L'Amant de la Chine du Nord*
UB	*Un Barrage contre le Pacifique*
LD	*La Douleur*
MDM	*Marguerite Duras à Montréal*
MR	"Marguerite retrouvée"
MA	"Mes Amours, c'est moi"
RLVS	*Le Ravissement de Lol V. Stein*
LP	*Les Parleuses*
LC	Mascolo, *Le Communisme*
AEM	Mascolo, *Autour d'un effort de mémoire*
ARSB	Mascolo, "Autour de la rue Saint-Benoît"
IP	Mascolo, "Un itinéraire politique"

Introduction

*The politics of knowledge often lies in the structure
of our ignorance. . . . Ignorance, like knowledge, is a
manufactured product: it is important to know why
'we' know certain things, and don't know others.*
—*Robert N. Proctor, 1995*

Several years ago, I envisaged this project as a monograph on Duras. I
believed then, as I do now, that Duras's ultimate political and scriptural aim
was not (simply) to define a "feminine subject" or undo patriarchy, but to
destroy the cartesian subject and its bourgeois, capitalist, colonial, and
patriarchal social orders, thus clearing the way for a new social form whose
contours will become visible only as they come into being. Then, as now, I
was also convinced that all creative work can be properly understood only
when considered in relation to the contexts from which it emerges, the
questions to which it responds, and the contradictions with which it
wrestles. So, with psychoanalytic feminist accounts dominating our perception of Duras, I set out to examine her work in the light of those
contexts critics had previously ignored, especially her colonial cultural
background and postwar politics, in hopes of showing, among other things,
that Duras enlists Lacan in the service of Marx.

But if I was certain of the importance of Duras's contexts, I misgauged
their force. I thought I would use their insights to illuminate Duras:
instead, they entered the scene, upended my project, and stole the show.
This inversion called to my mind the similar transformation of Beauvoir's
mid-1940s autobiographical project. Setting out to write her life history,
she discovered that to do so required understanding what it meant to be a
woman under Western patriarchy. The more she researched women's

contexts and sought answers to questions they raised, the larger those contexts loomed. In the end, rather than an autobiography, she wrote *The Second Sex,* an essay on patriarchal representations and the social construction of "woman," from her "place" as a white bourgeois intellectual woman in mid-twentieth century France. Similarly, having set off to understand Duras's creative project, I found that that would require understanding what it meant to be a woman whose sense of identity and place in the world were shaped exactly when and where they were and who wrote in the times and places she had. And the more I inquired into her contexts, the more surely my monograph became this cultural and literary history of twentieth-century France, written with a particular eye to, and "as if" looking out from Duras's "place" in it. Although unanticipated, this transformation was both felicitous and oddly in line with Duras's politics: it gave rise to a dialogue between Duras and her contexts that produced, as she might have predicted, a new understanding of both. In hindsight, Duras's "place" was ideally suited for such a study. It spans nearly the entire twentieth century, from the colonial to the postcolonial rule era, moves around and across French colonial geographies and borders, from lower-class and hinterland colonial borders to the most authoritative regions of France's intellectual and literary fields.

From the beginning, Duras's case presented paradoxes and contradictions that piqued my passion to investigate. How to explain her stellar success? How to account for the gap between many critics' lack of esteem for her literary talents and her status as, to recall Selous's accurate assessment, postwar France's grande dame of belles lettres? How to understand the chasm between her lower class and culturally borderzone colonial provenance and the received image of her as a French *bourgeoise?* How to read the apparent abyss between her radical left-wing journalism and her purportedly apolitical or solely psychoanalytic-feminist creative œuvre? The chasm between the widely held view of her textual politics as feminist or nonexistent and her claims of life-long marxism and its originary and abiding relation to her creative work? What to make of the dismissal of her political claims as uninformed, unenlightened, and/or inauthentic? The violently misogynist critical attacks on her? How to comprehend the inconsistencies and contradictions in her own statements and positions? What to make of the staunchly polarized patterns of her critical reception; her vilification in some quarters and the equally over-blown adulation in others? How to understand the fact that our binarily structured critical battles over Duras have consistently neglected an entire gamut of narrative threads and textual voices? Worse still: that these elements regularly refer to the same colonial, immigrant, and otherwise marginalized populations that were being excluded from French social discourse in the same decade in which Duras first attracted critical attention and we first gave her mass public visibility: the 1950s?

As finding answers to such queries persistently referred me to the 1950s, they established that decade as one of this book's central objects of study. The responses I discovered therein confirm the growing scholarly consensus that the 1950s continue to shape our debates and perception. In the mid-1990s, Alice Jardine suggested that the question "progressive scholars" worried with the deep structures of the 1990s must put to the "First American Fifties" (1945-1955) is: *"How did this country get from Hiroshima and Nagasaki to Disneyland in ten years?"* (108). On my reading, this question concerns the role of representation in the construction of our national historical narratives and national identity. As Benedict Anderson shows in *Imagined Communities*, while nations emerge from bloody events that break continuity and produce rupture, the national historical narratives that guarantee our sense of national identity require serial continuity. This continuity is achieved by way of a strange dialectics of ellipsis, in which the "tropological" function of signifiers (words), especially nouns, enables us to *both* forget *and* remember the events constituting our national historical series. In that process, the actual historical events, the violence, blood, killers and killed are forgotten and the *names of the events* are recalled, in the language of the victor, as the glorious events in its history. Emptied of their gory material and not-yet-national entrails, nouns such as "la Saint-Barthélemy," to recall Anderson's example, or "Hiroshima and Nagasaki," in Jardine's, take their place in the series of historical events that stand together, arm-in-arm and back into time, as the events in French or U. S. cultural memory.

The questions about Duras that I put to mid-century France are of the same nature as Jardine's: How did Duras, a lower-class *colon* offspring, Communist activist, and revolutionary intellectual of the groupe de la rue Saint-Benoît, come to stand in our perception as *Duras*, a woman writer obsessed solely with sentimental issues, especially and increasingly, sexuality and desire? In whose service and to whose gain did this transition take place? What is the social function of the icon *Duras?* What is its part, if any, in the silencing of disruptive cultural, political, and historical meanings in Duras's work and more broadly in the postwar French cultural and literary fields? In the separation of left-wing politics from intellectual work that took place in France, as Ellen Schrecker showed it did in the United States, "as if" spontaneously? What part did literary critics play in the construction of such icons, which emerged in the 1950s "as if" to form a specifically postwar and modern-era repertory of *lieux de mémoire*, in Pierre Nora's term; sites of collective imaginary identification *and* productive objects of cultural consumption? What part does these mass-circulated icons play in shaping modern French cultural and national identity?

But if the 1950s have an important place in this book, they are only one moment in the longer durée of two (at least) century-long dynamics that form, along with Duras, its principle objects of study. The first of these dynamics are the *representational efforts* designed and deployed to conserve (or to destroy) the French colonial order and its subject. The second dynamic is *displacement*, whose intentional forms assured nineteenth-century France's colonial implantation, but (this books shows) whose more accidental and directionally inversed twentieth-century manifestations increasingly subverted the French colonial subject and its cultural orders to produce their ongoing "Francophone shifts." In both dynamics, Duras had an important place. A colonial-era part of the century's inversed, colony-to-métropole *displacement*, she established herself within its *representational* dynamics before the war. At its end, she became an active participant, on the side of opposition, in the postwar's representational struggles whose ultimate stake was the French cultural subject. From 1950 on, Duras was postwar France's principal literary representer of *Indochina*, the discursive construct that Norindr believes shaped the deep structuring and generative instance of the French colonial subject. In the Francophone transformation these dyamics helped produce, Duras had a part similar to the one Elvis had at the same time in the United States: that of a crucial intermediary between, in her case, the French cultural field and its Francophone successor.

From Duras's thus multiply central place, this book maps the Francophone shift in three distinct movements. Its first two chapters reconstruct the history of *Duras*. The first examines Duras's personal and political self-positionings in the 1950 *Un Barrage contre le Pacifique,* the dialectical creation of *Duras* as a tool of response, containment, and success, and that icon's emergence, 1950-1958, onto domestic and international cultural consumer markets. Chapter 2 traces *Duras's* trajectory from its 1960s U. S. introduction in *Yale French Studies* to its 1992 appearance on the global screen in Annaud's *The Lover.* It examines Duras's relation to George Sand and others, her treatment of (her own) colonial cultural aspects in *Le Ravissement de Lol. V. Stein, India Song, Son Nom de Venise dans Calcutta désert, Le Camion, L'Amant,* and beyond, her lacanian and neolacanian feminist receptions, the early 1990s battle for the right to define her meanings, and that battle's 1992 resolution. Together, these chapters show *Duras* to be not the creation of literary critics alone, but the product of the dialectical interplay between Duras and her work, critical accounts of them, and her response to those accounts. Although they do not understand

Duras as a "false" image one could tear off to reveal the "true Duras" behind, they do perceive it as an ideological product; as partly shaped, that is, by the dominant conservative interests in the 1950s French social field. Rather than pure artifice, they establish *Duras* as partial, inaccurately stressed, and profoundly distorted. Imbued with that form of falseness that characterizes the incomplete, this icon appears as it does because it shows what it does and hides what it does; encourages us to remember and forget what it does; in short, because, in Mr. Proctor's apt epigraphical phrase, it structures the patterns of our knowledge and ignorance as it does.

Next, chapters 3-5 begin the process of recuperating and incorporating into our perception of Duras the exclusions effectuated in *Duras's* creation. Chapter 3 reads "together" Duras's autobiographical narrative of her formative Indochina years and the discourses of colonial education planning and reform of that same era. Where, it asks, would these discourses have encouraged a child of Duras's profile to position herself psychically? Chapter 4 begins "as if" from that psychic position and studies its displacement by the mid-century war traumas. First, it examines the "communist ethics" Duras and her closest interlocutors elaborated at the postwar, as announced in Robert Antelme's camp testimonial, *L'Espèce humaine*, and elaborated in Dionys Mascolo's philosophical treatise, *Le Communisme*. Then, in their light, it reads two crucial Duras texts: the linchpin of the psychoanalytic account of her work, *Le Ravissement de Lol. V. Stein*, and the alleged war journal, *La Douleur*. Building on the previous chapter, this one asks: what is the relation between Duras's cultural background, her postwar psychic and political realignments, and her creative project? Next, opening up our cartographic frame onto the transatlantic axis, Chapter 5 explores Duras's diasporic connections to the African-American writer Richard Wright. It studies, comparatively, their critical histories, reads *Un Barrage* in the light of *Black Boy*, documents her debt to Wright, and reveals his primary enabling place in the Francophone literary and cultural shifts.

Turning to that shift itself, chapter 6 takes the measure of its displacements "as if" on the face of *Indochina*. In its first chapter, this book studied Duras's introduction, in *Un Barrage contre le Pacifique*, of cultural difference and oppositional politics into the colonial representation *Indochina* and their silencing. Now, it concludes by showing that their "disappearances" notwithstanding, those differences and politics did not cease playing behind the scenes; in the dark. Indeed, midway between colonial writers like Malraux and the late 1980s-1990s Vietnamese diasporic artists, Duras's work assured the articulation between their colonial and Francophone positions. This chapter maps the responses Duras's *Indochina* has elicited from two artists of the Francophone Vietnamese diaspora, writer Linda Lê and filmmaker Tran Anh Hung. Its fundamental interrogation is: Do these responses extend Duras's challenge to the colonial ideological construct, *Indochina*, or not? If so, in which areas? If not, what does their retreat suggest? What is the relation between the transformation of this representation and the imaginary structures of the French cultural subject? And most broadly, what appears to be, based on this limited evidence, the function of at least this mass-circulated representation in the postwar and postcolonial rule era's modulating phases of consumer capitalism?

For me, writing this book confirmed the wisdom of the primary insight Duras and those around her took away from the 1940s war traumas: the need to think in inclusionary (both/and) terms. This insight is clearly consistent with her own positioning: born and raised on multiple borders, she ceaselessly identified herself with the marginalized; wrote from and to the borders. For half a century, we tried to pin her down, categorize her, determine once and for all precisely where she belongs. And for half a century, she confounded our efforts with her inconsistencies, positional inadequations, contradictions, permutations. On hindsight, the problem was in many ways ours: for she did not cease being what she always was—a complex, contradictory, and mobile composite, a woman of the borderzones, or to borrow Lionnet's term, a product and producer of *métissage*. As such, I suspect, she will be most adequately understood in all of her unresolvable ambiguity when we manage to leave behind our oppositional thinking; cease and desist from seeking to make her *either* political *or* not, *either* feminist *or* marxist, *either* revolutionary *or* reactionary, for instance. In the spirit of a first endeavor in that direction, this book seeks, in all of gestures, to undo divisions, make connections, identify complements, and establish dialogue.

On the broadest level, it reads across disciplinary and theoretical boundaries, borrowing tools from economics to interpret the discourse of colonial ideology and education, from social theory and cultural anthropology to illuminate psychic positions, from psychoanalysis to read literary and filmic texts. While its repertory of theoretical tools reflects my own desire to map between realms, it was also shaped by the shifting demands of the texts under consideration and the questions or problems they presented for resolution. Thus, it combines certain of Bourdieu's social theoretical notions, including field, competition, and *habitus*, with cultural anthropological notions, historical, economic, and colonial educational research to map Duras's profoundly complex and contradictory borderzone position and its relation to, for instance, the also, but differently, borderzone places of Wright and Lê as well as the centrist position of Sartre. Or, to introduce movement and temporarily onto its scene, it combines this interlevel mapping (social, psychic, textual) with the African American notion of "call and response." This permitted me to track the dialectical interplay between generations and cultural formations and to rethink the literary notion of "intertextuality" in terms of competition and struggle, cultural placing and displacement, conservation and change.

More narrowly, in addition to moving between Duras's case and the broader French cultural and literary fields, this book looks across the borders separating Duras from her critics to trace their dialectical creation of *Duras*. Developing new readings of Duras's work in relation to *Duras's* exclusions, it offers them not as substitutes or replacements for *Duras*, but as complements and partial completions that must be put into dialogue with what we already know about Duras (that is, largely, with *Duras*) so that, from their dialectical interplay, there might emerge a more adequate account of her project. Similarly, it reads Duras across the U.S. and French borders, discovering a decisive Wrightean influence that must be placed alongside the connections already known and those yet to be discovered. But while this study looks across generations and cultures to chart contemporary responses and extensions of Duras work, myriad others undoubtedly remain to be discovered. Moreover, it is clear to me that each of the routes this analysis follows precluded its taking other paths, that each of its readings could have been conducted differently, each connection articulated elsewhere or at another moment, yielding other and more compelling or important insights. But if my years of "living with Duras" left me with one truly transformative insight, that is that the task of understanding (and thus of understanding her work or any other) is not only daunting, but beyond the grasp of any one human being. Indeed, it demands exactly the kind of work Duras herself believed in, profoundly, as the only possible route to meaningful thought or radical social change: collective intellectual work, work in common, dialogue between us, between our discoveries and our insights.

Once in the early 1980s, Duras despaired that any of the revolutionary textual or practical activities in which she or others had engaged since the midcentury could ever lead, as they had hoped, to a new social form. By then, it looked to her, as she says to Dominique Noguez in 1984, as if the West had moved too far from the rest of the world; as if that most crucial of connections between the former colonizers and colonized could no longer be made by anything short of an earth-shaking world historical event, in which, here at least, she finds the only hope for a more egalitarian tomorrow:

The world is lost. It didn't work. It is finished (and I hope it is). We must rejoin this vacillation of the world in horror, in misery—never has one seen as many deaths by starvation. We are not contemporaneous with our world.

We need a catastrophe to equalize it all. The hegemony of the West is finished . . . The only way to rejoin the world, to rejoin misery, to get out of the shame/ infamy *[honte]* that we are in, is to rejoin the world. Not in a mechanical or messianic fashion . . . but in a cosmic way: let it change. Let perdition spread itself out everywhere *[que ça change. Que la perdition se répande partout]* ("La dame," 43).

And yet, overcoming that despair, Duras continued, much to her credit it seems to me, to write in the service of social change until her death. It thus seems only fitting that a book that began as a monograph on her work should end its self-presentation by inviting readers to join it in dialogue, to rethink twentieth-century French culture and her place in it, and, perhaps, to help modulate what Proctor calls the "structures of our ignorance" in ways that will expand and enhance those of our knowledge.

Jane Bradley Winston
Evanston, June 2001

Chapter 1

The Rise of the Spectacle: Critical Practice in a Modern Age, 1950-1958

*The imposition of a term and its connotation is
often the stake in a power struggle.*

—Anna Boschetti

In 1958 Gaëtan Picon suggested that in speaking of Duras's writing, "one must speak of an art of the call" (309). Picon's counsel was apt but tardy. Critics had been speaking about Duras for eight years by then. Rather than elucidate her writing's "call" as he apparently had in mind, however, their talk was working, by design or not, to contain its full signifying range. Duras had been noticed by critics in 1950, in the midst of France's postwar nation rebuilding, its attempt to reassert itself as an imperial power, and its domestic reordering as a modern consumer society. That year, she wrote against French colonialism from her place in French society—near the bottom of its colonial hierarchies, where she had been raised in Indochina, and in the margins of its continental bourgeois form, where she had moved in the early 1930s. Her most authoritative critics responded efficiently: containing her meanings within the sole bounds of French literature and culture, they silenced her political and cultural challenges. In the process, they created and put into mass circulation a representation I term *Duras*. Shaped by pressures of then-rising procolonial and bourgeois interests, *Duras* blocked perception of the culturally eccentric and politically oppositional range of Duras's call, thus mitigating and forestalling her work's socially transformative potential. Indeed, this was the case even with

Picon himself, who no sooner posed his apt words than he went on to develop his reading along the lines of what was already, in 1958, the hegemonic "cultural containment" trend in Duras criticism.

The efficacy of the cultural icon *Duras* emerges in the light of Pierre Bourdieu's social theoretical account of field competition and change. As Bourdieu discusses them in *Sociology in Question* and elsewhere,[1] field dynamics resemble those of the African-American tradition of "call and response." To enter any competitive field, he contends, one must respond to its most authoritative issues, trends, and demands, if only to contest them. It follows, then, that to open a given field to voices of other cultures or younger generations, that field must already contain within it "sites" that fledgling players are able to recognize and to which they can respond. Such "sites of response" might be situated in the Symbolic register of consciousness and language (as characters, themes, scenes, signifiers) or in the unconscious, or Imaginary *(imaginaire)* register of unconscious fantasies, desires, and bodily relations (as form, syntactic dislocations, rhythms, and so on). The various elements comprising a corpus's full range of calls—hence, the full range of sites to which new players might respond so as to enter into the competition in that field—are recognized or silenced, valued or devalued by critics and commentators who stand between the writer and prospective readers and "interpret" her work for them. In Duras's case, 1950s critics silenced her creative work's non-French cultural and left-wing revolutionary political calls, including the anticolonial and anti-imperialist.[2] The effect of their neglect and devaluation was far-reaching: it helped maintain the repression of political and cultural difference in the French literary and cultural fields, thus protecting them from the threats of broad-based and still more radical responses to and extensions of that specific range of Duras's "call."

Thus, far from the narcissistic product of Duras's sole desire for control or self-promotion, from even before its first emergence, *Duras* was a product of struggle. The 1950 players who had their way in defining *Duras* in culturally and politically conservative terms were the most powerful in the 1950s French critical field. With their win in the *Duras* critical subfield, they established themselves as the hegemonic instances to which the writer Duras was obliged to respond. Their victory thus set in motion a dialectical interplay between their analyses and her creative writings that proceeded, under changing historical and social conditions and amidst modulating relations of power, from book to critical account to each subsequent authorial riposte or strategy of response (the next text, or interview statement, for instance) to the end of her life. Henceforth, *Duras* stood as the object and the subfield of struggle on which players including the writer, her creative works, and interview statements, as well as her commentators, critics, reviewers, and their analyses competed for the right to define the legitimate discourse of *Duras*. A variable yet coherent visual and discursive constellation, *Duras* is comprised of photographic images (of varying and aging faces, poses, clothing, gestures, friends, family, homes), textualized geographical and Imaginary places, topoi, textual and semantic gaps, spaces, rhythms, silences, music, characters, ambiance; certain texts, films, and novels, and certain narratives within them. *Duras* is the matrix through which we know, or to borrow her more accurate term, *"croient savoir"* or *"believe* we know" ("L'Inconnue," 92) Duras and through which we construe her texts, her films, her theater, their meanings. If it was constantly susceptible to triage, selection, interpretation, and partial readings, *Duras* nonetheless remained remarkably consistent in its fundamental lines from 1950 until at least the early 1990s.

Produced at the early 1950s nexus of France's moribund colonial order and nascent modern consumer capitalist society, *Duras* went on to become one of France's widest and longest circulating cultural icons. In a nation where, as Pierre Nora and Benedict Anderson taught us, images of intellectuals and writers rank among the most crucial cultural places in which the community imagines itself, *Duras* became one of the most omnipresent places in which the mid- to late-twentieth-century French community did so. As one of the most productive sites on the domestic and international French culture markets, it came to stand as a site of transmogrification. It functioned simultaneously as the place in modernizing French culture where Duras's cultural and political differences were assimilated and made to produce, and as one cultural nodal point where the French community's self-imaging morphed into cultural, symbolic, and financial capital. *Duras's* cultural and capitalist efficacy derive from its redoubled structure: from its incipience, *Duras* has foregrounded narratives of desire and sexuality and repressed those relating to the writer's cultural and political differences. Incompletely repressed, however, these differences remained to inflect *Duras's* aspect. In fact, it is they that permit *Duras* to play with feminine artifice and deceit, myths of surface and depth, and the productive efficacy of lies and hidden truths. It is also they that imbue *Duras* with the ambiguous, edgy, vaguely exotic aspect that drives our desire to know, explore, excavate, unveil—that drives, in other words, the critical projects that assure, in their turn, *Duras's* reproduction and survival. Whether it enrages or enthralls, excites or exasperates us, *Duras* has captivated us, and it continues to make us speak. As Alain Vircondelet found, "What is astonishing, is that it [the dead body of Duras, her œuvre, her life, its/her places] exercises an intense vibration that gives us the desire to write, to better understand, to know more still about it" (*MD*, 189). All evidence corroborates Vircondelet's impression: *Duras* does fascinate, even in death. But, it behooves us to ask, to what political, cultural, and social ends? What self-image does *Duras* reflect back to the French "community"? What history does it permit that community to tell itself? What history does it prevent from being told? What truth claims does it support? What exclusions does it sustain?

The following pages work to respond to these questions by resituating *Duras* in relation to the social, cultural, and historical contexts from which it emerged. Because it is a product of selection and exclusion, recontextualizing this icon sheds light on the tools with which it was produced, the exclusions its creation required, the stereotypes that shored up its production and popular acceptance, and the role it continues to play in guaranteeing the psychic structures of the French colonial subject. Most locally, this process, historicizing *Duras,* reveals the crucial transitional place that Marguerite Duras and her work occupied between the French cultural and literary fields and their Francophone successors, and lays bare the part professional readers had in preventing her work from realizing its intermediary role. But it also shows that under the pressures of rising immigration and beyond even Duras's own demonstrable failure, her work managed to dodge the critical hold and prevail in the end.

More broadly, historicizing *Duras* uncovers the crucial diasporic connections it helped silence. It reveals, first of all, something we know but have yet to realize: the direct influence on Duras's early work of her fellow lower-class child become Communist Party member—Richard Wright. Indeed, historicizing *Duras* does more than that: it shows that rather than merely illustrating Sartre's theory, Wright formulated the crucial first-order response to Sartre's privileged "objective" literary engagement from the yonder side of the power line, the subjective place of the oppressed. Historicizing *Duras* not only establishes Duras's 1950 novel *Un Barrage contre le Pacifique (The Seawall)* as a response to Wright: by showing that Simone de Beauvoir's *Le Deuxième Sexe (The Second Sex)* and Franz Fanon's *Peau noire, masques blancs (Black Skin, White Masks)* respond to his call as well,[3] it provides the beginnings of a revised mapping of mid-century France in which each of these writers, and undoubtedly others as well, extended Wright's response to Sartre in his or her own autobiographical direction. For their part, Duras extended that call in the direction of her lower-class *colon* (to use the French term for whites in the colonies) place under French colonialism, while Beauvoir extended it toward her white bourgeois female place under western patriarchy, and Fanon took it in the direction of his place as an educated and professional black man of the Caribbean African diaspora under western racist colonialism. Crucially, then, Wright emerges from the pages of *Duras'*s historicization as the unacknowledged linchpin of an emerging and still disparate late 1940s "subaltern" challenge (Gramsci, 199-202 *et passim;* Lowe, 17) to the French cultural field ruled by Sartre.

But if Duras wrote from a place proximate to Wright's, the public image/cultural icon *Duras* came to stand as a crucial site in three ideological constructions that worked at counterpurposes to both Duras's and Wright's own to shore up their respective but interlocking conservative status quos. It became a "monument" in what International Situationist Guy Debord critiqued as the modern consumer capitalist "Spectacle," a central element in *phantasmatic Indochina,* the ideological and imaginary principle Panivong Norindr believes guarantees the psychic structures of the French colonial subject, and one of the key literary representations used to guarantee the survival of the western patriarchal subject and its social order by confining women writers to feminine literary spaces. *Duras* was created by division and displacement, thanks to racial and gender stereotypes, in a discourse derived—as Duras's style also was—from the discourse of French colonial propaganda. Returning, now, to that common "originary" ground, let us trace the history of *Duras,* paying particular mind to formerly silenced meanings, interlocutors, and intertexts, without forgetting this icon's resolutely dialectical provenance, in which Duras and her creative work also played a crucial role and by which they were, in their turn, shaped and transformed.

Duras and the Discourse of French Colonial Propaganda

From four to 26 years of age, Duras was bathed in the discourse of French colonial propaganda. In the 1920s she attended colonial schools freshly structured by it; in the 1930s she moved to France just as its cultural space was also just being structured by and saturated with it. She was in the Paris suburb Vanves preparing her *baccalauréat* from late summer 1931 to 14 September 1932, when she and her family returned to Indochina (Adler, 111). She was thus in the Paris region in the period of the famous 1931 Exposition Coloniale Internationale at the Bois de Vincennes, whose six-month run opened on 6 May 1931. After a final year in Indochina, Duras moved definitively to Paris on 28 October 1933. Shaped by the 1920s educational discourse of French colonial propaganda and perhaps by the 1931 Exposition, she became a shaper of the 1930s forms the governor general of Indochina Albert Sarraut insisted "must be reborn the very instant the Exposition dies" ("La Propagande," 4). As was also the case with Sarraut, who played the crucial part in propagandizing education in

Indochina and France,[4] the timing of Duras's displacement across the Indochina-France border greatly enhanced her competitive posture in France. If, as we will see, his travels between France and Indochina helped shape Sarraut's 1917 colonial education reforms, her move to France allowed her to procure a higher education and embark on a career in which her personal and cultural backgrounds would have been expected to diminish or even preclude altogether her chances of success.

Duras's adolescence in Indochina did not provide the tacit competencies and knowledge (Bourdieu's *habitus)* required to enter French higher education or compete successfully in the French intellectual field. In light of Bourdieu and Passeron's research findings, in fact, her geographic origins, socioeconomic class, and gender drastically reduced her chances of gaining entry to post-secondary educational institutions (8-12). Had she bucked the odds and got herself admitted, as a female student she should have been relegated to the Faculté des Arts (6). Instead she got accepted to the Ecole des sciences politiques and the Faculté de droit, one of Paris's most bourgeois faculties and its most gender-resistant; as Bourdieu and Passeron note, "women appeared latest in the Law facultés" (108). Entering law, Duras embarked on one of the two routes to power under the Third Republic, the other being journalism (Sherwood, 6). Raised in the lower echelons of the colonial hierarchies, she attended university when doing so was a luxury: tuition doubled and enrollment fell dramatically from the year she began her studies, 1935, to 1939 (Weber, 211). She was of the generation of female students who helped push female enrollment in law from 12.3 percent at the beginning of the 1930s to 20.3 percent by 1940 (Bourdieu and Passeron, 108).

But as the discrepancy between Duras's handicaps and success in entering university and then at procuring a position at the French Colonial Ministry suggests, her background imbued her with something significantly more important than the ideal habitus: it gave her what the discourse of French colonial propaganda was encouraging the French populace to desire ever more ardently—knowledge of Indochina, France's *Belle Colonie,* its places, images, sights, sounds, rhythms, and cadences. The 1930s discourse of French colonial propaganda cathected French popular desire in the métropole onto an Empire whose contours most ignored. The French still traveled little—four-fifths ignored what tourism was; most found travel "unfamiliar" and "daunting" (Weber, 162). The Empire inhabited most continental French minds as "an Elsewhere with quite fluid geographical contours and cultures still quasi-unknown" (Adler, 137). For that era's "average Frenchman," Weber believes, "the colonial image, if any, was that of a grinning black man advertising a sweet chocolate drink: Banania" (180). Nor were Duras's university peers better informed. Studies at the Faculté de droit "ignored the realities that laws affected"; those at the Ecole des sciences politiques "heeded neither political nor economic life" (210). "Trained to think in logical sequence, not in context (which might disturb the elegance of the logic)" (211), students were incapable of connecting the information they learned with personalities, institutions, circumstances, or history. Where Indochina was concerned, Duras could and would flesh out those contours and fill in those contexts.

If, as she contended, Duras got a job at the Colonial Ministry thanks to her deceased father's colonial connections (*MA*, 59),[5] her own knowledge of Indochina assured her rapid promotion. A "populizer of empire," to borrow Thomas G. August's term (65), she marketed Empire to France's electoral masses. She worked in the Service intercolonial d'information et de documentation and served on propaganda committees for the French banana and for French tea. Intent on making the colonies a primary national priority so as to create a "sacred union for the defense of the Empire" (Sarkozy, 224), her employer Colonial Minister Georges Mandel handpicked his principal collaborators for that project (225). When he needed a press attaché to promote his proposed use of 600,000 native colonial troops to help defend France, he took Duras from the Service intercolonial; when he decided to publish an essay to garner support for that project, he returned her to that Service where she began working on *L'Empire français* on 1 May 1939 with the also hand-picked Philippe Roques. The Colonial Ministry made two significant contributions to Duras's future writing: working there, she both met the prewar model for her postwar personal, literary, and political referent, the Jew, and took her apprenticeship in writing.

Duras learned to write composing "colonial information and documentation" intended to inform "capitalists about the risks and benefits of colonial speculation with the hope of stimulating the flow of investment to the overseas dependencies" (August, 63), and "colonial propaganda," which was designed to strengthen popular belief in the value and the legitimacy of the Empire. In both cases, she learned to create representations capable of attracting, augmenting, and sustaining popular desire. In cowriting *L'Empire français*, she took an additional step, learning not only how to cathect popular desire onto a textual image, but also how to mold that desire to a predetermined end (in this case, support for Mandel's project). As she produced propaganda, Duras helped both to compensate for her inferior class background and to shape her postwar enemies, the procolonial elite. Although she was not from the bourgeoisie, her job permitted her to shape the desires of students who were. And as she shaped them, she also honed her writing so that it was perfectly suited to meet their demands, as well as those of later generations shaped within that same

student culture. By 1962, when the Empire ended, French student desire
for the colonies would have modulated from a desire to possess the Empire
into a desire to study exotic cultures, but the colonial desire itself remained.
And, crucially for those capable of meeting that demand and seeking to
amass symbolic capital, it increased as one moved up the social ladder:
"When sociology students are asked whether they would rather study their
own society or Third World countries and anthropology, the choice of
'exotic' themes and fields becomes more frequent as social origin rises"
(Bourdieu and Passeron, 15).

Working at the Colonial Ministry provided Duras with the opportunity
to develop her writing skills creating a discourse that, on the evidence of its
effects on 1930s print press and publications, was structured around three
techniques: silencing, displacement, and saturation. To shore up flagging
support of Empire, the Ministry held colonial expositions—the 1931
International Colonial Exposition, the 1935 Salon of Overseas France at
the Grand Palais, the 1937 Gala of Overseas France, the Tricentennial of
the French Antilles, the overseas section of the Paris exposition, the 1940
Second Salon of Overseas France—and paid for its positions to be reflected
in the mass print press.[6] Both efforts helped to create a discursive
environment that silenced perceived threats (by means of noncoverage or
censorship), displaced attention onto false scandals and exaggerated threats,
and inundated readers with positive images of Empire.[7] The print press
failed to provide information on Germany's military rebuilding, newsreels
shown in movie houses "completely suppressed" (Weber, 126)[8] images of
Nazi demonstrations and parades, and translations of Hitler's *Mein Kampf*
that identified France as Germany's hereditary enemy and insisted it had to
be crushed before his projects could be fulfilled were ordered destroyed
(128). The print press simultaneously displaced attention from politics and
world historical events onto concocted and highly publicized political-sex
scandals (129) and alleged U.S. threats—its cultural attraction to French
youth, its exportable cultural goods such as jazz and soda fountains, and its
claimed preference for Germany, which was said to derive from German
Jewish domination of U.S. press and opinion (94-100).[9] A "modernizing,
rationalizing influence that upset the traditional order and landscape of
life" (94), the United States loomed in the 1930s French print press as the
menace of automation, automatons, rationalization, and depersonalization. Such Ministerial efforts helped provoke a quintupling of colonial
novels in winter 1930-1931 (August, 150),[10] the appearance of films
"clearly affirmative of the French colonial presence" (150), and an increase
in books textualizing and illustrating the U.S. threat, including Georges
Duhamel's dystopian *Scènes de la vie future,* Paul Morand's *Champions du
monde,* and Robert Aron and Arnaud Dandieu's *Le cancer américain,* an

account of the alleged U.S. colonization of Europe by credit, unfair competition, and taylorism.

Duras and Roques's *L'Empire Français* appeared in 1940. At the time, politicians exploiting the Empire for wartime propaganda were stressing its capacity to transform France from a "42,000,000 weakling" into "a giant 109,000,000 strong" (Weber, 180), and 53 percent of the French population indicated that they "considered the cession of colonial territory as distressing as the abandonment of any part of the motherland" (August, 157-8). *L'Empire Français*'s positive treatment of Empire suggests that, despite her colonial background, Duras's politics were consistent with those encouraged by politicians and espoused by her age cohort. In 1939 the strongest support of Empire came from people under 30 years of age and over 60 (158); Duras turned 25 in April. But to Duras and to Mandel, the timing of its publication transformed the meaning of *L'Empire Français*. It appeared on 25 April 1940 (Adler, 136): beginning three weeks later, the tragic events of Mandel's final years transmuted this textual embodiment of their shared faith in Empire into an embodiment of his place in the abjected margins of the French and European social fields. Derided as "the Jew" throughout his career (Sarkozy, 15), Mandel was already being marginalized when Duras worked at the Colonial Ministry. As she helped write *L'Empire Français*, his French citizenship was questioned; one leftist weekly went so far as to demand a copy of his birth certificate (Sherwood, 1). When Ribbentrop came to Paris in fall 1938 to sign the Franco-German Nonaggression Treaty, Mandel and other Jewish ministers, including Jean Zay, were invited to the German Embassy reception, but they were not asked to the French reception at the Quai d'Orsay (Weber, 177). On 14 June 1940 Mandel's exclusion assumed World War II dimensions. Having fled Paris with other government officials, he was arrested the following day, prompting Léon Blum to call Mandel "the first Resister" (Werth, 134) and one of Mandel's biographers to call his arrest the Vichy government's first discriminatory measure (Sarkozy, 275). Quickly released, Mandel fled to North Africa and recorded an Appeal from Casablanca, which was prevented from being broadcast. Rearrested at Rabat as a "threat to the exterior security of the State" (284), he was expelled from "the French zone of the Christian Empire" (285) on 7 September 1940. Convicted by the Vichy government on common law charges, he was first handed over to the Nazis, then returned to the French, and, finally, executed by volunteer paramilitaries in the collaborationist French Militia on 7 July 1944 in the Fontainebleau forest, three weeks after Jean Zay's execution at Molles (Sherwood, 289).

Consistent with the process of deferred signification or revision Freud terms *nachträglickeit* (LaPlanche and Pontalis, 111), these events resignified

Mandel's place as *having been* the place of most radical exclusion, or abjection. As used by Freud, the term *nachträglickeit* refers to a real working over of past events or situations in light of new situations or events or new stages in development. In this process, the new experiences allow the older ones, which had been impossible to incorporate into a meaningful context in the first instance, to be understood in their new contexts. *Nachträglickeit*, this process of deferred understanding or revision, is thus occasioned by events and situations (or maturation) that allow the subject to access a new level of meaning. Crucially, the new experiences not only permit the earlier ones to signify: they permit them to be signified as traumatic and thus to have psychical effectiveness. We recall that in Freud's case history, for instance, the Wolf Man's dream resignified his earlier sighting of intercourse as traumatic and precipitated his phobia. In Duras's case, Mandel's fate from 1940 to 1944 resignified his place as having been that of "the Jew." As it did, it resignified her place at the 1930s Colonial Ministry, a place embodied in the *Empire français*, as *having been* proximate, contiguous, and conjoined with his. To her, the war-related death of Philippe Roques in February 1943 (Sherwood, 359n19) further intensified the resignifying effects of Mandel's exile, imprisonment, and execution. And, less than a year after Mandel's execution, the traumas of spring 1945 retroactively revised his fate once again, provoking, in its turn, the deferred revisions of both Duras's place at the 1930s Colonial Ministry and of her situation in French colonial Indochina.

Image, Epiphany, Containment

From February 1945, as Allied forces began opening the Nazi camps, war correspondents sent photographs and film footage of the camps to French newspapers. Camp survivors soon began entering Paris as well. To intellectuals in France, these images had the effect of signifying the preceding war years as (having been) traumatic. Their sense of trauma is widely recorded. Duras's postwar friend, historian and academician Jacques-Francis Rolland recalls:

> There were Jews in Dachau before 1939 who made it to England. What impact did that have? None. It was only when people actually saw the camps that things blew up, not before, even though quite a few things were known. People say they didn't *know*, but knowing is a very complicated concept. I remember when I was working underground during the Occupation I was a personal friend of Marcel Aymé, a right-wing writer who, while not a collaborator, frequented those who were. I remember he said, in the spring of

1944, 'You know, I've heard rumors. It seems that there are camps in the east where they take people in trains and they aren't work camps, they're extermination camps.' And even I thought to myself, although I was a Communist at the time, 'That's just propaganda.' But when film footage arrived, I was shocked.

Similarly Duras's partner at the time, philosopher Dionys Mascolo, recalled "from the end of the war, I was scandalized" (*IP*, 36), and Duras herself identified spring 1945 as the origin of her writing: "I became an adult at that moment. I haven't swallowed that. I have been obsessed/haunted *[hantée]* since that time. There is no writer without a haunting/obsession and the nonresolution of that haunting/obsession. For years after the Liberation [of the camps], I was unable to go into the Jewish district without crying" (*MA*, 59).

Spring 1945's stunning revelation of the war's catastrophic dimensions destabilized the founding "thesis" of the post-Revolutionary French subject. As described by Kristeva, the speaking subject, its symbolic order, and its social system all emerge from a moment of violent sacrifice she terms "thetic." The post-Revolutionary French subject emerged from the French Revolution, which was, in Kristeva's terms, the moment of violence and sacrifice on the basis of which it constituted itself "as signifying and/or social" (*Revolution*, 67). It emerged as the subject of a symbolic order organized around rational and liberal thought and of its attendant social orders. It thus emerged around a founding contradiction: the contradiction between French liberal thought's notion of universal rights and the actual exclusion of certain sectors of the population from those same rights that structures its patriarchal bourgeois capitalist and colonial social orders. For the post-Revolutionary subject to stand firm, this contradiction had to remain hidden. Making it visible, the traumas of spring 1945 threatened that subject, whose destabilization is registered symptomatically in the widespread sense intellectuals who lived through this period have of suddenly having access to previously inaccessible insights or knowledge; of epiphany or revelation. Duras, for instance: "My spirituality was turned upside down. I started seeing things clearly after the extermination of six million Jews" (*MA*, 59).

Interpreting their wartime epiphanies in terms of marxist thought, most intellectuals in France believed that Nazi atrocities revealed the contradiction between the notion of universal rights and the class-based restriction of rights underpinning bourgeois capitalism. Even most of those who had been to the political right before the war moved into opposition in respect to a bourgeoisie intent on reasserting its rule; some, including Duras and her postwar friends Claude Roy and Maurice Blanchot, moved into the

French Communist Party (PCF). As Edgar Morin recalls, "there shone forth from Stalinist Communism, martyr and wartime victor, a solar radiance. Those who dared call everything into question were doomed to scorn or indifference" (*AC*, 77). This political realignment provoked a social redefinition of intellectual work. Sartre, for instance, charged the engaged intellectual with bearing witness to oppression; with recognizing, analyzing, and communicating its conditions to the oppressed. Convinced that the "perfected model of humanity" was the committed intellectual, a "free man" writing to "help the masses free themselves" (Boschetti, 112), he argued that the intellectual's action of revealing the world would be "sufficient to change it" (109). Henceforth "to write [was] to demand freedom for all" (Sartre, "La Littérature"). Following Sartre's lead, politically committed writers moved into the social field to challenge the bourgeoisie by creating and circulating aesthetically pleasing counterimages to bourgeois capitalist ideology.

Duras's circle took their 1945 epiphanies further still. Nazi atrocities showed them the contradiction in French liberal thought and the threat of rational thought. In their minds, Nazism stood as the logical end product of the division of post-Revolutionary rational thought from the nonrational modes of knowledge and corporeality. Reworking archaic western myths in terms of scientific, philosophical, and anthropological concepts, Nazism had rendered them, in Mascolo's 1987 phrase, "conceivable . . . universally admissible" (*AEM*, 64). Labeling modern rational thought the "chthonic reason of the new modernity" (65) to reflect its kinship with Evil, the infernal, and the chthonic deities, they indicted it as "not simply corrupted in the Swiftian sense, therefore, nor simply closed to that which it is not (its blindspots, which it is in its nature to ignore), but developed to the point where it produces new powers, and something like a second nature, that it does not control" (64). Believing that modern rational thought and its capitalist social order were logical precursor forms to fascism, they affirmed, as Morin writes, that "bourgeois democracy was not the antidote to fascism, for it was from it that fascism was born, for everywhere it collapsed under fascism. Only Stalinist Communism was the antidote to fascism" (*AC*, 35). Looking for nonrational means of disrupting rational thought and upending the social orders it subtends, they found them in madness, "playing, laughter, anger, indignation, revolt" (Mascolo, *ARSB*, 203).

World War II also clarified crucial aspects of post-Revolutionary French thought and society for Vietnamese nationalists. Under the Occupation, French officials based their demand that France's sovereignty be recognized and restored on the Revolutionary premise that all nations and peoples have an inalienable universal right to self-determination. Their demand suggested a presumption of blindness on the part of their address-ees, whom officials apparently supposed did not see the contradiction between the Revolutionary ideals and the actual structures and relations of oppression in France's capitalist and colonial social orders. Clearly, this contradiction was no news to Vietnamese nationalists who had learned it in their firsthand experience of colonialism, the writings of the Revolutionary theorists of universal rights, and/or the marxist critique of bourgeois capitalism. But what they were perhaps less cognizant of was the possibility that the *continental French populous* might not fully "see" that same contradiction. This possible blindness suggested that popular support of Empire might be grounded not only in self-interest, but in propaganda-induced ignorance as well, and this possibility suggested yet another: by revealing the actual colonial relations and conditions to the continental populous, one might manage to have them see those contradictions and, in so doing, change some of their minds on colonialism. In the war's wake, Vietnamese nationalists redoubled their efforts to present their accounts of French colonial repression in Indochina to the continental French. Ho Chi Minh "missed no opportunity to appeal to public opinion in France" (Buttinger, *VPH,* 267). When he presented his new government on 2 September 1945, for instance, he supported his claim of Vietnam's right to independence with citations from France's Declaration of the Rights of Man and the Citizen and the U.S. Declaration of Independence (210).

Drawn from "the bloodiest period in the entire history of French Indochina" (Buttinger, *VPH,* 215), France's second war for Indochina, the images that Vietnamese nationalists tried to insinuate into French cultural space may well have had the potential, given World War II's destabilization of the French subject, to unmask colonial ideology, destroy the psychic configuration of the French colonial subject, and provoke a significant reduction in popular support of Empire. The gap between the procolonial project and popular opinion was at its historic widest during France's attempted reconquest of Indochina. If they were "absolutely not disposed to allow the slightest attempt at succession" (Sorum, 58), the French generally lent merely passive support to the colonial project in Indochina, except when they perceived colonial issues as having a direct impact on them. Failing such evidence in 1946, the public's largely passive consent permitted this war to be waged despite the fact that "the majority of the public that voted for the governing parties either opposed or refused to express an opinion on it" (11). To admit the part of apathy in popular sentiments on Indochina is not to diminish the public's share of self-interest or its responsibility for colonialism: indeed, its apathy contributed to the more generalized sense of "indifference" that was, as *Les Temps modernes* put it, "the metropolitan form of colonialism" ("Ceci n'est pas," 1543). But unlike the more active support the French public lent to French colonial projects elsewhere, its passive support of Indochina seems to have helped mid-century Vietnamese nationalists envisage changing its mind. They thus appealed to Parisian intellectuals in hopes that, by integrating the nationalist critique into their antibourgeois stances, they would serve as conduits and funnel images of colonial repression to the crucial voting public.

Besieged on one side by left intellectuals and on the other by native nationalists, French bourgeois and "procolonial elites" (Sorum, 11)[11] endeavored to solidify French discursive space along the lines of its prewar configuration. They deployed to that end the same means that had been used by colonial propagandizers during the interwar years—silence, displacement, and saturation. Procolonial interests no longer paid the press, but they did apply their significant pressures on it. At a time when both mass and intellectual print presses depended on foreign news agencies and government communiqués for their international news, the procolonial elite blocked the inflow of information on the colonies, provided false accounts of the ongoing war in Indochina,[12] and saturated the mass press with lofty iterations of France's *mission civilisatrice*. Venues including *Le Monde* printed High Commissioner of Indochina General Georges-Thierry d'Argenlieu's declaration of France's "sacred duty . . . to reestablish order in Vietnam": "We came here because Indochina still needs France and France loves Indochina. France did not come guided by material or financial interests, but with humanitarian aims *[par l'humanité]*" (2). They also published General de Gaulle's warning that "united with the overseas territory, which she opened to civilization, France is a great power. Without these territories, she would risk no longer being one" (3). As early as February 1945, the mass press displaced popular attention onto a purported U.S. threat that had been "laundered" (Bourdieu, *PO,* 4) of its interwar anti-Semitism and refashioned to meet the native nationalist challenge. In response to the Allied proposal to establish an international colonial oversight committee, for instance, the mass press circulated images of U.S. imperialist designs and U.S. white racism:

> Ever in the avant-garde of human progress, France does not need anyone to commend the natives of her Empire to her. By remaining faithful to her in the course of these war years, they have proved to her that she understood them and knew how to be "humane" toward all, in the widest and most elevated sense of the word, by having no racial prejudice, by not subjecting people of color to a discrimination as painful as it would be unjust, in contrast

to what sometimes occurs elsewhere, by educating them and by having them attain more and more to the administration of the affairs of their country ("A propos de la conference").

In both the mass and intellectual presses, procolonial pressures provoked misreadings of ongoing colonial events. *Le Monde* misread U.S. reports of 10,000 victims at Sétif as an "Anglo-American offensive to discredit France in the eyes of Arabs of the Middle East" (Sorum, 35) and construed the U.S. refusal to transport French forces to Indochina at the end of the war as evidence of an Anglo-American plot to exclude France not only from Indochina but from the Empire (35). Although it criticized the Empire and argued that it could only survive if it were based on equality and justice (Sorum, 32), the left-wing journal *Combat* also voiced its fear of U.S. designs on Indochina and its hope that Indochina would remain federated with France. Even the PCF mistook native nationalists as agents of U.S. imperialism and campaigned in favor of a weak French imperialism over what it perceived as the strong American alternative. In fact, procolonial interests exerted such pressure on public perception in late-war and postwar France that they managed to have an effect on intellectual production even at the organ of intellectual left-political engagement, *Les Temps modernes*. As if overriding what one might assume to have been the political intentions of its staunch left-wing editorial board, those pressures caused even this journal's coverage of colonial issues to be silenced, its political interventions to be delayed, and its political engagements to be displaced onto the United States.

Because *Les Temps modernes* was constrained, like most in France, to rely on government communiqués for world news, its editorial board remained largely in the dark as to ongoing events in Indochina. One discernible effect of its lack of information was that, while French repression in Indochina escalated dramatically from September 1945, this journal did not publish anything about it until February 1946. Even then, the editorial board's relative ignorance of ongoing events in that colony constrained it to preface that article by a native nationalist with a disclaimer stating that, although it could not give its endorsement to the information and views in the article, it was publishing it in the interest of getting the word out. Moreover, each subsequent piece *Les Temps modernes* ran on Indochina in 1946 was so delayed in respect to the events and/or situations it addressed that it had little hope of achieving any real political efficacy. Tran Duc Thao's "Sur l'Indochine," appeared too close to the 6 March treaty, Pham Van Ky's firm indictment of French colonialism, "L'Ogre qui dévore la ville," was published too close to the Haiphong massacre, and the editorial board's anticolonial position paper, "Et Bourreaux, et Victimes" *(Henchmen and Victims)* appeared the same month the Indochina war broke out.

Convinced that "the Vietnamese cause would receive a better hearing in the more liberal atmosphere of the French capital" (Buttinger, *VPH,* 249), Ho Chi Minh requested negotiations in France; for the same reason, General d'Argenlieu agreed only to preliminary talks at Dalat. Having finally secured continental negotiations, Ho arrived at Orly on 2 June 1946. His proximity provoked overreaction in procolonial ranks: not only did pressures to silence, displace, and saturate reach an apex; they were deployed simultaneously on the representational and material-geographical levels. At Orly, Ho was informed that the talks had been postponed until after national elections and sent away to spend the interim in Biarritz. After Georges Bidault of the colonial party (MRP) had become head of government, the talks finally opened. Rather than in Paris, however, they opened in Fontainebleau, where they continued throughout the summer. By displacing Ho and then the talks themselves, procolonialists succeeded in maintaining as separate the Vietnamese nationalist critique of French colonialism and the Parisian intellectuals' marxist critique of fascism and bourgeois capitalism. Thus, as talks heated up at Fontainebleau in August, *Les Temps modernes* remained silent on their subject, issuing instead a 400-page double volume special issue titled: *U.S.A.* To distract the summer public, this issue explored American democracy, history, economics, worker consciousness, sexuality, psychology, and U.S. myths. It featured Philip Wylie on "Mom," Clement Greenberg on twentieth-century art, David Hare on "Comics," Boris Vian on Norman Cowin, an essay on Navajos, an editorial on the relation of race and the death penalty, "La Mort a une couleur" ("Death has a Color"), and thick sections on African-American culture—Negro Spirituals, the New Orleans music tradition, St. Clair Drake and Horace R. Clayton's "Black Metropolis," and Richard Wright's "Débuts à Chicago."

Richard Wright

Richard Wright did more than "symboliz[e] the political engagement of Parisian intellectuals after the liberation" (Stovall, 190): he moved literary engagement from the "objective" place of Sartre's privileged "free man" to the other side of the power line—the autobiographical and subjective place of the oppressed. This displacement was crucial: it permitted those excluded from the Sartrean position to appropriate the legitimated form of engaged literature and turn it against the engaged literary form itself.

Wright's response to Sartre was the first-order response that could open the flood gates of literary engagement to anticolonial, anti-imperialist, and feminist critiques of the French bourgeois and colonial orders; the enabling move for members of the still coalescing subaltern challenge to begin to come together as each one bore witness, from his or her subjective place, to the oppressions of the French status quo. From 1945 procolonial pressures bore down on this threat, shaping a French critical reception that appropriated Wright's work to its own conservative ends.

If gender would be used to contain Duras's threat, race was used to contain Wright's: indeed, his significant French literary capital was consistently based on a racial reading of his textual politics. Those critics who portrayed him as a "black Dostoevsky" (Brauër) or a "spokesman for his race" (Merceron) also heaped symbolic capital on him, praising him as a "brilliant literary artist" (Astre) or "one of the best American writers" (Merceron). Those who found other politics in his writing devalued it as primitive, feminine, unsophisticated, communist propaganda, or bourgeois mystification. One critic presented it as part of "the great family of social sentimental novels" (Coindreau, 104), a genre that had been feminized and devalued for more than a century, for instance, while another described it as "a clumsy apology for crime and communism [with] some value as a detective story" (Thiébaut). In 1948 the conservative Le Figaro's André Rousseaux went so far as to explicitly criticize Wright for having overstepped the boundaries of the racial problem. Standing nearly alone against the race-based containment of Wright's political meanings was Duras's friend and fellow Communist Party member (as Wright also was)— Claude Roy (see "Pourquoi").

Where Duras would emerge as a monument in the Spectacle and a principal support of the ideological and imaginary construct Norindr terms phantasmatic Indochina, the public persona/cultural icon Wright would become a crucial support of postwar French colonial ideology. Wright's presence in the French mass and intellectual presses coincided with the period of greatest tension in Indochina, which was also the period of greatest threat to French popular belief in Empire. Wright was introduced in France in February 1945 by Léopold Sédar Senghor in Poésie 45. From September 1945 to December 1946, French procolonialists pushed Vietnam from Ho Chi Minh's declaration of independence to war. From before to beyond that period, as procolonialists worked to silence native nationalist voices, Wright was invited to speak out on his life, his work, and American race relations. In summer 1946, when Ho was at Fontainebleau, Wright was in Paris; and as Ho tried in vain to get his views into the French press, that same press put before the French public a wealth of interviews with Wright. If from 1947 on, Wright would revise his political thought in an international direction, prior to then his work and statements tended to focus, without doing so exclusively, on U.S. race relations. Foregrounding his analysis of U.S. white racism, the French print press developed an image of *Wright* that shored up procolonialist aims by displacing French attention onto the United States, saturating French public discourse with indictments of U.S. white racism, and silencing the pressing issue of French colonialism.

From October 1945 to June 1947, *Les Temps modernes* not only followed, but arguably led, this trend in foregrounding Wright. In fact, it opened its two inaugural issues with a short story by him, printed his work regularly, and consecrated it as the emblem of engaged writing by printing a French translation of *Black Boy* in its entirety from January through June 1947. In this journal as in the broader print press, Wright's foregrounding bore witness not only to his writing's clear political force and literary merits, but to the sheer weight of procolonial pressures as well. Foregrounding Wright had the effect of displacing the journal's most valued genre, politically engaged writing, onto U.S. black-white race relations and of relegating the issue of French race relations and colonialism to the less valued testimonial essay genre. More broadly, Wright's French reception saturated French discursive space with negative images of the United States, from which there sprang forth inverse and positive images of France. Wright was cited as "describ[ing] Americans as the unhappiest people on earth because easy material life does not compensate for lack of balance and spiritual zest" (Escoube), asserting that "Americans know what to do in a time of crisis but they are depressed after victory" (12), and comparing "the humanist sentiment that penetrated everyday French life, literature, architecture, and art, with the materialism of American life" (Gordey, 1). He was further reported to have suggested that one "call Europe, which represents culture, the New World, and America, which represents material civilization, the Old World" (1) and to have contended that "it is in Paris that a young black can discover an atmosphere of freedom" (Molbert). He was said to have experienced for the first time in his life, during his eight months in France, the "atmosphere of a country exempt from the violent racial and color prejudices whose burden his brothers have carried in America for two centuries (Gordey, 1). Such images helped hide from sight (block or veil) the disruptive images of a colonially oppressive France then being made on the battlegrounds of Indochina and articulated by Ho Chi Minh. *Wright's* racist United States purified France, transforming it from oppressor to victim. Identifying with *Wright*, French readers read their position through his: he was a victim of U.S. white racism; they were victims of U.S. economic and cultural imperialism. *Wright* helped readers perceive France as a nonracist hub and position themselves as "European[s] puzzled by American racism" (*"Enfant du pays"*). At the height of French repression in Indochina and amidst rising racism in the hexagon, the cultural icon *Wright* helped maintain France's self-image as the place of civilization, universal values, racial equality, and unrestricted hospitality.

Duras's Response

In March 1947 *Les Temps modernes* consecrated Sartre's theory of engaged writing and Wright's emblematic instance of it.[13] In April Duras began writing *Un Barrage contre le Pacifique*. If as Boschetti believes Sartre's competitive genius lay in his combining of the two principal roles in the French intellectual field in which he struggled for power—the writer and the philosopher (Boschetti, 3-4), Duras's competitive genius lay in her combining of the two principal positions consecrated in the March 1947 *Les Temps modernes*—the objective place of Sartre's "free man" and the subjective place of Wright's oppressed.

On the levels of class, race, gender, and culture, Duras's childhood background positioned her in a difficult complex and contradictory fashion variously on the sides of the oppressor and the oppressed, without placing her on either side consistently, completely, or unambiguously. She was thus constrained and enabled to respond to the demands of the just-consecrated engaged field with a mobile and shifting narrative voice that weaves together these witness-bearing positions without embodying either. It was as if, ensconced in the ambient Kojevian hegelianism, she sought to sublate these positions; to maintain both the Sartrean thesis and the subaltern antithesis and move them to higher ground. *Un Barrage's* aptly "semi-autobiographical" narrative voice met the objective and subjective demands of the March 1947 engaged literary field by bearing witness to oppression from a place once removed from both—that of a daughter bearing witness to her mother's oppression and that of a lower-class *colon* girl bearing witness to native oppression. Where Wright bears witness from the place of the unambiguously oppressed, Duras bears witness from the contradictory position of a figure modeled on her younger self—the poor *colon* daughter. Displaced from the unambiguous subjective witness bearing place of Wright, this position permitted her to disrupt the allegedly "unified" subject both he and Sartre maintain. Disconnected, passive, *en attente* (in a waiting state), her novel's daughter serves as a relay and a conduit: in and through her (textual place), Duras introduces multiple perspectives on and accounts of colonial oppression, elaborated from various positions of race, culture, and gender. Rather than actively bear witness from a distanced position, her daughter sits distractedly and passively waiting, as through her eyes and ears the reader sees and hears voices relating relations and conditions of oppression under French colonialism—the voices and stories of, for instance, the native *caporal*, his wife, the French mother, and the wandering Asian Beggarwoman who leaves her moribund child with the daughter's family.

The voices woven into *Un Barrage* by way of the daughter's place are not mere products of memory or fiction alone: they are drawn from the March 1947 issue of *Les Temps modernes*. More accurately, they are response-extensions of voices in that issue, as articulated through and from a textual place proximate to, but distanced by time, geography, memory, and writing, from the writer's former place in Indochina. In addition to Sartre's articulation of the demand for politically engaged writing in the second installment of "Qu'est-ce que la littérature" ("What is Literature?") and Wright's emblematic but subjective instance of political engagement in the third installment of *Jeunesse noire (Black Boy)*, that issue included a 110-page section on Indochina. This section opens with "Indochine S.O.S.," the editorial board's response to François Mauriac's stunned response to its anticolonial position paper of December 1946. In that response, the editorial board clarifies its position on colonialism: "a priori we are wrong if after eighty years we are still hated as enemies, and if a military reconquest would be, *à la lettre*, our humiliation" (1039). That issue's remaining articles analyze Indochina—Tran Duc Thao's historical piece, "Les relations franco-vietnamiens," Claude Lefort's "Les pays coloniaux: analyse structurelle et stratégie révolutionnaire," Jean-Pierre Dannaud's "Service Inutile," Jeanne Cuisinier, "Détails," and N..., "Regard sur notre action politique en Indochine."

Duras refashioned the perspectives, analyses, and voices articulated in this Indochina layout into the content and form of her novel. Arguing the needs to confront French atrocities and to speak of the Vietnamese, Jeanne Cuisinier provided possible models for *Un Barrage*'s native characters and mother figure. Tran Duc Thao's claim that two horizons of view exist in Indochina and that only the native horizon is capable of envisaging an independent Vietnam is registered in *Un Barrage*'s narrative movement away from the French horizon and toward the Vietnamese. The editorial board's statement, "If the Germans had remained in France for three-quarters of a century, they would indeed have ended up building factories in which the French would have worked, roads and bridges that we would have used" ("S.O.S.," 1040) is similarly registered in the novel's main structuring device: the French colonial road system in Indochina. In the same way, the board's assertion that "the face of the French in Indochina is the face of the Germans in France" (1040) combines with the Nazi camp testimonial of Duras's ex-husband Robert Antelme, *L'Espèce humaine*, to create portraits of native road crews that resonated strongly in 1950 France with then recently published survivor depictions of the camps.

Duras designed and deployed *Un Barrage* as what she would later term a *mot-trou* (word-hole) (*RLVS*, 48; 38)*:* it would lay out the discursive veil of French colonial ideology iterated by the protagonist's mother; then, like the crabs it thematized, it would eat holes in that *barrage*—or rather, it would have its various witness bearers do so. Extending Duras's spring 1945 epiphany, *Un Barrage* would permit the French reading public to see (through its holes/through it as hole), the real conditions of French colonial oppression and their parallels with the fascist and capitalist forms. Destabilizing the psychic structures of the French colonial subject, it would precipitate a withdrawal of popular support of Empire and help end French colonial rule. *Un Barrage* combined the critiques that procolonialists had long sought to keep divided—the marxist and the native nationalist—and used them to counter procolonial propaganda strategy-for-strategy. It refocused French intellectual engagement on French colonial issues, saturated French discursive space with images of French colonial oppression, and cast the United States as an object of adolescent desire. It promoted revolution in the midst of the attempted reconquest, portrayed French resistance to French colonial rule, and gestured toward a post-French colonial revolutionary tomorrow rising up on Indochina's horizon. If the novel's marxist revolutionary project stopped short of its goal, its perhaps less consciously devised "combinatory challenge" has not.

Geneviève Idt claims Sartre wove insights from intellectuals outside of French culture into his work, creating "a vast palimpsest, an entirely second-order literature held together by pasteups and props, unacknowledged quotes and plagiarisms, tacit references and unconscious reminiscences, pastiches and parodies" (Boschetti, 25) that solidified his position and enriched the French literary and cultural fields. In *Les Temps modernes*, he published a wealth of voices from the margins of those fields, or, as in the case of Wright, from "outside" of them. Some of them, including Wright or Pham Van Ky, illustrated and performed his notion of engaged writing, while others, such as Tran Duc Thao, provided historical or political insights or testimonials. Legitimated by publication in *Les Temps modernes*, these voices marked the beginnings of the shift that would move the French cultural fields, in the next half century, away from Sartre's emblematic place of class, race, and gender privilege toward their own positions of marginality; from the alleged cultural homogeneity of his field toward their own heterogeneity. If their challenge was not of Sartre's making, it was nevertheless by way of him that their voices came together in a common textual "place" to enter into communication with one another in a way that is retrospectively recognizable as having been a subaltern challenge to his hegemony.

Responding to and extending their "calls," Duras introduced those voices, which Sartre's journal had relegated to the essay genre, into the French literary field. Her introduction of their calls helped expand and diversify the spectrum of sites to which future writers could respond in their attempts to enter and compete in that field. In this way, her novel helped establish the preconditions for the eventual expansion of the range of semi-autobiographical narratives such as hers within that field and for their expanded, if uncoordinated, challenge to the place of the traditional white male French bourgeois literary subject still occupied at mid-century by Sartre. Duras's project in *Un Barrage* thus intersected with work that had been ongoing since 1946 at the Centre d'études sociologiques, where her postwar friend and roommate Edgar Morin was involved in social science's "difficult task of disengaging itself from the task of studying ways to maintain an old exclusive cultural heritage for its conservative values and seeking ways to theorize a new variegated world, and perhaps a nation, in which there are many ways of being French" (Lebovics, 48-9).

Duras, or Displacement

When *Un Barrage* appeared in Spring 1950, the French social field was midway through the radical shift that would take it from the 1946 leftist surge of which it was born to a decisive right-wing "rule" by 1955 (G. Wright, 3). If as we have seen the French public was generally only "passively imperialist" in respect to Indochina (Sorum, 10), that spring the Communist victory in China and the beginning of the Korean War provoked in it a brief but intense "burst of determination" (246n9) to defeat the Vietminh. Opinion polls reflected this trend: in July 1949 only 19 percent of the French populace strongly wanted to reestablish colonial rule in Southeast Asia; by October 1950, 27 percent did (10). Shaped by mounting pressures to contain the postwar leftist challenge, *Un Barrage*'s reception was produced by a critical field that was itself emerging, within the context of modernization's "generalized compradorization" of the French middle class, as a "comprador class" (Ross, 8).[14] All in remaining part of the literary field, that is, the critical field was working, wittingly or not, in the interests of the increasingly hegemonic conservative political instance in the social field, to bring its pressures to bear on, in this case, Duras, her work, and its leftist revolutionary challenge. As France became more conservative, her first critics laundered *Un Barrage* of its anticolonial politics, its encoding of "stress" from the French cultural margins, its probably inadvertent intersections with women writing in the wake of Beauvoir. Rather than dismiss Duras, they prepared her work to amass profits for French publishers and booksellers and for the French cultural and literary traditions. From 1950, their conservative account of *Duras* continued to be contested by leftist readers: some were Duras's friends, many were Party members, all remained convinced that her work must be read in terms of marxist revolutionary politics.

Duras's leftist critics read her work in terms of the "time-places" of history, geography, everyday life, politics, and action. Her conservative readers abstracted her meanings away from the local and material and read them in terms of the ahistorical and atemporal "spaces" of, consecutively, women's fate, feminine literature, feminine desire, the feminine. Left-wing critics read her work as process and product; conservative readers read her textual meanings into the timeless space of the product and the commodity.[15] Her major leftist (time-place based) readers included Claude Roy, Monique Lange, Olivier de Magny, Maurice Nadeau, Geneviève Serreau, and Michelle Porte. Her principal conservative (space-based) readers included Jean-Henri Roy, Gennie Luccioni (Eugène Lemoine-Luccioni), Jacques Guichardnaud, Jacques Lacan, Marcelle Marini, Alain Vircondelet. In the 1950s her leftist readings were printed in *L'Observateur, Les Lettres Nouvelles,* and *France-Observateur;* conservative readings in (surprisingly enough) *Les Temps modernes, Critique,* and the moderate Catholic *Esprit.* Conservative readings of Duras remained hegemonic through the 1950s, although their center of power shifted from the *Les Temps modernes-Critique* nexus to the *Critique-Esprit.* Thus, as Duras's left political meanings moved toward the (merely) journalistic, her literary meanings moved toward the metaphysical. This apparently spontaneous separation of her literary and political meanings paralleled the trend in the United States, where McCarthyist pressures were forcing and encouraging the separation of intellectual work from left-wing politics even in traditionally liberal universities (see Schrecker; McCumber). By the early 1960s leftist readings of Duras moved to *La Nouvelle Revue Française;* conservative readings, to the United States and *Yale French Studies.* In France, as Duras's authority rose, the struggle to define her moved to the most authoritative literary venues: in December 1965 it dominated *Les Cahiers Renaud-Barrault;* in 1977 it elicited multiple competing publications from Les Editions de Minuit.

The first Duras struggle took place in 1950. Its competitors spoke from three principal journals: the organ of French anti-imperialism, *L'Observateur,* the organ of left-political engagement, *Les Temps modernes,* and the experimental literary venue, *Critique.*

Les Temps modernes was at the height of its authority; *Critique,* the only other acceptable venue in those years for politically "free" intellectuals whose views were incompatible with those of *Les Temps modernes* (Boschetti, 151) was poised to succeed it in 1953 as France's most authoritative literary journal. In Spring 1950 *L'Observateur's* lack of power was symptomatized by its editor Claude Bourdet's expulsion from his editorship at *Combat* under the sole pressures of one French Tunisian colonialist stockholder (Sorum, 51). The first professional readers of Duras's 1950 novel came from the political left—Maurice Nadeau in *Combat,* Monique Lange in *L'Observateur,* Claude Roy in the communist *Les Lettres Françaises.* They compared Duras to Caldwell, with Claude Roy claiming, for instance, that "as Caldwell denounced the abjection of the social system in the American Southern states, Marguerite Duras here writes the book of colonial denunciation" ("Le barrage," 3). They presented her novel as an indictment of French colonialism, finding, as Lange put it, "the trial of colonization present from one end of this book to the other" (19). These critics pointed out the analogies Duras made between French colonialism and Nazism, noting, as Roy does here, that the "immense concentration camp that colonization had made of Indochina is [figured in] the slimy, atrocious, and damp setting in which Marguerite Duras's astonishing novel situates itself" (3). They invited their readers to read *Un Barrage* as a call to revolution; a novel about "the Indochina of before the nationalist uprising—the Indochina that calls for, explains, and *necessitates* that uprising" (3).

In August 1950 Jean-Henri Roy responded to these readers from the pages of *Les Temps modernes.* If he had little power within the journal,[16] this ex-soldier with first-hand knowledge of Indochina had the authority to speak on its subject and had often done so in *Les Temps modernes.* Indeed, he had been part of the negative response to the editorial board's December 1946 anticolonial position paper, "Et Bourreaux, et victimes," to which the board had subsequently responded, in its turn, with its hefty March 1947 Indochina section. Reprinted at the end of that same Indochina section, his letter appears to be both its provocation and, in a circular return, a response to its clarification of the board's anticolonial politics. "Dear Sir," J.-H. Roy wrote, "For the first time, to my knowledge, your review publishes an article signed *Les Temps modernes* and for the first time since I began reading *Les Temps modernes,* I cannot approve its content without reservation" ("Correspondance," 1150). J.-H. Roy went on to plea with readers not to demoralize French troops on the grounds that, "engaged in combat for which they are not responsible, heirs of a past of errors that unjustly weighs them down, they are, in the full sense of the term, victims. We must not be, even by the pen, their henchmen" (1151). And yet, despite the fact that at *Les Temps modernes* his was the voice of internal opposition to the very politics that *Un Barrage* radicalizes, Roy was permitted to stand as the *Les Temps modernes* voice on that novel.

J.-H. Roy's review of *Un Barrage* made a crucial contribution to Duras criticism: it distanced *Duras* from Caldwell—hence from her textual politics (the American writer's textualization of U.S. white racism; her textualization of French colonial oppression). In the process, it provided insights into the perception of Duras and the critical use of race and gender for political containment in mid-century France. J.-H. Roy's first lines establish Duras as a site of ambiguity on the level of race. *Un Barrage* is "disquieting," he writes, because "we no longer know if Caldwell's characters are black or white" ("Un barrage," 375). Duras's race, too, was being noted at the time. Claude Roy recalled having been captivated by her "small vaguely oriental face, its gaze always distractedly hypnotizing, raised up toward the arriving person, who was always taller than she" (*Nous*, 121), and Beauvoir described her to Nelson Algren as "36 years old, half-white half-Indochinese, not beautiful but not disagreeable" (Adler, 286). But if, as Stuart Hall contends, we tend to read culture through the face of race, were such commentators actually remarking Duras's racial ambiguity or were their racialized remarks elicited by her cultural differences? Was J.-H. Roy's discomfort with her characters a discomfort with race or rather with something he reads, symptomatically, on the level of race? In the discourse of Duras criticism, at least, race does emerge as part of a chain of associations that links up, through gender and genre, to politics. More than that, when they are considered together, her critical history and Wright's reveal that race functioned as one way of reading (and containing) politics. In the late 1940s, as we have seen, French critics contained former American Communist Party member Wright's politics by "placing" them "as if" on the face of his race. Rather than being indicative of a parallel pattern in Duras criticism, however, J.-H. Roy's allusion to Duras's race is anomalous: it stands in his review as an early manifestation of the politics that her later critics would deal with not on the level of race at all, but on that of gender. Rather than "place" her meanings on the face of her race, as Wright's critics do, they would place this female writer's meanings "as if" on the body of her gender.

Recapitulating in advance this displacement, J.-H. Roy's review moves from its quick mention of race to an ultimately gendered reading cum political containment. His final phrase posed a query that bears the mark of France's ongoing shift to the political Right and was, for the engaged journal, an odd query indeed: Is *Un Barrage* didactic or is it literary? What, we might ask, provoked Roy to cast politics and literature as mutually exclusive? What motivated him to read its textual politics in terms of "didacticism"? Why does he not read them in terms of Sartre's combinatory term "politically engaged writing"? Made in a different context, Edgar Morin's remark that the "notion of engagement belonged to *[relevait de]* military psychology" (*AC*, 83) suggests one response: Roy posed his question because Sartre's engaged genre was per definition unavailable to a female writer. If that is the case, then J.-H. Roy's use of the term "didactic" was twice motivated in 1950 France—once by Duras's radical left-wing political connections (she was in the French Communist Party until January 1950); once by her gender connection to the didactic school marm Beauvoir and her just issued and still rage-provoking appeal to women to write in the 1949 *Le Deuxième Sexe* (See Moi, *Simone*). Both overdetermined and cautionary, his use of the term "didactic" registers the danger of *Un Barrage*'s being dismissed, whether as socialist realism or feminist rant. Using it, J.-H. Roy showed what must be sacrificed for Duras to succeed in the French literary field; then he proceeded to perform the sacrifice: "This novel would be an indictment of the colony, in the name of the poor whites inhabiting it as much as in the name of the native people, if it wanted to be didactic. As it stands, it is one of the best novels one can read" (376).

To the eyes of French readers, J.-H. Roy laundered *Duras* of politics (making her novel not an indictment of colonialism, but a tale of human misery), effaced its social and historical specificity (making it deal not in colonial oppression, but in universal human misery), reinstated colonial binaries (*Duras* may speak for poor whites and natives, but not from the disturbing ambiguous in-between). With this gesture, he placed *Duras* and her work within the categories of French literature and implicitly French culture. In terms of social-political function, his inaugural creation of *Duras* recalls that of *Wright:* reading Wright through his race and place (the United States), critics had prevented his textual politics from being read as Communist or extended, by way of race, into critiques of French race relations or colonial situations. In the same way, reading Duras through her gender, critics prevented her textual politics from being read as Communist or anticolonial. Thus in the era of McCarthy and the colonial wars did critical readings grounded in gender and racial stereotypes contain both writers' Communist and anticolonial threats "as if" within the "biological" trait that distinguished each one from the white male subject of the French bourgeois, patriarchal, and colonial orders. Henceforth, Duras's textual politics would be marked and managed by way of consistent complaints of her misgendered or virile writing.

In December 1950 *Critique*'s Jean Piel replaced Duras's former Caldwell reference with that of Marcel Proust by playing on the title of Proust's *Du côté de chez Swann:* "The novel of the mother, the lamentable epic of the mother," he proclaimed, *Un Barrage* might just as well have been called *"Du côté de la mère"* (270). This replacement shifted Duras's ambiguities from the colonial borders to the intra-European borders of the half-Jewish Proust. Asking readers to think of Proust when reading Duras, Piel displaced perception of her (work) toward the continent, French geographies, French culture, its internal borders, and the French literary tradition. Aligning Duras and her work with the heterosexually married homosexual Proust, he also shifted perception of her ambiguities from the cultural/racial plane to the sexual. By completing the transition from colonial cultural (racial) borders and politics to the borders of sexuality and their attendant surfeit of eroticism, Piel prepared *Duras* for entry onto the modern consumer market as an erotic and exotic object of consumption. Piel makes no effort to hide his capitalist approach to literature. Not only does he open his review article by proclaiming the novel to be "without any contest the most familiar form and the easiest to sell" (270), he concludes it by asking French readers to jump on *Duras:* "If the public is still looking for real novels, it should jump on this pasture" (270).

Recasting her ambiguities as sexual, Piel paved the way for *Duras*'s borderzone domestic marketing. From the nineteenth century on, as Andreas Huyssen has shown, modernist literary writing and mass cultural production had been gendered masculine and feminine, respectively. Following the male realist devaluation of sentimental themes as feminine, mass cultural writing—serialized feuilleton novels, popular and family magazines, bestsellers—had been devalued, and mass culture itself mystified as woman (Huyssen, 49). In yet another translation of Duras's ambiguous cultural borderzone aspect, *Duras* would be marketed on the borders of a masculine-coded French literary genre and the feminized and devalued pulp fiction genre. The pulp reference would mitigate and limit her literary worth; it would also help contain her politics. Pulp fiction was where the textual politics of women writing in Beauvoir's wake were contained, appropriated, and made profitable in the 1950s. The publisher most closely associated with women's pulp, René Julliard, was the first French publisher to deploy a heavy marketing campaign. Editions Julliard mobilized gender and sexuality in various ways to promote sales. It printed the names of young female authors on book bands and their photos on book jackets; Julliard himself paraded around Paris with young *protégées* to assure them mass press coverage. Pulp fiction was where the big money was, too: by 1956 Françoise Mallet-Joris's *Le rempart des Béguines* had been translated into 13 languages and had sold 30,000 copies; by 1962, Françoise Sagan's *Bonjour Tristesse* had sold more than 840,000 French copies and 4,500,000 translations. Traces of Duras's redoubled marketing as a competitor in both Sartre's field and Sagan's mark the French print press of the 1950s and 1960s, in which she is at times seen looking like Sartre—big glasses, vest, a masculine, distracted intellectual air; at others, like Sagan, gazing seductively, glamorously, and enticingly at the reader. [17] *Duras's* borderzone market position redoubled Duras's saturation of the press, broadened her readership, and increased her revenues; it also weakened her literary standing and permitted critics, especially of the early 1960s, to use her literary example to control the textual politics of (other) female pulp fiction writers.

The International Market

In February-March 1953 *Time* magazine circumscribed *Duras's* place in the emerging international culture market in relation to those of two French women whose books had also just appeared in English translation: the productive place of Madeleine Henrey and her *Little Madeleine: the autobiography of a little girl in Montmartre* and the unmarketable place of Beauvoir's *Second Sex*. Previously, in 1930s and 1940s, Henrey had published an impressive number of books under her husband's name, as Robert Henrey. Now, as her writing took a more transparently autobiographical turn and she began signing her books as *Mrs.* Robert Henrey, *Time* portrayed her as the emblematic French woman writer. In a review titled "French Without Tears," it cast her as a dutiful daughter who had once suffered hard times stoically, but who, by marrying her destiny to that of the Anglophones and reproducing their line, now succeeded brilliantly ("Today little Madeleine is Mrs. Robert Henrey, author of several well-written books, mother of the gifted Child Actor Bobby Henrey (The Fallen Idol)" [102]); a "French women writer [whose] saga of life and death in Paris is an endearing, peculiarly feminine mixture of gentleness and Gallic realism, a reminder that life has its quota of sentiment and that it can be conveyed without sentimentality" (102). Reflecting her market position next to other French female creative artists, *Time* completed its review with a photograph of Henrey that most U.S. readers would have had a hard time distinguishing from those of the writer Colette or the singer Edith Piaf. In the McCarthy and Marshall Plan years, Henrey's tale would ring in U.S. ears as an allegory of the situation of postwar France: by marrying its future to the United States and the Marshall Plan, they would have argued, France, too, could succeed. On the market, her *Madeleine* would benefit from its resonance with the already popular children's books of that same name by U.S. Austrian immigrant Ludwig Bemelmans, published by Simon and Schuster since 1939 and by Viking from 1958. Henrey's promise was to provide U.S. readers with "charming and readable" (102) panoramas of France; she went on to publish prolifically.

Reviewing *The Second Sex* two weeks later, *Time* viciously attacked Beauvoir. Where it had stressed Henrey's Frenchness, it did not mention Beauvoir's. Titled "Lady with a Lance," its review accuses Beauvoir of "tak[ing] a bead on a man and bring[ing] him down like a sack of hypocrisy," reducing "the warm aura of mystery that commonly surrounds woman . . . to a steely chill" (110), rejecting traditional western values (myth, religion, spirituality), and promoting contraception, legal abortion, and easier divorce as the foundation upon which the "real" woman will be built. Asserting that she has "a chip on her shoulder [that] makes her believe that every man is as autocratic as a Turk and every woman as malleable as a slave," *Time* dismissed *The Second Sex* not only as "pages of nonsensical epitaphs over her bleeding targets," but as *dépassé*—"Many of her protestations would strike even the inmates of a harem as being behind the times" (110). Combined with the advertisements chosen to share its page, *Time*'s attack on Beauvoir achieves the aspect of sheer unreality Alice Jardine finds characteristic of McCarthy era counterimages (see "Flash"). Portraying Beauvoir kissing her own ass—"Many authors of both sexes have bent their pens to the exploration of this subject [male-female relations], but none has bent so nearly double as Author de Beauvoir" (110)—*Time* placed its review vis-à-vis advertisements touting Phillips Milk of Magnesia's capacity to sweeten sour stomachs and, with scatological resonance, Samson folding chairs. It completed its composition with a photograph of Beauvoir in profile, positioned to look directly at the Phillips advertisement, as if into the face of her own abjection (see Figure 1).

Three weeks later, on March 16, *Time* sandwiched its review of the English translation of former Party member Duras's *Un Barrage* between an update on Joe McCarthy's House Unamerican Activities Committee and a retrospective on the just deceased Stalin. As implied by its title, "Outdoor Snake Pit," *Time* read *Un Barrage* not in relation to Caldwell or Proust, but to Mary Jane Ward's 1946 *The Snake Pit*. Ward explained the psychiatric provenance of her title in an epigraph to her novel: "Long ago

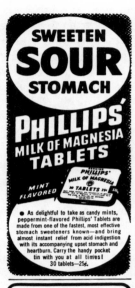

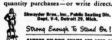
trifling interest. even to historians. Taken
together. the eight volumes show little of
the intellectual curiosity and range of the
writings of Thomas Jefferson (six volumes
published. 46 to come). But the character which builds in them. especially during the later years. is more impressive
than anything the legendmakers have
been able to fashion. The native wit. the
humility. the triumphant common sense
are as abundant as the 5,000-odd books
about him claim they were.

Lady with a Lance

THE SECOND SEX (732 pp.)—*Simone
de Beauvoir*—Knopf ($10).

*Numberless are the world's wonders, but
none
More wonderful than man; the storm-
grey sea
Yields to his prows, the huge crests
bear him high . . .*

Were Sophocles to croon this chorus
(from *Antigone*[*] below the boudoir of
Existentialist Simone de Beauvoir. she
would very likely fling wide her French
window and bomb him with *The Second
Sex* (weight: 2¼ lbs.). For Sophocles'
measures stand for just about everything
that Author de Beauvoir considers most
hateful in human life. As she sees it,
the male's conquest of the earth. the sea.
etc. is just an analogue of his smug conquest of the little woman.

Many authors of both sexes have bent
their pens to the exploration of this subject. but none has bent so nearly double
as Author de Beauvoir. or painted the
plight of woman on so large a canvas.
She begins her book. in time. with a discussion of Eve in the Garden of Eden.
and carries right on from there through
recorded history to the age of Dr. Kinsey.
By the time she has finished her biological. psychoanalytical and historical-ma-
terialist dissection of the situation of her
sex. the warm aura of mystery that commonly surrounds woman has been reduced
to a steely chill.

The Invention of Woman. As Existentialist Jean-Paul Sartre's major disciple
and friend. Author de Beauvoir deplores
the fact that much of mankind draws
spiritual nourishment from myth. religion.
legend and unthinking optimism. Man.
argues the existentialist. must be more
than a mere passive "being." He must
be an "existent." *i.e.*. one who boldly
accepts the mortality of body & soul but
nonetheless resolves to pit his courage
(his only weapon) against the cruel reality
of life & death.

"Male-man." argues Simone de Beauvoir. is relatively lucky. He has raised
himself by the bootstraps from the quiter
of nonentity to the dignity of "human
being"; he may. at will. transcend even
this and rise to the stature of an "existent." But woman's uplift has barely begun. Far from being an existent. she is not
even a human being yet. She is a "lie" and

* As translated by Dudley Fitts and Robert
Fitzgerald.

a "treason" to her own reality. because she
is "in large part man's invention." Her
plight in a man-made world is summed up
in two of Author de Beauvoir's characteristically sweeping statements: 1) "The
most sympathetic of men never fully comprehend woman's concrete situation." and
2) "The most mediocre of males feels himself a demigod as compared with women."

"One is not born. but rather becomes.
a woman . . . It is civilization . . . that
produces this creature. intermediate between male and eunuch . . ." From childhood she is "fated . . . to be the passive
prey of man." to awake in him "an unknown being whom he recognizes with
pride as himself." What man dreads above
all. Author de Beauvoir believes. is woman's ceasing to be his most priceless "idea"
and becoming very much like himself. For
this reason. he never pries into the re-
cesses of her mind; it might give her the
notion that she has a mind. On the other
hand. there is no tribute he will not pay
to what he considers her finest qualities—
of which "renunciation" is the one he
loves best.

The Building of Brotherhood. As these
samples show. Author de Beauvoir knows
how to take a bead on a man and bring
him down like a sack of hypocrisy. More :
the pity that she writes pages of nonsensical epitaphs over her bleeding targets. The
chip on her shoulder makes her believe
that every man is as autocratic as a Turk
and every female as malleable as a slave.
Many of her protestations would strike
even the inmates of a harem as being
behind the times.

Contraception. legal abortion. easier divorce are the foundations on which Author de Beauvoir hopes to build the "real"
woman. The structure—which is to bring
about "brotherhood" between men & wom-
en—will rise the sooner if men will only
stop chanting about the wonder of their
works.

Figure 1. Review of Beauvoir's *The Second Sex*, February 1953. © 1953 Time Inc. Reprinted by
Permission. Photographic reproduction courtesy of the Newberry Library, Chicago.

they lowered insane persons into snake pits; they thought that an experience that might drive a sane person out of his wits might send an insane person back into sanity." *The Snake Pit* relates the story of a female writer married to a practical rural man who leaves her husband and "decorous small home town"[18] for Greenwich Village where urban hardships provoke her nervous breakdown, and it traces that woman's journey from the first glimmer of post-crisis self-awareness to full recovery. *The Snake Pit* reads as an allegory of the war experience, of heightened white U.S. fears of urban spaces and the racial and ethnic "others" concentrated there, and of the radicalization of especially black men during their service abroad. It warns white women to renounce the urban jobs they had filled during men's wartime absence and return to the traditional western gender roles and racial and ethnic homogeneities associated with mid-1940s rural America. The title of *Time*'s review article also positioned *Un Barrage* in the U.S. popular eye alongside Twentieth-Century Fox Studio's 1948 film adaptation of Ward's novel. Directed by Anatole Litvak, the film *The Snake Pit* starred Olivia de Havilland, shocked audiences, and won considerable critical acclaim. De Havilland nearly took the Academy Award for best actress; the film received an Oscar for best sound recording (Mowrey, 353).

By aligning *Un Barrage* with *The Snake Pit, Time* demotes French colonial Indochina to the status of a snake pit and Duras's story from the level of politics to that of psychology. It elides the ambiguity of Duras's cultural background by establishing her characters, including her young heroine stand-in, as outsiders to colonial spaces: like Henrey, *Time* magazine's *Duras* is a French woman telling tales of French women suffering hard times and trying to prevail. It then goes on to reinstate Duras's ambiguity on borders more propitious to sales: standing on the borders of France and Indochina and of sanity and insanity, she promises to provide French and U.S. readers with scenes of exotic colonial places and images of psychological states. In the United States, *Time* contends, "Duras' characters will have something of the fascination and strangeness of people from an exotic, outdoor *Snake Pit*" (120). As France's second Vietnam war raged, *Time* counseled the French to read Duras's anticolonial *Un Barrage* as a nationalistic cautionary tale confirming the dangers of colonial spaces and validating the "natural distrust" that "most Frenchmen" have "of living anywhere except in France" (118). On its reading, *Un Barrage* tells of a teacher and his wife who were swayed by a colonial propaganda poster into going to Southeast Asia. Showing "what happened to these babes in the Cambodia woods" (118), it traces the decline of the widowed French wife and mother, who is reduced to the state of "a paranoiac in the jungle clearing, screaming revenge on her whole life, while the tropics close in on her like an ant horde" (118-20). "In France, where the book has already been published," *Time* concludes, "it should confirm the widespread French conviction that there's no place like home" (120).

Like those of Henrey and Beauvoir, Duras's meanings and consumer market niche were reinforced by a photograph of her and by advertisements on her review pages. Holding a large furry cat (shades of jungle), she is shown apparently in France, gazing dreamily off as if—the cat leads readers to imagine—into an exotic jungled distance. Her photograph is positioned so that it looks at promotions for the Ditto D-10 Duplicator and Full Color Processor's ability to reproduce in up to five colors, while on the facing page a full-page advertisement promotes thermopane windows for school classrooms. Its wall-length window gives out over flat and undeveloped lands not unlike those of Southeast Asia, an image that reinforces Duras's capacity to open up for her readers vistas onto remote exotic places (see Figures 2 and 3, pp. 42 and 43).

Perseverance and Failure

If *Un Barrage*'s reception taught Duras that she could not *declare* her politics and succeed (Duras and Gauthier, 184), she does not appear to have understood her de facto interdiction to textual politics per se. Obliged to respond to the hegemonic terms of her reception, she worked to discover a viable way of combining politics and literary form. From 1952 to 1955, her work varied widely from realist narratives with vague allusions to the colonies, such as *Le Marin de Gibraltar*, to explicit references to Marx, such as *Petits Chevaux de Tarquinia*, to metaphorically figured accounts of colonial oppression, like her short story "Le Boa," to a marxist class analysis framed as a humorous anecdotal tale in "Madame Dodin," to a study of Marx's theory of needs in a minimalist and theatrical discursive form in *Le Square*. As France continued its shift to the political right, conservative pressures helped shape unfavorable reviews, decreasing sales, and ever smaller first printings of each subsequent book. Critics received *Le Marin* tepidly, *Les Petits Chevaux* harshly, *Des journées entières dans les arbres*, which included "Le Boa," unenthusiastically, and *Le Square* coldly. Sales and first printings decreased accordingly: after *Les Petits Chevaux*, Gallimard reduced the first run of Duras's next book, *Des journées entières dans les arbres* from 5,000 to 3,000 copies; after *Des journées*, they printed only 2,200 copies of the next text, *Le Square* (Adler, 290-301).

At the same time, rising conservative pressures resulted in a withholding of financial and symbolic capital from left-wing readings of Duras produced by her critics, by her adapters, and by Duras herself. In 1954, the year of Dien Bien Phu (May) and the *Front de libération nationale's* (FLN) declaration of the Algerian War of Independence (November), Geneviève Serreau decided to take *Un Barrage* to the stage. Serreau believed that, "profoundly imbricated in the personal drama of a poor white family (victims of the colonial system in the same way as native people), the political themes of *[Un Barrage]* escaped all didacticism: it was not a defense counsel's speech, but a slow rage which, simultaneously meditated and warm, gains adherence" ("L'adaptation," 41). Unable to find anyone willing to finance her project, Serreau abandoned it "for lack of means" (Adler, 316). Only two critics praised *Le Square*—Maurice Blanchot and Olivier de Magny. Magny presented *Le Square* as Duras later would: as a marxist analysis of class oppression in explicit linguistic terms and from an implicit feminist perspective.[19] His review had no impact. In contrast, Blanchot read the historical and political meanings out of *Le Square:* what first struck him about this play was not politics but "this kind of abstraction, as though two people . . . who meet by chance in a public garden, had no other reality than their voices" ("Painfulness," 199). If Duras captures the moment she was trying to in this play, he contends—"the moment at which people become capable of dialogue" (204)—she owes that success to the fact that she situates her characters *outside* of all historical or socioeconomic situation; isolates them, that is, "from the ordinary world in which none the less they dwell" (204). Used in the playbill for *Le Square's* September 1956 stage adaptation, Blanchot's reading prefaced and shaped the viewing public's encounter with Duras's play.

Increasingly from 1950 to 1956, a practice of capital withholding rendered Duras financially dependent on Gallimard. She owed the publisher 97,000 francs when she signed the contract for *Le Marin,* but they advanced her another 120,000 francs anyway. When that novel appeared, she requested and Gallimard added another 80,000. By December 1952, *Le Marin* had sold only 2,800 copies. She requested 250,000 francs in advance of her next book, *Les Petits Chevaux de Tarquinia.* Even after six years on the market, it would sell only 2,023 copies. She wrote *Le Square* indebted to Gallimard for 150,000 francs and wanting financial independence from Mascolo. Duras voiced her desire to earn that independence writing journalism; her male friends objected that doing that would be tantamount to prostitution. She asked for an advance from Gallimard, who gave her 50,000 francs. After *Le Square's* low first run, cold reception, and poor sales, she was 89,665 francs in debt to Gallimard (all figures from Adler, 295-320). When she and Mascolo ended their relationship in Summer 1956, Duras sent what Laure Adler describes as a "heart-rending SOS" (312) to

Outdoor Snake Pit

THE SEA WALL (288 pp.)—*Marguerite Duras—Pellegrini & Cudahy* ($3.50).

Most Frenchmen have a natural distrust of living anywhere except in France, but the poster swayed the schoolteacher and his wife. It showed a colonial couple elegant in tropic white, taking their ease in a banana grove, while eager natives bustled at tasks around them. "Young people," assured the poster legend, "a fortune awaits you in the Colonies!" Ma and her husband applied for teaching posts in Indo-China and, one day in 1899, sailed to take them.

The Sea Wall, a first novel by French-woman Marguerite Duras, is the story of what happened to these babes in the Cambodia woods.

Pa survived only a few years, but Ma was made of fiercer things. Having quit

International Press
NOVELIST DURAS
In the jungle, a paranoiac.

her teaching job to take care of the two babies, Joseph and Suzanne, she began to give private lessons in French and to play the piano at a moviehouse named the "Eden." In twelve grim years she saved enough money to buy a government land concession on a plain bordering the sea.

Ma began to work her acres with joy, only to find that her land was literally a washout. Every summer, just before harvest time, the ocean burst over the whole farm and destroyed the crops. The first time Ma saw it happen, a little of her reason was carried away too. Against all advice, she borrowed to the limit of her credit and built a sea wall to keep the ocean out. But in one season, the crabs ate through the mangrove pilings, and one night the sea carried everything away. Soon after, Ma began to throw fits.

The rest of the book is a close-up of a paranoiac in a jungle clearing, screaming revenge on her whole life, while the tropic

TIME, MARCH 16, 1953

Figures 2 and 3. Review of Duras' *The Seawall* and facing page, March 1953. © 1953 Time Inc. Reprinted by Permission. Photographic reproduction courtesy of the Newberry Library, Chicago.

Rush-Henrietta Central School, Rochester, N.Y., Benedict M. Ade, Architect.

Whether you have children or not...

You're paying for new school buildings in your community. And if you're concerned with any other type of building, you can be doubly interested in the cost, savings and other advantages of the Daylight Wall in the school shown here. The architect says (italics are ours):

"The Rush-Henrietta Central School was built at a cost of 62 cents per cubic foot which is low compared with other recent public schools in this area. Yet the building has radiant heat, ventilation, glazed tile wainscote, terrazzo floors, metal acoustic ceilings in corridors and *Thermopane* insulating glass.

"Children love these bright rooms that seem to be part of the great outdoors. (*Wouldn't this be true of adults, too—office workers, factory workers, hospital patients?*) They don't feel shut in, but as free as the sky itself. (*Note how the glass goes from sill all the way to the ceiling.*)

"The high level of natural daylight admitted by the large *Thermopane* windows provides excellent illumination. On desks farthest from the windows, we get light meter readings of 50 foot-candles on bright days. That is well over the accepted American Standard Practice minimum of 30 foot-candles."

SOMETHING SPECIAL FOR SCHOOL EXECUTIVES

For a complete appreciation of this statement, so that you can apply the thought to your new schools, we offer a free copy of *How To Get Nature-Quality Light For School Children*. It is a brief, authoritative booklet which everyone interested in school lighting should read.

Write to Libbey·Owens·Ford Glass Company, 4633 Nicholas Building, Toledo 3, Ohio, for your copy.

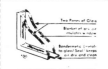

THERMOPANE QUICK FACTS

Thermopane insulating glass with " " of dry air hermetically sealed between two panes has twice the insulating value of single glass. This reduces chilliness, drafts and heat loss at windows in winter. Thermopane cuts air conditioning costs by reducing the amount of heat entering during summer. It cuts out 44% more noise than single glass. Write for Thermopane literature.

THERMOPANE · PLATE GLASS · WINDOW GLASS

DAYLIGHT WALLS
...THAT DON'T OBSCURE VISION

OTHER L·O·F GLASS PRODUCTS: Vitrolite* • Tuf-flex* Tempered Plate Glass
Tuf-flex Doors • Safety Glass • E-Z-Eye Safety Plate Glass • Fiber-Glass

Gallimard; it failed to move Claude Gallimard. On 17 September 1956 the dramatic version of *Le Square* opened at Le Studio des Champs Elysées, where it came and went almost unnoticed. The Théâtre de la Huchette backed out of its obligation to house the play during the spring season. Le Studio des Champs Elysées agreed to do so, provided Duras pay. She begged Gallimard to finance that run; "You can't imagine, Gaston, how much this manner of proceeding can be unbearable to me" (317). Gallimard agreed. Critics reiterated their cold reception.

May '58 Coup d'état: *Duras*

Nothing Duras did guaranteed the stellar success she enjoyed in spring 1958. Not of her own making, that success was not either, properly speaking, her own. Accruing rather to the conservative icon *Duras*, it was assured by several white bourgeois French men, most notably the Gallimards and René Clément, who had purchased the film rights to *Un Barrage* in 1956. Considered the most promising French filmmaker to emerge at the end of the war (Andrew, 172), Clément had directed France's "only great resistance film" (172), the 1945 *La Bataille du rail*, studied Germans and refugees aboard a submarine in the 1947 *Les Maudits*, and made the great antiwar film, *Jeux interdits* in 1951. Named Best Director at Cannes for *La Bataille du rail* in 1945 and in 1948 for *Au-dela des grilles (The Walls of Malapaga)*, he had received Academy Awards for best foreign film for both *Au-delà des grilles* and *Jeux interdits*. Touted as France's answer to neorealism, he was "with Claude Autant-Lara, the most important figure in the French film industry during the 1950s" (172). In fall 1957 Clement's *Gervaise*, an adaptation of Zola's *L'Assommoir* with Maria Schell, was released in the United States. On its subject, the *New York Times*'s Bosley Crowther proclaimed that if anyone could manage to faithfully adapt Emile Zola's blistering textual political discourse to the screen, then that was without any doubt the French director Réné Clément. By 1958, when *Un Barrage* appeared, U.S. critics were praising Clément's films as "consummately French" (Andrew, 174). Reviewing *Un Barrage* in France, however, François Truffault reacted quite differently: he accused Clément of having sold out. Once Clément had made movies, he wrote, now he directed "his career" (53); once his films had followed his ideas, now he followed only fame and fortune, and his films doled out only exoticism and enticing stars. In Truffault's words: "For Clément, the essential thing is that the film he is making costs more than the last one and less than the next" (53).

A Hollywood-Italian coproduction, Clément's *Un Barrage* was designed as an international success. It was financed by Columbia and Dino de Laurentiis, released in Italian as *La Diga sul Pacifico*, and marketed internationally as *The Seawall, This Angry Age*, and *Un Barrage contre le Pacifique*, with different *montages* for each version. Its male lead was to have been James Dean, but he was replaced by Anthony Perkins; its female lead, playing Duras's adolescent stand-in, was the 28-year-old Italian actress and de Laurentiis's wife, Silvana Mangano. Clément's *Un Barrage* was not created as a colonial equivalent of his political film *Gervaise:* it was designed to compete with the rush of French films focused on love, sexuality, and young starlets being released in the United States that year. In the 12 months preceding *Un Barrage's* release, the *New York Times* reviewed more than 25 such titles, including *Maid in Paris* with Dany Robin, *Lover's Nest* with Françoise Arnoul, *The Light across the Street* with Brigitte Bardot, three more Bardot films (*And God Created Woman, Please! Mr. Balzac,* and *The Bride Is Much Too Beautiful*) and three with Danielle Delorme, star of the film adaptation of Colette's *Gigi—Deadlier Than the Male,* the adaptation of Colette's *Mitsou,* and Columbia Pictures/Otto Preminger's *Bonjour Tristesse,* based on the bestseller by Françoise Sagan.

Amidst rising tensions and violence in France and Algeria, such French films distracted audiences and displaced their attention. On 8 May 1958 Pierre Pflimlin, an advocate of negotiating with the FLN, was asked to form a new government in France. Tensions rose, mass demonstrations were staged, riots broke out. On 13 May, as Pflimlin was sworn in, General Salan announced he was taking charge in Algeria and General Massu announced the formation of a Comité de Salut Public in France, where both men asked de Gaulle to take power. As these events unfolded, a barrage of sexy French films filled French and U.S. cultural space, attaching the signifier "French" not to scenes of oppression, but to exciting—and in the United States, at least, exotic—scenes of titillation, sexuality, and eroticism. On 10 May *Folies Bergères* tantalized *New York Times* readers and U.S. spectators; days later, the preeminent entertainer of U.S. troops, Bob Hope, beckoned them to see his *Paris Holiday.* Then, one day after the stunning French political developments of 13 May, René Clément's film was released in the United States. In contrast to *Gervaise,* whose black and white shooting reinforced its serious political content, Clément shot *Un Barrage* in brilliant technirama-technicolor, which both earned Truffault's disparaging review title "Notre techniramage" and enthralled big-screen U.S. audiences. Were that not sufficient, its U.S. version, *This Angry Age* appeared on the same bill with a second Columbia release: *Screaming Mimi* with Anita Ekberg and Gypsy Rose Lee.

By his own account, Clément's film "displaced the center of interest" of Duras's novel. Unable to film in Indochina, which had ceased to exist in 1954, or in Vietnam, where the nationalist struggle continued, he reconstructed *Indochina* at a displaced location: Thailand. Clément thereby displaced Duras's anticolonial narrative from the colonial geographies that give it its meaning to a nation that had never been colonized by the West and which, moreover, had been a U.S. ally since 1945. Consistently, his film was interpreted without the least colonial referent. Its tale was that of a European widow and mother blinded by her dependency on her already grown children, thwarted by the merciless conditions of life in Thailand, undone by her vain attempts to retain her children by involving them in her "self-ambitious" (Nason, 3065) efforts to sustain a run-down rice plantation on the banks of a muddy and unmanageable Thai river. Its setting furnishes no more than colorful and exotic "background" for its central story—the "internal disintegration" (3065) of the three European protagonists. Shifting Duras's ambiguities from the colonies to Europe, from the cultural to the sexual plane, and from the intra-subjective to the intra-heterosexual dyad, Clément's *Un Barrage* concentrates a surfeit of erotic appeal in two couples—one formed by the half English, half Sicilian Mangano and a compromised merchant-marine officer played by Richard Conte; the other, by Anthony Perkins and Alida Valli in the role of the older, beautiful, philandering female. Inversing Duras's textual politics, it depicts the mother's death as "the last means of bringing back her son and daughter" (3065) and has that son return after her death to complete her dam project with better materials. The *New York Times*'s review of Clément's film completes the elision of Duras's textual politics. Casting Clément as a "specialist" in that form of "tragedy" that devolves from "deeply-pained" people's inability "to face their own feelings" (3065), it recasts the family's suffering, which Duras roots in western patriarchal colonial relations, as the result of one woman's emotional manipulation and mental weakness.

Thus, where Duras designed *Un Barrage* as a word-hole that would help bring down French colonial rule, Clément made a film through which the French could continue to imagine themselves in Indochina four years after it had ceased to exist. His *Duras* gave French audiences what they had been encouraged to desire since the 1870s but had already lost by 1958: *Indochina*. Maintaining that linchpin of the French colonial imaginary, his *Duras* helped solidify and maintain the actually disrupted structures of the French colonial subject. It not only permitted France to establish itself on the international culture market: it helped France establish itself in the international cultural imaginary *in the same place* where *Indochina* stood in the French colonial imaginary—as an exotic and erotic object of desire capable of spinning fantasies, sustaining desire, and molding that desire to a predetermined action; in this case, the purchase of cinema tickets, theater tickets, books, and other related consumer objects.

Identifying *Un Barrage* as one more worthless attempt to woo U.S. audiences, François Truffault predicted its international financial failure. He was not wrong. Ironically, however, *Un Barrage* was lauded in France as "a complete success, a flawless chef-d'œuvre" (Adler, 337) in spring 1958 French popular press—the same discursive venue where Norindr believes the discourse of French colonial ideology had created, most heavily concentrated, and most effectively mass-disseminated the ideological representation *phantasmatic Indochina* for 60 years. In fact, fortunately for Duras's literary career, Clément's film was so well received in France that it overrode the strongly political meanings she was herself attaching to her name at the time. From February 1958, with French popular opinion deeply divided by France's bombing of the Tunisian village of Sâqiet sidi Yûsuf, she doubled her *France-Observateur* contributions and aligned them with political and minority issues. On 6 February 1958 she published "Un train de mille cadavres qui nous arrive du Pakistan" ("A train of a thousand cadavers arrives to us from Pakistan"); on 20 February, "La Reine des Nègres vous parle des blancs" ("The Queen of Blacks Speaks to You of Whites"), an interview with Sarah Maldoror on Genet's *Les Nègres;* on 27 February, "Des samourai d'un type nouveau"; on 13 March 1958, "Confucius et l'humanisme chinois;" on 27 March, "'Poubelle' et 'la Planche' vont mourir" ("'Trash' and 'Plank' are going to Die"), on socioeconomic class as it inflects the demographics of the death penalty. Yet no matter how loudly Duras shouted her revolutionary politics, the success of Clément's film drowned out her voice, permitting *Le Square* to enjoy a stunning success in Germany that summer and to be taken on by the Théâtre de Poche in Paris for 30 representations. Not only that: Clément's film created new demand for Duras's novel. As Adler put it, "Numerous spectators discovered *Un Barrage contre le Pacifique*. The press echoed this new interest for the book, which found a second youth" (337). But, to reinsert the politics into this takeover, rather than *discover* Duras's book thanks to Clément's film, the French public read it henceforth through (the face of) his film. As if to materially mark Clément's spring 1958 signifying coup, before Gallimard reissued its stock of unsold copies from its first run of Duras's *Un Barrage,* it ripped off the original cover and replaced it with an image drawn from a poster promoting Clément's film. By 8 May 1958, when Clément and Duras both discussed *Un Barrage* in the pages of *France-Observateur,* she may have insisted that

Figure 4 Duras, "Le 'Barrage' est mon histoire," May 1958. Courtesy of Roger Viollet.

"Le Barrage est mon histoire," but the French public heard her to say—the story of Clément's *Duras.*

Had she been consulted on the sale of *Un Barrage*'s film rights, Duras would have disapproved. She believed in theater and documentary film, which promised to unsettle the subject, teach it something new, even perhaps produce social change. Anticipating Debord's society of the Spectacle and Baudrillard's simulacrum, Nietzsche had called theater a "revolt of the masses" (Huyssen, 51). Duras concurred. She believed theater remained relatively free of modern consumer capitalist pressures, and she marked her confidence in documentary film in 1955 when suggesting to fellow members of the Comité des intellectuels contre la poursuite de la guerre en Algérie that they "make a film on the lives of North Africans living in France that would show the extent to which they are disregarded

Figure 5. Indian Woman set in the line of Duras's sight and above the subtitle "Comment va Tatiana?" in *L'Express*, May 1958. Photo Astrid Bergman Sucksdorff. Reprinted by permission.

[méprisés] and make the French sensitive to their situation" (Adler, 309). But Duras did not believe in cinema: it was, to her mind, a means for alienating and disempowering the masses; the opium of the people in modern consumer capitalist society.[20] She may have approved Serreau's project: she would not have agreed to Clément's.

Duras said she felt "betrayed" and "dishonored" (Adler, 336) by Clément's film.[21] To be more accurate, she was *displaced* by it from her French colonial borders and anticolonial politics. This displacement was marked

symptomatically in the film and in the print press of the time. If casting
Mangano in the role of Duras's textual stand-in brought her cultural borders
to within Europe's parameters, it also set them at a distance from Duras,
inscribing them "as if" on the face of Mangano, which at least one U.S.
Italian scholar describes as having the look of a woman wearing a detachable
Oriental mask.[22] From this period on, Duras herself began to be figured in
the French print press in a relation of proximity-distance vis-à-vis images of
colonized peoples, issues, and themes. Reviews of her books began to be
regularly positioned near advertisements related to colonial consumer or
cultural items; images of her were regularly positioned so as to gaze dreamily
toward the exotic colonial, as she had in *Time* magazine. Indeed, this
practice structured even the layout of the article in which Duras herself
insisted that *"Un Barrage* is my story," which was set on the page in a way
that has her gazing, as if nostalgically and longingly, toward an apparently
"native" woman and child (see Figures 4 and 5, pages 48 and 49).

On 1 June 1958 Charles de Gaulle took power in what Duras considered
a coup d'état. In July Dionys Mascolo and Jean Schuster launched their
vehemently antigaullist *Le 14 Juillet*. As Duras responded that month by
publishing "Assassins de Budapest" in *Le 14 Juillet* and promoting *Le 14
Juillet* in *France-Observateur*, Gennie Luccioni sealed the enthronement of
Duras in *Esprit*. Luccioni's critical means were simple and effective: she
proclaimed the existence of a break in Duras's corpus between the works of
her youth and maturity. Devaluing her pre-*Le Square* works as immature,
she secured *Duras*'s meanings from the threat of Duras's own textual
history. Henceforth, Duras's *Un Barrage* circulated in French cultural space
as mere juvenilia, leaving Clement's *Un Barrage*—and the *Duras* it en-
throned—to strut its chef-d'œuvre stuff. On the international level, Luccioni
served as a conduit for *Duras:* she prepared the psychological and cautionary account promoted during the McCarthy era for adoption by gender
conservative critics in the United States, by Jacques Lacan in 1965, and
even by neolacanian "feminists" in the 1970s. Luccioni's personal trajectory
embodied this transitional role: after *Esprit*, she went on to author the
neolacanian *Partage des femmes*. Like her predecessors in the *Duras* critical
subfield, Luccioni cordoned Duras off from politics and cultural difference
by reading her work in terms of traditional patriarchal gender stereotypes.
As early as 1956, Luccioni had introduced the "intuitive Duras" topos
Lacan would adopt in 1965: "Whatever [Duras] writes, one feels, on each
line, the regard of a woman who knows" (150). In 1958 she went on to link
Duras's alleged intuition to maternal protectionism and to make it serve
conservative social interests by claiming that, fully cognizant that "man
only wants to be free to destroy himself" (75), Duras believes that society
cannot and should not be changed. Luccioni capped off the 1950s

depoliticization of *Duras* and sent it into the 1960s with these firm claims: knowing that all revolutionary politics are futile, Duras writes in a cautionary mode to protect would-be future revolters and her own textual offspring from the infinitely futile, ever unreflective, immature, and indeed "adolescent" acts of rebellion.[23]

In France, the defeat of Marguerite Duras's anticolonial textual meanings was confirmed in 1959, when Geneviève Serreau decided to try, once again, to mount her leftist adaptation of *Un Barrage*. In the wake of Clément's 1958 film, Serreau feared that the French viewing public would miss the anticolonial engagement of both Duras's novel and her play. More specifically, she feared that it would follow the now hegemonic trend and read *Duras* away from the specific material places of her politics and into the abstract and universal spaces underpinning French culture and literature. In her words, "It was essential that audiences not misunderstand: *Un Barrage* did not deal with Eternal Injustice but with a specific, precise, and proximate injustice, whose fires continued to burn (it was 1959 and the Algerian War was in full swing" ("L'adaptation," 43). To avoid the recuperation of her engaged Duras by the now hegemonic conservative icon *Duras,*

> I added a brief prologue that revealed that specific situation in its simple evidence by way of a *rapprochement* whose irony was totally objective: in front of the mother's bungalow, a Vietnamese peasant couple reduced to total misery congratulated themselves on not having died as so many of their compatriots had during the construction of the white people's roadway, while a childish voice-off from the side of the stage innocently recited a geography lesson drawn from a chapter on French Indochina. I had borrowed the student's text without changing a single comma from an actual geography book (from 1946) that had been awarded a prize by the Académie française. The resulting effect was a pretty aggressive black humor (43).

As it had been in 1954, Serreau's project was countered by producer pressures and subjected to a withholding of capital. Indeed her producers might just as well not have gone to the bother of removing her preface (43), for even without it, the play closed the 1950s as a relative financial failure due to what Vircondelet calls "a loss of affection on the part of spectators because of the events in Algeria" (*DB*, 264).

Chapter 2

Going International: *Créoles,* Criticism, and the French Colonial Subject, 1960–1996

What matter who's speaking, someone said, what matter who's speaking.

—*Samuel Beckett*

Finally in September 1959, Charles de Gaulle upheld Algeria's right to self-determination and sovereignty. Turmoil ensued in France, Dionys Mascolo recalls, as "the entire nation was plunged into a malaise to which no instance of power or knowledge, no public organization, no moral or cultural institution, attempted to respond" (Adler, 355). As the Empire disintegrated from 1959 to 1961, three expatriate French scholars at the most prestigious universities in North America introduced Duras to U.S. academics in this nation's most authoritative journal on French literature: *Yale French Studies.* Those scholars were Henri Peyre, Sterling Professor of French at Yale since 1938 and chair of Yale's French Department since 1939, his colleague at Yale, Jacques Guicharnaud, and Princeton's Armand Hoog. Reading them today as they present Duras to a U.S. audience reveals what the disparate and cumulative critical readings of the preceding decade do not: that 1950s French critics effectively contained the political and cultural threats in Duras's writing by reading it into the space of French sentimental fiction, a genre characterized, Margaret Cohen reminds us, by its antimaterialist approach, its avoidance of material and social detail, its refusal of broad social panoramas, the emplotting of its constitutive conflict in family terms, its narrow plot focus, its adherence to traditional gender expectations, and, for its heroines, its tragic resolutions. By 1950 sentimental writing had been devalued in France for more than a century, since the nineteenth-century male realist challenge to post-Revolutionary women writers who dominated the genre. Enlisting it to ward off the threat of yet another female writer, Duras's 1950s critics read her work, too, into the sentimental literary genre. In the process they created, in dialectical interplay with her work, a public persona or "cultural icon" with a clearly conservative political and cultural function: *Duras*.

Importing *Duras* into the United States in the pages of *YFS*, Jacques Guicharnaud rejected Duras's alignment with politics and stressed, as Luccioni before him, the tragic aspect of her scriptural project. Guicharnaud reads *Duras* as a "social sentimental" novelist: he has her expanding sentimentalism's narrow focus, as women writing during the male realist challenge had, to include a wider female collective and issues pertaining to it. As he sees it, Duras's "novels do not deal with the hypothetical future of humanity; they deal with the personal, individual experience of women who live *hic et nunc*, their present boredom, their very personal hopes or despair" (107). Guicharnaud dismisses the notion that Duras might write toward social change by contending that to do anything other than describe women's actual conditions "would mean writing science fiction or trying to imitate men" (107). He then inserts her writing into the sentimental category of female tragedy: "The world is unlivable for women because, such as it exists, by its very structure, woman is always dispossessed. . . . Yet [women] live in that world and make a certain number of gestures and pronounce a certain number of words because if they did not make those gestures and did not pronounce those words, one wonders what else they could do. That world is their world; they are inseparable from it, and any manifest rebellion or systematic refusal is no more than an abstraction. They might as well take a large knife and cut their bodies in half" (107-8).

Two years earlier in the pages of *YFS*, a fourth French expatriate, Johns Hopkins's René Girard expressed a view Henri Peyre would echo: in French literature, at least, the "sexes are becoming more alike" (7). Women's liberation had turned heteroerotic relations into "a battle of equal and identical selves trying to outdo each other in their display of callousness and insensitivity" (6). Girard not only considers "homosexual obsessions" the "paroxysmal form" (7) of this widely generalized disease: he identifies its emblematic textualizer as Marcel Proust, the figure in which, in Duras criticism, colonial cultural ambiguities and politics are repressed and through which they reemerge as the exotic sexual ambiguities of the cultural icon *Duras*. *Proust*'s appearance in a *YFS* overview of the contemporary French novel, rather than an analysis of Duras alone, suggests that as the *YFS* expatriates were talking about gender as the Empire disintegrated, they were also worrying through the ongoing dissolution of French colonial binaries. That they were not actually *talking* about the colonial disruptions suggests that the structure of repression and displacement characteristic of Duras criticism was part of a more general trend in which the anxieties and ambiguities deriving from the end of Empire were being repressed in French literary (and perhaps cultural) discourse generally and that, once repressed, they were driving and shaping the production of, for instance, the *YFS* expatriate discourse on female emancipation, feminine writing, sexuality, and, in Girard, homoerotics.

Furthering the goals of French colonial propaganda, this structure displaced attention from French colonial issues. Advancing the aims of capitalists, it enhanced the competitiveness of French cultural products—especially those featuring female stars, characters, and writers—on the domestic and international markets. In *YFS,* Princeton's Hoog most clearly transmutes Duras's politics and cultural ambiguities into the fetching stuff of the French culture niche. Recognizing, like *Les Temps modernes*'s Jean-Henri Roy before him, the ambiguous borderzone aspect of Duras's *Un Barrage,* he describes it as a "somewhat disconcerting narrative, a curious mixture of the farmyard and Saint-Germain-des-Prés, of urban nausea and rustic odors, of Erskine Caldwell and Jean-Paul Sartre" (69). Relying on traditional patriarchal stereotypes of feminine vulnerability, he reads Duras's alleged similarities to Caldwell as symptomatic of the male's influence on her and devalues that influence as one instance of the U. S. cultural imperialism about which the French had been anxious since the 1920s: "We have all too often been presented with sham Steinbeck and pseudo-Caldwell. In the years following the Liberation, the evil was at its height" (68). Dismissing all allegedly Caldwellian aspects of her work ("we recognize all that. We have seen it elsewhere" [70]) and all allegedly Sartrean aspects, he leads one to suspect that what is at issue in his reference to Liberation evils is not only U.S. cultural influence, but left-wing textual politics as well. Having devalued Duras's narrative threads dealing with the social, historical, and political, Hoog slows her textual time to a soft and sensual rock, "the movement of time, at once isolating and creating personality: the tilting of time toward a past which a second later is transformed into an empty nothingness" (71). Remolding the scriptural traces of her cultural borders into equally ambiguous corporeal borders—"Neither completely of flesh and blood nor altogether disincarnate, [her writing] floats midway between geography and pure space" (73)— Hoog, like *Critique*'s Piel before him, presents *Duras* as erotic pastures on which modern reader-consumers can experience "a sort of sensual intoxication (the hands that touch, the breasts and shoulders of women, the nocturnal aroma of flowers)" (73).

But if male critics relegated Duras to sentimental literary space "like" the male realists had nineteenth-century French women, Duras was not a "French" woman writer. Like Belgian-born Marguerite Yourcenar and half-Russian Nathalie Sarraute, she was a cultural borderzone female, and like them she was being ushered into French literature and culture. Rendering that assimilation explicit, Peyre proclaimed that all three women must be included "on any listing of the thirty finest French writers of the present time" (57). The precise means to Duras's displacement to within the French cultural and literary fields was the social sentimental *Duras*, which served several other crucial functions in those same fields. Devised to contain Duras's oppositional politics and cultural differences, it was deployed by 1961 to contain both the feminist challenge to male dominance articulated in Beauvoir's *Le Deuxième Sexe* and the women writers who were then responding to its call. Enlisting the same argument *Time* magazine had used against Beauvoir in 1953, the *YFS* expatriates proclaimed female emancipation a *fait accompli*. In fact, Peyre repeated *Time*'s portrait of Beauvoir as a phallic female with a chip on her shoulder in a way that allowed his claim that women writers no longer had chips on their shoulders to be understood as meaning that they were no longer feminists: "The rights of a woman whose career is in literature have been bravely and brilliantly vindicated in our age by Virginia Woolf and by Simone de Beauvoir. The fight is won today. The very many women writers of contemporary France have ceased to carry a feminine chip on their shoulders" (47).

In a similar way, Jacques Guicharnaud praised *Duras* as an emblematic feminine writer in words that simultaneously discredited women writing in Beauvoir's wake. Take, for instance, this phrase of praise—"The novels of Marguerite Duras, a woman writer, are especially refreshing in that the heroines have no need to become soldiers, intellectuals, social workers, or lesbians in order to live or love or suffer" (106)—which tacitly devalued Christiane Rochefort's challenge to patriarchy in *Le Repos du guerrier*, Beauvoir's challenge to male intellectual dominance in *Les Mandarins*, and Françoise Mallet-Joris's challenge to heterosexual norms in *Le Rempart des béguines*. Moreover, consistent with the established trend in Duras criticism, Guicharnaud read *Duras* not as merely distant or different from, but as writing at strict political counterpurposes to Duras, who joined both Beauvoir and Rochefort that same year as first signatories of one of the first and most important intellectual actions against French colonial rule in Algeria, *La Déclaration sur le droit à l'insoumission.*[1]

Assimilated into the French literary field in a process recalling Geneviève Idt's account of Sartre's scriptural "pastiche" (Boschetti, 25), the work of cultural borderzoners like Duras, Sarraute, and Yourcenar helped expand the available sites in the French niche on the international culture market and assuage the imminent loss of the French colonial exotic. Duras's cultural assimilation (as *Duras*) helped prevent the women who responded in the 1950s to Beauvoir's appeal to write narratives about women's lives from destroying, as the 1953 *Time* reviewer said Beauvoir did, the "warm aura" surrounding "woman" ("Lady," 110). So doing, it helped prevent those women from diminishing French cultural competitiveness on the domestic and international markets. *Duras* also significantly enhanced at least one already existing market site: "French colonial Indochina." Portrayed as dealing with the Indochina of her childhood rather than the mid-century nationalist and anticolonial struggles, *Duras* refocused the site "Indochina," giving it a retrograde aspect capable of meeting what would soon become nostalgic demands for the lost colony. Finally, *Duras*'s de facto colonization of "Indochina" helped forestall the French cultural and imaginary encounter with the more radical voices of cultural difference from France's former colonies. Duras's especial susceptibility to be transmuted into a cultural icon with a conservative cultural function derived from her own borderzone cultural position. That position made it possible to read her (work) into French culture while also retaining in a repressed form the structures, anxieties, and ambiguities of the disintegrating French colonial order and using them to amass symbolic and capital gains on the emerging modern French consumer and international culture markets.

1964: Response, Resistance, Subversion

Like all writers questing legitimation and authority in the literary field, Duras was obliged to respond to the issues and demands of her hegemonic critics. Symptoms of this constraint became visible in her work by 1964, when the doubling and displacement characterizing her public image emerged into the fabric of her own creative work as a doubling and displacement of the heroine. That year, *Le Ravissement de Lol V. Stein* separated Duras's previously solitary semi-autobiographical heroine into two figures, Tatiana Karl and Lol V. Stein, who provide, on the level of their names, a complex set of borderzone cultural coordinates. The name

Lola Valérie Stein transforms the Italian referent René Clément introduced into *Duras* when he cast Sicilian-English Silvana Mangano for the
female lead in his film version of *Un Barrage*. Together, Lola Valérie Stein's
Spanish-sounding Christian name combines with her Jewish surname to
create cross-ethnic and cross-cultural connections that exceed the category
of French *bourgeoise*. The character Tatiana Karl is coded as exotic: the text
lingers at length on her long and heavy dark hair and links her thematically
to mysteriousness, sexuality, and eroticism. Her given name introduces
into Duras's corpus a name we have already seen printed in boldface in the
May 1958 issue of *France-Observateur*, near Duras's claim that *Un Barrage*,
"C'est mon histoire," above a piece on the Italian actress Sophia Loren and
below the picture of the native woman, apparently Tatiana, holding a child.
Tatiana Karl's first name thus combines a tacit colonial reference with the
marxist connotation of her last name, Karl (Marx). Her full name transforms the name of Théodora Kats, a figure Duras claims entered her corpus
in the mid-1940s,[2] although her first published appearance, to my knowledge, is in *La Douleur*, where she is said to have been the daughter of a
woman the narrator knew and to have died in a Nazi camp. Tatiana Karl
thus combines and transforms three sets of political signifieds—colonialism, the Holocaust, and marxism—as they were combined for Duras in
spring 1945, when she recognized for the first time her place as (proximate
to) that of the Jew. Bodying forth Duras's own sense of identity, Lol and
Tatiana therefore appear to loosely represent her European and colonial
cultural aspects, respectively.

   Le Ravissement de Lol V. Stein stages the temptation of the French
colonial object of desire, embodied in the alluring figure of Anne-Marie
Stretter. A narrative of loss, quest, and attempted reconciliation, this novel
responds both to the critical silencing of Duras's cultural differences and to
her own temptation to integrate into French bourgeois and colonial society.
Duras's narrative of *cultural passing*, it wrestles with the desire to fall for
Duras, give in to the French cultural imaginary, let oneself be ravished by
the French colonial object, lures of money, and promises of fame into
forgetting Tatiana and becoming *Duras*. It opens with Lol's loss of both her
proximity to Tatiana (behind the plants, beneath the flowers) and of the
capacity to narrate her own story, and it traces her attempt to find the
"word-hole" that would bring down French bourgeois and colonial psychic
structures and permit Lol to reintegrate her alienated cultural aspect. It
ends on near success: "There was no longer any difference between her and
Tatiana Karl except in her eyes, free of remorse, and in the way she referred
to herself—Tatiana does not state her own name—and in the two names
she gave herself: Tatiana Karl et Lol V. Stein" (189; 179, mod.).

1965: Jacques Lacan and Lol V. Stein

Duras's increasing capital in the field of French cultural production was marked by the near total dedication of the December 1965 *Les Cahiers Renaud-Barrault* to her work. Contributors appeared in order of authority: Jacques Lacan and his article on *Le Ravissement de Lol V. Stein*, which achieved instant hegemony and defined the legitimate discourse of Duras as psychoanalytic, came third; Geneviève Serreau and her forgotten essay on adapting *Un Barrage* to the stage came near last. Lacan's competitive genius lay in his combining and bringing to completion the main positions in the Duras critical field. He completed the narrowing of Duras's plot focus from the broad social panoramas of French colonial Indochina to the thoroughly intra-individual and intrapsychic. He completed the antimaterialist rejection of social and material detail with a concise and self-assured assertion that "sociological considerations referring to varia-tions from one epoch to another" are "of little importance" compared to the apparently immutable structural relations of the subject, the Other, and desire (14). He completed the elision of history and historical time by casting social change as leading to chaos, violence, and the death of the subject. By abstracting Duras's characters into the functions of his universal "structures of desire," he evacuated the specificities that make it possible to distinguish Lol and Tatiana on the grounds of cultural, class, race, or ethnic difference.

Like Luccioni before him, Lacan read Duras as intuitive; like Guicharnaud, he read her as transfixed by sentimental issues, love, ro-mance, and sexuality, but in their psychoanalytic forms. Under his pen, *Duras* became a female writer exploring the immutable structures of a Symbolic Order predicated on the irreparable exclusion of feminine desire and hence of any notion of a *sujet au féminin*. With no hope of provoking revolutionary change, his *Duras* does all she can: she continues to write and, in the process, she continues to produce capital. Asked to comment on Lacan's praise of her as a writer who "proves she knows *[s'avère savoir]* what I teach without me" (9), Duras rightly notes: "That's a master's word. He is the reference. It's an enormous homage, but it is a homage that ricochets back on him" (*MDM*, 61). In fact, Lacan's reading did perform what Hélène Cixous refers to as the economy of the return: it elevated *Duras* in terms that guaranteed that her financial and symbolic gains would return to shore up the patriarchal order he himself explores, the French culture he casts as universal, the emerging international consumer capitalist order in which his reading of Duras, undertaken at the height of his intellectual authority, permitted *Duras* to amass significant French cultural and literary capital. Consistently, going against his otherwise total evacuation of history, Lacan inserts Duras into only one historical context: that of the French literary field, its courtly love tradition, and the lineage of Marguerite de Navarre and her 1559 *L'Heptaméron*.

1973–1975 *India Song:*
Power, Demographics, Coming Out

Culturally empowered by Lacan's reading, Duras was politically emboldened by the near revolutionary events of May '68. As her cultural authority rose with post-May '68 neo-lacanian "feminism," so did her capacity to resist containment and survive. Thus, when asked for a theatrical piece by Peter Hall, director of London's National Theatre, did she seize the chance to further her political agenda and subvert the literary critical trend that had culminated in Lacan's 1965 insertion of her into French cultural and literary history next to Navarre. In its 1973 *text, theatre, film* version and its 1975 film version, *India Song* is a work of cultural, linguistic, literary, and political self-positioning. In it, Duras situates herself vis-à-vis George Sand even more forcefully than she had in *Le Ravissement de Lol. V. Stein* or *Le Vice-consul*. Whether recognizing or not her own self-positioning, she had in fact considered calling *India Song* either "Indiana Song" (Duras and Gauthier, 167-8; 121) or "Indiana's Song," in reference to "the song that the vice-consul had taken up with one finger as a child, to imitate his mother at the piano, the melody that came back to his memory with the letter from his Aunt in Neuilly" (Marini, 138). Explicitly in these titles and in the more subtle and otherwise useful "India Song" (which extends Duras's indictment of colonialism to the British case, and, through it, to western colonialism tout court), Duras appropriates Proust's mechanics of rememoration and deploys them against the conservative critical use of the icon *Proust* by establishing her lineage as that of George Sand and her textual concern not with courtly love, but with issues of race, class, and colonialism.

Duras's and Sand's critical receptions have much in common. Composed a century apart, they share a staunch refusal on the part of male critics to read their textual politics. Taken together, they suggest the outlines of a gendered critical practice in which, without uttering the word politics, critics indict and silence women's textual politics by casting their writing as misgendered and virile. George Sand first entered the literary field during the male realist challenge to female sentimentalists. Although she aligned *Indiana* (1832) with realism in an attempt to gain the legitimacy associated with it (Schor, x), critics read her as an idealist writer with a virile pen, as Naomi Schor catches Edouard d'Anglemont doing in his description of that "novel [as] written with all the strength of a man's grip and all the grace of a woman's pen" (ix). As Schor suggests, reading Sand as an idealist silenced her work's relation to the socialist and humanist writing of Victor Hugo and Emile Zola. In a strikingly similar way, 1950s critical accounts of Duras's writing as misgendered or virile silenced her textual politics and, with them, her writing's relation to Richard Wright's as well as to the work of, for instance, the Vietnamese native nationalists who had and were being published in *Les Temps modernes.*

Unlike Sand, however, Marguerite Duras wrote with the power of Lacan's 1965 consecration in a social field in which the revolutionary élan of May '68 remained strong, post-May '68 feminism, including the neo-lacanian, was in the period of its first effervescence, and rising immigration from the former colonies was increasing the level of stress from the French cultural margins. Duly emboldened, Duras set out, as her 1969 title put it, to "Destroy." In *India Song,* she aimed to destroy French colonial ideology in general and its impact on public apperception of her work in particular. To that end, she deployed the means of ideology-critique she had first devised in *Un Barrage:* first she laid out French colonial ideology and then she destroyed it. In 1950 Duras had figured colonial ideology along marxist lines, in a figure that also named a short-lived Communist journal of that period, as a barrier standing in the way of the rising masses; a seawall, *Un Barrage.* In the 1960s she refigured colonial ideology psychoanalytically in the guise of the alluring erotic and exotic feminine object of desire, Anne-Marie Stretter. Played in *India Song* by the pale blond Delphine Seyrig, Stretter bodies forth a colonial object along the lines Jean-Claude Carpanin Marimoutou finds characteristic of the French literature of Réunion: that is, she figures the object of French colonial desire for a westernized and Aryan Asia. In a narrower sense, Stretter embodies the object of French colonial nostalgic desire for its lost model colony, Indochina. In this sense, Stretter incarnates the monument constructed around Duras and used to contain her political and cultural meanings: *Duras.* Indeed, in *India Song,* Duras takes on *Duras* and its temptation to the French public and to herself. She often said that she had always written to Stretter, the object of desire in relation to which she first learned to shape her writing at the 1930s Colonial Ministry; she also said that she had to kill her off so as to liberate her writing. Consistently, *India Song* is a "swan song" in which Duras lays Stretter-*Duras* out languorously and seductively before the viewer's gaze, then stages the suicide by drowning of both this French colonial object of desire and the representational tool of Duras's conservative intellectual and critical opponents.

Echoing Hegel's master-slave scenario, Duras established the death of the French colonial object as following from and enabling the rise of a second female figure: the Beggarwoman. First textualized in *Un Barrage* as a young Asian, this girl gets pregnant, is thrown out of her home, wanders by the French *colon* family's bungalow, leaves her dying infant daughter, and continues on her nomadic way. Silent since 1950, the Beggarwoman reemerges in *India Song*, with voice. In a scenario shaped by the neo-lacanian feminist decade of its production, as Stretter's suicide subtracts the visual object of desire from the French colonial gaze, the Beggarwoman comes to voice in the margins of the film as, Duras insists, "*India Song*'s main character; the character around which everything revolved" ("La couleur," 25). If at the beginning of *India Song* Anne-Marie Stretter is the star of the show, "the woman from Calcutta," by its end, the Beggarwoman has stepped into that role.[3]

Like *Indiana* and *Le Ravissement de Lol. V. Stein*, *India Song* has redoubled heroines. As Schor points out, Sand figures the social distance between her heroines linguistically: Indiana can write; her foster sister from Reunion, Noun, cannot (xvii). Duras borrows Sand's means in both *Le Ravissement* and *India Song*: Tatiana Karl can narrate Lol's story while Lol cannot; Stretter can speak only in a very restricted way (not at all within the diegesis and rarely in its voice off) while the Beggarwoman chants, laughs, and sings. Since at least 1950 Duras had been promoting laughter, song, and music as revolutionary forms that exceed the status quo, resist its constraints, promise to subvert its structures. Asked the year of *India Song*'s release why she believed women had not used their intelligence or their silence, and why they possess that silence in the first place, she responded:

> Because men have established the principle of virile force. And everything that emerged from this virile force—including words, unilateral words—reinforced the silence of women. . . . It is as if you asked me: "Why aren't there writers in the proletariat? Why aren't there musicians among the workers?" That's exactly the same thing. There are no musicians among the workers just as there are no musicians among women. And vice versa. To be a composer, you must have total possession of your liberty. Music is an activity of excess, it is madness, a freely consented madness ("An Interview," 430-1).

Duras had portrayed music and laughter as subversive and potentially revolutionary practices against bourgeois patriarchal and colonial orders since 1950. That year, she ended *Un Barrage* with a *colon* family laughing in the face of French colonial agents and native children's revolutionary voices rising up on the horizon. More than two decades later, she began *India Song* by combining *colon* and native voices to create a laughing, chanting, singing, and implicitly *créole* Beggarwoman.

The Beggarwoman clearly derives from Duras's early cultural experiences, postwar revolutionary politics, and memory. Her empowered resurgence and coming-to-voice in *India Song* register not only Duras's increased authority, but also the rising pressures of immigration from the former colonies, which was already transforming the social and cultural landscape of 1970s France. In a very material sense, this character's vocalizations depended on the increased presence of Southeast Asians in Paris. Rather than searching out a voice that would be the Beggarwoman, Duras's crew found it in French cultural space and brought it to the studio: the Beggarwoman "didn't exist. There was a little sound track that someone had picked up, that a female Laotian student had recorded for television" (Duras, "La couleur," 25). In the months preceding the 1975 Communist takeover of Saigon and the "boat-people" exodus, the Laotian student's voice amassed increased power in *India Song*'s studio, where "the actors, the film crew, needed to hear her, that girl. We played that sound track very often. She became taboo, sacred: when she spoke or sang or talked nonsense, that is, everyone stopped talking" (25). As Duras had once transformed the analyses of Vietnamese nationalist essayists found in *Les Temps modernes* into the structure of *Un Barrage*, she now transformed the student's voice into *India Song*'s Beggarwoman. With the native beggars and lepers said to hover outside the walls separating France's Embassy from native sections of Calcutta, the Beggarwoman figures the increasing instability of French colonial boundaries in the period of this film's production: they cross that border physically to get food scraps at the Embassy's back door; her voice wafts over it as it weaves its song, chant, and nonsense.

Like *Indiana*'s heroines, *India Song*'s Beggarwoman is a site of *créolité*. Following French lexicology, Sand differentiated her heroines on the basis of race: Indiana is a colonially born Caucasian and thus, in one of the two French definitions of the term, a *créole*, while Noun is considered to be *créole* because she is taken to be of mixed race. At first, Duras's filmic heroines appear to be laid out along oppositional rather than *créole* lines: Stretter is white; the Beggarwoman presumably Asian. When read as such, their fates appear to merely inverse those of *Indiana*'s *créoles*: Sand's nonwhite *créole* Noun commits suicide by drowning while the white *créole* Indiana survives; Duras's white heroine Stretter drowns herself while the Beggarwoman survives. But in the 25 years from *Un Barrage* to *India Song*, Duras had introduced significant movement into the Beggarwoman on the level of race by having her most emblematic attributes, including wandering and madness, move (or wander) across racial lines. Where *Un Barrage*'s Asian Beggarwoman wanders past white *créole* Suzanne's home, for instance, *Le Ravissement*'s white heroine wanders past that of Tatiana Karl, who is coded non-white. By having these practices move across racial borders, Duras established the practices themselves as mobile and shifting forms of *créolité*. Progeny of Sand's and Duras's previous *créole* heroines, *India Song*'s Beggarwoman is herself a mobile and shifting, racial and cultural *créole*.

India Song's Beggarwoman and Anne-Marie Stretter entertain a relation of interdependence and succession rather than of opposition and simultaneity. The Beggarwoman's marginality devolves from Stretter's centrality; Stretter's suicide is the sine qua non of the Beggarwoman's foregrounding. The embodiment of the object of French colonial desire, Stretter guarantees the status quo. As psychoanalytic and postcolonial research suggests, as the object of desire of the subject of post-Revolutionary bourgeois patriarchal colonialism, she serves as psychic guarantor of that subject and, through it, of the Symbolic and social orders that emerged alongside it. In so far as that subject and those orders are structured around binary oppositions, as Cixous showed in her 1975 text, "Sorties," Stretter sustains binaries, including the racial binary that sunders the French signifier *créole* into two significations and two *créoles*. Clearing the path to the dissolution of those binaries, Stretter's suicide permits the Beggarwoman to escape the sandian situation, in which one *créole* must perish for the other to survive. Duras manages Stretter's demise and the Beggarwoman's succession with an emblematically Sandian device: lifting the mirrors from Indiana's bedroom, she relocates them to the French Embassy—as if to whisper *"le bordel"* (the brothel). Formerly in Sand's mirrors, the confusion of Noun and Indiana had precipitated Noun's suicide by drowning; now in *India Song*'s mirrors, Noun's fate becomes Stretter's and, beyond her, that of the French colonial order. Bringing that order down, these mirrors become the place where Noun and Indiana's Durassian progeny intertwine to create and empower, as a racial and cultural *métisse*, a Beggarwoman who is not, for as much, self-identical or "one."

Identifying her literary lineage with *Indiana*, Duras gestures back further still to a novella that appeared a decade before *Indiana* and served as one of its models. Written by Duras's nominal forebear and a *créole* from Martinique, Claire de Durfort, duchesse de Duras, the groundbreaking *Ourika* (1824) related an African girl's adoption by a French couple and the social alienation she experienced as an outsider in France. Aligning her semi-autobiographical writing with the fiction of Sand and de Duras, Marguerite Duras identifies herself, by way of the Beggarwoman, with

Noun, Indiana, and the more distant figure of *créolité*, Ourika. Not surprisingly, when asked if she identified with any *India Song* character, she rejected Stretter with a firm "Non" before declaring: "Me, that's Calcutta, that's the Beggarwoman" ("La couleur," 22). Significantly, she also identified the Beggarwoman as her film's only nontragic character; the only one to escape the constraints of predetermined fate, the only subversive character: "They are all tragic characters. Except the Beggarwoman" (25).

India Song's place in French culture and literary history can itself be measured in respect to *Indiana*. In 1832, as France moved into Algeria, Sand decorated Indiana's bedroom with print illustrations from Bernadin de Saint-Pierre's narrative of idyllic young love in exotic places, *Paul et Virginie*. Rather than portray exotic places as sites of idyllic love, Sand cast them as places of last instance flight and desperation, establishing her first novel, *Indiana* as the end of the French primitivist solution (Schor, xxi). Nearly 150 years later—25 years after World War II, 13 after the end of French colonial rule, and the year Communist forces took Saigon—Duras set *India Song* in the Rothschild Palace in the Bois de Boulogne, which, she explains, is the former Jewish family home that Nazi occupational forces confiscated and used as "the residence of Goering and part of the German headquarters, too" ("Son nom," 36). By setting the suicide of the object of French colonial desire in the Rothschild Palace, Duras reiterates a perspective that, formulated years ago in *Les Temps modernes*, informed *Un Barrage*'s anticolonial critique: "the face of the French in Indochina is the face of the Germans in France" ("S.O.S.," 1040). In a term of analysis that was coming into favor in the 1970s, and which Duras would enlist 20 years later to describe her writing's relation to politics, by setting *India Song* in the Rothschild Palace, she established the "place" of Nazism and the "place" of colonialism as rigorously the same. By choosing the Rothschild Palace, she refused to "other" either Nazism or colonialism by "placing" them outside of French geographical, cultural, or psychic bounds. Quite the contrary: identifying the "place" of Nazism and colonialism as an actual material, social, cultural, and historical site of oppression and decay in the very heart of post-Empire France, she established *India Song* as the swan song of the French colonial "solution."

In 1976 Duras consecrated this demise in *Son nom de Venise dans Calcutta désert*, a film that kills off both *India Song*—"I had to make *India Song* endure that ordeal, being destroyed" ("Son nom," 35)—and Anne-Marie Stretter: "I no longer see her . . . in *Son nom de Venise* . . . That which was begun in *India Song*, death, showing death, is completed in *Son nom de Venise*" (35). *Son nom de Venise* was shot at the Rothschild Palace in the same sequence and with the same rhythm and soundtrack as *India Song*. Filmed actorless amidst the palace's broken mirrors and crumbling ceilings, walls, and fireplaces, it pushed the era of French colonialism into a more remote and unavailable past, as if to erect putrefaction as an obstacle to any residual and nostalgic French colonial desire. *Son nom de Venise* was received as the sacrilege it was designed to be. Speaking to Duras, for instance, Dominique Noguez recalls feeling, when he saw this film, "almost a sense of sacrilege. I was not alone in this. I had the impression that you were putting your hands on *India Song*" (35). But Duras's conservative critics saved their vitriol for the dramatic version of the more explicitly engaged *Abahn Sabana David*, whose theatrical version, performed the same year, caused *Le Figaro*'s François Nourissier to complain in a review titled "Sixty-Eighter Lament": "Hermetic, nocturnal, entirely devoted to an exhausted political discourse, the play made our heads spin with weariness. We had the impression of encountering once again—set to the repetitive and haunting rhythm of Durassian poetics—all of the tiresome drivel of the ends of leftist dinners: to have or not to have confidence in the Party, anti-Semitism in popular democracies, 'we are all German Jews.'"

1977: Opposition and Resistance

From 1975, interest in immigration increased "exponentially" in French intellectual circles (Noiriel, 2). From 1950 to the mid-1960s, only 15 doctoral dissertations dealt with immigration. From 1965 to 1975, a decade surrounding May '68, that number rose to nearly 80, and in the next decade, 1975 to 1988, doctoral theses related to immigration nearly quadrupled to 300 (2). In the United States and France, this period was marked by an increased scholarly interest in the unconscious structures of the western colonial subject and their textual manifestations—reiterating figures, patterns, and structures of thought, for instance, and textually discernible "places" of memory. Edward Said's *Orientalism* broached this intellectual arena in 1978; Pierre Nora's multivolume social-historical study, *Lieux de mémoire* began appearing in book form in France in 1974. Consistent with this trend, in 1977 the critical struggle over Duras's meanings returned to Editions de Minuit, where two of the three critical titles on her work that year registered the social and intellectual stress on "place"—Marcelle Marini's *Territoires du féminin avec Marguerite Duras* and Duras Michelle Porte's *Les Lieux de Marguerite Duras*.[4]

Part of the post-May '68 feminist challenge to Lacan, *Territoires du féminin* reads Duras in terms of the neo-lacanian feminist critique elaborated by psychoanalyst Luce Irigaray in, most notably, *Speculum de l'autre femme* and *Ce Sexe qui n'en est pas un*. Marini pays particular attention to the figure of the Beggarwoman. Reading her away from her social, cultural, and ethnic specificity into the universal categories of myth and lacanian thought, she construes the Beggarwoman as the figure of Woman's fate under patriarchy. Her analysis follows a logic of territoriality in which territoriality is taken not in a geographic sense, but in relation to the psychoanalytic structures of desire, the topographies of feminine desire, and the female body. Where Lacan had Duras excavating his structures of desire, Marini sees her excavating their gaps, holes, and absences in search of the feminine relation to desire she believes they foreclose. If she clearly would undo patriarchal structures, Marini ends up repeating the main positions that conservative critics had laid out over the preceding 27 years, introducing them, as she does, into the domain of neo-lacanian feminist analysis. In the end, Marini's *Duras* continues to explore only personal and sentimental issues, sexuality, and desire. Trapped in the role of eternal tragedian by an immutable status quo, she, too, fails to produce the social change she seeks: "Did not the immense collective discourse she encountered at birth reject her, make her, as a woman, banned from language? Elan stopped dead in its tracks. Tragedy is the register of Marguerite Duras's texts. Whatever the efforts to modify the rules of the game, the outcome is inscribed, ineluctably, in the opening deal of the cards" (27).

The Durassian project that Marini had hoped would be revolutionary therefore devolves in her analysis into a useless but inevitable act of denunciation (Marini, 27-8). Like Hoog before her, Marini slows the time of Duras's writing to an exotic-erotic soft spin, as "going and coming from a lost past to the present, a woman [tries to] access the phantasm that restrains her desire in the relation to the other" (25). As had those of Piel and others before her, Marini's eroticized discourse of *Duras* establishes Duras and her heroines as objects of desire and sets them before the reader's gaze. Reading the textual traces of Duras's complex and contradictory formation in the social, cultural, and historical borders in terms of ambiguous and highly erotic psycholinguistic borders, Marini locates her heroines "*between* the phantom of the penis-phallus that the other imposes on us . . . *and* the phantom of our sex, murdered, denied, abhorred" (71). There, she portrays them peering provocatively, "on the threshold of [their] night" (18) beneath the "subjective dress the other lends" them, asking Lacan's question, "What to be/being beneath? *[Quoi être sous?]*" (Lacan, 10), searching for a response that would be "a representative of [their] body-sex," that would have "something to do with the enigma of the female body as a desiring body" (Marini, 45), and that would answer the question: "How to associate female sex and desire?" (26).

Consistent with her title—historically and semantically, the term *territoire* is linked to the nation-state[5]—the capital production of Marini's neo-lacanian sentimental *Duras* accrued to the French nation, French culture, and the French cultural niche on the international market. Published in large format with its title in lower-case chic, Marini's *Territoires* was a visually discernible French intellectual product. Its air of belonging was augmented by its inclusion in Minuit's collection *autrement dites* (otherwise said), which marked it as a competitive strategy for increasing the publisher's share of the neo-lacanian "feminist" market dominated by the publishing house, Editions des femmes. *Territoires* entered the international market just as the work of the neo-lacanian theorists known here as "French feminists" was entering the U.S. academic field. Although none of the intellectuals most closely associated with this rubric was French—Julia Kristeva is Bulgarian, Hélène Cixous is an Algerian Jew, and Luce Irigaray is Belgian[6]—their work, like that of Yourcenar, Sarraute, and Duras before them, was appropriated into the French intellectual field. Read as French in this country, it helped rejuvenate U. S. French departments. It gave a sexy new appeal to the study of French, transformed some literature departments into centers of feminist theoretical research, provided some female scholars with academic positions in "French theory." It assured French studies a place in some Women's Studies departments, honed out places for psychoanalytic feminist thought in English departments and comparative literature programs, and helped provoke an international exchange of information (more translations, publications, articles) between researchers in France and the United States. It sold books by and about Duras. But if it sold abundantly of books such as *Moderato Cantabile* and *Lol V. Stein,* it did not sell the books Duras's left-wing supporters had historically foregrounded, including *Un Barrage.* The qualities accounting for the market appeal of the successful works can be discerned in Marini's evocation of the neo-lacanian *Duras*'s capacity to provide an infinite wellspring of discursive production: "One could play indefinitely: the quest goes on and on. Marvel of these autoerotic games" (265).[7]

In contrast to Marini's critical study, Marguerite Duras and Michelle Porte's *Les Lieux de Marguerite Duras* emphasized Duras's relation to the real material and cultural places of Indochina. Shaped by the rising stress on place, memory, and identity in late 1970s French intellectual production, its form registers her understanding of the porous relation between place, memory, and text: "As I see it, memory is something diffused/distributed *[répandue]* in all places *[lieux]* . . . I perceive places in this way . . . I tell myself it is places that receive and contain memory . . . that if we did not offer any cultural or social resistance, we would be permeable" (Duras and Porte, 96). As if miming Duras's ideal instantiation of permeability, the *fou,* or madman, a "head-colander *[tête passoire]* traversed by the memory of everything" (96), *Les Lieux de Marguerite Duras,* an open and mobile text, moves between the abstract spaces of intellect, memory, and writing, and the real material social, cultural, and geographical places in which Duras had lived or did live. Constructed of excerpts from her plays, images of their actors, photographs of Indochina, and Porte's interview with Duras, it weaves together the writer, her texts, and her changing contexts.

Les Lieux de Marguerite Duras* was one piece in a de facto 1977 triptych whose constituent works teased apart the creative genres *India Song* had combined—text, theater, and film. In addition to the text, *Les Lieux,* that triptych included the play, *L'Eden Cinéma,* and the film, *Le Camion.* In these three creative pieces Duras reasserted control over the same life stories René Clément's 1958 film adaptation of *Un Barrage* had appropriated. In *Les Lieux,* Duras retold her story and that of her mother, in *L'Eden Cinéma,* she focused on the mother's, and in *Le Camion,* she identified herself with its avatar of the Beggarwoman—the woman it has wandering the routes of France, the *dame du Camion.* Talking with Noguez seven years later, Duras asked if he, too, was wondering "whether she's me?" before announcing: "She is perhaps my model, that woman. What I would have preferred being. . . . The physical description of that woman corresponds to my own. I see her as me. It is the only time that has happened to me, in literature and in film. I saw myself. With that suitcase. The banality. I thought of me" ("La dame," 45, 47). In sharp contrast to Marini, Duras does not associate the Beggarwoman with "Woman," but with real people from her Indochina childhood; the "beggars who built fires and slept near the fountains, by the basins of tropical creepers at night" (Duras and Porte, 27). When she aligns herself with *Le Camion*'s Beggarwoman, she thus declines alignment with the sole European bourgeois subject and stresses her relation to its Others—its borderzoners, its *créoles,* its colonized, its women, its Jews: "When I talk of Jewish nomadism in *Jaune le soleil* . . . of fires extinguished everywhere . . . I think that is linked to what I lived as a child" (27); "In *Le Camion,* Jews are evoked all the time. They are evoked all the time in all of my films, practically in the form of the woman. *Le Camion*'s woman partakes of that, too, you see." (38).

As if liberated, Duras threw herself into the production of diversely "engaged" works on immigration *(Les Mains négatives,* 1979), Jews and the Holocaust (including *Aurélia Steiner, Aurélia Steiner, Aurélia Steiner,* the films *Aurélia Steiner, dit Aurélia Melbourne, Aurélia Steiner, dit Aurélia Vancouver,* and *Césarée* in 1979 and the war journal, *La Douleur,* in 1985), eroticisms *(L'Homme assis dans le couloir* in 1980, the film and text *L'Homme Atlantique* in 1981 and 1982, *La Maladie de la mort,* 1982), incest *(Agatha* and the film, *Agatha ou les lectures illimitées* in 1981). She issued a volume of selected mostly mid-century journalism under the name of her cultural place, *Outside*, in 1981, the year she also stressed the relation of her writing to the traumas and events of the mid-century war—"when that has taken place within your own country, in as close a physical proximity as the one I lived, it is unforgettable, it is abominable" (*MDM*, 27). She named the temporal and geographical concurrence of her life and the Holocaust as the defining trauma of all who had lived the war as she had and insisted that she writes "in the dimension [of the camps] even if the words themselves are not articulated" (27). In 1984, she again stressed her position "outside" French culture: "I was born in the Far East. I am *créole*. I lived there until I was seventeen. In Vietnam. I thus spoke Vietnamese as well as French. And when I was eighteen, they told me: 'You are French, you must complete your university studies in France.' I had a great deal of difficulty getting used to your country" ("La Classe," 11). That year, she also published *L'Amant*, which was widely read as the autobiographical revelation that her own first sexual relations had been interracial; in respect to the relations of power in French colonial Indochina, that is to say, that those relations had been—as they have not been widely read—collaborative.[8]

Of the 28 creative works Duras put into circulation from 1977 to 1984, one earned unprecedented publisher confidence, wide reviewer praise, heavy and immediate public consumption: *L'Amant*. Minuit issued a first run of 25,000 copies, more than doubling its previous publishing high of 10,000. Following Duras's 28 September 1984 appearance on Bernard Pivot's literary talk show *Apostrophes*, demand for *L'Amant* rose to 10,000 copies per day. Constrained by paper stocks, Minuit issued 15,000 additional copies and then another 18,000 (Adler, 520-1). In the end this work of its author's winter was so successful that it won the literary prize designed to recognize the first work of a young unknown: the prix Goncourt. Duras considered her 1984 Goncourt a political gesture: finding no reason to deny her the prize, she contended, the jury had seized the opportunity to impress her postwar friend, then President of France François Mitterrand: "Everyone is trying to imitate Mitterrand, to do things as they think he likes, that is, and in domains as distant and out-of-synch with current events as the Goncourt" ("Ils n'ont pas," 30). But if Duras recognized the politics of the prize, she failed to ask the crucial question: Why *L'Amant?* Out of all of her books, why had this one been chosen for the Goncourt? What exactly did the jury recognize in this particular book?

Duras's 1984 Goncourt probably did not recognize *L'Amant* for its unusual or promising literary attributes: its author was too old for it to have portended well for her future production, and the novel itself is relatively poorer proof of her skills than earlier works, including *Un Barrage*, which had been nominated for the 1950 Goncourt. It may have recognized the unavoidability of recognizing a writer who had produced so much, earned an international reputation, been around so long, sold well at home and abroad. In that case, the prize would have measured the rising capacity of consumer pressures to shape the decision of at least that year's Goncourt jury. But if Duras's Goncourt suggests that relations of power were shifting between producers and consumers of French literary goods, it more clearly reflects the recognition, on the part of French cultural producers (and juries) that if *L'Amant* was not even Duras's best instance of literature, it had precisely what it would take to meet the demands of culture consumers in France and abroad. It marked their recognition, conscious or not, that as she had in the late interwar years, Duras could supply what the French public was increasingly being encouraged to desire: in the 1930s, enticing evocations of the Empire and its capacity to help defend France; in 1984, enticing and nostalgic images of the eroticism and grandeur of Empire lost. It also marked the recognition that on the international market Duras's *L'Amant* could supply both the exotic-erotic consumers had come to expect and desire of the French culture niche, partly thanks to Clément's film adaptation of *Un Barrage*, and the representations of Empire that U.S. academic audiences would increasingly desire in this period of the beginning of postcolonial studies. Most importantly, perhaps, Duras's Goncourt signaled an awareness that this Duras book provided near perfect raw material for a big budget Hollywood-style but resolutely French cultural extravaganza film. Duras may have believed that she had got the Goncourt because the jury found no reason to deny it: it looks instead as if that jury had every reason to give it to her.

   L'Amant was an ideal text for shoring up the French colonial imaginary and France's international culture-market profile. Drawn from *Un Barrage*, it tells of a *colon* girl's first sex with an older Chinese man in a fragmented and postmodern style that pays no mind to the historical, social, and cultural contexts that the 1950 novel rendered explicit. Nor were most readers able or encouraged to supply those contexts: the French cultural forgetting of Duras's *Un Barrage* was so complete that one 1984 critic, Danièle Brison, found cause to explain to her readers that "in 1950, Marguerite Duras published another very great text: *Barrage contre le Pacifique*" ("Duras"), provide a synopsis of that novel, and conclude by admitting that "René Clément made a magnificent film out of this story, but Duras's name remained impressed in few memories of it" ("Duras"). Judging from marketing patterns, at least one alternate route to those same social, historical, and cultural contexts, the one available in *Les Lieux de Marguerite Duras*, was being discouraged: advertisements for Minuit's other books by/on Duras listed Marini's *Territoires* and Blanchot's *La Communauté inavouable*, but they rarely (if ever) mentioned *Les Lieux*.

Read in isolation from those contexts, *L'Amant* was not only consonant with French colonial fantasies: it elaborated a thinly veiled allegory of French colonial ideology's account of the French experience in Indochina—its imagined Franco-Asian coupling (marriage), the native population's rejection of the French suitor, the departure of the French, the abiding longing of the people of Southeast Asia for the departed French, and the French lover's nostalgia for its lost object of desire.

Bestowing the *prix de jeunesse* on an elderly Duras was a performative and a symbolic gesture. Ironically, by transforming what she considered to be an annotated family photo album into a bona fide literary work, it *diminished* Duras's literary status from that of author to mere autobiographer. It increased the power of her lover's tale, which critical pens elevated to the rank of the origin of her writing; "the story from which all of the other stories come" (Alphant). Once so bored by *Abahn Sabana David*'s outdated leftist engagements, *Le Figaro*'s François Nourissier verily glowed over *L'Amant:* "Here, in the proper sense of the term, Duras returned to her source, her 'primary scene': the moment circa 1930, when, on a ferry crossing a branch of the Mekong, an extremely rich Chinese man approaches a small fifteen-year-old white girl he is going to love" ("L'Amant"). Giving the Goncourt to *L'Amant* performed the replacement of the common origin Duras attributes to her politics and her writing (her early childhood and the spring 1945 traumas) with an exclusively personal-sentimental scriptural origin—the lover's tale. Duras's Goncourt thus feted not an *œuvre de jeunesse,* but the textual matrix of the apparently clean and perfect parthenogenetic birth, as if from the sole pen of Duras, of the conservative cultural icon *Duras.* It was, to paraphrase Fanon's words on North American colonization, a perfect crime.

Replacing the origins of Duras's work shifted her textual time into the retrograde mode of nostalgia. French readers were encouraged to enter her corpus via *L'Amant*'s erotic tale, "then descend the great river with its Asian slowness and follow the novelist into all of the delta's meanderings, into the moistness of rice paddies, into the shady secrets where she developed the repetitive and haunting incantation of her novels, her films, her theater" (Nourissier, "L'Amant"). Late 1950s readers had been encouraged to read *Un Barrage* through Clément's depoliticized film adaptation of it; now early 1980s readers were encouraged to discover Duras's work through a sentimental *L'Amant.* Laundering the politics from her creative work once again reduced Duras's threat, permitting critics to reassure "lovers of novels until now intimidated by Duras" that even they could "discover [her] through *L'Amant*" ("L'Amant"). Integrating Duras into French culture, French literary history, and French feminine writing, *L'Amant*'s critics "placed" her alongside Edith Piaf; "in the indisputable filiation [that is, as the daughter] of Maurice Blanchot" (Laplace).

Nor did critics portray *L'Amant*'s success as Duras's: it was a coup for French publication, French culture, French literature. The 1984 Goncourt really belonged to Blanchot—"Whatever the intention of the Academicians, it was Blanchot's victory that their choice yesterday consecrated" (Laplace); its capital gains accrued to Editions de Minuit: "The fact that the laurels bestowed on *L'Amant* confer little or nothing on Duras matters little, finally, if they help sustain Beckett's publisher. For a rumor . . . had it in Paris that the publishing house of rue Bernard-Palissy [Minuit] was having serious difficulties" (Iommi-Amunategni). As they had not, to my knowledge, since the 1950s, critics spoke of Duras in stark capitalist terms. Brison, for instance: "besides recognizing success, the function of literary prizes is to increase sales. Drop everything. If you don't have it already, run out and find *L'Amant*" ("La bonne"). Even French fashion found a way to profit by transmuting the cultural ambiguities that had once founded *Un Barrage*'s politics into a consumer product. *Duras* became a "social phenomenon," as Parisians walked around Saint-Germain-des-Prés in her hallmark turtleneck collars, sleeveless vests, and short boots (Adler, 522). And as it had since 1953, her work continued to enhance the French *standing* on the international culture market: indeed, for the first time in its history, *Newsweek* magazine dedicated a full-page article to a French [sic] author: *Duras*.

Of course, the Goncourt had its advantages for Duras, too: greater international visibility, increased symbolic capital, more exposure in the mass print press, on the radio and television. Even before the prizewinner was announced, Duras seized the chance to contest the exotic-erotic account of *L'Amant* and realign her name with left-political signifieds. As previously noted, she appeared on Pivot's *Apostrophes* to discuss *L'Amant*, and she stressed in an interview with Hervé Le Masson her wartime experiences, her role in the Resistance, and her connections with Mitterrand. In 1985 she followed up that interview with her alleged war journal *La Douleur* and the film, *Les Enfants*, which, the fruit of a project dating back to 1971 and her children's book, *A Ernesto*, invited children to refuse familial and educational institutions and interpellations so as to become agents of social change. As she had in the late 1950s, from April 1985 to June 1986, she published journalism regularly and much of it was explicitly political. Those articles included interviews with Mitterrand, a comparison of factories and concentration camps, an appeal for one Vietnamese political prisoner's release, and the much-discussed Christine V. piece linking infanticide and class oppression. In 1990 Duras returned to children and revolution in *La Pluie d'été*. This time, as if to close the circle on her corpus, she picked up the native children's revolutionary voices from the final lines of *Un Barrage*, wove them together with that of the *colon* girl (her own young textual stand-in), and created a text in which the promise of social change lies in the immigrant children of late-twentieth-century France and their refusal of the French status quo.

As Duras continued to affirm her marxism, critics mocked her left-wing politics as superficial and opportunistic.[9] As postcolonial immigration and French racism continued to rise, others complained, as they had since the 1950s, of her alleged grammar mistakes, while still others ridiculed her style. In 1988 Patrick Rimbaud printed a book-length parody of her style. Vulgarly titled *Virginie Q.*, a play on the French term for "ass" *(cul)*, his book appeared under the pseudonym Marguerite Duraille, itself a play on the French verb "dérailler"—to drivel, to talk through one's hat, to be off one's rails or rocker. *Virginie Q.* reads as an appropriation of the strategy of subversion Luce Irigaray defined as "mimicry" and its redeployment against both Duras's use of the French language and the textualizations of feminine desire neo-lacanians like Marini found most subversive in her work. A masterful exercise in style, *Virginie Q.* apparently sought to show the ease with which a (real) French man can replicate this woman's simple and vacuous style. As she continued to battle age and alcoholism, other critics castigated Duras for being irrational, inconsistent, and intent on controlling her public image, while still others engaged in the critical violence that characterized the 1987 reception of *Emily L.*, which, as Duras said, "was not literary criticism, it was an attempt to put to death. . . . It was not literary criticism, it was a attempt to hurt me from a distance, to prevent [my book] from being read" (*MR*, 62).

The remarkably more hostile and aggressive tenor of Duras criticism registered both Duras's increased symbolic capital and transformations in the political climate from 1950 to the 1980s. Nineteen-eighties critics wrote of Duras after the 1970s neo-lacanian challenge, which, if it failed to revolutionize the French gender landscape, significantly altered both Duras's international stature and conditions in U.S. French studies. These changes were reflected in the pages of *Yale French Studies*. As we have seen, from 1959 to 1961, *YFS* provided the venue in which three expatriate male scholars had their way in introducing Duras to U.S. readers in their terms, which was as *Duras*. In stunning contrast, three decades later, two authoritative North American female scholars, Alice Jardine and Anne M. Menke coedited a special 1988 issue of *YFS* titled "Exploding the Issue: 'French' 'Women' 'Writers' and 'The Canon'?." And yet three years later, feminist inroads in U.S. academe notwithstanding, Duras still insisted to Jardine that women were at risk in France: "In France, if you don't pay attention, you get eaten up." Jardine: "As a woman or as a writer generally?" Duras: "As a woman writer" (Interview by Jardine, 73). Questioned on her chances of being included in the twentieth-century French literary canon, Duras recalled her PCF affiliations, leftist politics, and refusal of traditional gender roles before admitting, "I don't know . . . who will be deciding. The only thing that reassures me is that, now, I've become a little bit of an international phenomenon—even a pretty big one. And what France won't do, other countries will. So I'm safe. But those are the terms that I have to use. I'm not safe in France. I'm still very threatened" (77).

Nonetheless, Duras continued to affirm the connection between her writing, her cultural position, and her politics. She responded to allegations that her grammar is imperfect by showing them for what she believed they were: rejections and attempted purgings of cultural difference in its linguistic manifestations. She described her writing not as French, but as a culturally *métisse* discursive fabric woven of French and Vietnamese: "Vietnamese is a simple and monosyllabic language that has no coordinating conjunctions and no verb tenses. You don't say 'I went yesterday,' you say, 'I go yesterday.' And you use a great deal of this type of inversion: rather than say 'That woman, I liked her very much,' you say 'I liked her very much . . . that woman.' My style is very much that: a carrying forward to the end of the most important word. The word that counts" (*MR*, 62). She continued to insist that literature could be political: "Political texts could be in a novel" (60). She proclaimed in fact that her own politics and writing came from precisely the same "place": "My writer's place and my political place are the same. I speak from the same place, rigorously." (60). She said that she had no regrets about her PCF membership, credited it with having taught her revolutionary hope, insisted on her abiding faith in marxist analysis and described her political position: "I am and I remain marxist"; "I am a sort of nonaffiliated leftist militant. I am as I hope everyone will be tomorrow: free and on the Left" (60). Although she and others who had joined the Party after the war had certainly been proved wrong about the Party, she said, actual conditions in capitalist societies demonstrated that they had not been wrong about everything or about marxist theory: "I agree with what Antoine Vitez said shortly before dying: 'Perhaps we were wrong (we, [PCF] members), but in light of what we see happening now in capitalist societies—the monopolizing of goods and the systematic exploitation of low-wage earners—we must not have been completely wrong" (61). Where critics had sexualized her (work) and invoked readers to partake of its pastures for decades, she now invited readers to partake of the political pastures bequeathed by Communism: "The Communist error has become a pasture, an internal reference with regard to political power, whatever it may be, to the rotting, to the terrifying, horrifying degradation of all other political tentative. Nothing has been proposed this century, but really nothing that is more pure, more elevated than that which is dead. . . . Now, after the universal joy of the deliverance from the Communist error, comes Doubt" (61).

The Last Stand

The final struggle in the writer's lifetime for the right to define the legitimate discourse of *Duras* took place from June 1991 to January 1992. It played itself out on the grounds of Duras's highest authority—*L'Amant* and its definition of her life story and her textual meanings. This battle's principal players were academic and Duras scholar Alain Vircondelet, filmmaker Jean-Jacques Annaud, and Duras herself. Their strategies, *Duras: biographie, The Lover,* and *L'Amant de la Chine du Nord,* respectively, implicated three publishers in the struggle: Editions Julliard (1950s hub of women's pulp fiction), Editions de Minuit (home of experimental fiction and publisher of *L'Amant),* and Editions Gallimard (bastion of traditional French literature and Minuit's historic competitor for Duras meanings and market shares). This round of Duras struggles resembled that of May 1958, but it also revealed the extent to which Duras's cultural and symbolic capital had increased in the interim. In the 1950s Gallimard had sold the rights to *Un Barrage* without as much as consulting Duras. In 1987 it was she who sold the rights to *L'Amant* in order to realize the financial gains she believed necessary to assure her son a decent inheritance. Faced with Clément's 1958 appropriation of her story, Duras had had no recourse. While she did not have sufficient power in the 1980s to write the film scenario to *L'Amant* as she had hoped to do, she did have the power and the competitive skills to pen a counterscenario to Annaud's film and get it into bookstores before his film's release. Appearing in the preemptive position, *L'Amant de la Chine du Nord* remained on the bestseller list all summer long.

Seizing the opportunity she thereby opened up for herself—the opportunity to associate her public persona with her signifieds of choice—Duras spoke in the French press that entire summer long about her textual politics, her dislike of cinema, her desire for social change. Just as Blanchot's interpretation of her 1955 *Le Square* had preceded and shaped the French public's encounter with that play, she now prefaced its encounter with Annaud's film. But where Blanchot's preface had laundered *Le Square* of its politics, her discourse of summer 1991 verily saturated French discursive space with affirmations, clarifications, and explanations of her (textual) politics in preparation for the January 1992 premier of *The Lover.*

That summer, critics represented Duras as furious with Annaud, although this view is not confirmed by the textual evidence, which shows her stressing both her sympathy for Annaud and the fact of their divergent conceptions of cinema. She insisted that her problem was not with Annaud but with "cinema, its limits" ("Vous faites," 18). As she described them, his conception of cinema was to hers as Debord's ideological and alienating "spectacle" would be to its destruction: Annaud admires and creates cinema; she hates it and seeks its demise. Looking back to the period of her filmic production, she proclaimed, "I certainly was a killer of cinema. Cinema, I detest it!" (19). Conceptualizing their filmic approaches in terms of foreground/background, she contends that by foregrounding lush surfaces, stories, and stars, he produces "obese cinema," the cinema of the victorious capitalist order, "the farthest place *[lieu]* from literature, from 'letters,' as they say, from language" ("Dans le parc," 27). Based on the fact that Annaud aimed to create a biographical film and had cast a beautiful star for the lead, she argued that rather than put spectators at risk, as true art does, his star and his film would distract and enthrall them: "If the little girl is too pretty she will not watch anything, she will let herself be watched" ("Vous faites," 18); rather than seeing, she will only be seen, rather than showing, she will be offered up as spectacle. Far from creating conditions capable of provoking positive social or subjective change, his film would turn spectators into sheep in the same way in which—whether by authorial design or critical mediation[10]—her novel, *L'Amant* had devolved into a sheep-forming enterprise. She gestured to a photo of penguins on a beach, "Voilà, these are the readers of *L'Amant*" (19). That summer, Duras described *L'Amant de la Chine du Nord* as a reappropriation of her life story and her 1984 novel; as "for me the true *Amant*" ("Vous faites," 18). In terms of her own poetics, her description is accurate. *L'Amant de la Chine du Nord* is a "translation." That is to say, it works with the background of the story; the place of her politics and her writing—"The background of all of that, the ground, is the colony, and by colony I mean the space of Lol V. Stein as well, in which she moves, the fabulous [or fictitious] names, S. Thala, U. Bridge. A novel exists from the moment I penetrate into those zones, which are perhaps childish zones of my life, but very serious, very important and dangerous *[grave]*, and which are also political places, you can see that for *Un Barrage*" ("Dans le parc," 27). Functioning as a counterimage to Annaud's *The Lover*, *L'Amant de la Chine du Nord* provides a scenario for obese cinema's ideological inverse—"Skinny film *[le cinéma maigre]*, the least possible cinema. Film said, rather than spoken, like *India Song*, and not million-dollar cinema. That cinema is obese, and they cannot hide that" (27). On 5 July 1991, seven years after she had appeared on *Apostrophes* to discuss *L'Amant*, Duras appeared on the show that had replaced it, Bernard Rapp's *Caractères,* to discuss *L'Amant de la Chine du Nord.* Speaking with difficulty, she gave voice to political despair. Rapp: "And the desire for vengeance remains in you today?" Duras: "For injustice, yes. I am political because of that. I will never change . . . I am still communist, but I know . . . that it's finished, that that will never arrive, because it is impossible that it could arrive. It will never be possible."

Three months later, Alain Vircondelet's *Duras: biographie* was poised to appear. Shaped by rising French interest in intellectual biographies, his project intersected with that period's growing academic research into the wartime textual politics of French-speaking intellectuals. In 1984 U.S. academic Jeffrey Mehlman described prewar writings by Duras's postwar friend Blanchot as "activist, fascist, a protracted apology for terrorism" (39); in 1986 Alice Yeager Kaplan extended the investigations in *Reproductions of Banality,* and, one year later, Belgian doctoral student Ortwin de Graef's discovery that Paul de Man had published more than 140 articles in the Belgian collaborationist newspaper *Le Soir* moved the investigations closer to France. Vircondelet's 1991 biography would make major revelations about Duras; most stunningly, that she had been employed by the 1930s Colonial Ministry, written the late prewar procolonial essay *L'Empire français,* and worked at the Vichy government's Commission de Contrôle du Papier.[11]

Days before Vircondelet's book appeared, the popular literary magazine *Lire* prefaced its French public reception with a ten-page section on Duras. Attributed to Pierre Assouline, this layout pit, wittingly or not, Vircondelet and Duras for the right to define, as its title put it, the real life *(la vraie vie)* of Marguerite Duras. By that time, Assouline was a well-established journalist and biographer. In the 1980s alone, he had published *Monsieur Dassault* (1983), *Gaston Gallimard : un demi-siècle d'édition française* (1984), *Homme de l'art : D.-H. Kahnweiler, 1884-1979* (1988), and *Albert Londres, vie et mort d'un grand reporter, 1884-1932* (1989). Clearly, he had earned the symbolic capital required to decide the issue of Vircondelet's value as a biographer. For his part, as the author of the first master's thesis and book-length study on Duras, Vircondelet had amassed the capital required to speak on her subject; as a fellow *colon* child (born in French colonial Algeria), he had the authority to speak on the colonies as well. Vircondelet also had what it took to enable Assouline to accept his version of Duras's life as the truth, despite the journalist's significant reservations about other aspects of the biography, and to read her own account of her life, politics, and writing in terms of the traditional feminine discursive attributes—lies, deceit, and dissimulation. Vircondelet's capacity to speak the truth of Duras, hence to be the voice of revelation on her subject reflects a privilege accruing under western patriarchy to his race and gender, but it also derives from his affiliation with the Catholic line of Duras readers dating back, most importantly, to Gennie Luccioni's crucial *Esprit* contributions of 1956 and 1958. Partly because he was on faculty at the Institut Catholique de Paris, Vircondelet's research on Duras could be received as "exact and verified," and his version of her story could purport to "make *revelations* about certain aspects of [her life] that had been hidden by the interested party" (Assouline, "La Vraie," 50; my emphasis).

As he is cited and paraphrased in this *Lire* layout, Vircondelet works to discredit Duras's claims that French colonial Indochina shaped her sense of identity, politics, or writing. To the contrary, he contends, Indochina taught her only avarice. Vircondelet rejects Duras's claims for her textual politics in particularly harsh terms: "I asked myself the question of the authenticity of her engagement many times. In fact, her only engagement was writing. A totally selfish and egocentric engagement that rendered her generosity abstract" ("Les pistes," 52). He suggests that her prewar tenure at the Colonial Ministry and her procolonial essay establish her postwar writings on Indochina as opportunistic, that her part in the Resistance was too little too late, and that her links with Nazi collaborators were too suspicious. Vircondelet's account of Duras encourages Assouline to read her critique of cinema as mere sour grapes and her reservations about Annaud's film as the rancor of a spited female whose secrets it reveals. By devaluing the textual political claims that had provoked 1950s critics to cast Duras's writing as virile and misgendered, Vircondelet and Assouline guaranteed, consciously or not, that when confronted with Vircondelet's imminent political revelations about Duras, the French reading and viewing public would override that evidence and continue to perceive her as the French female sentimental writer, *Duras*.

Consistent with the historic trend in Duras criticism, *Lire*'s layout creates and purveys its meanings in a dialogue between written text and image. Its text-image dialogue reveals the layout as a work of containment with long-standing precedents in Duras critical history. It further shows that in this layout, wittingly or not, Vircondelet functions as a powerful and distilled instance of the French culture police, a role figured in Duras critical history by the figure of Proust. As if symptomatizing the acute threat his own impending revelations posed to *Duras,* Vircondelet verily bodies Proust forth in his elegant and widely recognizable proustian pose (See Figures 6 and 7). This layout's text-image dialogue also reveals the threatening "Duras" that Vircondelet's biography risked revealing and the feminine sentimental *Duras* the layout deploys to preemptively repress it. As one might expect, the layout opens with the first image, performs its displacements and repression, and closes with the latter, as if to seal its victory.

Figure 6. Alain Vircondelet in *Lire*, October 1993 © F. Ferranti/Opale.

In *Lire*'s first shot, Duras looms menacingly above the title that promises to reveal to the reading public Marguerite Duras's real life. In sharp contrast to the lush natural background and soft air of the Vircondelet image, Duras is shown standing on the borders of France, apparently somewhere along the north French coast, against gray concrete and cool blue water. As they had been since the 1950s, her revolutionary politics are encoded as virilization. Looking cold-hearted and mean, she wears an oxford cloth shirt and a blood-red jacket registering her PCF affiliations, the Communist blood bath, her abiding Marxism. This Duras is both an older version of the postwar's "little militant activist" (Rolland) and politically committed writer, and the figure of the colonially born, culturally borderzone Duras, whose faux leopard-skin foulard, mark of her colonial connections, seems finally to unmask the real and menacing visage of the apparently harmless little kitty cat that U.S. readers had seen four decades earlier, in March 1953, cradled in the younger Duras's arms in *Time* magazine (see Figure 2, page 42).

    Lire's victory over this menacing "Duras" is marked by the layout's final Duras photograph, which sits above her interview with Assouline. The dialogue between this interview, its title, and Duras's photograph suggests that its photograph and title sought to preface and shape the public's

Figure 7. Marcel Proust, 1896. Cl. Otto et Pirou.

encounter with its text. The vast majority of the interview concerns Duras's colonial background, the wartime traumas, her reactions to Vircondelet's book, Annaud's film, the cinema, and other adaptations of her work. In jarring contrast, its title, "Mes amours, c'est à moi" ("My Loves are My Business") reiterates the only words uttered in that text on either love or sexuality—Duras's firm insistence on her right to privacy: "What I will always hide are my loves [*mes amours*]" (58). Above this title an especially diminutive-looking Duras in a short gray skirt, chic black coat, and high-heeled boots appears to skip out toward the reader, while a fountain (a symbol of male sexuality since at least Chrétien de Troyes) spews behind her. This Duras greets us with a smile, looks kind, receptive, and unthreatening; an elderly woman in her "place" in this Parisian square, in the imaginary heart of France. This face of *Duras*, the feminine sentimental writer, stands at the end of the *Lire* layout as symptom and sign of its victory over Duras's leftist textual politics and cultural differences.

Rather than exclude those meanings entirely, however, the *Lire* layout treats them as the erotic exoticization of *Duras* dictates it must: it retains them in a distanced and displaced fashion. Three pages before this image of *Duras*, Assouline prefaced its reception by insisting that Marguerite Duras's "face, which she says is ravaged, the body that she sees as shrunken, are not only those of an old Indochinese woman *[une vieille Annamite]*" ("La Vraie," 53). His words prepare the public to see the closing Duras shot through an interpretive grid that had remained silent, to my knowledge, since Beauvoir had described Duras to Algren, J.-H. Roy had expressed malaise with her racially ambiguous characters, and Claude Roy had recalled having been enthralled by her vaguely "oriental" visage. These words both retrieve the colonial cultural referent whose repression is required for the erotic-exotic structuration of *Duras* and invite readers to perceive in Duras racial ambiguities promising more secrets to come.

As for Marguerite Duras, she uses her interview with Assouline to reiterate her political and cultural positions. She again states that she has nothing against Annaud, but that they have different views of cinema, and she contends that her sense of identity derives from her formative years on colonial borders. She again identifies herself as *"créole*, native of Cochin China. . . . I took my *baccalauréat* exam with, as second language, Indochinese, or as one says, Annamite. I got a twenty in Annamite and a zero in history" (*MA,* 59). In phrases we recall, she insists on her writing's debt to the Second World War: "My spirituality was turned upside down. I started seeing things clearly after the extermination of six million Jews"; "I became an adult at that moment. I haven't swallowed that. I have been obsessed/haunted *[hantée]* since that time. There is no writer without an obsession/haunting and the nonresolution of that obsession/haunting" (59). But coming at the end of nine full pages establishing her as narcissistic, deceitful, and apolitical, Duras's words merely resonate as further evidence of those same negative attributes. That evidence confirms a notion and creates a desire in the reader—the notion that Duras continues to hide enticing truths and the desire to throw down one's *Lire* and rush out to discover them. Established as unavailable from Duras, however, those truths must henceforth be quested elsewhere—in Vircondelet's biography, for instance, or Annaud's film. Indeed, the competitive genius of the *Lire* layout was its ability to promote their cultural products without damaging *Duras*'s marketability. Emerging intact as a site of feminine deceit and veiling (Assouline to Duras: "You don't like it that one speaks of what you want to hide?" [58]), *Duras* presents itself as a place of infinite hermeneutic interest whose meanings are no longer menaced by Duras's revolutionary politics or colonial background, for the Truth in these matters has been spoken.

The Lover: Parting Shots

In August 1987 Duras submitted a scenario for the film version of *L'Amant* to Claude Berri: Berri immediately asked Jean-Jacques Annaud to direct his film (*A2*, 10). It is hard to imagine that Berri could have had a Duras-Annaud collaboration in mind given their radically different investments in the project. To her, *L'Amant* was not about sexual relations between a white girl and her Chinese lover, but about how their relation had taught her that she would write. She did not believe that her book about writing could be made into a commercial film nor did she desire that it be. She did not wish what she called an international extravaganza repeat of Clément's *Un Barrage*. Quite different desires drove Annaud, the director of international extravaganzas including *La Victoire en chantant (Black and White in Color)*, *The Name of the Rose*, and *The Bear*, and, according to Pierre Billard, the "champion of French cinema on the international market" (Annaud, Int., 51/61).[12] Berri approached Annaud where their desires converged: on the grounds of female sexuality. Said Berri to Annaud on 8 September 1987: "the film rights [are] for you. You who want to make a film about women" (*A2*, 10). Annaud found two reasons for accepting the offer: to assuage what he describes as his guilt at not yet having focused on feminine sexuality and to satisfy his nostalgic longings for the French colonial empire (Annaud, Int., 52/62). After his studies at l'Institut des Hautes Etudes Cinématographiques, he explains, he had served as a delegate in the Service des arts et du commerce de l'industrie cinématographique of the Federal Republic of Cameroon. He had left that experience "unsettled" by Africa and imbued with "nostalgia" for the colonial era of "French presence and grandeur" (52/62), despite the fact that he had not lived through that era. His decision to direct *L'Amant* derived directly from his African experience: "it was not just a love story: there was the encounter of two races, two cultures," which had "fascinated" (*A2*, 12) him since the day he had left for Cameroon. In this account, Annaud attributes motivations to his filmic engagement with Indochina that echo, in a postcolonial-era colonial nostaglic mode, those André Malraux attributed (in 1967) to his colonial-era personal and literary engagement with that same region: "Asia fascinated me. She represented the Other. For me, Asia played the role that the woman plays for most men. She was absolutely different, and I wanted to know her" (d'Asiter, 59; Norindr, 75).

No longer able, in his postcolonial rule era, to travel to Indochina, Annaud's project appears to have been shaped by a desire not merely to resurrect Indochina, but to experience *grande époque* Empire by replacing Duras. More specifically, it appears to have been shaped by a desire to construct a filmic simulacrum of her Indochina and her experience there, to situate himself within them, and to know the ecstasy of her pleasures. Apparently shaped, then, by what postcolonial critics describe as the western male desire of conquest in its patriarchal and colonial modes, it also appears to respond to a desire to witness her female experience from the exterior position of the male voyeur; to combine, in a metaphysical gesture, her feminine pleasure and the masculine one to be had watching it. Unlike Clément in the 1950s, Annaud could and did go to Vietnam. With a budget of 150,000,000 francs, he worked as would an encyclopedic collector or curator. He searched out the sights, places, and people textualized by Duras. His on-site team of 500 French, Vietnamese, Filipino, English, Scottish, Canadian, and Italian members constructed an immense storage facility, filled it with refurbished or reconstructed *pousse-pousse*, tilburys, bikes, cars, and carts, restored building façades, room interiors, and restaurants. They painted tree trunks, built workshops for dying, embroidery, and sewing, searched out period cloth from as far away as Cambodia. Crew members searched shipyards, boat cemeteries, and ports around the world before finding an authentic and acceptable *Alexandre Dumas* in Cyprus and transporting it to Saigon. They looked for a Morris Léon Bollée limousine, found one in Seattle, sent it to Paris, refurbished it, added platforms for technicians and cameras, and transported it by air to Saigon. Annaud's desire to rebuild Duras's Indochina pushed him so far as to find and use in his film members of her former lover's family (*A2*, 10-30).

On his own account, Annaud aimed to transform Duras's novel into spectacle. "In spite of Vietnam, in spite of the epoch, in spite of colonialism, I knew that the wager of this film was located elsewhere: it was a question of describing in images the mounting of desire, the intimate relation, the ecstasy of pleasure" (*A2*, 16). Its success would require enrapturing the audience with scenes of desire; "lead[ing] spectators to the spectacle of pleasure, and mak[ing] them love without reserve the image of desire, the image of love" (35). To that end, Annaud sent scouts to France, England, the United States, and Asia to find the young girl and her Chinese lover. They searched Bangkok, New York, Los Angeles, and Shanghai before finding Tony Leung, a Hong Kong star (30). In three months they interviewed 7,000 girls between 14 and 19 years of age (17). They videotaped 800 of those girls; Annaud interviewed around 100 without success. Finally on 20 March 1990 he found Jane March on a British magazine cover (18). Believing she and Leung would work together, he deemed it urgent to conduct trial runs: "It was essential that the girl and the Chinese man 'desire one another.' Tests were thus conducted in a Paris studio" (20).

When the cast returned from Southeast Asia to shoot the film's sex scenes in Paris, this voyeuristic impulse gave way to a transformational project. *The Lover*'s intimate scenes were shot in a tiny and sultry Paris studio (20 square meters at 40 degrees Celsius and 100 percent humidity) that Annaud termed "the temple" to reflect the seriousness of the work being done there. If sex scenes are usually shot with the couple in bed and the camera by the door, Annaud not only filmed *The Lover*'s intimate scenes himself, he "took off from the door, accompanied the couple to the bed, and stayed with them in amorous emotions without, for as much, showing what one does not see when one makes love" (*A2*, 35). In an interview published in *Le Monde*, he went so far as to declare: "I was in the bodies, in the most secret parts of the bodies, but that does not show" (Heymann and Froden). Getting into bed with them, he appears to have been trying, as Vircondelet does in imitating her writing style, to insinuate himself into Duras's "place"; to take her place in that place. On this reading, his film project assumes mythic dimensions: fearing the fruit of his union with her, Zeus ate Mêtis; Athena was later born from his brow. In similar fashion, Annaud ingests Duras's textual matrix in order to produce his offspring, his film's young girl—discovered by him, groomed by him, even, to believe the film production shots, made-up by him and transformed by that make-up into a racially ambiguous figure; a displaced replacement for Duras's novel's young heroine stand-in *la Blanche*, the white girl (see *A2*, 31). Nor are these the only signs that, consciously or not, Annaud's project was shaped in part by a desire to replace Duras. The textual evidence suggests, in fact, that he imagined *The Lover* as a repetition, transformation, and replacement of the 1959 Alain Renais film for which Duras had written the screenplay, *Hiroshima mon amour*. If this is the case, then here, too, *The Lover* stands as an absolutely depoliticizing replacement. Duras has explained her approach to the *Hiroshima* screenplay in terms of discovering some way to breach the incommensurability that separates our everyday personal and intimate lives from their contemporaneous world historical events, as her life in wartime Paris had been tragically separated from the so proximate world historical reality of the Nazi concentration camps (*MDM*, 26-27).[13] As Norindr suggests, *The Lover* treats this relation between the intimate and the world historical in a way that is politically opposed to Duras's own. In contrast to his first feature film, *Black and White in Color*, Annaud's *Lover* ignores both world historical and contemporary Vietnam in order to reconstruct colonial Indochina "as an elaborate stage where a love affair can be filmed" (Norindr, 144). And where Duras speaks of the guilt and trauma involved in having continued one's everyday life and loves, unawares, as the Holocaust took place next door, Annaud seems to don a certain triumphal tone as he inserts *The Lover* into a similar problematics: "As newspapers around the world carried headlines concerning the imminence of the Gulf War that would break out on 16 January, two days before it did, somewhere in the Cochin China of 1927, on a ferry in the middle of the Mekong, a Chinese billionaire approached a white girl he was going to love" (*A2*, 26-8).

One month before *The Lover*'s release, Annaud published a commented photo album under the same title as Duras's novel: *L'Amant*. But where her *L'Amant* was an annotated family album *sans* photos, his was an annotated album of *The Lover*'s production with abundant photo illustration. It featured images of the French director, his camera, and his colonial gaze, as well as numerous erotic shots from his film. A simulacrum, displaced in the erotic direction, of Duras's *L'Amant*, Annaud's *L'Amant* was designed to replace her novel as the pre-text to his film. It was, in fact, a counterstrategy to Duras's own preemptive counterstrategy to his film *The Lover*—her novel, *L'Amant de la Chine du Nord*. Perhaps the most crucial move in Annaud's *L'Amant* was its deft appropriation of the final pages of Duras's novel.

Duras ends *L'Amant de la Chine du Nord* by transforming the closing lines from her *L'Amant,* which describe the telephone call its then aged heroine received from her former Chinese lover. Her 1991 version expands and updates that scene in light of the perspectival shifts that had taken place in the near decade since *L'Amant,* especially those related to the resufacing of World War II-related issues and Duras's textual engagements with them in, for instance, the 1985 *La Douleur* and her 1986 talks with Mitterrand. Thus, where *L'Amant*'s final lines began, "Years after the war, after marriages, children, divorces, books, he came to Paris" (141; 116), *L'Amant de la Chine du Nord*'s commence: "Years after the war, the hunger, the dead, the camps, the marriages, the separations, the divorces, the books, the politics, the Communism, he called" (231; 225 mod.). The following year, Annaud transformed Duras's fragments to produce his *L'Amant*'s final lines:

> Years after the war, after the marriages, the children . . . the divorces . . . the books, he had come to Paris with his wife. He had telephoned her. He was intimidated, his voice trembled. In the trembling, she had recognized the Chinese accent. He knew that she had begun to write books, he had also learned about the little brother's death, he had been sad for her. And then, he had not known what else to say. And then he had said to her. He had said

that it was as before, that he loved her still, that he could not ever stop loving her, until death (65; ellipses in original).

Like the subversive "mimicry" Luce Irigaray theorizes, Annaud's closing text appears to repeat Duras's own, but it in fact transforms it in ways that subvert her 1991 voice and return reader perception of her (work) to the confines of *Duras*. Although his text largely reverts Duras's closing fragment to its original 1984 contours, by signaling elisions made from the 1991 version, its (incorrectly placed) ellipses prevent it from being construed as *dépassé*, outdated in respect to her updating, and establish it, to the contrary, as the most recent and thus (one is invited to suppose) most authoritative version. Annaud's most crucial changes to Duras's 1991 text are historical, political, and positional: he removes the political and historical signifiers she had added to her first line (the hunger, the dead, the camps, the politics, the Communism), the relative reciprocity and equality she had introduced into her heroine-Chinese lover relation, and the voice and active agency she had attributed to the latter. In *L'Amant de la Chine du Nord*, the Chinese lover *taught* the heroine something new about her brother's death; Annuad's Chinese lover had merely *learned* of her brother's death and felt sad for her. In *L'Amant de la Chine du Nord*, the lover's declaration that he will love the heroine until his death is reciprocated by her emotional reactions, as she bursts out sobbing, drops the receiver, runs into her room, and flings herself, crying uncontrollably, onto her bed. In Annaud, the Chinese lover's undying love stands alone. In *L'Amant de la Chine du Nord*, the Chinese lover fears everything; in Annaud, his fear reintegrates the dimensions of intimidation, which we are invited to understand devolves from the fact that he is talking to a former *colon* woman. That reintegration resituates their relations within the unequal structures of colonial hierarchies.

To guarantee the authority of his closing fragment and its story of Duras, Annaud transforms the strategy Lacan deployed to establish his 1965 reading of *Le Ravissement de Lol. V. Stein* as the Truth of Duras. Lacan established his authority to speak for Duras by referencing her own alleged words: "I introduce Marguerite Duras here with her consent"; "Marguerite Duras told me with her own mouth that"; "I want to note *[entends faire état]* here that I have this from Marguerite Duras herself"; "I limit myself to what Marguerite Duras testified to me that she had received from her readers" (9-14). In his *L'Amant* as in his film, *The Lover*, Annaud devised a subtler visual means to shore up his own authority to speak the Truth of Duras: a Duras simulacrum. On his book's penultimate page, which faces its final fragment, he set a photograph of Jeanne Moreau, an actress long associated with Duras and her work. Dressed à la Duras, shot from behind in semidarkness, and looking quite like Duras, Moreau sits at a desk, "as if" writing in front of a window giving on to a view stunningly similar to the one available from Duras's 5 rue Saint Benoît apartment (which it may well be) (see *A2*, 164-5). Establishing *Moreau-Duras* as his text's apparent source and guarantee proves more effective than the lacanian antecedent: it allows Annaud to tell Duras's story (laundering out its unmarketable oppositional politics; reintroducing the structural inequalities of the colonial subject) in a style nearly indistinct from her own. Taking her (speaking) place, albeit at a distance, lying next to her place on the bed, he sees all (to wit, the ellipses), but does not show all. And with that gesture, he becomes the one with the secret. It is through his perspective, so proximate to the eye of the camera, all but indistinguishable from her own, that spectators were invited, from winter 1991 on, to read Duras's life story and her work. In his *L'Amant* and in *The Lover*, Annaud put into circulation enticing objects of desire—Leung, March, and their couple—designed, consciously or not, to captivate and enrapture audiences, sell tickets, shore up the French culture niche on the international market in a postcolonial rule era driven by nostalgia for Empire and the erotic fantasies that had always driven the French colonial subject, whose desires Duras had learned to attract, and whose psychic structures she had learned to help maintain by honing her writing skills imitating the discourse of French colonial propaganda at the 1930s Colonial Ministry.

Imitating her style, even insinuating themselves "as if" into her place of enunciation, French critics from Jean-Henri Roy to Vircondelet and filmmakers from Clément to Annaud thus had their way in securing the victory of the cultural icon *Duras*. As the 1958 victory of Clément's *Duras* had been, Annaud's was signaled by the replacement of her novel's 1984 cover photograph with an image drawn from his film on subsequent editions of that same novel. Especially on the international market, Annaud replaced more than an illustration: he replaced Duras herself. As we recall, his annotated photo album, *L'Amant*, features a photograph of Jane March posing next to the young Duras's face on her 1984 novel's cover (see Figure 8). On the cover of HarperPerinnial's 1992 English translation of Duras's novel, March, made up *en métisse*, moves into the place of Duras (See Figure 9). All but indistinguishable to the general reading public from the writer herself, this photograph replaced Duras as the source of *The Lover*'s tale and recoded her cultural *métissage* as racial, thereby enhancing her exotic-erotic appeal to western audiences. With those who had preceded him, Annaud thus helped establish the conditions that had permitted them and would permit those who followed to use Duras's 1930s propaganda skills to continue to attract those same desires and shore up the

Figure 8. Jane March posing next to Duras's *The Lover*, 1990. Courtesy of Jean-Jacques Annaud.

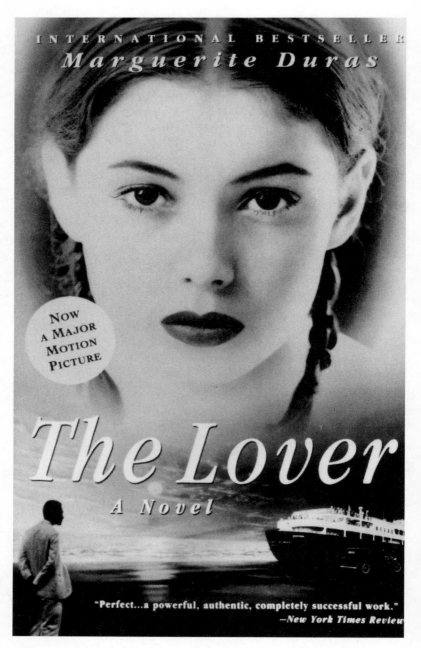

INTERNATIONAL BESTSELLER
Marguerite Duras

NOW
A MAJOR
MOTION
PICTURE

The Lover
A Novel

"Perfect...a powerful, authentic, completely successful work."
—*New York Times Review*

Figure 9. Jane March on the cover of Duras's *The Lover*, 1992. Courtesy of Jean-Jacques Annaud.

French colonial subject decades past her own shift to the revolutionary political; past even, perhaps, her death.

On 13 January 2001, as I prepared this manuscript for publication, the *New York Times* announced that Jeanne Moreau had just become the first woman to be inducted into France's Academy of Fine Arts. Asked by the *Times* correspondent about her works in progress, Moreau noted that in addition to other projects, she would be starring in Josée Dyan's film adaptation of *Cet Amour-Là*, Yann Andrea's memoirs of his 16-year relation with Duras. After noting that Duras and Andrea's relations were "unusual" since he is "gay" (Riding, 2), Moreau went on to contend that this film, in which she plays (an unnamed) Duras and Aymeric Demarigny, Yann Andrea, is, as one might expect, "beautiful" (2).

Chapter 3

Rationalizing Empire: Scientific Management, Colonial Education, and Cultural Placing

*On part pour écrire avec des petits bagages de quatre
sous, que les autres ont ficelés pour vous, on ne part
pas dans la liberté.*

—*Marguerite Duras 1977*

*Laws restrain for a while,
education alone enchains forever.*

—*K'ang-hsi, second emperor of the Ch'ing Dynasty
cited by French Colonial Ministry attaché Poirier 1913.*

Following her conservative 1950s critics, most of Duras's subsequent critics have read her creative work as if she were *Duras*. On the social, cultural, and geographical levels, that is, they have interpreted her work as if it had been produced from the "place" of a Paris-born Paris-educated middle-class French female. Their readings required and sustained the neglect of her formative years, their psychic consequences and scriptural effects. As they laid themselves out between the writer and her work on one side, and her readers or spectators on the other, these critical interpretations rendered less perceptible or even imperceptible those aspects of Duras and her work that exceeded the parameters of French bourgeois culture and its subject. This chapter is the first of three designed to begin the process of retrieving and incorporating into our perception of Duras the symbolic and imaginary materials that were thereby silenced.

Duras often described herself as marginalized and "outside" in respect to French culture. She identified herself with society's underclasses, its marginalized, its prostitutes, its criminals, its insane. Admirers and detractors alike tended to dismiss or diminish her claims. Her postwar friend Jean-Jacques Rolland, for instance, defined her relation to the oppressed and to populations in less developed or formerly colonized regions in terms of pity-based *misérabilisme* and the distance from the oppressed that it implies; her former lover Mascolo rejected her claim that she was marginalized, insisting that she was *bourgeoise*. These pages inquire into Duras's "place" by putting a series of questions to the historical, socioeconomic, cultural, and geographical contexts in which she came of age. Most crucially, they ask: into what "psychic place" would her early social and cultural contexts have "placed" a child of her profile? On which grounds, if any, could she have "legitimately" staked claims to marginality?

Borderzones

From birth through late adolescence Duras's "situation" was consistently "borderzone": each of the social, cultural, and geographical contexts in which she lived and thus in relation to which she was constrained to define her self was, in accordance with Renato Rosaldo's definition, "crisscrossed by a plurality of languages and cultures" (163). In Gloria Anzaldúa's fuller definition, "borderlands are physically present wherever two or more cultures edge each other, where people of different races occupy the same territory, where under, lower, middle and upper classes touch, where the space between two individuals shrinks with intimacy" (pref., 1). A child of the borderlands, Duras was among those children who build their senses of personal and cultural identity out of threads from the various constituent cultures, as Rosaldo sees Esperanza doing in Sandra Cisneros's *The House on Mango Street:*

> Esperanza inhabits a border zone. Multiple subjectivities intersect in her own person, where they coexist, not in a zone of free play but each with its own gravity and density. Moving between English and Spanish, her name shifts in length (from four letters to nine) in meaning (from hope to sadness and waiting), and in sound (from being as cutting as tin to as soft as silver). In contrast to Gregorio Cortez, she does not stand in one place, looking straight ahead, and shout, "Yo soy Esperanza" (163).

Duras was born in 1914 to an upwardly mobile French colonial family in semi-urban Gia-Dinh northeast of Saigon. Her parents had both been raised in France's lower classes—both of their families had been provincial peasant farmers—but they had raised their social statuses with the move to colonial Indochina. An *institutrice,* her mother taught younger native children; an upper-level mathematics teacher, her father managed to get himself promoted to a prestigious mathematics position in Phnom Penh in 1918, when Duras was four. His promotion elevated the family's social status to the point where it was inferior only to the colony's professional and administrative elite. Duras's earliest social position thus repeated in the colonial setting that of Jean-Paul Sartre's family in relation to Paris's professional elite. His parents certainly would have outclassed hers on the continent, but her parents' relocation to the colonies permitted her to enter life as he did: in the lower ranks of her birth society's elite. This partial equalization of their respective social statuses illustrates the colonial advantage for lower-class provincials and helps explain Duras's capacity to challenge and enter into competition with French literary and intellectual elites, beginning with Sartre, when she moved to France.

But with her father's death in 1918, Duras's family lost the social status that had been attached to him.[1] In his life, her mother had moved from the French peasantry to, in the term used for the French living in the colonies, French *colon* bourgeois respectability: from his death, she moved as a single woman, a widow, and a mother in a French colonial fabric whose constituent cultures were all unrelentingly patriarchal. Duras believed that she had fallen to the *colon* hierarchy's lowest rung, and her assessment appears to be accurate. As an *institutrice* of native children, the mother had no institutional power. She was thus constrained to relocate frequently to wherever the administration transferred her—from Phnom Penh, Cambodia, to Vinh Long and Sa-Dec near Saigon. The mother stopped teaching in 1924, whether by choice or as a consequence of native school reforms, and moved to Kampot in rural Cambodia. Henceforth, her family fell in with the rhythms and lifestyles of the southern Vietnamese population, whose tendency to farm the land and move on had undermined early missionary efforts and whose continuing nomadism was being remarked in the 1920s.

Duras's trajectory in 1920s Indochina traced a nomadic pattern quite similar to the one that structures *Un Barrage contre le Pacifique.* She lived in rural and urban areas, in regions with different demographic densities, racial and ethnic profiles, languages, cultures, and practices of everyday life. Then as now, Indochina's population was predominately Vietnamese. In 1937 when the first accurate counts were finally made, 87 percent of its population was Vietnamese, 11.5 percent belonged to other native groups, and 1.5 percent was immigrant. That immigrant population included 217,000 Chinese, 40,000 to 50,000 French, 6,000 East Indian, and a small number of non-French Europeans and non-European *assimilés*, most of whom were Japanese with a European legal status. Most Europeans and 80 percent of the Chinese lived in urban Cochin China; most Vietnamese lived in rural areas and were poor. Numerous hills people (mostly Moi) inhabited the isolated regions of Cochin China, while in the Mekong Delta region of Cambodia where Duras lived for some time in 1924, 250,000 Khmer lived in "self-contained groups" among the Vietnamese peasant farmers (Tate, 337-43).

Framed by this context, Duras recounts the following personal cultural history. As if returning her mother to the low social rank she had occupied as a farmer's daughter in France, her oppression at the hands of French colonial agents established her as "much closer to the Vietnamese . . . than to the other whites" (Duras and Porte, 56). Nevertheless, not having moved to Indochina until she was a young adult, the mother did not ever make the linguistic transition. She taught native children, she lived a rice farmer's life, but she did not speak Vietnamese; "she was never able to learn it, it's very difficult" (60). In this, she conformed to the dominant white trend; "in 1910 only three Frenchmen in Tonkin could speak Vietnamese fluently and correctly, only 9 per cent could speak it enough to satisfy urgent necessities in the restaurant or the field, and 91 per cent knew no Vietnamese at all. Unable to converse with educated Vietnamese who had no way to learn French, the Frenchman learned about the country from his 'boy,' his mistress, or from his visits to the opium den or other morally degraded spots" (Bain, 335). To believe Duras, in her family, at least, the cultural and linguistic transformation occurred in her own *créole* generation: she and her brothers spoke Vietnamese "like Vietnamese children" and lived a Vietnamese peasant everyday life—"we didn't ever wear shoes, we lived half naked, we bathed ourselves in the river" (Duras and Porte, 60). This cultural integration took place on the Cambodian plains, in the absence of their French cultural referent, the mother, who was so "occupied by despair" that she left her children in "complete freedom" (60), which they used for spending entire days in the forests and swimming in little streams *(racs)*. "Very different" than in France, their childhoods made them "more Vietnamese children, you see, than French" (60).

Duras narrates her removal from the cultural borderzones and her installation into a French cultural position along Lacanian psychoanalytic lines. Bursting onto the scene of her life (as the mother of her 1964 heroine Lol V. Stein would erupt into the scene of the S. Thala ball), her mother severed her identification with the Vietnamese and forced her to assume a French cultural identity. In her account, French cultural line-toeing is enforced linguistically: language separates the mother from the Vietnamese, and discursive iteration hammers Duras into a French identity—"My mother often repeated to us: You who are French" (Duras and Porte, 60). Two years before Julia Kristeva's *Pouvoirs de l'horreur* was published, Duras cast her initial rejection of the French cultural identity along the lines of the Kristevan *abject*[2] in a recollected scene closely resembling the 1958 textual scene in which *Moderato Cantabile's* Anne Desbaresdes rejects the French bourgeoisie: "One day she went to Saigon and brought back some *pommes reinettes* . . . she forced us to eat them. We couldn't swallow them, we said that they were like cotton, that they weren't edible, that we couldn't eat French food. I suffered from a sort of anorexia when I was 10 years old, in Phnom Penh, she *[on]* forced me to eat beef steaks, I vomited beef steaks" (60-1). One begins to get sense of the traumatic efficacy of her mother's injunction and the ensuing complexity and contradictions in Duras's psychic position and sense of self in the fact that she does not appear to have become *conscious* of the inaccuracy of her mother's claim until half a century later: "That is what I am discovering now," she said to Porte in 1977: "that it was false, that belonging to the French race, excuse me, to the French nationality" (60).

Both cultural anthropologist Renato Rosaldo and writer Gloria Anzaldúa explore cultural borderzones in the late-twentieth century's postcolonial era and globalizing U. S., at a time and in a place when cultural borders are beginning to be acknowledged or even praised in some quarters. Even then, Anzaldúa emphasizes their difficulties: "It's not a comfortable territory to live in, this place of contradictions. Hatred, anger and exploitation are the prominent features of this landscape" (pref., 1). Marguerite Duras came of age in a time and place where borderzones were more difficult to live; in a liminal situation that was shaped by and subject to the pressures of French colonial rule. In that context, *métissage* in the *colon* population did not represent a "third way," a route to new cultural vistas, an embodied dialectical leap: it was miscegenation, that fatal step "back" down the slippery slope to savagery. It represented the retrograde movement against which France's entire *mission civilisatrice* was designed. It would have been difficult for a "non-colored" (pref., 1) borderlands girl such as Duras to find solace, compensation, or joy in the knowledge that she was part of "the further evolution of humankind" (pref., 1). Nor does Duras textualize her imaginary engagement with her early borderzone situation in terms of a "multiplex personal identity" (Rosaldo, 166) or a "shifting and multiple identity" (Anzaldúa, pref., 1): she structures it as a pattern of distance and alienation, desire and loss.

Duras insists, "I only had Vietnamese girls as friends until I was fourteen or fifteen" (Duras and Porte, 56); "my first games were Vietnamese games with Vietnamese children" (61). And yet, distance constantly separates her fictional stand-ins from the native children with whom she recalls having been so close. She depicts her brother playing with Vietnamese children; says that he "was in the habit of playing with them" (*UB*, 20). But at no time in her Indochina fiction *(Un Barrage contre le Pacifique, Eden Cinema, The Lover, The North China Lover)* does she portray herself actively playing with Vietnamese children. Rather, she depicts her fictional self, as here in *Un Barrage*, looking on—"Suzanne didn't swim as well as [her brother] did. From time to time she got out of the water, sat down on the bank, and watched" (21)—as if, *en voyeur*, she were trying to live their intercultural interaction vicariously or envisage some means of integrating herself into their scene. Still, her fictional selves play only with their brothers, interact only with a *colon* girl at the Saigon boarding house for Vietnamese girls, have sex only with *colon* or Chinese men.

Duras gestures toward what she supposes must be more general patterns: "That must happen often . . . you are born in a milieu, you speak the language of that milieu . . . and then one informs you that you are not Vietnamese and that you must stop seeing Vietnamese children because they are not French and that you must wear shoes, that you must eat steak and fries and stop behaving so badly" (Duras and Porte, 60). As a matter of fact, her narrative of cultural displacement manifests autobiographically a dynamics of cultural separation that was specific to French colonial Indochina in the period of her childhood. From 1906, colonial administrators not only worked to strengthen the boundaries between colonizer and native populations in Indochina: they focused on an institution with which Duras was doubly bound, by way of her parents' professions and her own perhaps inconsistent matriculation—the French colonial school system.

Education and Bordercrossing:
The Discourse of French Colonial Education

Educational issues carried a more "highly charged political connotation" in Indochina than they did in other French colonies (McConnell, 3). Education's central cultural and political roles in the Vietnamese social order that the French sought to supplant required them to pay it particular mind. Both the Vietnamese and the French used education as a means of unifying the nation. In the Vietnam unified by emperor Gia-Long in 1802, education was the route to political power. All "officials were scholars, and all scholars, whether in government service or not, were morally obliged to teach the young. No village was without its school, no school without its qualified teachers, and no gifted pupil was denied the chance to attend an institution of higher learning" (Buttinger, *VDE*, 46). These traditional teachers gave students nationwide a common written language (Vietnamese transcribed in Chinese characters) and a Confucian moral and cultural base. When necessary, they served as advocates of the masses against ruling class injustice, diverting the vast interregional networks to which their positions gave them access into an effective means of fomenting rebellion. By means of those same networks, they organized and led the most effective and long-lived early anticolonial resistance efforts against the French invasion and implantation. If some administrators believed anticolonial resistance had been crushed by 1890, with the teacher networks in place well into the twentieth century, the mandarin scholars remained a source of considerable concern.

Many French officials considered the cultural and communicative tools that these traditional teachers purveyed—their interdependent inculcation of Chinese characters and Confucianism—more menacing than such overtly anticolonial practices. Vietnamese national and collective identities were bound up in characters, which linked them culturally among themselves and with the former Chinese invaders. Unable to read characters, most French colonial administrators could neither evaluate curricular materials used in character-based education nor identify and purge subversives from the teaching staff. Knowledge of characters gave native students potential access to materials the French colonials considered threatening to their colonial order, including Rousseau's *Contrat Social* and Montesquieu's *Esprit des Lois*. As early as 1862, when France took control of Cochin China, French officials thus advocated replacing character-based education with an education in *quoc-ngu* ("national language"), the roman script transcription of Vietnamese devised by earlier Christian missionaries. This scriptural change was discussed as a means of containing the teacher threat, assuring communication between French and Vietnamese, and beginning the progressive cultural assimilation of the Vietnamese population, a project whose necessity, Le Myre de Vilers, the first civil governor of Indochina, affirmed to subordinates, "imposes itself . . . foremost in your preoccupations and should inspire all your acts" (Bain, 268). At least one military leader presented the replacement of characters with *quoc ngu* script as the first step in that assimilation: "The development of Franco-Annamite schools which will substitute alphabetic writing for characters is the surest way of arriving at change: after a generation it must be hoped that one will be able to communicate ideas of progress and humanity in a language that all Franco-Annamite people will understand" (*Bulletin*, 37). By the *début du siècle*, however, such early colonialists ended up discomfited by their own positive results: no sooner had *quoc ngu* education realized some success than Vietnamese students and intellectuals appropriated the roman script to promote nationalist sentiment and proclaim Vietnam's right to independence.

Their demands emerged amidst the growing anticolonial unrest following Japan's defeat of Russia in 1904-1905. Sending a "thunderbolt [through] the Asian world" (Bain, 339), Japan's victory gave new validity and urgency to nationalist and anticolonial thought in Vietnam. It stimulated an important flow of both anticolonial ideas and those carrying them across national, intellectual, and linguistic boundary lines. In 1905 Phan Boi Chau, "the most vociferous Vietnamese rebel-nationalist of the time" (McConnell, 10), crossed out of Vietnam for China, went from China to Japan to print anticolonial pamphlets, and sent those pamphlets back across Indochina's borders to students and parents in the northern regions of Indochina, especially. As did other anticolonialists, Phan read Japan's victory as proof that the route to Vietnam's independence lay in the "bricolage" promises, to use Levi-Strauss's term, of a modern western education: if one learned the European's modern scientific tools, one could use them to beat him at his own game (Bain, 339-40). He thus urged Vietnamese students to cross the borders that cordoned them off from western knowledge, procure a modern education in Japan or the Philippines if necessary, return to Indochina and use that knowledge to push the French out of Indochina and back across the borders from East to West. In Indochina, lecturers traveled widely, assuring "listeners that education was a means of liberation and that Vietnam would rise again if it followed the path chosen by Japan" (Buttinger, *VPH*, 121). From its opening in March 1907, Hanoi's Dong Kinh Free School, the anticolonial movement's "organizational center and spiritual home" (122), offered students a curriculum that reads like an intellectual bordercrosser's mess kit—studies in Vietnamese, Chinese, French, political science, and geography—and it provided them with study abroad opportunities in China and Japan.

In the French colonial population, increased native bordercrossings provoked fears of infiltration and contamination and a desire to police and solidify boundaries. Documents of the period reveal a *colon* sense that the Vietnamese were escaping their places and must be put back. Too close to the French, they threatened to "infiltrate" (Rosello); too distant, they risked being contaminated by foreign ideas and insinuating them into the colonial order. Taking steps to resolidify borders, French metropolitan and colonial administrations engaged in violent repression and moved on the educational front. Any native effort to procure a modern western education was deemed a political act against the French colonial regime; "even reading Montesquieu and Rousseau, whose works the Vietnamese obtained in translation, was considered an act of rebellion, since these books, although not formally banned, were not made available to the Vietnamese" (Buttinger, *VDE*, 122). Indochina's colonial administration closed the Dong Kinh Free School, arrested many teachers, and encouraged Vietnamese parents to insist that their children return home; France made its aid loans to Japan contingent on the expulsion of Vietnamese students (Kelly, "Colonial," 97-8).

From the mid-1800s, French colonial officials discussed education as a key means, with political, military, and social institutions, for consolidating colonial rule. Governor General Paul Bert "believed in education as a political weapon" (Buttinger, *VDE*, 120); twice Governor General Albert Sarraut called native schools "the counterpart of the authoritarian act that installed us in foreign countries" (Léon, 23). In 1906 it was thus per usual when, in the midst of increasing unrest, Governor General Paul Beau decreed immediate short-term education reforms and the formation of a Conseil pour le perfectionnement de l'enseignement indigène for the long-term planning of native education. After reviewing the issues for seven years, this council submitted its final recommendations in 1913, one year prior to Duras's birth. Before she turned four, Sarraut issued his December 1917 Code of Public Instruction legislating the creation of Franco-Vietnamese schools for native students.[3]

Sarraut reassured the French *colon* population that the new schools would provide a safe modern education (Bain, 367).[4] He insisted that they would neither create *déclassés* nor encourage domestic or international demographic shifts in the Vietnamese population. To the contrary, they would educate native students to stay in their actual socioeconomic classes and rural populations to remain rural, and they would allow both the students and the *colon* population to avoid the dangers of contamination abroad. But what Sarraut failed to realize or at least neglected to mention was that his own thinking on native education had been contaminated in the course of his recent bordercrossing. Forced to return to France for medical reasons in 1914, he had remained there until 1917. And as he convalesced, his desire to calm anticolonial unrest and create a stable and productive French colonial Indochina had met up and commingled, as if one lonely night, with the ideas of the U.S. engineer F. W. Taylor for ending labor unrest and creating a peaceful and productive Factory.[5]

Taylorization, Colonization, Civilization

As early as 1900 French thinkers, engineers, politicians, and union leaders discussed Taylor's scientific management, or rationalization as a solution to the labor problem; "an agent of social peace" (Moutet, 81).[6] But the crucial "colonial extension" of early century discourse on taylorism that permitted Sarraut to make the conceptual leap from production-related concerns to Indochina's "native problem" was made by Henri Le Chatelier. In the period of Sarraut's Parisian convalescence, Le Chatelier occupied the power center of the emerging field of scientific management. In the view of many historians, he almost single-handedly shaped the terms of taylorism's introduction and dissemination in France. Editor of the *Revue de metallurgie* in which the first translation of Taylor's work appeared in 1907 and author of the preface to the French version of *The Principles of Scientific Management,* Le Chatelier was the expert on whom Minister of Armament Albert Thomas called to orchestrate the government's wartime intervention into private industry. Le Chatelier's authoritative version of scientific management inserted it into an historical narrative and world picture (Heidegger's term) that, when read by one focused on colonial matters, as Sarraut was, served to redefine the French colonial *mission civilisatrice* and, with it, the very goal of native education:

> *In civilized countries men have a great desire for happiness; they seek all the amenities of life, and are willing to make strenuous efforts to procure them.* Restraint is indispensable in civilized countries. Often the Negroes of the African tribes are satisfied with primitive homes; they go without clothes and have no other ambition than to lead a vegetative existence in the sunshine, without bestirring themselves. . . . On the contrary, in civilized countries the desire to enjoy the pleasures of life, each day more numerous, to possess the good things in increasing degree, to make more money . . . is certainly the most powerful motive to force men into action (preface, 849; italics in original).

Le Chatelier's words translate French colonialism's ideological rationale, the *mission civilisatrice,* into capitalist terms. Unleashing it from its religious and cultural moorings, they anchor that mission to capitalism, production, and consumption. Being civilized becomes synonymous with desiring, seeking, and being willing to make strenuous efforts to procure ever more "good things"; civilizing others becomes a matter of teaching them, by restraint or force if necessary, to desire, seek, and make strenuous efforts in pursuit of that same goal—"good things." (As Greil Marcus put it in a different but relevant context: "You are nothing unless you have everything: that was modernity. Modernity was the shifting of the leverage point of capitalism from production to consumption, from necessity to wish. It was a difficult project: all desires had to be reduced to those that could be put on the market, and thus desires were reduced to needs and experienced as such" [129]). Le Chatelier's words provide a means for translating colonial relations into capitalist relations, especially those inhering in the scientifically managed factory. In his words as in Sarraut's context, taylorism's fundamental categories, "creators" and "executors" of tasks slide into Albert Memmi's colonial categories, *le colonisateur* and *le colonisé*. Le Chatelier thus provides a model through which a governor general could imagine the possibility of resolving native unrest and creating a harmonious colony using the analytic categories and means of scientific management.

Sarraut arrived in France on the eve of World War I, just as the labor unrest that rocked France from 1910 to 1912 yielded to the needs of mobilization and the need to produce a varied war arsenal of high quality. He thus arrived just in time to watch taylorist rationalization become the solution to France's national defense problems. Sarraut had a particular interest in this transformation since it was taking place in armament factories whose wartime labor shortages had been compensated not only by new French female hires, but by more than half of the 100,000 Vietnamese who had been sent to France to help in the war effort. Sarraut's practicum in rationalization provided an inspiring illustration of its potential for success: by rationalizing its arms production, France resolved its defense problem without rekindling labor unrest. To many in France, it thereby proved "the universality of this method of problem resolution" (Nelson, 62). Riding the wave of its wartime success, taylorism realized a "very large penetration into diverse sectors" (63) of French industry and business. Coming in the midst of a national crisis, its success convinced most in France that increased productivity would be the key to France's postwar economic prosperity (Moutet, 67). Not surprisingly, in the 1910s taylorism became "one of the conceptual bases [of] ministers like Albert Thomas or Clémentel, engineers and experts, reform-minded trade-unionists" (67), as well as of Albert Sarraut, a regular habitué of ministerial milieus in the period of his Paris convalescence.

Taylorist methods included material and discursive tools. They conjoined actual transformation of conditions and relations in the workplace with a strategic deployment of its characteristic rhetoric. On the material level, the scientific ordering of work (rationalization) instilled "vertical" divisions between conceivers and executors of tasks (managers and workers) and "horizontal" divisions between workers. Wage policies promoted both divisions: higher wages induced workers to accept re-education and workplace constraints; differential wages (higher pay for products made using taylorist methods) undermined worker solidarity and collective resistance and strengthened worker-employee ties. Formerly centralized, management tasks were parceled out to section heads ("functional foremen"), who divided each task into its smallest units, identified the most efficient means (in motion-time) for completing each one, selected the best worker for the task (the "first class man"), and educated him into its "perfect" completion. New positions were created for inspectors and disciplinarians whose job it was to *surveiller et punir* all factory personnel and operations.

Like the discourse of French colonial propaganda, taylorist discourse contrasted sharply with its unequal factory conditions and relations. Its discourse resounded with the happy cross-class feelings prescribed by Taylor's fourth principle—*"Intimate friendly coöperation between the management and the men"* (Thompson, "Literature," 13)—and reiterated his view that "close, intimate, personal coöperation between the management and the men [was] the essence of modern scientific or task management" (Carlton, 721). As described by its own advocates, taylorist discourse was designed and deployed to hide the relations and conditions of worker inequality from the workers themselves. Taylorism's own literature describes its discourse as instrumental: it claims that it could "rende[r] labor unions and strikes unnecessary" (Thompson, "Literature," 9), for instance, and describes the ideal shop disciplinarian as the "man who understands when the best results will be accomplished by means of a 'jolly,' or when sternness is a necessity" ("Foreman's," 402). Taylorism's discursive strategies ranged from "happy talk" to a differential coding of signifiers. Terms including Le Chatelier's "good things" carried different meanings when used in creator-creator and creator-executor communications. For instance, when a creator spoke to an executor, the term "prosperity," the concept-term that drove creator desire, did not signify "financial profit," as it did to creators themselves, but rather a higher moral purpose; each "man's . . . best use of his highest powers" (Clark and Wyatt, 811). Such discursive strategies were designed to reorient worker attention away from the unequal relations and conditions that defined them as an oppressed class, toward an imagined ideal image of community with management—the harmonious, peaceful, and productive fantasies of a cooperative and congenial Ideal Factory. As Taylor put it, "Life which is one continuous struggle with other men is hardly worth living. . . . Soon after being made foreman, therefore, [I] decided to make a determined effort in some way to change the system of management so that the interests of the workmen and the management should become the same instead of antagonistic" (808). But if taylorist discourse functioned as designed, then while employers looked to the Ideal Factory as a place to profit, workers would envisage it as the place where they could most perfectly and efficiently realize their specified tasks.

From the moment he returned to Indochina in 1917, Sarraut distinguished himself by his rhetoric. As McConnell notes, "If he was not the first French official to claim that humanitarianism and altruism were the main forces driving the French colonial enterprise, he was the first to place such claims at the heart of his political discourse" (2). Described as lofty, inspired, even grandiloquent, Sarraut's colonial discourse won him wide support on the continent and in the French colonial population in Indochina. But at least one historian points to the chasm between his rhetoric and his policies: "Characteristically," writes McConnell, "he used uplifting progressive language to describe policies that were modest, even conservative" (12). For his part, Buttinger believes that "it is safe to assume that Sarraut knew what he was doing when his actions failed to conform to his words" (*VDE*, 98). In fact, Sarraut's colonial discourse, which shaped "the language in which Frenchmen talked about their empire" (McConnell, 2), resonates like textbook "taylorese." Sarraut said, for instance, that the need for "a method of action that is precise and based on a better division of work" had provoked him to undertake the "revision and recodification of the statute regulating the totality of our educational services" ("Indochine," 39). To explain the goal of the new schools for native students, he proclaimed, "It is public education's role to perfect the productive value of this indigenous human capital" (39). To justify his spending program and otherwise reassure anxious *colons,* he also affirmed that native education must increase the "indigenous attachment" to the French by setting their sights, too, on the stability and well-being of the French colonial project:

> This goal, indigenous attachment, leads me to consider a third form of obligation toward this human capital that we have resolved to conserve by medical assistance and perfect with education. We must do something else: we must, I repeat the expression, attach it to its labor, its social duty, as to its duty toward us, indeed these two duties must combine to form one sole. The education we give the indigenous population would be, as some have believed, a real peril, yes, if it helped that population liberate itself from us, separate itself from us. . . . It will not be a danger but a strength for us if it helps the indigenous people better understand our constant striving toward good and progress and if, in that way, it better inclines them toward the noble cause of tutelage or protectorship [*tutellage*] (40).

As scientific management did factories, Sarraut's education reforms divided Indochina's social fabric horizontally, within and between regions, and vertically among social strata (Kelly, *FVS,* 2). As decreed, implemented, and modified in response to native resistance, the new colonial schools forged linguistic, intellectual, and conceptual divisions between *colon* and native students, elite and nonelite native students, and students in rural and urban areas. As he centralized colonial education, Sarraut created a system of regional directors ("functional foremen") responsible to the head of Public Instruction in Hanoi, opened new positions for controllers and inspectors of education, and standardized curricular materials and schoolday schedules nationwide. Judging from education articles of the period, his reforms were undertaken with a firm eye to economics. Most articles explaining the reforms to the *colon* and metropolitan publics begin by describing them in terms of generosity and positive impact on students, but end by emphasizing their projected economic benefits to French colonialists or the métropole. Many of these articles go so far as to explicitly identify specific lacunae in the colonial productive sphere that they promise the new native schools will fill.

As it encountered scientific rationalization, education planning in Indochina took on a new teleology and a convoluted temporality, both of which it shares with taylorism's practice of selecting the "first class man" for a given task and then educating him for that task. Henceforth, colonial education planners approached colonial education as taylorists approached factory operations: they imagined a smooth-running colony of the future and then endeavored to materialize that ideal image. The discourse of education reform is consistently structured around this double temporality— the grammatical present tense in which the new education provisions are explained and the "future anterior" tense in which journalists, colonial administrators, or Colonial Ministerial officials plot the students who "will have been formed" by the new schools into their designated places on their imagined virtual map of a restabilized and productive French colonial Indochina of the future. Their fantasy of that future Indochina was shaped by the male colonial desires of conquest that underwrite the French colonial project, by French colonial propaganda's ideological and imaginary image of Indochina (Norindr's *phantasmatic Indochina)*, and by taylorist images of the ideal factory. In turn, the native school system that fantasy of future Indochina helped shape was devised, consciously or not, as a matrix through which the actually unstable and anxiety-producing Indochina would be passed and from which it would emerge as the peaceful and productive future colonial society. In taylorized factories, education was deployed to mold workers into predetermined places and functions in a schematic representation or organizational chart, or organigram, of the ideal future factory. As depicted in Sarraut's Code of Public Instruction, colonial education in Indochina had analogous aims: "In accordance with the social destination of each person [our general educational work] will satisfy some with a primary education, others with professional educations, still others with complementary or secondary educations, offering finally, to those who can climb yet higher, higher degrees of education" ("Indochine," 39).

By 1914 scientific management's selection of workers was being discussed in relation to phrenology. Dr. Katherine Blackford and Arthur

Newcomb argued that one should apply a system of selection that Clarence Thompson considered no more than "a slightly refined and modernized phrenology" ("Literature," 38). Other researchers studied anatomy, identified its variations, and, in works such as Frank B. Gilbreth's *Motion Study*, compiled lists of the traits alleged to most effect "the efficient performance of manual work" (34).[7] These included many variations inflected by race, gender, and ethnicity, such as "anatomy, brawn, contentment, creed, earning power, experience, fatigue, habits, health, mode of living, nutrition, size, skill, temperament, and training" (35). In the same period, French colonial education planners were speaking of meeting the educational needs of Indochina's student populations in terms of what they cast as the essential, unchangeable, and inherent attributes of those populations: all but two members of Governor General Beau's planning council believed, for instance, that French education was "ill-adapted to Vietnamese mentalités" (Kelly, *CSV*, 100). As their talks slide into a discussion of professional destinies, the education planners can be seen enlisting racial and ethnic stereotypes in the service of an ultimately taylorist argument. Thus, council members argued that French education was antithetical to the goal of giving Vietnamese students "a simple education, reduced to essentials, permitting the child to learn all that will be useful for him to know in his humble career of farmer or artisan to ameliorate the natural and social conditions of his existence" (100). The contradictions inherent in appealing to allegedly ahistorical and immutable racial or ethnic traits to make a socioeconomic case appear quite clearly in one French Ministry official's view that "the Annamite *[sic]* has only one desire: to instruct himself in the European manner. He quests science with the force of a vital necessity and the atavistic passion of a race in which, from time immemorial, science was the key to ambition/success" (Poirier, 265). Formulated in relation to French colonial needs, such views varied widely according to their vicissitudes, but native school planning maintained its consistently taylorist aim: "to transform the primitive peoples of our colonies . . . to render them as devoted to our cause and useful to our enterprise as possible" (Léon, 21).

Due especially to their stunning failure, French colonial education planning and Sarraut's Code of Public Instruction played a crucial part in shaping the conceptual, social, and imaginary contexts of Duras's childhood. She was four years old when Sarraut decreed his Code. For the rest of her Indochina years, the native school project was disrupted and modified as native resistance forced the *colons* to amend their legislation. Her acculturation took place at the nexus of the colonial cultural battles, at the temporal and geopolitical place where the French *colon* and native populations fought for the cultural and linguistic identities of Indochina's youth.

She has said both that she didn't attend school and that she attended school irregularly. Clearly, though, she did attend regularly enough to pass the rigorous *baccalauréat* exam with the help of only one preparatory year in France. More than that, this daughter of colonial educators, employed or not, could not have escaped the pressures or formative effects of the educational system as the vast majority of rural Vietnamese children actually did.

Most Vietnamese peasants refused to send their children to the Franco-Vietnamese schools, opting instead to join with neighbors and give them a Confucian education. Most Vietnamese rural bourgeois sent their children to the more prestigious urban Franco-Vietnamese schools. Most Vietnamese elite in Cochin China, where Duras lived most often, paid for their children to attend the best Franco-Vietnamese school, a French lycée for *colon* children, or a metropolitan institution. In fact, far more native students attended the traditional village schools of characters that were closed down by the 1917 education reforms than re-enrolled in the new schools those reforms established for them. Indeed, at no time in the remaining French presence did more than a meager 10 percent of any Vietnamese age group attend the Franco-Vietnamese schools (Kelly, *FVS*, 32).

The Franco-Vietnamese schools' stubborn failure to succeed merely increased French colonial desire for them; demanded ever greater French colonial intellectual, psychic, and social investments in them. As their failures forced education officials to plan and replan the two-tiered educational program, the conscious and imaginary colonial ambiance of Duras's childhood and adolescence became saturated with ever revised images of projected ideal scenarios. Daughter of first generation French educational functionaries, she spent her psychically formative years ensconced in the persistent imaginary structures, desires, and expectations of the *colon* community. Her sense of self and cultural identity derived not only from the real material and social conditions of her youth but from that community's imaginary fantasies of the social destinies of Indochina's youth populations. The question thus becomes not only how did her social, cultural, and historical contexts shape her imaginary sense of herself, but how did the ambient imaginary context shape it? Clearly, traces of early education discourse appear to have inflected her writing style. Most notably, perhaps, the future anterior of its perspective appears transmuted, after the end of colonial rule, into her characteristic use of the past conditional, as in, for instance, *Le Camion*'s opening line: "This would have been a film" *("Ç'aurait été un film").* Insofar as they suggest that Duras's psychic position, her sense of place in the world, was shaped in part by the ambient and increasingly insistent colonial imaginary context, such textual traces encourage us to ask: Where would a lower-class *colon* girl of her profile have fit into their ideal and hierarchized virtual map of future Indochina? Where would the planners have imagined her? Where would she have come to imagine herself, in the virtual organigram they so persistently endeavored to materialize into a future stable and productive French colonial Indochina?

Mapping Indochina: The Education of Vietnamese Boys

The ethos in the *colon* community on the eve of Sarraut's 1917 Code was one of widespread suspicion that the Vietnamese were escaping their places and had to be put back. French schools on the metropolitan model, established for *colon* children and administered by the French Ministry of Education, accepted on a space available basis those offspring of Vietnamese midlevel functionaries, landed gentry, and traditional elites who could pass the qualifying examinations. Vietnamese students had recently begun to outperform *colon*s on the exams and thus to outnumber them in some French schools. Blaming the Vietnamese presence for their own children's poor performance, *colon* parents demanded that Vietnamese admission be restricted or eliminated: one had to draw the line between colonizer and colonized populations more sharply, they insisted, or the Vietnamese who were today usurping *colon* "rights to elite status by crowding the benches of French schools" would soon demand and obtain "equality in access to government jobs, in how the government treated them, and in the long run, in making political decisions" (Kelly, *CSV,* 98-9).

Sarraut's Code reads like a virtual floor plan for re-educating the Vietnamese into a cultural space that would limit the horizons of their desires, as if naturally, to a subordinate social place in the French colonial system. This cultural division and hierarchization was effectuated by way of a differential signification of the term "modern" in educational discourse and in the curricular materials used in the schools for *colon* students and for Vietnamese students. As the education planning council's members were the first to insist, both school systems were designed to prepare students for their roles in the "modern" world. But these schools presented the modern world to the two student bodies in stunningly different guises. The French school "modern" looked forward to new science and technology, new communications and means of transportation, new industries and factories, innovative cultural forms (cinema, records), modern political, social, and urban organizations. It cast its gaze past Indochina and the East toward the metropolitan *patrie,* western Europe, and North America. French schools offered a curriculum replete in science, mathematics, history, geography, literature, and philosophy. Their general modernizing élan was shored up by constant reference to the métropole as the emblematic modern industrial country. In sharp contrast, the Franco-Vietnamese school "modern" looked back to the future, offering native students a vision of the future that conformed to the French colonial ideological account of the "authentic" (pre-Chinese) Vietnamese past, culture, and lifestyle, duly fleshed out by an occasional reminder of Vietnam's French colonial salvation—a shiny automobile or a bus, for instance, or a paved road. Consistently, the curriculum used in these schools offered not a voyage to the historical past but a transversal foray through the timeless space of the French colonial *imaginaire.* From 1925 to 1939, all but two of the readings that the *Bulletin Général de l'Instruction Publique* suggested for use in Franco-Vietnamese schools were "written by Frenchmen or Eurasians. Some were administrators, such as Governor-General Pasquier, who glorified the Vietnamese past. Still others were anthropologists whose interest was in depicting primitive cultures" (Kelly, *CSV,* 108).

The native school day was largely devoted to literature and language. One-quarter of the readings that formed the basis of those lessons from 1925 to 1931, when Duras and her peers were middle- and high-schoolers, focused on rural Vietnamese everyday life. Even their odd slice-of-metropolitan-life corroborated the traditional values message by presenting modern French existence as life in the France "of small hamlets and people who loved their mothers" (Kelly, *CSV,* 113). Textbooks for native students rarely if ever depicted French cities, factories, science, or technology. They portrayed modern commerce as rural Vietnamese markets, modern industry as traditional rice farming, modern means of transportation as pedicabs *(cyclos; xich-lo).* All newer modes of transportation were cast as horrifying or fantasmatic—trains were drawn as monsters, for instance, and airplanes as fantastic birds (110). Like female students in France at the time, native students attending these schools were educated in the arts not the sciences, with the arts referring, in this case, to traditional handicrafts and rice farming (110). Of 145 lessons devoted to professional life from 1926 to 1931, 45 percent counseled rice farming, 29 percent artisanal crafts, and 3 percent suggested administrative work. No lesson at any level in any native school showed the scholar as a professional model. These books presented the writer-poet, which Duras would turn out to be, "as a starving person who sat in a garret spinning out verses that no one read or heard and that had little utility for anyone" (111).

Had it been effective, Indochina's two-tier school system would have created two separate youth cultures. In intellectual tools, worldviews, professional potential, and social status, these youth cultures would have fallen into traditional western patriarchal gender categories, with native students the passive feminine yin to the *colon* student's masculine yang in the educational planners' organigram. French school curriculum both provided *colon* students with the intellectual tools needed to obtain high-level jobs and social status and worked to form them psychically into an imaginary equivalent of the "monarch of all" position that Mary Louise Pratt identifies as the colonizer's promontory vantage (209; 223). While native schools formed their students into a nonexistent rural past and limited their language competence accordingly, French schools gave *colon* students two discrete discursive and conceptual registers. One was aligned with their own modern futures; the other, with the colonizer's version of traditional Vietnamese culture. If colonial schooling had proceeded as planned, those formed in these two youth cultures would have been incapable of communicating with one another on modern grounds, where the student educated in the Franco-Vietnamese schools would have been unprepared to travel discursively or conceptually. To communicate with one another in French, they would have had to limit their discussions to the native students' subject matters of competence; largely, that is, to the French colonial ideological version of Vietnamese tradition. Even then, the native school student would have come to that space from a radically different place than the French school student: where the native child would have come to it as if upwards and toward the future, the *colon* student would have learned to cast her gaze backwards so as to capture this quaint but picturesque mode de vie.

As they divided Indochina's youth cultures, the colonial schools also effectuated a *rapprochement* of the native male and *colon* female positions. When addressing elite native crowds, Sarraut often boasted—symptomatically, it turns out—that elite native males were now sitting on French school benches next to the colonizers' daughters. This feminization of the native male both registered a certain homoerotic desire chez the colonizer and flattened out traditional heteroerotic relations of desire (in so far as they are dependent on unequal male-female power) between the female *colon* and male native populations. Despite the failure of the Franco-Vietnamese schools, the structure of this imaginary scene, which drove education planning and Sarraut's reforms, shapes Duras's semi-autobiographical representations of her childhood "place" on the Cambodian plain. It permits us to respond to the question of why she does not represent herself at play with native males as she does her brother: because her representations follow the flow of desire being encouraged in the collective *colon* imaginary by colonial school systems in the period of her Indochina childhood. She does not show herself playing with native boys because as a *colon* female her desires were being discouraged by ambient educational, cultural, and imaginary dynamics from directing themselves toward that cathexis. With no desire in the *colon*-native boy games, she simply sat, as she represents herself doing, bored, waiting, and alone, watching the boys play.

On Female Education

There is such an absence of representation of native girls' education in colonial documents and newsprint media of the period that one might assume that native girls attended boys' schools or that female education was too trivial a matter to merit the thought, ink, or paper stock. Quite the opposite is the case: from the turn of the century, tensions ran so high around native girls' schooling as to make it a locus of cultural struggle between elite Vietnamese fathers and colonial officials.[8] French officials complained that as soon as Vietnamese elite fathers "had procured new schools for their sons, they would not stop before obtaining the same for their daughters" (Poirier, 266). The colonial officials themselves argued against providing Vietnamese girls and boys the same education on the grounds that one had to "protect the native woman" (266). Vietnamese elite fathers countered their refusals by deploying whatever means they could to get their daughters educated. In 1900 one exiled chief had his daughter cross-dress to gain entry to a boys' school in Constantine, Algeria, where she studied for three years before being discovered and expelled. In 1907 another elite father, Nguyen Van Mai, took his daughter's case to the Société d'enseignement mutuel in Cochin China, where he "expounded on the disastrous effects that abandoning girls to the old culture and educating boys into an entirely different one would have on native families" (266). Other elite fathers circulated petitions and sent them to the head of colonial education, while the *tong-doc* of Cholon, one of the most important figures in Cochin China, "took the initiative of a private subscription to obtain a school in Saigon" (266). In this context, the relative silence of colonial officials on the issue of girls' schools measures the importance and sensitivity of what Colonial Ministry envoy Poirier explicitly identified in his nearly unique article on the subject as "the most original part of our work, and perhaps the most profound, as much from the point of view of our political security as from that of the labor yield and amelioration of the native people in this country" (266).

If native girls' education was the most silenced and crucial aspect of the 1917 education reforms, the *discourse* on native girls' education has the half-veiled, hat-over-one-eye aspect generally associated not with pedagogy, but with intelligence operations. Their treatment of this issue suggests that colonial education planners valued not educating native women "in itself," but rather for the relations that a proper education could establish between native females and other players in Indochina's colonial field. Consistent with western patriarchal stereotypes and practices, native female education was designed to prepare girls to become placekeepers in the French colonial social fabric: holding other players in their designated places, they would guarantee the stability of the French colonial order. In two years of school (from age 10 to the threshold of puberty), they would learn domestic skills (Vietnamese and French cooking, clothes and dish washing, vegetable gardening, animal care, sweeping, ironing), professional skills (sewing), basic academics (one year each of *quoc ngu* and French, basic mathematics, history, geography, and one year of Confucian moral thought in *quoc ngu*). Instruction in prenatal skills was to be given in the *maternités* that had been springing up since the turn-of-the-century. This educational regimen would prepare native "woman" to contain both the threats posed by the Vietnamese male and those associated with the Chinese population of Indochina.

To early twentieth-century French colonials, Indochina remained, French efforts notwithstanding, "a Chinese colony under French armed police *[gendarmes]*" (Poirier, 269). Except for "a dozen families," they contended, "Indochina is composed of an administrative and military feudal system that governs a Chinese bourgeoisie that trades and revels and native commoners who work and die of hunger" (269). Indochina's French colonial population and administration had what Tate considers a "formidable" (339) prejudice against the Chinese, whom they perceived as "cysts" or "excrescences" in that colony. If colonial officials confronted the Chinese with a "wall of official prejudice" and a "general policy of restriction and discrimination" (339), judging from their educational discourse and provisions, Albert Sarraut and the colonial education planning council also designed native girls' education to combat point-by-point the perceived Chinese Threat. As they envisaged them, the new schools would provide Vietnamese women with the skills required to counter the dominance of "the speculator from Cholon, from Hong Kong, from Canton" and the menace of the "insolent and unmanageable Chinese labor force whose unions, the *towkays*, had made their salaries rise excessively" (267). Courses in nutrition and cooking would teach Vietnamese women how to nourish their husbands and children so that they would produce *like the Chinese*, for as experience had shown, rather than the unmodifiable "degenerate Chinese" the French had all too hastily supposed him to be, the Vietnamese man who regularly "receives with his rice a suitable portion of meat, vegetables, and pasta prepared with fat takes on muscle and energy and furnishes a labor yield equal to that of the Chinese, whose sole superiority is knowing how to eat" (267). As for the new *maternités,* they would teach Vietnamese women modern childbirth techniques needed to expand the Vietnamese population and thereby assure France's projected *grande colonisation* of Indochina's vast uninhabited territories. Adding western business skills to her innate business sense—the native woman was said to be a "born merchant" (266)—the girls' schools would give Vietnamese women the tools to compete with the Chinese on the market, increase family coffers, and control family finances.[9] Instructing Vietnamese women in Confucian thought and moral code, colonial administrators argued, would go far in countering the menaces of Chinese characters, Chinese educations, and Chinese translations of Revolutionary writings. Colonial administrators realized that the rising native insurgency derived in part from their own previous policy of separating colonized populations from the Confucian moral base. They believed that one way of countering current native unrest and precluding it in the future was to reintroduce Vietnamese youth into the Confucian worldview. They looked to Vietnamese women to complete this task, convinced that "in matters of nationality, a passionate matter if ever there were one, the mother's sentiment wins out over the father's idea . . . in all countries, the woman is the conservative force and tenacious guardian of tradition even when she is its victim" (266). Such views led colonial officials to hope that, once inducted into Confucian thought, native women would instill politically quietist (quieting) values in their children, thus precluding their radicalization by a father's potential nationalism or anticolonialism.

But to keep others in place, native women had to remain in their own. Education planners worried about their penchant for doing the contrary—for *wandering,* a trait embodied decades later by Duras's Beggarwoman and her transformation, la dame du *Camion,* of whom we recall Duras contending, "she is perhaps my model, that woman. That which I would have preferred being" ("La dame," 47). The Colonial Ministry's Poirier blamed the native woman's wandering for her wasted sexual energies and failed maternities. To his way of thinking, she may have proved herself fertile but she remained a "mediocre childrearer *[éleveuse]*" (266). He holds native woman's rural-to-urban wandering responsible: it took her from reproductive sexuality to the debauched squandering of her sexuality in lacemakings and prostitution; from the roles of wife and mother to the "malicious skills" of the "petite *congaï*"(266). Once, he said, the native woman had witnessed proper childbirth techniques, but having let her mind go a-wandering, she now completes birthing in a distracted, mechanical, and unsuccessful way. For the colonial project to succeed, her desire must be channeled into commercial gain and reproduction: only then would she cease expending her energies on Chinese lovers as she currently did, only then would she begin combating the Chinese on the market, only then would she return home to her husband and reproduce an expanded, robust, and productive Vietnamese workforce. Poirier: "In this country where immense empty spaces spread out behind the swarming hedge of people, the first thing we need is people. The first usefulness of the woman is to be a mother" (266).

If the new girls' schools were to introduce native women to modern technologies of reproduction and motherhood, the task of maintaining that focus befell *colon* women. Especially in rural regions, *colon* women were encouraged to form mixed study groups or school councils with native women in which to complete their interpellation into western wifedom and motherhood. They were to serve as models toward which native women would be encouraged to strive (an irony given France's demographic inadequacies on the continent and in colonies like Algeria, which some argue it lost for failure to reproduce and fill the land). In so far as *colon* women's role in the education planners' organigram was the strategic *bridging* of colonial categories, Duras's mother, a teacher of native girls and a fabricator of *barrages* manqués would clearly have qualified as a "first class man" for the job—"to make our influence penetrate intimately into native society" (Poirier, 270).[10] As French colonial women like Duras's mother instructed native girls in western ways, the male colonial gaze construed those same girls not only as objects of desire, but as superior substitutes for the French colonial females themselves. Poirier's narration of one 1910s colonial classroom scene stands as a case in point:

> During our inspection tour, we observed this many times: a class of 60 to 80 young girls not forewarned of our arrival, all dressed in immaculately white Vietnamese shirts and pants that they had cut out, sewn, and cleaned themselves. We asked that a sewing test be conducted on the spot. A few little girls ten to twelve years of age were chosen at random and asked to cut out a blouse: they sat gracefully *[gentiment]* down, cut out their patterns very quickly, pinned them, tried them on, all in fifteen minutes. The cleanliness of their round faces, their necks, their nails, their bare feet, their beautiful straight black hair free of coconut oil, their teeth without *laque* or betel nut, rendered them pretty (267).[11]

As Poirier's gaze penetrates clothing of western design, caresses little girl faces, necks, nails, moves down to their bare feet, rises to pass through their unoiled hair and over their betel-free teeth, the drive to substitute finds its breathless voice: "In what primary school of any French town could we/ would we have found as much?" (267). The logic of substitution driving this desire had a firm socioeconomic base. French officials perceived native women as natural fits for the precise socioeconomic place occupied by the mother, and they sought to educate them into that place. In their eyes, native women's destination was identical to what Duras describes as her mother's fate: "the true destiny of the Vietnamese woman is to work on her home, on the agricultural destiny of the country and on the national tradition" (266). Indeed, in Poirier's phrase, their value was rigorously analogous to that of her mother, a Flemish farmer's daughter: "The Vietnamese woman represents in the agricultural life of Indochina an economic value equal to that of the Beauceron or Flemish farm woman" (266). Colonial officials sought to educate the native woman into the *colon* woman's place in the structures of desire and in the social field; to have native teachers succeed French *institutrices* as "the conservative force" (266) reproducing the social and cultural status quos. Figuratively, then, one might say that colonial education official worked to create a stable future Indochina in which the native woman would cultivate *French* bananas (for like "Humbolt assured . . . on an equal planted surface bananas produced 133 times more nutritive substance that wheat" [268]), as Duras so provocatively portrays the mother doing in *Un Barrage contre le Pacifique*.

The Mother's Place

In the discourse of colonial education reform, the place inhabited in Indochina's social fabric by women like Duras's mother thus emerges in the time of Duras's youth as a site of competition and struggle. Its competitive dynamics were motivated by the pressures of a male colonial logic of female interchangeability and substitution. The imaginary competition that male colonial desires installed between native and *colon* females manifested itself materially as a struggle for the teaching positions in the native girls' schools provided for by Sarraut's Code of Public Instruction. The male French administrative position on this struggle is clear: both the Colonial Ministry's Poirier and the new educational provisions weigh in strongly against *colon* women. For his part, Poirier casts female *colon* teachers as French colonial education's weak link and native female teachers as "the mainspring of the school" (270). On the social and material levels, the education reforms went further still, envisaging the replacement of the *colon* female teachers by the native girls studying under them and encouraging the *colon* teachers to seek out their futures—after training their own replacements—in the nonremunerated volunteer public relations positions being created by/for them.

The administrative move to replace *colon* women registered the structural and imaginary French *colon* need, demand, and desire for firm boundaries between colonizer and colonized. In the 1920s and 1930s Indochina's *colon* community was in the grips of an increasing anxiety concerning its own future. "If I were to choose a single word to describe French perceptions of their position in Viet-Nam" at the time, writes historian Milton Osborne, "that word would be 'uncertainty,' with uncertainty sliding on frequent occasion to anxiety" and "this pervasive anxiety . . . at times bec[oming] fear" ("From Conviction," 17-8). Osborne believes the mounting *colon* fears emanated from *colon* "awareness of an almost total divide existing between the indigenous and the colonial communities" (18), but the examples he provides suggest that they derived from a growing sense of too intimate proximity, border permeability, imminent encroachment, and contamination. Osborne notes, for instance, that some *colon*s feared the Vietnamese would penetrate their home and murder them (in bed),[12] while others were afraid that the Vietnamese soldiers and workers who had been sent to wartime France had been "infected" by Communist revolutionary ideas there and that, on their return to Indochina, they would "pass this infection to others" (17).[13] Such *colon* concerns about the intentions of the Vietnamese were heightened by the near total *colon* inability to understand what was being said or written by the Vietnamese in the Vietnamese language.

Of all *colon* positions, the "mother's place" at the bottom of the *colon* social ladder was the most proximate to the native population. The positional closeness of their positions would have been greater than in France's other colonies, due to the relatively mitigated distance between colonial categories Osborne and others find in Indochina:

> A key difference between the situation [Otare] Mannoni describes for Madagascar, and that which existed in Viet-Nam . . . was the fact that having arrived in Viet-Nam the French could see, and did see, a culture that had claims to importance just as significant as the culture of the colonials themselves. This perception must be seen as qualifying any sustaining sense of the master in a master-servant relationship" ("From Conviction," 24)

Consistent with this proximity, in her discourse and in her writing Duras imbues the mother with clear and increasing signs of cultural contamination; her mother was, we recall, "much closer to the Vietnamese . . . that to the other whites" (Duras and Porte, 56). Depicted in Duras's writing as the place of "wrong-way" cultural movement, the mother and her place marked that most menacing material and imaginary place where the French colonial subject found itself beckoned by the temptations leading back "down the slippery slope" to savagery. They marked the place, that is, where that subject found itself tempted by the path against which the entire

French colonial project, its subject, its *mission civilisatrice*, Henri Le Chatelier's taylorist worldview, and Sarraut's Code of Public Instruction defined themselves. They figured the most highly charged place of potential contamination, miscegenation, cultural and/or racial *métissage* in the social and imaginary fabrics of French colonial Indochina; the place that most "disturb[ed] identity, system, order," least "respect[ed] borders, positions, rules," remained resolutely and intransigently "in-between, the ambiguous, the composite" (Kristeva, *Powers*, 4). As depicted by early century education officials and by the mid-century Duras, the mother's place is the social and cultural place where *métissage* takes place, the psychic place where one's sense of being a subject threatens to dissolve, the linguistic place where meaning evanesces, as *mère* runs into *mer* and even *merde* (Duras, *UB*, 58-9); that is, as mother runs into sea and even shit. Indeed the "mother's place" in Duras, like the poor *colon* institutrice "place" in early twentieth-century colonial education discourse, marks the spot of that which Julia Kristeva aptly names: the abject.

Produced alongside the psycholinguistic subject and its social order, the abject is comprised of those early affects and thoughts with which they are not associated. In contrast to the allegedly masculine and human affects and thoughts from which the subject and its social order are said to emerge, the materials comprising the abject are categorized as maternal and nonhuman. As Kristeva understands it, the primary enabling condition of both the subject and its attendant social order is the jettisoning, or abjecting, of the abject. As we have seen, prior to and during Duras's childhood, Indochina's colonial social order was being disrupted and the psychic structures of the French colonial subject threatened by world historical events including Japan's 1905 defeat of Russia, World War I, the Bolshevik Revolution, the bordercrossings of native men sent to aid wartime efforts and native students sent to study in France, the continental mass print press coverage, however inadequate, of native insurgency and French colonial repression in Indochina and, in the colony itself, by unrest, violence, and growing fear. Colonial education planning and reforms emerged as a proposed resolution to questions that context posed: How to maintain French colonial rule in Vietnam? How to maintain the integrity of the *idée coloniale* in both colonial and continental French populations? How to create a stable and productive French colonial Indochina?

The response of the colonial education planners to these queries was: by rationalizing social and imaginary relations between colonizing and colonized populations; by readjusting the psychic structures of the French colonial subject in ways that would meet changing world historical and social conditions, from the October Revolution and the Third International to the mounting unrest that would lead to the peasant and student strikes and demonstrations of the mid-1920s and the turn of that decade in Saigon, including those that took place at the school Duras would attend, the Lycée Chasseloup-Laubat. Read together, the educational discourse of the period and Duras's textual engagement with that period furnish a revelation: located at the intersection of the *colon* proletarian and *institutrice* positions in 1910s-1920s Indochina, the "mother's place" was the precise position in education planners' virtual organigram that would have to be jettisoned if their visions of the future French colonial subject and its stable and productive social order in Indochina were to cohere and materialize. As one might thus anticipate, the mother's place was not only a focal point of 1920s *colon* fear: it was the object of administrative focus and official action. Returning to Indochina for his second term as governor general, Sarraut argued for the proximate removal from Indochina not only of lower-class *colon* teachers but of the entire *colon* proletariat: "Messieurs, I often said in former times what a mistake it would be to maintain a too numerous and too poorly paid French personnel in Indochina. The proof no longer needs to be made: a European proletarian is nonsense *(non-sens)* in the adminis-tration of such a country" ("Indochine," 38).

To be abjected is not, however, to be removed: it is to be repressed and to remain. Jettisoned to the borders between the human and the nonhuman so that the subject and its social order can emerge, the abject remains hovering there, neither me nor not me, installing ambiguous oppositions between I and Other, Inside and Out, beckoning me to recognize it, to approach the place where meaning, the subject ("I"), its social order, begin to collapse. It hovers "on the edge of non-existence and hallucination, of a reality that, if I acknowledge it, annihilates me" (Kristeva, *Powers*, 2) as "something rejected from which one does not part, from which one does not protect oneself as from an object. Imaginary uncanniness and real threat, it beckons to us and ends up engulfing us" (4). Against this threat stand the apparently spontaneous visceral reactions that move me out of the path of danger; the nausea, vomiting, dizziness, or fainting that "thrus[t] me aside and tur[n] me away from defilement, sewage, and muck" (2). From the perspective of the subjective, social, and cultural status quos, both the abject and abjection are protective mechanisms; the safeguards and "the primers of my cul-ture" (2).

Where Sarraut declared the place of women like the mother as subject to removal from Indochina, three decades later in *Un Barrage*, Duras fiction-alized a death of the mother in Indochina. Leaving her cadaver lying to rot in that colony, she leaves a corpse suspended at the beginning of her postwar corpus and in the French colonial order. This scriptural gesture transformed the mother into the abject par excellence: having been a site of cultural ambiguity and contamination in life, in death she became and remained "the utmost of abjection" (Kristeva, *Powers*, 4): "the corpse (or cadavre: *cadere*, to fall), that which has irremediably come a cropper . . . cesspool and death" (3). In this way, Duras established her novel, and, through it her corpus, as a place of political engagement, revelation, and epiphany: showing the French colonial subject that which had been and continued to be shoved aside so that it could cohere, it would put the subject at risk, as Duras contends true theater does; take it to the borders and temptations of its own dissolution and that of its colonial order. Duras understood, as Kristeva also would, that "as in true theater, without makeup or masks, refuse and corpses *show* me what I permanently thrust aside in order to live" (3). Leaving the corpse and its evidence lying in the midst of Indochina and of the French literary field, Duras designed her "theater of the corpse" to "unmask" the French colonial "theatre of the colonies" that had been an integral part of French life since the late nineteenth century (Norindr, 18). Hovering over Duras's corpus from 1950 on, the mother's corpse was designed to take French readers to the border of their condition as colonial subjects; the borders from which that subject "extricates itself, as being alive" (Kristeva, *Powers*, 3). Encroaching upon everything, it would take readers to the place where the French colonial subject would cease being the "expeller" to become the expelled, the dispatched, the disappeared. It would take them, in Kristeva's phrase, to the place where "It is not longer I who expel, 'I' is expelled (3-4). Lying rotting in her corpus, in French literature, in France, the mother's cadaver suspended its revolutionary (or apocalyptic) potential, its enticing promise to bring down that nation's colonial subject, choosing to manifest itself occasionally, as if to recall to our minds its looming presence—as, for instance, the dead dog in *Le Ravissement de Lol V. Stein*. But the revolutionary project was the daughter's revenge: appropriating her mother's fictional death to her own political ends, she would defeat her mother's assassins. For its part, the mother's cadaver could but remain there, jettisoned and abject, waiting to be discovered, whether on the beach or in the bungalow.

Duras's Place

Daughter of an abjected mother, Duras was apparently untouched by the native student strikes in Indochina not only in her school years but at times at her school. By the mid-1920s, nationalist consciousness was spreading in the elite Vietnamese student population, and student protests were taking place colony-wide. Both derived from Vietnamese nationalist efforts to build ties with younger students and from the actions of French educators in elite schools, who "basically drew the lines of French versus Vietnamese and contributed to emergent student national consciousness" (Kelly, *FVS*, 49). Thus, in 1926, did a French teacher at the Collège des jeunes filles indigènes order one Vietnamese girl to give her seat to a French girl and move to the back of the room. When she refused, her uncle, a municipal counselor in Saigon, tried to comply in her stead. Outraged by the girl's mistreatment and her uncle's subservient conduct, native students went on strike. They later met with the Educational Service's Georges Taboulet, who left this account of their position:

> They felt themselves increasingly insulted by the directress, the *surveillant*, and all of the European personnel of the *collège*. Mlle Santoni (the directress) had addressed the students quite regrettably, like this "I will crush all Vietnamese under my feet. Ah, you wish my departure? Know well that I will leave only after I am assured that Vietnamese no longer exist in Cochinchina (48).

Similar incidents provoked student strikes at the Lycée Chasseloup-Laubat in 1920, 1921, and 1926; massive student strikes erupted in central Vietnam in 1927 after a French teacher slapped a native student. Even though such events might have been expected to at least raise the issue of colonial injustice in an adolescent of Duras's age and social profile, she insisted that before World War II "I didn't even ask myself the anticolonial question" (*MA*, 58).

Duras's disconnection from the native student strikes was more than a personal reaction: it was (also) a local manifestation of the *desired* effects of the Code of Public Instruction and its colonial education system. Her lack of involvement was consistent with the design intent of the schools shaped by French colonial propaganda and scientific management: to separate *colon* from native students on the socio-geographical, intellectual, and psychic planes so as to help maintain, among other things, the division between the European working class's consciousness of class oppression and Indochina's native population's consciousness of race oppression, and preclude the particularly menacing threat of their joining forces. Duras's failure to see parallels between her family's oppression and that of native populations (and vice versa) symptomatizes an apparent intellectual and imaginary success of colonial education designs, even in the face of and beyond their demonstrable material failure. Displaced from one another, their respective positions materialize the "imagined places" of *colon* and native students in the colonial education planners' virtual organigram of future stable French colonial Indochina.

But Duras's difference vis-à-vis the elite native students is not only a question of colonial efficacy: it also pertains to the discrepancy between their respective senses of relation to the material grounds and geographies of French colonial Indochina. The native students grounded their sense of self and community in Vietnam: they understood and "imagined" their "self" and community, as Tran Duc Thao would assert in a 1946 *Les Temps modernes* essay, from the Vietnamese horizon, as the Vietnamese subjects of the (past and) future independent nation, Viêt-Nam. Duras portrays her relation to Indochina in a very different register. Although she explained her failure to ask the anticolonial question by the fact that "the colonies were my country" (*MA*, 58), she consistently depicted her relation to Indochina's architectural and geographical places as nomadic and transitory: she moved all over its surfaces, from Tonkin to Cambodia, Cambodia to Cochin China, the Plaine des Oiseaux to Sa-Dec, and Sa-Dec to Vinh Long, and she lived in myriad changing *maisons de poste*, but she never possessed "a home of my own" ("La Classe," 11). Rather than identify herself with any one colonial group, she casts herself ambiguously, in terms of two injurious epithets, as both *la petite blanche* (little white trash) and *une sale petite annamite* (filthy little native); rather than situate herself within any one colonial group, she portrays herself in stark isolation from *colons* and displaced from native students; at a distance, "outside." Speaking to Gauthier in 1974, she revealed the ways in which colonialism had positioned her outside of the girls in her age bracket; friends she otherwise "might have had," with whom she otherwise "could have played": "I remember a grace, a nearly collective grace, you see, circulating, of these girls who were . . . made of a sort of receptivity to nature. They spoke little, they amused themselves among themselves, and they received the rain, the heat, the fruits they ate, the baths in rivers, you see, a receptivity that was apparently very, very elementary" (143; 104; ellipses in original). Only 15 years after having left Indochina would the traumas of spring 1945 finally permit Duras to perceive that which colonial and bourgeois interests were exerting redoubled efforts to hide: the connections between her place outside and those occupied by the Indochinese students alongside whom she had studied, but with whom she had not managed to play.

Chapter 4

Holocaust and Revolution: Communist Ethics, Lol V. Stein, and *La Douleur*

What sticks to memory, often, are those odd little fragments that have no beginning or end.

—*Tim O'Brien*

The traumatic events of 1945 retroactively resignified Duras's place in Indochina as proximate to the Jew. Raised in the place of wrong-way cultural movement, miscegenation, ambiguous and composite identities, henceforth, she perceived herself as outside. Before the war, Duras had married a fellow student and French poet; during it, she transferred her desires onto a half-Sicilian autodidact; in its wake, she defined herself and her politics in dialogue with a close-knit group of fellow French Communist Party members and borderzoners, most notably her husband, the poet-become-Nazi-camp-internee Robert Antelme, her half-Sicilian lover Dionys Mascolo, and Edgar Morin, the son of Jewish immigrants. From their oppositional political and culturally marginal places, these intellectuals responded to the wartime traumas with philosophical treatises and textual political projects, which both emanated from and were relegated to the margins of French culture. Duras's textual politics were silenced and Mascolo's philosophical treatise all but disregarded: indeed, the inattention to his philosophical work helped guarantee the silencing of the politics in her creative work. From our vantage, these intellectuals were, as they believed, ahead of their times: they responded to the war traumas with a challenge to the post-Revolutionary rational subject and its bourgeois capitalist and colonial social orders, which, silenced by the conservative forces of 1950s modernizing France, reemerged only two decades later, transformed, in the work of Jacques Derrida, for instance, and that of neo-lacanian theorists Julia Kristeva, Luce Irigaray, and Hélène Cixous. This chapter analyzes Mascolo's philosophical thought, in dialogue with which Duras developed her textual politics. It then reads Kristeva's revolutionary poetics in its intersections with Mascolo before going on to read, in the light of both of their accounts of textual politics, two of Duras's most important texts, *Le Ravissement de Lol V. Stein* and *La Douleur*. Beyond its local aim of retrieving the revolutionary politics 1950s critics silenced in Duras, it also seeks to bring back into the light the philosophical positions and textual politics that were silenced more generally in 1950s France by means of ideologically designed and deployed cultural icons such as *Duras*.

The Place of Writing and Politics

Duras claims that her writing and her politics emanate from exactly the same place: "My writer's place and my political place are the same. I speak from the same place, rigorously" (*MR*, 60). She aligns that place with the spring 1945 camp revelations and their demonstration of the failure of the modern rational subject, the Cartesian "I think therefore I am," beginning with her own: "I had Jewish friends, I had had a Jewish lover, two of my best friends were Jews, they had Jewish children, I had a very dear friend who was a Jewish writer. Then suddenly they had yellow stars. And I didn't think about it. I didn't think about what I could do for them" (*MDM*, 27). She casts her relation to writing as haunted or obsessed and identifies the source of its haunting as the revelation, by the spring 1945 camp disclosures, of her own wartime failure to think: "I think that the obsession into which I have been plunged since the war, and which is the case of my friends, too, is the fact that we did not realize what was going on" (*MDM*, 27).[1] But if she believes that all who lived the war as she did share her sense of being implicated in the camps—"You know, everyone who lived the war as I lived it became like that. It is impossible otherwise" (27)—she also believes it is impossible for human beings to engage directly with events on the general world historical level. For those who did live the war closest to Duras, including Mascolo and Morin, the scene that actually revealed to them the failure of the rational subject was not the Holocaust per se, but the local mediating scene of the return of Duras's husband Antelme from Dachau. As they narrate it, "Antelme's Return" unified them as a group, redefined their senses of identity, their friendship, their politics, and their intellectual projects.

Mythic Primal Scene in Six Acts

(Act I: Miraculous bordercrossings). It is 12 May 1945, "the day of the peace" (*LD*, 62; 51). Robert Antelme lies near death in the section of Dachau where U.S. soldiers quarantined those considered too weak to be saved or too contagious to risk treating. An untouchable in a land cordoned off for death, he is saved by a secular and banal miracle grounded in materialism, camaraderie, and communication. Member of a mission organized by one Father Riquet, François Mitterrand enters Dachau where, unbeknownst to him, Antelme lies dying. Recognizing his friend and fellow Resistance fighter, Antelme whispers "François." Recognizing Antelme by his dentition, as if a cadaver, Mitterrand and a colleague "wra[p] him up in a sheet, as people wrap up a dead body" (62; 51) and take him across the border separating the doomed from the survivors. Mitterrand telephones Mascolo and a friend, tells them to go to his office in Paris, retrieve uniforms, passports, mission orders, and gas ration cards stored there, disguise themselves as officers, go to Dachau and rescue Antelme. After driving all night, they arrive at Antelme's side. As had Mitterrand, they recognize their friend only when he whispers "Dionys." Removing him from the camp, they complete Antelme's journey to the upper world.

(Act II: *Ecce Homo*). Antelme leaves Dachau, writes Mascolo, "not simply gone astray *[égaré]* in the absurdity of a nonplace or limbo but rather abandoned or already elevated to the dimension of a temporal effacement or uselessness" (*AEM*, 57); "an Ecce homo without a subject, exposing no one, not exposing a man but Man reduced to his irreducible essence. Which is therefore not representable" (55).

(Act III: Revelatory Speech). Antelme's speech flows forth, logorrhea: "As soon as they'd left Dachau behind, Robert L. spoke. He said he knew he wouldn't reach Paris alive. So he began to talk, so that it should be told before his death" (Duras, *LD*, 63; 52). His speech reveals the mystery "without mystery of the unity of the species, always evident and always blinded" (Mascolo, *AEM*, 53); "that the variety of the relations between men, their color, their customs, the classes they are formed into masks a truth that appears here, at the boundary of nature, at the point where we approach our limits, appears with absolute clarity: namely, that there are not several human races, there is only one human race" (Antelme, 229; 219).

(Act IV: Traumatic Vision). In a Verdun cafe, customers are awed by the sight of Antelme; in Paris, Duras fails before his sight: "He was looking up. I can't remember exactly what happened. He must have looked at me and recognized me and smiled. I shrieked no, that I didn't want to see. I started to run again, up the stairs this time. I was shrieking, I remember that" (*LD*, 64; 53). Later in memory-image, she recognizes Antelme as the others had, by his mouth: "In my memory, at a certain moment, the sounds stop and I see him. Immense. There before me. I don't recognize him. He looks at me. He smiles. He lets himself be looked at. There is a supernatural weariness in his smile, the weariness of having managed to live till this moment. It's from this smile that I suddenly recognize him, but from a great distance, as if I were seeing him at the other end of a tunnel" (65; 54).

(Act V: *Ecce Homo* Interpreted). Antelme returns in a state Mascolo calls "indetermination" and "depersonalization" (*AEM*, 62). Under present historical and social conditions, human beings have access to two modes of thinking—rational thought and a "consciousness, a second understanding that does not belong to the thought of the thinker controlled by reason" (20). Normally, one speaks from one sole mode, "leaving the other to silence" (32), but as Antelme later insists, the Nazi camps were limit situations, "the moment when the distance between beings is at its greatest . . . when the subjugation of some and the power of others have attained such limits as to seem frozen into some supernatural distinction" (229; 220). As such, they were the most radical instantiation of the divisions characteristic of post-Revolutionary rational thought, its subject, and its social order; "a magnification, an extreme caricature—in which nobody wants or is perhaps able to recognize himself—of forms of behavior and of situations that exist in the world, that even make up the existence of that older 'real world' we dream about" (229; 219). Reworking archaic Western myths in scientific, philosophical, and anthropological terms, fascist ideology rendered them, in Mascolo's phrase, "conceivable . . . universally admissible" (*AEM*, 64). Exaggerating the archaic Western myth of human progress toward ultimate perfection ("It's an SS fantasy to believe that we have an historical mission to change species, and as this mutation is occurring too slowly, they kill" [Antelme, 229; 219]), fascists subjected camp inmates to "the condition of the proletarian in its extreme form" (101; 95). Under these conditions, Mascolo believes, Antelme's rational and nonrational modes (and the worlds, or *mondes,* to which they belonged), "came, for a time and as if for him alone to be joined together again" (*AEM*, 32). Their rejoining put Antelme at risk; situated him in the "inaccessible intermediate space, place of exception, perdition, or election for him . . . where the one who speaks is but is not, where there is only his speech *[parole]*" (32-3). It established him in a state of "death to oneself *[mort à soi-même]*" (53) or "dépersonnalisation" (62). Issued from within that state, his voice, "no longer *of* anyone, could be received by all others . . . as that of another self, more than alike and more than fellow *[plus que semblable et plus que frère]*—capable of saying that which each one seeks in vain to say to himself" (33).

(Act VI: Group Effect). Antelme's speech depersonalizes Duras and the others. It severs them from Enlightenment faith in rational thought and the myth of human progress; "There will be no return to the old form of Humanism, to naive 'Humanity.' . . . In Hell, he was in the home of human beings. Indeed it is that that he 'brought back from Hell'" (Mascolo, *AEM*, 37). It defines their politics; "from there . . . we found ourselves, before having understood anything about it, judiazed and communized forever" (62); "Judiazed means departed from unconsciousness, from the relative security enjoyed by those who are not threatened in their essence, as are the Jews" (Mascolo, *IP*, 36). Indeed as Mascolo later affirms, Antelme's "intuition of the unity of the race, which also relocates it into the unknown, turns out to be all that our communism will have been made of" (*AEM*, 64). Casting their particular form of communism as a "communism of thought, a shared thinking, a community of thought" (*ARSB*, 199), Mascolo situates it at the nexus of Antelme's revelation of one species, Marx's critique of bourgeois institutions, Hölderlin's claim that thought exists only in dialogue and his embodiment, with the other poet, Antelme, of simplicity. In spring 1947 Duras and her friends meet the Italian communist Elio Vittorini, author of *Uomini e no* (1945), who provided the terms in which they would frame Antelme's revelations. Henceforth, they would think in terms of man and "the 'nonhuman' of man, the possibilities of inhumanity in all men" (Mascolo, *AEM*, 75) and construe the Nazi as "the nonhuman of man, armed with reason, informed of ethics, and anxious *[soucieux]* about perfection, who erects the great labor of dishumanity of the camps" (75).

(Epilogue: Borderzones). Antelme's physical and psychic bordercrossing experience would enfold their politics and writing within a logics of borderzones. Having begun life as the least marginal of them all, he was precipitated into the farthest reaches of the psychic borders by his camp experiences. After his return, the others would all strive to attain, then to maintain or reattain the borderzone psychic state they believed he had occupied. In 1947 Duras, Mascolo, and Antelme began their first (for Antelme, only) major textual engagements with their wartime epiphanies—Duras's *Un Barrage contre le Pacifique*, Mascolo's immense treatise *Le Communisme: Révolution et communication, ou la dialectique des valeurs et des besoins,* and Antelme's camp testimonial, *L'Espèce humaine.* Each of these works is most productively read as it was produced: in dialogue with each of the others. This is especially the case with Duras's creative approach in its ever more minimalist rendering. Mascolo's treatise stands not as the key to her novel or corpus, but as a crucial companion text, a systematic laying out of the ethical premises to which she also adhered, from which she too worked until at least May '68, and from whose basic tenets, textual evidence suggests, she did not diverge sharply even until death.

An Ethics of Refusal: *Le Communisme*

In 1947 as the French Communist Party (PCF) hardened its cultural policy, Mascolo and Antelme struggled within it to procure the right of revolutionary intellectuals, writers, and creative artists to complete cultural freedom. Mascolo also began working out, in the light of Antelme's insights, a revised conception of the intellectual's role in the revolution. Compelled to respond to dominant instances and trends in that era's intellectual field, he distinguished his positions from those of Jean-Paul Sartre. In matters of speaking position, Sartre writes from within Enlightenment rationalist and philosophical traditions; Mascolo defines his position as antiphilosophical and nonrationalist. In the realm of ontology, he opposes what he considers Sartre's idealist view that the human being is born a free consciousness in situation, with his own materialist view that the "undoubted human minimum *[minimum humain certain]* is the man of material need" (*LC*, 433). Rejecting the Cartesian account, he defines the subject, with Lacan, as that which it lacks: "I am that which I lack" *["Ce que je suis c'est ce qui me manque"]* (*AEM*, 84). Far from reaching out spontaneously into the world as Sartre would have us believe, he contends, the human being is forced to reach out to satisfy real material need: "The discovery of material need alone forces him to take an interest in the outside world and makes him exist" (*LC*, 418). Taking aim at Sartre, Mascolo rejects all attempt to circumvent this primary human material aspect:

> To feign *[jouer]* transcendence is to escape the reign of need, and escape from the reign of need is always done by surrendering to the state of things. To remain on the level of the thing, of need, is what requires an effort. To leave the level of things, to feign an escape out of need, which is *never* real, it suffices to merely let oneself go, to abandon oneself to the situation, to the 'force of circumstances' (458).

Mascolo's revolutionary intellectual does not present himself as a theoretical judge in the way he sees philosophers, educators, moralists, and literary writers doing. Indeed, "the oppression that must be most feared is the oppression of theory" (*LC*, 29). Unlike Sartre's engaged writer, Mascolo's revolutionary writer does not use language instrumentally as a means to communicate his thoughts: he works on language itself in an attempt to break down all obstacles to communication. Nor does he write to or for the oppressed masses in an attempt to enlighten them, but to and for himself and all other human beings in an effort to establish communication with the "common man" in us all. Finally, Mascolo contends, the intellectual cannot become revolutionary by studying materialist thought and absorbing materialist theory (as Sartre did): he must discover material need by discovering himself (as the poor autodidact Mascolo had) as a man of material need: "That is the work of revolution. The person who seeks truth directly will not find it. . . . The truth will not be found, it will be made by man who will make it *in the process of making* himself. The man who makes himself at the same time as he makes truth, is *the man of need*" (423). The revolutionary intellectual must thus pursue revolution on her own behalf, too, and at her own risk and peril; "All revolutionaries who are revolutionaries solely for the liberation of others are bourgeois idealists" (506).

Rather than revise Communist political theory, Mascolo develops a communist ethics. Due at least in part to Antelme's experience and to the crucial role of communication in his rescue and the propagation of his insights, Mascolo grounds his ethics in both material needs and communication. In his view, material and communicative needs are the only possible foundations of ethical thought and universal values. If they are so closely linked as to be one and the same, they also represent different phases in the movement to realize man's "true anthropological nature" (435). Material need makes all communication possible: recognizing its material need, the human being reaches out into the world to satisfy it and enters into communication. Material need thus founds the realm of communication, which is the realm in which all values are decided. However, since all common (universal) values must be grounded in the full satisfaction of material needs, no universal value can be decided until the success of the revolution. Envisaging an unending production of new material needs, Mascolo elaborates a notion of revolution as unending process in which material need and communication function as sine qua non means: "The revolutionary movement does not have communication as its goal. It has the need that demands satisfaction as its means, and that is all. It is for that reason that it is materialist. That every need that demands satisfaction is in addition a need of communication, that appears to us the most certain thing in the world" (475).

At the mid-twentieth century, Mascolo believed, something was blocking communication and the movement to satisfy material needs. It was thereby denying "that which cannot be denied: needs, communication, the only foundations of the quest of the true and of the good" (422). As Guy Debord also would, Mascolo attributes that blockage to the emerging bourgeois consumer capitalist society; "the material strength of thing-to-thing relations established between men by the play *[jeu]* of nonmastered economic nature" (422). As he understood it, both Cartesian rational thought and its attendant capitalist and colonial social orders block the satisfaction of these fundamental human needs by installing boundaries and divisions within and between human beings, by dividing the human race into races, and by dividing human actions and interactions into those proper to the private and the collective spheres.

To Mascolo and others at the rue Saint-Benoît, revolutionary action must occur on both sides of these multilayered divisions. Most broadly, it must be taken in both the collective sphere to which bourgeois society relegates material needs, and in the private sphere, to which it relegates values. In the collective sphere, political activists and proletarians must engage in the practical movement for the satisfaction of material needs; at the same time in the private sphere, intellectuals must engage in the practical research of communication. Both revolutionary tasks have the same ideal function: "to blow up the partitions the state of things establishes and which prevent us from seeing . . . to establish communication or make it possible by destroying all existing impermeability . . . to force the exterior world to lay down the appearances with which it disguises itself . . . to discover/reveal the world" (476). These revolutionary tasks meet up on the grounds of their deep meanings. The deep meaning of political action is "to assure communication in the realm of collective economic and social relations, thus under the reign of needs. The deep meaning of art and intellectual activity in general is to assure communication in the order of private relationships, thus under the reign of values" (487). So, too, are their tasks complementary: as the revolutionary movement works in the collective sphere toward the full satisfaction of material needs, it must suspend all values; in the period when values are suspended, intellectuals must work in the private sphere "to maintain their ideal existence" (514). To do that, they must endeavor to become "proletarians of the spirit," "intellectuals of simplicity" (to Duras, banality); the counterparts of proletarians, "men of the simple need" (433). In order to become proletarians of the spirit, they must undo the bourgeois division of their destinies from that of the proletarian and realize that their destinies are, in terms Duras uses to define the relation of her politics and writing, rigorously the same. Alone and with friends, they must recover man's material being, beginning with the common (material) man within, and replace material need where it should be in human thought, which is "the first place" (432). But what real material or intellectual form might such revolutionary work take?

Mascolo once said: "The fundamental principle of my thought (the thought shared rue Saint-Benoît) is negativity" (*ARSB*, 200). He went on to define negativity in terms of an ethics of refusal: "The negation of what exists. Nietzsche said, 'I know truth only as the contrary of a real and living nontruth.' And I say, 'I have absolutely no idea what I want, I have no positive will [*volonté*], but I know what I don't want at any price and which exists and against which I will fight'" (200-1). But negativity took a second form as well in Mascolo's ethical thought. Without escaping the ethics of refusal or gesturing toward a utopian future, he develops negativity as an insistence of the second and nonrational consciousness, which he casts both as "a nonsupervised system of refusal, hope/vow [*voeux*], interrogation," "a straying/wandering in which one's intellectual faculties find themselves intact without law," and as "the movement of a 'new ignorance'" (*AEM*, 20-1). Convinced that rational thought and its "clear" language render humans incapable of accounting for materiality, he contends that "to be equal to the revolution's lack of clarity, one must have first renounced the rational illusion of clear language" (*LC*, 509). Defining the intellectual's revolutionary work as an insistence of the nonrational mode of thought into the rational mode, his ethical thought intersects with his postwar friend Georges Bataille's work on sovereignty and prefigures Julia Kristeva's search for a revolutionary ethics in *La Révolution du langage poétique*. As she would, he both believes that the artist must bombard rational thought with the nonrational in order to provoke the "conflagration of knowledge" (433) and privileges poetry as intellectual work's "highest reality" (461). With Bataille, Mascolo locates the private sphere of intellectual work outside the law, describes it as sacred, and claims that the intellectual might "get ahead of the revolution" (513) in the same way that "ecstasy permits one to get out of the hell of discourse" (470). Intellectuals might take a lead on the revolution, he believes, provided "they departicularize nothing. . . . These escapes are particular and instantaneous, not able to be imitated, not generalizable" (513). In the end, the only possible *political* efficaciousness of a work of art is its potential to save time for the revolution. The division of collective and private spheres creates a need for terror, he explains, which the intellectual might help diminish by removing obstacles to communication and creating new transboundary knowledge.

In contrast to marxist orthodoxy, Mascolo does not identity the revolution with the power of the proletarian: instead, revolution will occur only when "the man of universal history" is "the master of things," which will be "when the distinction between proletarian and nonproletarian will have become impossible, and in consequence, when it can no longer be a question of anyone or any class whatsoever being 'in power'" (506). He rejects all preconceived notion of the psychic or social configurations revolutionary work might eventually yield—all utopia, that is—on the grounds that any project "that lets itself be projected is limited in advance by the condition of the person projecting it, which is the condition of the object" (*LC,* 443-4). He neither advocates nor believes that the revolution would yield perfect unity or equality: "The revolution will not abolish all oppression" (468-9). If one must therefore engage in revolutionary work in the service of no predetermined goal, then "to say the revolutionary movement has no goal means that it does not prejudge what the human being should be, that it is not a humanism, or that it could only ever be a provisional humanism" (472). If the revolution will not yield perfect unity, perfect equality, or a perfect human being, consistent with his understanding of the marxist idea as "the idea of what *else* there is than thought in thought" (447), it will involve a recognition and embrace of difference.

With Bataille, Mascolo casts the revolution and the intellectual's revolutionary work in terms of sovereignty: "The communist revolutionary movement is the movement of general sovereignty. The sovereign man is not the master but the man who no longer has need of slaves to be sovereign" (*LC,* 470). Revolution will be made not on the grounds of power but on those of our common human weakness. Its happiness will not be the bourgeois variant: it will be "the mutual avowal by each human being of his material nature, that is, his own weakness and the complete recognition of material nature, thus the weakness of the other" (475). Revolutionary work will bring happiness only as it restores the (singular, not plural) tragic: "If we take revolution to be indispensable and the abolition of the reign of needs necessary, that is because revolution, need dominated, must restore to every human life its true tragic. Man reduced to a thing is not tragic. His liberation must render him susceptible of being tragic, or: of having a life. That must be the case from the beginning of his liberatory movement. Such is the only tenable revolutionary optimism" (467). In contrast to his own postwar epiphany, this revolution will not erupt as an enlightening of consciousness: it will require the sustained practical activity of successive generations (505).

Duras's Textual Project

Defined at the postwar, Duras's textual politics can be explained in Mascolo's terms: to access the place of "depersonalization," destroy all existing impermeability, blow up the partitions that prevent us from seeing, break down all obstacles to communication, including those between the rational and nonrational modes, and bring down the post-Revolutionary subject of rational thought and its bourgeois capitalist and colonial social orders. But Duras developed her style through the 1950s, as her friends composed their "auto-critiques"[2] and Jacques Lacan expounded his psychoanalytic theory. Shaped in relation to them, her textual political project increasingly took on the form of a sustained and reiterated self-analysis *(auto-analyse)*. Rather than reflecting a retreat from the political, her self-focus is consistent with Mascolo's account of the intellectual's revolutionary work in the private sphere, on the level of personal and intimate relations, and toward the definition of new values. Indeed as Duras contends, in focusing on her self, she aims at the collective social-political: "I cannot directly approach things in general, it is by going to the most particular of things that I attain the other things" *(MDM,* 74).

Two decades after Mascolo's *Communisme,* Kristeva's *Révolution* developed a theory of the intellectual's role in the revolution that is remarkably close to his. When it comes to reading Duras's creative work, Kristeva's model is in some ways better suited than Mascolo's, for developed in the period of Lacan's hegemony, it appropriates his model (as Duras also does) in the service of politics whose philosophical referents and larger lines are quite close to Duras's (and Mascolo's) own. Kristeva gives Mascolo's rational and nonrational modes psycholinguistic dimensions and names: the "Symbolic Order" and the "semiotic processes." As Mascolo holds that rational thought and its social order incarcerate "man," she contends that the Symbolic Order arrests the subject's dynamic movement and incarcerates it in a preexisting "place of enunciation." Against Lacan's view that the subject is permanently placed in an unchangeable status quo, Kristeva says that castration results in a merely provisional first-order "thesis" of the speaking subject. This thesis leaves an excessive, fluid, and mobile subject-in-process *(sujet en procès)* flowing within language as process; a form of language that she defines in contradistinction to the Symbolic, as negativity. Where Mascolo's negativity is comprised of the mobile but lawless intellectual faculties excessive to rational thought, hers is the very medium of writing—language.[3] As she sees it, language is a crossroads, an intersection, a means of transportation that enables and effectuates communication between the Symbolic and the semiotic. Moving within it, the excessive subject-in-process works to expend the Symbolic's "subject of enunciation," the dead moment of its own first thetic placing, by introducing into its Symbolic "place" the semiotic's rhythms, cadences, silences, and spatializations. Like Duras, Kristeva considers writing an individual quest—"one of the most daring explorations the subject can allow himself, one that delves into his constitutive process" *(RPL,* 67); an individual quest that becomes political praxis as it "reaches the very foundation of the social—that which is exploited by sociality but which elaborates and can go beyond it, either destroying or transforming it" (67). Crucially, however, where Kristeva can see only chaos, violence, and death beyond the actually existing Symbolic, Duras and Mascolo see the promise of revolutionary beginnings. To them as to Lenin, negativity is, in Kristeva's apt paraphrase of the Russian revolutionary, the "liquefying and dissolving agent that does not destroy but rather reactivates new organizations and, in that sense, affirms" (109).

Reading Duras through Kristeva while keeping Duras's revolutionary difference *firmly* in mind brings the anticolonial dimensions of her project into view. Attempting to write within language and as a subject-in-process, Duras endeavors to pummel the first-order thesis of the post-Revolutionary subject with her semiotic processes. Defined against its conservative forebears,[4] Kristeva's semiotic is shaped by the ordering of a child's body, drives, and primary processes in the period leading up to the mirror stage and within the relation of the child's body to its mother, its family structures, and, I will add, its social, cultural, and historic contexts. Pummeling the Symbolic place of the Cartesian subject with her own semiotic processes, Duras thus pits—against the French colonial subject— the rhythms, musics, spaces, silences, and spatializations of a semiotic formed in her borderzone place in French colonial Indochina. As she works to expend the thesis of the French colonial subject, she thus also introduces the rhythms, textual spaces, gaps, absences, and syntaxes of her borderzone colonial cultural place into them. On the level of the writer, this dynamic shows her at psychic odds with herself; pitting the colonial borderzone sense of identity her mother's words once "repressed" against the French cultural identity those same words simultaneously forced her to assume.

This struggle plays itself out on the level of the text as a struggle between Duras's genotext and phenotext. As we recall, the genotext is shaped by the semiotic processes associated with the spatial intuition at the heart of the function of signification. It produces a textual space "in which the subject is not *yet* a split unity [but] in which the subject will be *generated*" (Kristeva, *RPL,* 86). Discernible within the text as gaps, silences, and absences, genotext is a nonlinguistic process that "moves through zones that have relative and transitory borders and constitutes a *path*" (87). The phenotext is produced by the Symbolic Order whose "multiple constraints—which are ultimately sociopolitical—stop the signifying process at one or another of the theses that it traverses; they knot it and lock it into a given surface or structure; they discard *practice* under fixed, fragmentary, symbolic *matrices,* the tracings of various social constraints" (88). The Symbolic proper to bourgeois colonial capitalism, Kristeva affirms, molds the semiotic processes into binaries, arrests the signifying processes in the stasis of the sign, and locks the subject into an "axial position that is explicitly or implicitly

called 'I' or 'author'—a projection of the paternal role in the family" (91).
Insofar as the phenotext organizes the place of an already generated subject
and its relations to its objects, it joins with the genotext to circumscribe the
space between the before and the after of the subject—the space of Duras's
writing.

Duras's Textual Forms

Putting herself in play and at risk, then, Duras works to textualize not
merely the structures of the post-Revolutionary subject, but her own
psychic structures—"I speak always of me, you know. I wouldn't get
involved in speaking about others. . . . I speak of what I know" (*MDM*, 36);
"One writes nothing outside of oneself" *(Bon Plaisir);* "I go from me to me.
That's narcissism" ("Vous faites," 19). If in the first part of *Un Barrage*, she
narrated the whole of French colonial ideology, she was also experimenting, from 1947 and in that novel, with the abstract model provided by
Lacan's account of the structures of desire. This experimentation produced
what I term her characteristic "cinema scenes." Generally, Duras's cinema
scenes have the contours of Lacan's mirror stage: they depict a heroine
confronting an *imago* in respect to which she might define herself. Some
focus on already existing relations ("Le boa," *Un Barrage's* cinema screen
image, *Moderato Cantabile's* cafe scene, *L'Homme assis dans le couloir's*
heteroerotic cinema scene) and others on potential relations *(Un Barrage's*
stream scene, Lol. V. Stein's ball scene), but all of those that are most
strictly in line with the views laid out in *Le Communisme* portray a heroine
waiting, *en attente,* for a revolutionary future whose contours are foreshad-
owed by no predetermined *imago*. The heroine in "Le Boa" stands
transfixed in the French colonial "zoo" by her cinema scene—the subject
consuming its object (a boa/a chick)—while *Un Barrage's* young heroine
confronts at least four cinema scenes. At a stream, she watches her brother
swim with native children, by a bridge, she stares at a diamond ring, on a
bench, she waits for an unforeseeable future; at the Eden Cinema, she
watches as heterosexual relations proceed as boa-chick relations had—
along the lines of digestive logic, in the Western bourgeois tradition of the
subject's consumption of its object, devolving, then, from what looks like
desire into a horrific prefiguring of the subject's off-screen consumption of
its object. After *Un Barrage*, Duras rendered her cinema scenes in the more
abstract terms of, for instance, *Le Square's* bench scene, *Moderato Cantabile's* cafe cinema screen, and Lol. V. Stein's S. Thala ball scene. But whatever
their variations, Duras's cinema scenes are consistently set in the space

between the before and the after of the subject, where the subject is at risk and in play. If they intersect the subject at various psychic moments, all work to effectuate its rupture with the rational mode, its entry into the depersonalized state, and its access to the second mode of consciousness, or semiotic. All endeavor to infuse the Symbolic scene with semiotic rhythms and desire in an attempt to modulate its stasis into mobility—wandering, shifting roles, genders, voices, and genres, for instance—and discover new beginnings.

In reference to the psychoanalytic scene of analysis and cure, Duras calls her writing "translation." Convinced that compulsions to repeat derive from the inability to narrate a repressed traumatic scene, Freudian analysis endeavors to cure obsessive behavior by "translating" that scene into two discursive registers. First the patient draws it out of her unconscious by "translating" it, bit at a time, into the language of speech, which permits her to experience it as a real and present event; then the analyst "translates" it into the language of the past, so that the patient can forget it. Consistent with Kristeva's description of Duras's writing as noncathartic ("La Maladie"), Duras refuses the second (or analyst's) translation. To her mind, memory is composed of "isolated lit points or else clear passages toward somber inextricable regions. One sees oneself going toward, but one doesn't know toward what" ("L'Inconnue," 68). As she writes, she moves from memory's lit passages toward the dark and inextricable regions she considers the most important, and toward the encounter with the rhythmic, musical, maternal, and corporeal shapings/traces of her own borderzone colonial provenance. Writing in the depersonalized state of the *fou*—"When I write . . . I am no longer in possession of myself, I am a colander, I have a hole-filled head *[j'ai la tête trouée]*" (Duras and Porte, 98)—she tries to establish communication between the French colonial Symbolic and her own colonial borderzone semiotic. If this project is to have revolutionary effect, it must go further still: it must permit her (heroines) to "see" that which is currently invisible, to name it, and thus to translate it into the Symbolic. That is to say, it must permit them to name that which was abjected and repressed so that the existing subject and its social orders could emerge, and which stands today as a word-hole *(mot-trou)*. Because the existing subject and social orders emerged and survive thanks to that word-hole's abjection and repression, its "translation" would effectively bring them down. Duras often explicitly situates this revolutionary endeavor between dusk and dawn, figuring dusk as the potential end of existing psychic and social structures, night as the space between the before and the after of the subject in which revolutionary work takes place, and dawn as the crucial moment bringing either the debut of yet another bourgeois capitalist and colonialist day or the birth of revolutionary new beginnings. When dawn breaks, "it's over," whether "it changes" or "it continues." In all cases, illumination—the light of midday, the setting sun *Le Square*'s peddler identifies as "l'incendie," the S. Thala's ball's artificial light—figures the revolutionary dynamics of durassian *incendie* (*Le Square*, 44).[5]

As we know, in response to the events of World War II and to growing colonial unrest, postwar French society solidified and defined itself by reinforcing binaries. In response to that same war, Duras and her group defined their postwar identities and projects as on the borders and seeking to bring binaries down. As a result of the 1950s resolidification of the post-Revolutionary binaries, Duras was alienated, by her critics but also to some extent within her self, from her colonial aspect. Her corpus from 1964 on represents a sustained attempt, in the face of those ambient social pressures to divide, to recognize and reintegrate the psychic structures of the *créole* identity she had formed in Indochina. The following pages discuss two moments in that effort: *Le Ravissement de Lol V. Stein* and *La Douleur*. Published in 1964, *Le Ravissement* bears witness to the efficacy of France's 1950s modernization efforts—their elision of (colonial) cultural difference, domestic containment of women, silencing of nonpatriarchal forms of desire, division along class and especially race lines, and construction and circulation of a French colonial object of desire linked to Indochina and capable of maintaining the psychic structures of the French colonial subject that Norindr's *phantasmatic Indochina* long underpinned, even beyond the Empire's end. *Le Ravissement* inaugurates Duras's scriptural endeavor to overcome that alienation, effectuate psychic reconciliation across colonial binaries, reposition her scriptural voice within colonial cultural borderzones, as the *créole* daughter of an abjected mother.

Créole: Doubles

In 1975 Hélène Cixous spoke of the emergence in *Le Ravissement* of Duras's "fantasme fondamental"(Foucault and Cixous, 13). In fact, two fantasy formations emerge in this text—Anne-Marie Stretter and Tatiana Karl. Duras introduces Stretter as an object of desire so as to catalyze the personal revolutionary work this text tries to achieve—the effacement of the barriers separating Lol and Tatiana, their merging, and her heroine stand-in's "self"-definition, as it were, beyond the realm of the Cartesian and Lacanian subjects, as unalienated from the nonrational modes of knowledge, fully sexual, and *créole*. But what Duras does not appear to have realized as she wrote this text was that Anne-Marie Stretter figures the object of French colonial desire, and that, as such, her textual presence campaigned against Duras's own textual political project. Indeed, Stretter's eruption into this text makes a significant autobiographical statement: it reveals Duras tempted by that French colonial object of desire and locked in a struggle between that temptation and her left political and cultural textual project.

Le Ravissement works step-by-step through the process Le Communisme casts as the intellectual's work in the personal realm—breaking down all barriers to communication, within and between subjects. As it begins, its heroine is already sufficiently distinct from the psychic, cultural, and intellectual "stuff" that will have to be jettisoned so she can emerge as a subject and be called by a name. As her truncated name—not the full Lola Valérie, but simply Lol V.—suggests, she is already divided from the second mode of consciousness, including emotions, the body, musicality, and from her extra-French cultural aspect. But she has not yet emerged fully into the position bourgeois patriarchy reserves for a female of her profile. Still outside of rational psychic and bourgeois social structures, she is in the state Mascolo calls "depersonalized"; in the in-between of the subject, past the first moments of ego formation, but not yet past its emergence, she hovers on the threshold of what Lacan called the mirror stage.

The problematic Duras engages in Le Ravissement is: how might this girl Lol avoid being relegated to the bourgeois female position, which is, to her mind, one of the worst forms of oppression. Since the bourgeois Revolution, she explains, middle-class women have been constrained to pass their lives "chez elles, imprisoned, satiated, in a concentration camp universe" (MDM, 75). Today, they continue to find themselves in a socially and historically produced state of "infernal idleness [oisiveté]," of which Duras notes, "there is undoubtedly nothing more infernal than idleness" (75). To the feminists who criticize her for writing about "rich women in bourgeois comfort" and the communists who complain, "Oh là là, she runs around looking for good little middle-class women with all the advantages of money, clothes, toiletries, beauty, lovers, etc.," Duras proffers this political corrective: "That's not true. I show damned and scorned women. I don't know anything worse than that, even in misery. Women living in misery are happier than bourgeois women. It's an agent [facteur] of suicide" (75).

But as she sees it, bourgeois women's position under patriarchy also gives them certain revolutionary advantages, which they share with others marginalized under bourgeois rule, including women more broadly, children, and the mad (les fous). Not having had a social voice, they have a privileged relation to silence; forced to remain idle, they have a privileged relation to the potentially productive political posture of passive waiting, *attente;* excluded from rational discourse and education, they are less completely divided than men from the second, nonrational mode of consciousness. Thus, even before this novel begins, Lol possesses qualities that both derive from women's historical oppression and portend well for her revolutionary potential: she is porous ("she slip[s] through your fingers like water" [*RLVS,* 13; 3]), she is in a state of passive waiting *(attente),* and she is prone to wandering ("part of her seem[s] always to be evading you, and the present moment" [13; 3]). Duras claims that she captures bourgeois heroines "at the moment of . . . their crisis" (*MDM,* 75), when they might throw off bourgeois female constraints for as yet unknowable but more liberated psychic and social configurations. Accordingly, she picks Lol up at the beginning of her wedding engagement party, as she stands on the threshold of domestic containment to the position of bourgeois wife. Introducing into her engagement party scene that most revolutionary element—desire, Duras captures this heroine on the "day this infirm body stirs in the womb of God" (*RLVS,* 51; 41).

As Lol and her fiancé, Michael Richardson, enter the S. Thala ballroom to fete their engagement, Anne-Marie Stretter erupts onto the scene. Provoking a rupture, the sight of her propels Richardson and Lol (as, in 1945, the sight of Antelme had Duras and Mascolo) into the revolutionary modalities Mascolo identifies as "the dream, waiting, or need, initiated, of a new origin" (*AEM,* 25). It installs them, that is, in the state of depersonalization, in which they may take a lead on the revolution by briefly escaping oppression in the way "ecstasy permits one to leave the hell of discourse"(Mascolo, *LC,* 513). Depersonalization is the asocial, ahistorical, nondiscursive state in which they will work toward full communication, community, communism; the place in which Bataille contends one might attain sovereignty. It is the place where they might redefine themselves as "'entire,' 'integral,' 'total' or still sovereign," might recognize themselves in their irrationality, might accept to put themselves at risk and refuse, henceforth, to renounce playing their lives "on chance" (516).

This rupture occurs in the evening, leaving them the night to make revolutionary gains. As Stretter and Richardson move onto the dance floor, they form *Le Ravissement'*s first cinema scene. Far from embodying actually existing structures and relations of desire whose inequalities, digestive logic, and, for women, fatal consequences Duras had cast in earlier works such as *Un Barrage* and *Moderato Cantabile* in the forms of bloodied lips or dead bodies, the S. Thala cinema scene figures relations of desire that are abjected in bourgeois society, including the accidental, nonconjugal, nonreproductive, and homoerotic. As such, this scene presents itself as an *imago* in relation to which Lol might define herself not as an object of male desire, but in relation to unconstrained and free-flowing desire.

Taking her place closer to nature, behind some plants, Lol works with Tatiana, the sensually and ethnically coded embodiment of her "other," to define herself in a way that includes both that which is her current "self" and that which appears, excluded, as its "other." Between them, as well as from Lol to Stretter, homoerotic forms of desire emerge—Tatiana holds and caresses Lol's hand; Lol whispers, "I have to invite that woman to dance" (*RLVS*, 18; 8). In a ballroom saturated with free-flowing desire, Lol stares fascinated at her cinema scene, not as a jilted lover would, but as a woman "whose heart is wholly unattached, a very old woman, watches her children leave her: she seemed to love them" (18; 8). After the first dance, when Richardson comes back over to her, a plea for help or acquiescence in his eyes, she smiles at him, encouragingly. As the night progresses, she forgets the bourgeois logics of desire; "the age-old equation governing the sorrows of love" (19; 9). By dawn's first light, only three of the original four persons in the S. Thala ball's cinema scene remain, Tatiana having faded from view; reintegrated, as a result of their night's work, we are invited to surmise, into Lol. Showing the effects of that gain, Lol, Richardson, and Stretter have grown "centuries older" and "attained the wisdom of the ages; "that kind of age which lies, lurking within the insane" (19-20; 9-10).

To retain the S. Thala night's gains, Richardson would have had to have seen a "sign of eternity" (21; 11), of the promise of new beginnings that emerged in its course and brought it back with him—"translated" it—into the conscious realm; the light of day. Although "Lol V. Stein's smile . . . was one such sign," Richardson is so consumed with Stretter, that "he fail[s] to see it" (21; 11). Thus can post-Revolutionary bourgeois rational structures reassert their control: the music ends, the musicians take their places in rational linear order and "fil[e] past them, one by one, Indian-style, their violins enclosed in funereal cases" (21; 11 mod.). Their reassertion permits Lol's mother to erupt violently onto this scene. As had Duras's own mother, she attempts to triangulate her daughter's cinema scene in a conservative sense: severing Lol from the ball's revolutionary possibilities, she would enforce her assumption of an established incarcerated position in the patriarchal status quo. Throwing her body into the line of vision joining Lol to this scene, she divides her daughter from its revolutionary dynamics. Screaming epithets that define her as "the woman wronged," she attempts to hail or interpellate (Althusser) her into that patriarchal feminine position. Striking down her mother's hand, Lol manages to elude that interpellation, but with Richardson and Stretter jettisoned from the scene, she leaves the S. Thala ball in an intermediary state similar to the one in which she entered it: between the before and the after of the subject, she hovers still within the realm of the mirror stage, "not yet God, nor anyone" (*RLVS*, 49;39).

One decade after the ball, Duras figures Lol as Kristeva does the subject-in-process: having assumed the objectified bourgeois feminine place of wife and mother, she exceeds its confines. Her excess inserts itself as subject-in-process into the mobility of wandering *(errance)*, Duras's geopolitical equivalent of the negativity of language. Lol's *errance* permits her to rediscover and communicate with the figure that had faded away during the S. Thala ball, but with which she had not managed to merge: Tatiana Karl. As she sets herself a-wandering the streets of U. Bridge, Lol remembers Tatiana, whom she had forgotten in the interim. Going to her place on the edge of nature (the forest), she embarks once again, with her, on an attempt to reaccess the depersonalization of the S. Thala ball. Lol works to recreate that scene with Tatiana and her lover, Jacques Hold. Framed by the window in the hotel room where they make love, they form a characteristic durassian cinema scene; lying in a rye field, she watches, transfixed, a solitary spectator this time. As their efforts progress, Tatiana once again begins to fade, permitting Lol and Hold to return alone to S. Thala where, in the famous ballroom, then on the sandy beach, and, finally, in a hotel room, they work toward Lol's reintegration with Tatiana, the definition of a new relation to desire, and a new form of unalienated "subjectivity."

Their revolutionary project is profoundly entwined with memory. For Lol, to access Tatiana is to access the memory of the other within and, with it, the memory of a nondivided form of human interaction, communication, and community. Believing that memory is diffused in all places, Duras contends that cultural and social resistance alone prevent us from being permeable to it. To access memory, she says, we must open ourselves up, become porous, write. In the S. Thala ballroom, Jacques Hold attains, albeit incompletely, the porosity Duras finds in that epitome of the revolutionary writer: the madman; a "hollow form . . . traversed by the memory of all," "a colander-head who, being nothing, offers no resistance to anything" (Duras and Porte, 96). As he becomes permeable to the memories diffused in the ballroom, Hold catches sight of the knowledge that had alluded Richardson: he sees that a trace had remained of the S. Thala ball's revolutionary gain, although he does not see the actual trace itself: "One trace remains, one. A single, indelible trace, at first we know not where" (*RLVS*, 181; 170-1). Prodding them—"What? You don't know where?" (181; 171), an astounded, ironic, and intruding Duras moves them to the sands of T. Beach where they sleep, Lol a bit deeper in the sand, like *des fous.*

Le Ravissement's T. Beach scene cites and transforms the famous beach scene in the classic French novel *Manon Lescault,* whose eponymous heroine dies in the French colonial sands of Louisiana. This citation marks the memories to be had in the S. Thala sands as colonial, aligns them with sexuality and desire, and effects a complex colonial linkage. It links Manon (marginalized on the basis of her freely determined sexuality) and her abjected corpse to Duras's mother (marginalized despite her rejection of sexuality) and her abjected cadaver, both of whom were sacrificed so that the bourgeois patriarchal and colonial psychic and social orders could stand. It further suggests that by opening themselves to their memories, Lol and Hold might disrupt those orders so as to undo the separation of this narrative's still living female dyad, Lol and Tatiana. Awakening before Lol, Hold sees that a trace of their apparent gains exists and suspects what it might be: directing our attention to a crowd gathering around something lying dead in the sands, as Manon Lescault, *Un Barrage*'s mother, and Chekhov's seagull all had before it, he identifies it as "perhaps a dead dog" (184; 174). But just as Richardson had been so enthralled with Stretter that he failed to see Lol's smile at the S. Thala ball, on T. Beach sands Lol is so transfixed with Hold that she fails to see this sign. Once again, Duras narrates her failure as a failure to translate knowledge gained in the depersonalized state back into the conscious realm. As they awaken, Richardson and Lol are clearly outside of the structures of rational thought and language, but moving toward reentry: "We're astonished at first," writes Hold: "Then we rediscover the stream of our memory, marvelous, fresh from the morning, we take each other in our arms . . . without being able to utter a single word" (183-4; 174). Then there occurs, as they reintegrate conscious, Lol's failure to see: "to the beachside, the side where the swimmers are, Lol, her face in my neck doesn't see it . . . a crowd gathering around something, perhaps a dead dog" (183-4; 174 mod.).

Identifying the sign of their gains with the figure of the dead dog, Duras explicitly associates their project with the revolution. As she made clear earlier in *Le Ravissment*, the dead dog is itself a sign of the "word-hole" whose discovery would ring in a revolutionary new day. In this novel, the work of the revolutionary intellectual emerges as synonymous with finding the word-hole whose absence "ruins all the others . . . contaminates them," and that word-hole, it turns out, "is also the dead dog on the beach of high noon, this hole of flesh" (48; 38). As Duras describes it, the word-hole would name the newness that would emerge in the instant bourgeois divisions—of rational and nonrational, mind and body, thought and emotion, sane and insane, for instance—are overcome. No more than Duras or Mascolo does Lol try to envisage either the exact form of the word-hole or the new social form it would enable—as Duras puts it, she "does not probe very deeply into the unknown" (48; 38). But what she does believe, as they also did, is that finding it "would always have meant, for her mind as well as her body, both their greatest pain and their greatest joy, so commingled as to be undefinable, a single entity but unnamable for lack of a word" (47-8; 38).

Having failed to see the dead dog, Lol and Hold go to a hotel room where, enlisting the aid of sexual desire and the depersonalization to which it provides access, they continue their attempt to break down divisions. As Lol attains the peak of ecstasy, which is also that of depersonalization, she effectively merges with Tatiana. Articulated through the gaze *[le regard]*, language, and the crucial act of translation, her transition begins as Hold informs us that Lol recalls, undoubtedly, that she is making love with Tatiana Karl's lover. Quickly, however, as he becomes *her* lover, too—in linguistic terms, as her new status as Hold's lover places Lol in the same linguistic "place" that Tatiana already occupies (Hold is now *Tatiana's/Lol's* lover)—Lol begins to doubt her identity, "the only identity she recognizes, the only one she has used at least as long as I [Hold] have known her" (188; 178). As she does, Lol asks Hold, using a distanced third person singular pronoun to refer to what is no longer, properly, "herself," to name that which she has become/is becoming: "She says: 'Who is it?' She moans, asks me to tell her. I say: 'Tatiana Karl, for example'" (188; 178-9 mod.). Their gains are evident, thus far, only in the dialogue between language and vision: looking at the woman we have known as Lol but naming her Tatiana, Hold invites us to see their conjoining. Narrating those gains into the fabric of language, he goes on to describe, even after they have stopped having sex, the continuing quasi-conflation of Lol and Tatiana: "There was no longer any difference between *her* and Tatiana Karl except in *her* eyes, free of remorse, and in the way *she* referred to herself— Tatiana does not state *her* own name—and in the two names *she* gave herself: Tatiana Karl and Lol V. Stein" (189; 179 mod., my emphases). Clearly, however, if Hold translates their gains from the depersonalized, or in Bataille's term, sovereign state into the conscious register of language, he does not find the word that does not yet exist, which would have *named* the recombined and at least proto-*créole* form created by the merging of Lol and Tatiana. In its absence, he can but point to that form using subject and relative *pronouns:* even as they prepare to leave the hotel room, he says, "*she* continued to resemble *the one [celle]* she had been during the night" (18; 179; mod., my emphases).

With Mascolo, Duras figures the revolutionary process as requiring the progressive, step-by-step practical activity of successive generations. Already aware of their place in revolutionary history, Lol V. Stein and Jacques Hold had gone to the hotel room dreaming "of another time when the same thing is going to happen would happen differently. In another way. A thousand times. Everywhere. Elsewhere. Among others, thousands of others who, like ourselves, dream of this time, necessarily" (*RLVS*, 187; 177). In that room, Hold had joined the revolution: henceforth, he refuses the end that would separate him from Lol, opting instead to put himself at risk, in Mascolo's phrase, "to play his life on chances" (*LC*, 516), and to help invent "the end without end, the beginning without end of Lol V. Stein" (184; 175 mod.).

As *Le Ravissement* ends, Lol, Tatiana, and Hold resume their private realm work, she in the rye field; they in the hotel's window-frame cinema screen. Their efforts have their place within the larger context of "God knows how many affairs like Lol V. Stein's, affairs nipped in the bud, trampled upon, and . . . massacres, oh! you've no idea how many there are, how many blood-stained unrealized attempts [*inachèvements*] are strewn along the horizon, piled up there" (48; 38-9 mod.). Outside and beyond *Le Ravissement*, they assume their place within the *longue durée* of a revolutionary movement that Duras, as if turning around in her writer's seat and assuming a proselytizing tone worthy of *Un Barrage*, had already implored us, too, to join: "Among these unrealized attempts, this word, which does not exist, is none the less there: it awaits you just around the corner of language, it defies you—never having been used—to raise it, to make it arise from its kingdom, which is pierced on every side and through which flows the sea, the sand, the eternity of the ball in the cinema of Lol V. Stein" (48-9; 38-9 mod.).

Shit: deferred revisions

As discussed previously, Duras would finally recognize Anne-Marie Stretter as the object of French colonial desire and murder her a decade later, in *India Song*. If in 1964 Stretter's overwhelming attraction prevented Lol from merging with Tatiana Karl and defining herself as *créole*, her death in 1973-1975 and its consecration in the 1976 *Son Nom de Venise dans Calcutta désert* permitted Duras to align herself with the wandering Beggarwoman one year later, in the paratext to *Le Camion*. Reconciled with her other cultural aspect, Duras went on to name herself *créole* in one 1984 interview. Having so done, she finally returned to textualize in *La Douleur* the 1945 events that had retroactively revised her place in Indochina as having been that of the *créole* daughter of an abjected mother. In its turn, *La Douleur* retroactively reinserts Duras's personal textual project into the frame of the collective ethical and political projects from which it had emerged. Reflecting the importance the issue of place had assumed in the French intellectual field by 1985, *La Douleur*'s problematic is positional:

trauma, its disruption of the "thesis" of the subject, the quest for repositioning. Confronting trauma on both the personal level of Duras's husband's deportation and the general level of the Holocaust, it asks: Where can one situate oneself in respect to the pain and guilt provoked by the spring 1945 disclosures and survive; or as Duras formulates it in her war journal, "I don't know where to put myself in order to stand myself" (23; 16).

A rational first-person narrator opens *La Douleur*. From the beginning, Duras depicts it confronting spring 1945 disclosures and succumbing in the face of "this new face of death, organized, rationalized, discovered in Germany" (*LD*, 60; 49). This narrator would resolve that spring's psychic disruptions by suppressing its materiality, repressing its second consciousness (semiotic), and incarcerating itself more tightly in the sole Cartesian mode: "The throbbing in my temples continues. I must stop this throbbing in my temples. His death is in me. It beats in my temples. One cannot be mistaken about that. To stop the throbbing in my temples—stop the heart—calm it—it will never calm down on its own, I must help it . . . to stop reason from leaving its orbit, fleeing, leaving my head" (13; 6-7); "I must be rational" (12; 5). Using the "clear language" Mascolo says fails to account for materiality, it works toward self-control in short, choppy, self-contained and -containing sentences replete with reminders and imperatives. When the phone rings, it reminds: "Don't hang up, answer. Don't yell to scream to leave me alone" (12; 5); when she feels disoriented, it verifies spatial bearings: "Opposite the fireplace, the telephone, it is beside me. To the right, the living room door and the hall. At the end of the hall, the front door" (11; 5). When her psychic upheaval increases, it provides protection: "I turn out the lights, I go into my bedroom. I go slowly so as to gain time, so as not to stir things in my head" (17; 10).

In this rational first-person mode, Duras confronts her "mythic original" cinema scene. She is at the Gare d'Orsay working for the Service de Recherche, which she formed under the auspices of the Resistance group to which she and her friends belonged, Le Mouvement National des Prisonniers de Guerre, gathering news of deported persons for the movement's newspaper, *Libres*. As Lol V. Stein stood in the ballroom into which Stretter erupted, Duras stands in Orsay's Hall of Honor as the (mythic) first survivor from Weimar enters:

Suddenly two scouts emerge from the hallway carrying a man. The man has his arms around their necks. They carry him, their arms crossed beneath his thighs. He is dressed in civilian, he is shaved, he appears to be suffering a great deal. He is a strange color. He must be crying. One couldn't say that he is skinny, it is something else, there remains so little of him, so little that you wonder if he is still alive. Yet no, he is still alive, his face is convulsed in a terrifying grimace, he is alive. He does not look at anything, not the minister, not the hall of honor, not the flags, nothing. His grimace could be him laughing. He is the first deportee from Weimar to enter the center (*LD*, 28; 20 mod.).

Like Lol, Duras stares: unawares, she moves forward to "the middle of the hall of honor, my back to the loudspeaker" (28; 20). A government minister arrives in the room to greet the survivor; "The minister comes over and takes off his hat, he goes toward the old man, holds his hand out to him, the old man takes it, he doesn't know that it's the hand of the minister" (28; 20). As Duras stands staring at this couple, the minister and the Jew, a scenario unfolds that registers the war's division of Mandel as Minister/Mandel as Jew and his separation as Jew from those remaining in the ministerial ranks. A female Gaullist functionary erupts violently onto the scene, like Duras's mother, *Un Barrage*'s mother, and Lol's mother before her. Figuring the bourgeois capitalist power that reemerged to reassert its control in France after the war, she thrusts herself into the line of vision joining Duras to her Orsay cinema scene. Agent of yet another interpellation *manquée*, she screams: "It's the minister! He's come to meet you!" (28; 21).

Coming in the war's wake, this cinema scene yields epiphany. A young priest returns from deportation holding a little German boy in his arms. Entering Orsay's Hall of Honor and proclaiming to the women waiting there that "it was not the fault of this poor child" (31; 23), he "was arrogating to himself the right to forgive, to absolve, already" (31; 23). Recalling the final posture of Anne Desbaresdes in the 1958 *Moderato Cantabile*, Duras records both the women's epiphanic capacity to "see" that the priest is right and their inability to understand his language. By *Moderato*'s end, Anne Desbaresdes' experimentation with the male lead, Chauvin, had gone some way in depersonalizing her but not him. The resulting chasm between their respective places in relation to the revolution—the fact that by the end of that novel she has begun that process and left him behind—structures its final scene: "having already left the field in which he was located" (*MC*, 84), she could not see his hand beat the air and then fall back down onto the table. Similarly in *La Douleur*, the spring 1945 traumas and revelations—figured on the local or personal level as the sight of this first Weimar returnee—wrenches the women waiting at Orsay, including Duras, out of post-Revolutionary rational structures. Thus if the priest "alone was right," he was right "in a language that these women could no longer comprehend" (*LD*, 32; 24). He speaks in terms of external enemies, guilt and innocence, penance and absolution; they realize that "there is no exterior enemy" (Mascolo, *AEM*, 75).

Orsay's revelation—that innocence and guilt (priest and child) must be integrated into one same frame—pushes Duras's rational voice to crisis. It had attributed guilt and innocence unilaterally. Shaped perhaps by the position of innocence into which both Duras's decision to divorce him and have a child with Mascolo and his deportation put Robert Antelme, this rational voice attributed unilateral guilt to Duras and equally unqualified innocence to Antelme. But Gare d'Orsay's revelation provokes this premonition in the rational narrator: "As soon as [Robert L.] comes back I shall die, it can't be otherwise, it's my secret" (*LD*, 37; 28). Simultaneously, it repositions the autobiographical narrator, permitting her survival past the demise of her rational voice. This repositioning does not resituate her vis-à-vis a universal or "general" group she could not have knowledge of, but in relation to one woman known to her, Mme Bordes. Both are said to be "in advance" of "all the books"; *en attente*, where words fail: "All of the books are behind Mme Bordes and me. We are at the front of a combat without name, without arms, without spilled blood, without glory, at the front of waiting *[attente]*. Behind us stretch the ashes of civilization, of all thought amassed through the centuries" (44; 35). Depersonalized, they too leave behind the sole rational mode. Even before Antelme's return, Duras figures the war's destruction of the rational subject as the death of her own rational narrative "I":

It happened in a second. No more throbbing in my head. It's no longer that. My face forsakes itself *[se défait]*, it changes. I forsake myself, I open out *[me déplie]*, I change. There is no one in the bedroom where I am. I no longer feel my heart. Horror mounts in a slow flood, I'm drowning. I have such fear that I no longer wait. Is it over? Is it over? Where are you? How to know? I don't where he is. I no longer know where I am either. I don't know where we are. What is the name of this place? What is this place? What is this story? Who is that, Robert L.? No more pain . . . I do not exist (46; 37).

Before Antelme's return, Duras frames the Orsay epiphany in Vittorini's terms: "We are all of the race as those who were burned in the crematoriums and gassed at Maïdanek, we are also of the race of the Nazis. Egalitarian function of the Buchenwald crematoriums, of the hunger, of the common graves at Bergen-Belsen, in these graves we have our part, these extraordinarily identical skeletons, they are those of a European family" (57; 47). Given the indivisible fact of one sole human race, pain *(la douleur)* must be implanted in hope; guilt, in the priest. It can no longer be a question of *forgiving* a young German boy, or the Nazis, for that matter: rather, we must all must recognize the pain, assume the guilt, the other within. This insight resolves Duras's positional quandary—where to put onself and where to put pain in order to be able to "support" both it and oneself:

> If the Nazi crimes are not seen in world dimensions, if they are not understood on the collective plane, then the concentration camp internee at Belsen who died alone with a collective soul and a class consciousness . . . has been betrayed. If one gives Nazi horror a German and not a collective destiny, one will reduce the man in Belsen to regional dimensions. The only response one can give this crime is to make it the crime of all. To share it. Just like the idea of equality, fraternity. To support it, to tolerate the idea of it, share the crime (60-61; 50).

After Antelme's return, Duras's autobiographical narrator locates guilt within even him, thus resolving her conjugal guilt. To her as to Mascolo, any value that is not grounded in material need is idealist: indeed, to them, the very term idealist signifies those "systems in which values are taken separately from the needs that correspond to them" (*LC*, 437)—and all idealism is counterrevolutionary. But Duras does more than merely ground the values created at Orsay in materiality: in a characteristically ambiguous tone hovering between mirth and caustic political irony, she casts epiphany as endproduct, revelation as shit, illumination as issuing from darkness and putrefaction, the intuition that we are all "human" and "nonhuman" as the most foul and putrescent product of the still living human body. Seated on the chamber pot, Antelme will pass voluminous diarrhea, material sign of the Nazi crimes and his victimization. Just prior to its "enormous, unexpected, excessive glou-glou" (*LD*, 68; 57), however, his own nonhuman potential emerges, as if from his anus, wrapped in protective parentheses, brought to our attention by italics:

> *(The little Jewish girl of seventeen from the Faubourg du Temple whose elbows have broken though the skin on her arms, undoubtedly because of her youth and her skin's fragility, her joint is on the outside instead of being inside, it sticks out naked, clean, she suffers neither from her joints nor from her belly, from which they removed one at a time, at regular intervals, all of her genital organs) (68l; 57).*

Antelme's shit is, per definition, abject. Jettisoned to the borders of the human and the nonhuman so that the subject and its social order can emerge, it remains there, neither me nor not me, installing ambiguous oppositions between I and Other, Inside and Out, beckoning to me to approach the place where meaning, "I," and my social order with me, begin to collapse. More than that, Antelme's shit is the abject in motion: fluid, dynamic, it is the abject become negativity; the analog, in the realm of real material need where all values must be grounded, of language as process.

Fluid, mobile, and heterogeneous to the categories between which it flows, it permits communication between existing categories; it successfully transports contents from the invisible (repressed or suppressed) side of their borders out into the light, or consciousness, where they can be seen. Antelme's shit brings to the corporeal "outside" of this camp survivor and, in the eyes of his postwar friends, a man-saint, his potential, shared by us all, to be "nonhuman"; to produce, as here, even the most heinous Nazi war crime. As it does, it brings into the light, thrusts before our eyes, the epiphany Duras and the others who gathered at the rue Saint-Benoît had had in spring 1945: that all of us, as human beings, have the human and nonhuman potential; that we are thus one human race.

La Douleur tells the story of the 1945 resignification of the colonial abject Duras embodied textually as the mother's cadaver in *Un Barrage* and in relation to which she formed her early sense of her self, of her place in the world, and of her textual project. The war journal shows the spring 1945 traumas transforming the mother's cadaver into shit, shocking it out of stasis into movement, making it the means and the medium of the revelation that defined her postwar sense of self and her political (ethical) and scriptural projects. If in 1984, *L'Amant's* success provoked critics to promote the erotic-exotic tale of her first sexual relations to the status of the origin of her writing, in 1985, *La Douleur* rejected that account, identifying her scriptural origins not with idealized images of exotic eroticism, but with defilement in its most human material forms. In fact, *La Douleur* ends by capturing Duras's postwar textual project "as if" in the instant of its emergence (birth) from (the displaced canal of) Antelme's anus on an incredible wave of shit. With this figuration, Duras gestured back to her first post-spring 1945 novel, *Un Barrage;* the first of her novels to have been informed by communist ethics and designed as textual political praxis. From the height of her Goncourt and in the figure of Antelme's shit, she retrieved the political "stuff" that had been laundered out of her story since 1950 by her critics, yes, but also by her response to their demands. Antelme's shit reiterates and recapitulates a sequence of signifiers that had already slid in that first novel from her writing's colonial origin, through her displacement to France, and to that origin's retroactive revision and radical politicization in spring 1945. We recall that sequence: from the *mère* (mother) in Indochina across the *mer* (sea; ocean) to France and the spring 1945 revelation, transported no longer on the shitty soil of the Indochina concession, but now on Antelme's European *merde* (shit) (*UB,* 58).

Grounding their postwar sense of self, their ethics, and their scriptural projects in the French colonial abject transmuted into pan-European negativity, Mascolo and Duras wrote against the emerging hegemonic trends of their era. Under the reign of de Gaulle and the Marshall Plan, postwar France sought to strengthen itself by solidifying borders and reinstating binaries. Against that trend, Duras and the other intellectuals in her circle sought to displace binaries and borders, beginning with the most basic human versus nonhuman, to within the human race and each human being. Positioning their thought and projects "as if" on the hyphen between the categories of rational thought and its social orders, they placed them precisely where hegemonic trends in postwar France worked hardest to elide all traces of blurring, of the composite, the *créole*, the borders. It is not surprising, finally, that Mascolo's treatise on the intellectual's role in the revolution received so little critical notice in its day or that the most important literary critics in 1950s France silenced Duras's revolutionary textual politics. Abjected, their thought and projects remained in the margins of the French bourgeois capitalist and colonial culture that had succeeded in returning to power after the war, beckoning its subject to approach the place where it and its social orders would begin to collapse. After May '68, the main contours of Mascolo's psycholinguistic model of revolutionary intellectual praxis were picked up consciously or not by post-structuralists such as Kristeva, who enlisted them in the service of a merely liberal politics that could envisage no more than disrupting the status quo ad infinitum without bringing it down. The 1970s rewrites of his postwar communist ethics assume their place alongside Marini's 1970s liberal interpretation of Duras. One reduced the rue Saint-Benoît group's communist ethics to the dimensions of the same rational thought and capitalist order they sought to end; the other inserted Duras's revolutionary scriptural practice into a circuit of potentially infinite and infinitely profitable textual production whose profits fell to the financial and ideological coffers of the bourgeois capitalist system she wrote to bring down.

Chapter 5

Transatlantic Connections: Wright's *Black Boy* and Duras's *Colon* Girl

I AM the marginal man!

—Richard Wright

Ce que je suis dit qu'il faut commencer avec Barrage.

—Marguerite Duras

Marguerite Duras called *Un Barrage contre le Pacifique* a "book denouncing the colonial state" ("Bon Plaisir"). Claude Roy described it as a "great work of revolt and contestation" ("Sur Genet," 314). In my view, too, it would be difficult to imagine how Duras could have composed a more transparent critique of French colonialism. Nonetheless the fact remains: in more than 50 years since its publication, few critics have read *Un Barrage* in terms of anticolonial politics, or for that matter in terms of politics at all. The 1950s critical neglect of *Un Barrage* is not particularly surprising: published just as "the [Franco-Vietnamese] conflict entered into the frame of the [Cold War] struggle that opposed the western and Communist blocs," ("Chronologie," 471), it advocates political views that were to become increasingly unpopular during that conservative and nationalistic decade. But if they silenced *Un Barrage*'s politics through the 1950s, critics called for the novel's virtual elision from her mature corpus at the end of that decade, as the Algerian War of Independence raged, and Duras wrote violently antigaullist and anticolonialist articles for the journal *Le 14 Juillet*. A main proponent of that position, Gennie Luccioni, portrayed *Un*

Barrage as immature, stylistically dated, and eminently forgettable as such, then went on to posit the break that cleared the way for the selective recuperation of Duras's less transparently political texts alone: "It was necessary for Duras to first purge her family tragedy, murder the gods and demons of her childhood. *Barrage contre le Pacifique* allowed her to relive, by writing it, the maternal epic and become an adult" ("Roman abstrait," 73). From then until quite recently, *Un Barrage* has been registered in Duras critical discourse as a silence, a gap, a hole.

From today's perspective, *Un Barrage*'s lengthy critical marginalization seems disconcertingly commensurate with what critics have begun to suspect may be this novel's central importance to Duras's œuvre. In fact both textual evidence and Duras's insistent indications are so convincing that Alain Vircondelet called *Un Barrage* Duras's "foundational text. The one she will unceasingly rewrite, as if she really only ever wrote one sole book . . . and reworked the same motifs" (*DB*, 180). Vircondelet went on to the claim: "Despite the fact that it is written like a great classical novel, *Un Barrage* is paradoxically the inexhaustible novel, the canvass of the other novels, the essential weave" (181). Wholeheartedly agreeing, I would add but one caveat: *Un Barrage* is indeed fundamental to understanding Duras's work, but that is not despite its classic style, as Vircondelet believes, but in large part due to its unabashed realism.

The first novel written after Duras's 1940s political realignment, *Un Barrage* is the only novel in which she explicitly declares her revolutionary textual politics, for reasons she alludes to in this 1974 exchange with Gauthier: "When you write, you don't want to say, 'It's shameful, what's happening in India'": "I don't want to be declarative. . . . That's over, it's . . . because once I was . . . in the *Barrage*" (*LP*, 183-4; 134). If she clearly implies that *Un Barrage*'s critical reception taught her a lesson about critical practice and literary competition, she does not say that it forced her to renounce politics: in fact, she ceaselessly insists that the contrary is true. She does say, however, that after *Un Barrage* and its harsh reception, she chose not to overtly declare her textual politics. As she describes it, her move from realist to minimalist writing, which critics have often emphasized, is thus of a piece with a second transition, which they have consistently failed to note—from declared to undeclared political narratives.

But while it is clearly rooted in 1950s conservative political agendas or *partis pris*, the neglect of Duras's political narratives is also aided and abetted by the postwar evolution of her writing. When she wrote *Un Barrage*, Duras lifted themes and scenes from her earlier novels and, developing them along realist lines, presented them in their original socioeconomic, political, and historical contexts. After *Un Barrage*, she began chipping away at those contexts, paring her works down to minimalist dimensions. Unlike the vast majority of her critics and readers, however, she neither rejected nor forgot those original contexts. Quite the contrary: when she speaks of the politics in her writing, she clearly implies that as she reworks various textual fragments, she remobilizes their original and largely unchanging political significations as well. *Un Barrage* might thus be understood as a master code: entering Duras's postwar œuvre through it, one might "fill in" the politics she later supplies (by using the same politically charged fragments) and leaves "silent" (by depriving them of their contexts).

To read *Un Barrage* in relation to its silenced politics is, of course, to read it in relation to World War II, the Spring 1945 revelations, the ethics and understanding of intellectual work elaborated in response to them by Duras and the others rue Saint-Benoît. But it is also read *Un Barrage* in relation to Richard Wright and his writing, which saturated and amassed great symbolic capital in the postwar French literary field. In fall 1944 excerpts from Wright's "Big Boy Leaves Home," as well as from Zora Neale Hurston's *Jonah's Gourd Vine* appeared in *L'Arbalète*. In 1945 the first installment of Wright's "Fire and Cloud" opened the first issue of what rapidly became France's most prestigious literary journal, Sartre's *Les Temps modernes*. In 1946 *Uncle Tom's Children* was published in translation as *Les Enfants de l'Oncle Tom;* from January to June 1947, *Black Boy (Jeunesse noire)* appeared in installments in *Les Temps modernes*. The month before Duras began *Un Barrage*, *Black Boy*'s March installment in that journal was positioned next to Sartre's "Qu'est-ce que la litterature?," which conse-crated it as the most perfect illustration of engaged literature. That summer *Black Boy* was published in book form by Gallimard, and *Native Son* appeared from Albin Michel. Wright's work had a significant role in shaping the contours of *Un Barrage*, and, through it, those not only of Duras's entire creative corpus, but, in the context of her rise to France's literary heights, those of the postwar French literary field. Let us then return to *Un Barrage* and read it as it was produced: in dialogue with its social, cultural, historical, political, and literary times.

Spring 1945: Duras and the Jew

In the two novels she wrote before spring 1945, *Les Impudents* (1943) and *La Vie tranquille* (1944), Duras was clearly trying to write through and resolve the conflictual knots of her 1920s Indochina family drama. She appears to have had no sense that geographical or cultural contexts were central to her story (which she transposes onto continental soil) or that socioeconomic conditions had to do with her family's internal conflicts (neither fictional family is rich or upper class, but neither is oppressed or impoverished, either). Focusing solely on personal and psychological issues, she composed both of these pre-1945 novels along rather traditional bildungsroman lines. A single issue dominates both: the rivalry pitting a young heroine against her older brother for their mother's love and recognition. *Les Impudents* tells of a rebellious daughter who rejects the financially and socially attractive suitor her mother would have had her marry in favor of a wild affair with a wealthy man and subsequent forced marriage. In the end, its heroine breaks with her mother, moves away from Paris (as Duras had moved from Indochina), and leaves her brother squarely positioned to continue manipulating his mother. In contrast, *La Vie tranquille* presents a decidedly dutiful daughter. In its first pages, a scenario Duras more than once admitted imagining unfolds—the murder of her older brother (figured by an uncle) by the younger brother whose existence he had rendered miserable. That murder clears the way for the daughter to be loved by her mother, marry for her benefit, and offer her the happy ending Duras's own 1939 marriage and wartime pregnancy seemed to promise her mother, Marie Donnadieu.

But by the time Duras wrote *Un Barrage,* her world had been turned upside down. She had lost the child and divorced the husband who were to have guaranteed a tranquil resolution to her 1944 heroine's family drama. Late World War II events had precipitated her into politics, encouraged her critique of a status quo she had never before questioned, and instilled in her an undying hatred of Nazis: "I do not want to go to Germany. . . . There is nothing to be done. I do not forgive" (*MA,* 59). As the war ended and proof of Nazi atrocities surfaced, she was disgusted by her own wartime inaction, as she believes everyone else was who had lived the war as she had lived it (*MDM,* 27). However, if 1945 forced much of Europe to rethink its history, it also compelled Duras to reevaluate and contextualize her colonial Indochina past. This was the case for reasons one tends to forget: 1945 may have begun with the end of the Second World War, but it ended with the first beginnings of France's second Indochina war. By spring 1945, unrest had broken out and was being violently repressed in Algeria and Indochina. In August, control of Indochina passed to Ho Chi Minh and the Viet-minh.

Like Duras, most Viet-minh were communists who elaborated their politics along antifascist lines. Their analyses were directed not at German or Italian fascists, however, but at French colonialists and the Japanese who sought to supplant them. Extending Duras's French Communist Party analyses, their demands permitted her to *name* the agents of her (family's) suffering. That act of naming mobilized a set of analogies that encouraged her to lift her family "tragedy" out of the purely individual category. Just as

Nazis deported and imprisoned her husband Robert Antelme, for instance, French colonial powers had oppressed her family, and just as Nazis had marginalized and murdered her Jewish friends, so had French colonizers marginalized and murdered her native neighbors and playmates. In her discourse of the time, one such analogy is particularly striking: linking her brother's 1942 death in the colonies to the fact that the French had made antibiotics rare, she also links her infant son's death in Paris that same year to gas scarcities caused by the Nazi occupiers.

One can gauge the impact of these 1945 conflations on Duras and her writing by rethinking her representation of her primal political moment— La Douleur's Gare d'Orsay scene. If one reads that scene in terms of the European war alone, Duras seems to depict herself transfixed solely by France's first returning Nazi camp survivor. But when one reads that scene in terms of the complex conflations that actually comprised her 1945 epiphanies, a more complex dialectics emerges: standing transfixed, Duras watches as her 1920s fold into the 1940s, as Indochina merges with Occupied France, and as her image combines with that of the man before her eyes. Emerging at the point of those conflations, Duras's primal political image—the Jew, le juif—is coextensive neither with the Jewish man before her nor with Duras herself. A new and inclusive image, even, perhaps, an imagined community, it coalesced as the sight of that Jewish man at Orsay provoked in Duras the deferred revision of her Indochina place and story. In her psyche, that revision folded together their abjected places and their stories, solidifying in her the belief that "the Jew's story is my story" (MDM, 73). Product of that deferred revision, Duras's "Jew" marks the symbolic origin of her postwar writing; the personal and political "place" from which she writes. From that place, she composed a postwar corpus characterized by its consistent concern with "Jews"; that is, with all those that western bourgeois capitalist society marginalizes, excludes, and oppresses.

Fall 1945: Duras and Richard Wright

By Fall 1945 Duras was grappling in her writing with the psychic and political consequences of the wartime traumas. That October, her first scriptural engagement with Antelme's deportation, "Les Feuilles" appeared in the journal Confluences. Its publication coincided with Richard Wright's first appearance in Les Temps modernes. If Duras's encounter with the Orsay returnee shaped the place of her writing, her encounter with

Wright inflected its form. Wright's impact on Duras's writing is compre-
hensible in light of the strong similarities in their personal histories and
political views and the demands of literary competition. He, too, had been
raised outside of France by a former school teacher and single mother, had
attended school irregularly, and had finished at the top of the class—he as
valedictorian; she, with the highest mark in her year's *baccalauréat*. His
background had also failed to prepare him for literary competition:
indeed, it had resulted in a *habitus* inadequation that manifested itself
symptomatically, as hers also did, as an intense struggle to develop a style.[1]
And as Duras would, Wright identified himself as an "outsider . . . gifted
with a double vision . . . both inside and outside of culture at the same time"
(*The Outsider*, 119).

Wright's political positions were also stunningly similar to those of
Duras and her friends at the rue Saint-Benoît. A Communist Party
member from 1934 to 1942, he had opposed, as they would in the late
1940s, all Party attempts to restrict cultural freedom (Fabre, "Beyond," 48).
His experience of white racism, like Antelme's of the camps, had convinced
Wright that all men are potentially evil. As Duras and her friends would, he
believed the intellectual's role in the revolution was to create the values "by
which the race is to struggle, live and die" (Gilroy, 169). He, too, held
communication to be integral to that task; indeed he, too, considered it
both a "form of self-creation" and "a way of creating a universe of discourse,
a community" (JanMohamed, 224). Rather than develop an ideal image of
what "man might and ought to be" (Hakutani, 8), he situated his ethical
thought where they would theirs: "on the sheer edge of an old world going
to pot and the new one whose outlines are yet to be seen" (Fabre, *Unfinished
Quest*, 314).[2] Like Duras and her friends, he considered himself ahead of
his time: "My point of view is a Western one, but a Western one that
conflicts at several vital points with the present, dominant outlook of the
West. Am I ahead of or behind the West? My personal judgment is that
I'm ahead. And I do not say that boastfully; such a judgment is implied by
the very nature of those Western values that I hold dear" (*White Man*, 53).
As if echoing his words, Edgar Morin would describe the rue Saint-Benoît:
"Without any doubt we were people of the future socialist society rather
than people of the dictatorship of the proletariat" (Mascolo, *AEM*, 77).

But if they were together politically, Wright had a significant lead on
Duras in France's literary field. Before she could as much as begin her first
postwar novel, he had been consecrated as the emblematic instance of
engaged writing. Wright's high status established him as a model Duras
might follow: she was constrained as a fledgling writer to respond to the
literary field's hegemonic instance in order to enter the field and become
competitive; he provided a "site" to which she might respond. In Wright,

Duras found advantages she did not in Sartre. Obviously, Wright provided a site of response that was socially, culturally, and politically closer to her own. But just as surely, his work permitted her to compose autobiography without submitting to the longstanding French literary devaluation of that genre. To the contrary: by responding to Wright she could position herself vis-à-vis the African-American literary tradition, which was dominated by the autobiographical and bildungsroman genres (Stepto, "Literacy," 93) and at the same time amass the significant symbolic capital accruing to Wright. As importantly, Wright's work provided a psychoanalytic representation of subjectivity much better suited than Sartre's Existentialist model to Duras's own understanding of the psychic dimensions of oppression and liberation.[3]

Published in 1947, Duras's "Le Boa" made at last two things clear: the fact of Duras's response to Wright and, as reflected by its *Les Temps modernes* appearance, that response's beneficial effect on her struggle for legitimacy. A first and skeletal working through, or *précis*, of what would become *Un Barrage,* this story shows Duras enlisting the psychoanalytic approach and autobiographical genre to wrestle with her Indochina bildung (formation, or education; coming-of-age) and its deferred revision. More accurately it shows her focusing on the precise point in psychoanalysis that Wright did: the mirror stage. First discussed by Lacan at the 1936 Marienbad International Congress of Psycho-Analysts, the mirror stage is the moment when, seeing its reflection in a mirror, perhaps, the child of six to 18 months first apprehends, on the imaginary level, its body as unified. This moment is not that in which the subject emerges; rather, as the child identifies with the image in the mirror, or *imago,* it forms "the matrix and first outline of what is to become the ego" (Laplanche and Pontalis, 251).

In the mirror stage, Wright found a means of understanding how an "enslaved" subject is formed and of conceiving of ways in which it might liberate itself. Three texts in which he works through this problematic had a particular impact on Duras: "Fire and Clouds," *Native Son,* and the semi-autobiographical *Black Boy.* "Fire and Clouds," which Duras would have read in 1945, depicts the route to liberation in terms of progressive steps—trauma, dislocation from the enslaved subject position, retreat to the mirror stage, confrontation with identity *(imago)* alternatives, and the assumption (or not) of a more liberated personal identity whose articulation with a more liberated collective identity suggests the existence of a structural connection between individual liberation and radical social change. Beaten unconscious by white men, its hero Reverend Taylor awakens in a foglike state similar to Mascolo's depersonalization (chapter 4). Consistent with what JanMohammed shows to be Wright's correlation of enslaved psychic structures with immobility, marginalization, and social death, Taylor enjoys enhanced mobility in this semiconscious state. Fleeing through the white district to his home in the black section, he confronts two *imago* alternatives. One registers his enslaved identity under Southern U.S. white racism; the other, his identity in relation to the black community. Identifying with the latter, Taylor moves into the social sphere. Embracing his community's folk wisdom, he begins his liberation; recognizing itself in the more liberated *imago* he reflects back to it, the community commences its own (JanMohammed, 224-5).

Focused on the enslaved position, *Native Son* prefigures Debord's critique of the Spectacle and Althusser's account of interpellation. In French by 1947, it examines the mass media purveyance of subjugated *imagoes* and passive popular identification with them. Its hero, Bigger Thomas finds his *imago* both in the elite white Dalton family for which he works and on a South Side Chicago cinema screen, where white racist and capitalist ideology spins itself out. Michael Harper captures Wright's political use of the cinema screen in these lines from his 1973 poem, "Afterward: A Film." As filmic images of naked men, silver veils, and wild dancing pass before his eyes, Bigger has no need to imagine anything:

> it is all before him,
> born in a dream:
> a gorilla broke loose
> from his zoo
> in a tuxedo: baboon
> You pick your red bottom
> The Daltons are the movies (cited in Stepto, "Wright," 72).

In *Black Boy*, Wright multiplied *imago* alternatives, confronting his young hero stand-in, Richard, with images of his blazing home, his father killing a chicken, and a mostly black chain gang whose striped garb reminds him of zebras in a zoo. His crucial *imago*, however, positions him in relation to literacy as a means to liberation: in it, a black schoolteacher reads to young Richard, and his imagination takes flight. Erupting violently onto this scene, his grandmother severs him from that teacher and literacy (Stepto, "Literacy," 87). The boy refuses to submit to the enslaved position. Fleeing the house, he goes not *to* the cinema, but to a place outside of it. Using that site bricolage-style, he sells tickets in order to raise the funds needed to purchase both mobility and access to literacy by buying a train ticket to a Northern city.

As Duras composed "Le Boa," the semi-autobiographical story of a young heroine's attempt to escape women's imprisoned identities, she did not perceive literacy as their route to liberation. But as Wright had, she identified that route as the one actually denied the oppressed group on which she was focusing: where he identified literacy in the African American case, she identified sexual self-awareness and self-determination in women's case. Following Wright's precedent, Duras confronts her heroine with *imago* alternatives in respect to one of which she might define herself and her relation to existing structures of power. Aligned with the schoolmarm Mlle Barbet, her heroine's first *imago* offers her the possibility of lining up as Duras's own mother had: on the side of power as a sexually inactive woman who reproduces its structures unaware that she is their victim. Duras implicates her own 1930s occupancy of that position by figuring it in terms derived from her work on the Colonial Ministry's French banana and tea propaganda committees: each week, Mlle Barbet snacks on one French banana and French tea. Composed from two of *Black Boy*'s *imagoes*—the chain gang and the father with chick—her heroine's second *imago* has clear phallic dimensions: in a zoo, a boa ingests—or rather, has just ingested—a live chick. Unlike Wright's hero, her young heroine regularly misses the actual murder and, missing it, fails to identify with the feminine position in this scene—the place of the always already sacrificed chick.

Marking her difference from Beauvoir, Duras provides this young heroine with a means to identify with the masculine position. Two years later in *The Second Sex*, Beauvoir would contend that, in matters of transcendence, boys have an advantage over girls: "The major benefit obtained from [the penis] by the boy is that, having an organ that can be seen and grasped, he can at least partially identify himself with it. He projects the mystery of his body, its threats, outside of himself, which enables him to keep them at a distance. . . . Because he has an alter ego in whom he sees himself, the little boy can boldly assume an attitude of subjectivity; the very object into which he projects himself becomes a symbol of autonomy, of transcendence, of power; he measures the length of his penis; he compares his urinary stream with that of his companions; later on, erection and ejaculation will become grounds for satisfaction and challenge" (278). In stunning contrast, Beauvoir believed, "the little girl cannot incarnate herself in any part of her" (278). What Beauvoir would deny, Duras grants twofold: in her breasts, her young heroine finds forward-looking body parts that she can grasp, alter egos in which she sees herself, symbols of autonomy, transcendence, and power into which she projects herself and in relation to which she defines herself. The boy may size up his penis with his companions: she compares her breasts to the boa. It prevails in the social sphere, she concludes: but in the private realm— where the intellectual works for the revolution—her breasts rule. In her words: "Outside of the house, there was the boa, here, there were my breasts" (107). Having affirmed this young heroine stand-in's position of power, Duras put herself to the task of more fully elaborating her personal trajectory and its social revolutionary implications in *Un Barrage contre le Pacifique*.

Opening Tableaux, Inaugural Positions

Un Barrage contre le Pacifique opens with a spotlighted shot: alone with a dying horse against an otherwise blank setting, an undefined third person plural—an *ils* (they)—is isolated in what the text suggests might be a desert prison; severed from the rest of the world. From *Un Barrage*'s first clause, *ils* is established as redundant and claustrophobic. Piling one signifier of "them" upon another, Duras writes: "Il *leur* avait semblé à *tous les trois* que c'était une bonne idée d'acheter ce cheval" ["It had seemed to them, all three of them, that it was good idea to buy this horse"] (*UB*, 13). From this phrase on, a redoubled movement takes hold of *Un Barrage:* as contexts rise up and are rejected or retained to fill in the sparse inaugural image, a voice slowly emerges from within the *ils*. Individual at first, it will become multiple and heterogeneous before finally emerging as collective and revolutionary. In *Un Barrage* as in *Black Boy*, the narrative progression away from speechlessness and anger to articulation and hope (Thaddeus, 272) is of a piece with the progression from stasis to mobility (Stepto, "Literacy," 91-2).

But before moving on, *Un Barrage* emphatically establishes its position. Set on desertlike grounds, it replaces the famous dead mother of Camus's famous first line—"Aujourd'hui, maman est morte. Ou peut-être hier, je ne sais pas" ("Maman died today. Or maybe yesterday, I don't know") (Camus, 9)—with a dying (then dead) horse. With this replacement, *Un Barrage* establishes itself as a response from a female *colon* from Indochina to the male *colon* from Algeria: against both his image of the alleged absurdity of the Human Condition and his refusal to take a firm anti-imperialist stance, it throws down, as if a gauntlet, its dead horse. Responding at the same time to colonial writer André Malraux's description of Cambodia as a vast uninhabited region, "practically a desert" (30; Norindr, 91), it then tears away colonial ideological pretense to unmask colonial ideology with caustic irony. Behind the façade of the alleged *mission civilisatrice*, it shows, French colonialism works solely to French advantage.[4] A self-serving system of one-way transportation and exchange, it is designed to enable the colonizer "to extract something from this world, even if it wasn't much, even if it was miserably little, to extract something that had not been theirs till then, and bring it to their corner of the plain, which was saturated with salt" (*UB*, 13); "That's what transports were: even from a desert, where nothing grows, one could still make something come from it by transporting into it those who live elsewhere, who are part of the world" (13).

Going beyond mere critique, Duras's tableau opens *Un Barrage* by announcing French colonialism's death. For eight days—the biblical time of creation—that horse had tried to repeat God's feat and create a world in its image. But an exhausted centarian at the mid-twentieth century, as French colonial rule in Indochina was, it had died in the process: "The horse was too old, indeed much older than the mother for a horse, like a hundred-year-old man. He honestly tried to do the work demanded of him, which was well beyond any strength he had had for a long time, then he died" (13). As we know, this declaration of death turned out to be uncannily accurate—France would lose Indochina in 1954 and its Empire in 1962, exactly one hundred years after obtaining Cochin China in the Treaty of 1862. But in 1950 when *Un Barrage* appeared, this declaration was not yet a statement of historical *fact:* it was a revolutionary *promise.* Pronouncing the horse dead before the fact, it established colonial rule's living body as the site and source of its own cadaver; as the abject and site of abjection on this colonial scene. More than that: it placed around that dead horse, as agents of colonialism's demise, an evocative trio of characters—a mother, her son, and her daughter.

Modeled on the trio in *Indiana*'s inaugural tableau, Duras's characters, too, form a "bizarre Oedipal triangle" (Schor, xiii). Where George Sand's tableau features the young *créole* Indiana, her jealous, tyrannical, and paternal husband, and her asexual cousin, Sir Ralph, *Un Barrage*'s is built of the young *créole* Suzanne, her paternal and tyrannical older brother, and their sexually inactive mother. *Un Barrage*'s trio also cites the Holy Family: derived from Duras's own mother, Marie, its asexual mother assumes the role of (politically) Virgin Mother, its paternal older brother, Joseph, plays the part of a thoroughly un-Holy Stepfather of that name, and—with extreme audacity—Duras's own stand-in, Suzanne, steps into the stunning leading role as a secular and feminine Jesus, Lord and Savior. By aligning itself with *Indiana*, the novel with which Sand sought to establish her realist credentials, *Un Barrage* defines itself not as sentimental fiction, but as serious realism. Aligning itself with the Bible, it indicates that just as colonialists sought to supplant God, its heretical Family will bring the colonialists down. Positioning its trio alongside Sand's, it further indicates that in that revolutionary project, it will make full use of the transgressive potential of sexuality and *créolité*. Consistently, positioning themselves in relation to the abject, two *créole* voices arise: outside of the diegesis, Duras's postwar voice takes up its place vis-à-vis her own mother's abjection (chapter 3), while within the diegesis, Suzanne's voice prepares to emerge in relation to *Un Barrage*'s dead horse.

Articulating across the borders between the métropole and the colony, Duras and her stand-in would fulfill *Un Barrage*'s revolutionary promise. In 1950, as the Indochina war raged and France's mass media worked to silence news of it, they would propel that colony to the French cultural fore. Just as *Black Boy* had forced American readers to consider the U.S. South from the black perspective (Fabre, *Unfinished Quest*, 280), *Un Barrage* would force the French to consider Indochina, and through it the Empire, from the perspective of its oppressed populations. Rather than address colonialism on the world historical level, *Un Barrage* would proceed as Duras said she always did: going to "the most particular of things, [it would] attain the other things" (*MDM*, 74). Focusing on one particular *colon* experience in Indochina, *Un Barrage* would attain the general of Indochina; revealing the general of that colony's particular case, it would reveal French colonial oppression in general. Designed as a "word-hole," it would achieve that effect by laying out the discursive veil of French colonial ideology *(le barrage)* and then, like the crabs it thematized, it would eat holes in it. It would achieve its perspectival gestalt by handing off its narrative voice. In Part I, the mother's voice would lay out the most familiar French colonial ideological narrative. In Part II, her daughter would take over the narrative voice, displace it in the direction of feminist and marxist class critiques, then hand it off to the victims of French colonial oppression, who would move it, past their own victimized positions, to a more fully revolutionary final position. In *Un Barrage*'s readers, Duras hoped, the resulting gestalt would be Epiphanic and social transformative: eyes wide open, they would withdraw their support of colonialism and toll the bells on Empire.

The Mother's Tale

In Part I of *Un Barrage*, the mother's saga is narrated in the explanatory mode of French colonial ideology: defined by bourgeois liberalism, it enlists notions of individual enterprise, human progress, the Human Condition, and its trappings—destiny, fate, and collective tragedy. Born to provincial peasants in France, the mother is an exceptional individual. Overcoming her meager circumstances, she receives her parents' permission to continue studies at a Normal School, where she earns her period's equivalent of a *baccalauréat*. After teaching briefly in France, she is courageous enough to go with her husband to teach in Indochina. When his unexpected death leaves her with two young children, this exemplary product of the existing socioeconomic system falls back on the skills it had given her. At the Normal School, she had learned to play piano; after his death, she takes a position playing piano accompaniment at the colonial city's Eden Cinema. There, she is so intent on rehoning her skills that she fails to see the images passing above her head on the screen. While her job at the Eden Cinema preserves her from "new blows of destiny or human-kind" (*UB*, 25), it thus also subtracts her "from struggle and the fertile experiences of injustice" (25). After a decade, she leaves the Eden "as she had entered it, intact, alone, virginally innocent of all familiarity with the powers of evil, desperately ignorant of the great colonial vampirism that had incessantly surrounded her" (25; 19 mod.).

Still convinced by French colonial propaganda, the mother spends the money she had saved during her ten years at the Eden on a land concession she believes will permit her family to get rich. She moves to the Kam Plain, plants her land and waits for the harvest. When the sea washes away her crop, she blames fate, nature, and bad luck; when the same thing happens the following year, she blames the corruption of the cadastral agents who sold her the concession. Her explanatory modes thus take account of the most general and individual levels of things, without engaging with the social or historical. As a result, they prevent her from seeing the conditions of her own oppression, those of native oppression, or the connections between them. Not surprisingly, her interaction with Indochina's native populations recapitulates the French colonial interaction more generally. Like the early Christian missionaries, she began by trying to save individual native peasant children: "The mother always had one or two of them at her place during her first years on the plain" (119). Confronted with failure ("nor with the children had she had any luck" [119]), she curtailed contact with peasants and began working their stories into a narrative of Nature and the Human Condition.

Duras found formal inspiration for the mother's narrative, and especially its long and lyrical passages on native children, in Richard Wright, who floated factual details on "a sea of emotion" (Hakutani, 118) to produce powerfully ironic passages. Following him, Duras floats false and ideological accounts of native children's deaths on a sea of emotion to create lyrical passages whose caustic irony becomes clear in Part II of her novel. Repeated often to herself and her children, her story opens by aligning the conception of native children with natural seasonal cycles:

As long as she was young enough to be desired by her husband, every woman on the plain had her child each year. In the dry season, when work in the rice fields slowed, the men thought more of love and the women were taken, naturally. And in the months that followed, the women's bellies grew. Thus, in addition to those who had already come out of them, there were those who were still in the womb. This continued regularly, at a vegetal rhythm, from a long and deep respiration, the stomach of each woman inhaled a child, swelled, and expelled it so as to take in another (117).

It portrays the resulting babies descending overabundantly upon the plain, like monsoons or mangoes—"It was for these children as it was for the rains, fruits, floods. They arrived each year, by regular tides, or if you like, by crops or efflorescence" (117)—and dying by the scores: "For so many of them died that the mud of the plain contained many more dead children than there had ever been who had had the time to sing on the backs of buffaloes" (118). As her story goes, native children have been dying in this fashion from time immemorial: "So many of them died they were no longer mourned, and for a very long while already, they had put them to rest without a proper burial. Simply, on returning from work, the father dug a little hole in front of the cabin and laid his dead child in it" (118; 93 mod.). Attributing their deaths to natural causes, the mother's narrative concludes by casting them as necessary to the balance of nature:

It was necessary indeed that some of them die. For if for only a few years the children of the plain had stopped dying, the plain would have been so infested with them that undoubtedly, lacking the means to nourish them, they would have given them to the dogs, or perhaps left them exposed at the forest's edge, but even then, who knows, the tigers themselves might have ended up not wanting to eat any more of them. They thus died, and in every way, and more were born, always (118-9).

Deftly, the mother gives the children's deaths a positive aspect; justifies them in her own eyes: rather than being eaten alive, as they otherwise might have been, they "returned to the earth simply, like the wild mangoes from on high, or like the dead little monkeys at the river's mouth" (118). Native suffering thus emerges as timeless, context independent, eminently immutable.

Rather than waste energy on the unchangeable, the mother concentrates henceforth on personal finances. Using the system to better her family's lot, she tries to make it work in her family's favor. Unwitting mouthpiece of French colonial ideology, her efforts seem to corroborate the view of the

Colonial Ministry's Poirier: "in all countries, the woman is the conservative force and tenacious guardian of tradition even when she is its victim" (266). Constructing her in the textual lineage of "Le Boa's" Mlle Barbet, Duras aligns the mother, too, with bananas. Having been convinced to move to Indochina by idyllic propaganda posters featuring a couple relaxing in the shade of banana trees, she now tries to raise bananas on her own concession. When her dams fail, she displaces her hope onto her daughter Suzanne: making a good marriage, she believes, this girl might finally make banana cultivation profitable. But in its transfer from one generation to the next, the banana takes on decidedly sexual connotations. As she works on her banana trees outside, the mother glances back and forth between her trees and the bungalow where Suzanne entertains her wealthy suitor, M. Jo, thinking "with a satisfied air: the work being done behind that door was differently efficacious than the work she pretended to do with the banana trees" (*UB*, 68).

Waiting by the Roadside: abject and *attente*

At their mother's concession, her children dream, like *Native Son*'s hero, to the ideological representations provided by the social, cultural, and economic status quo. Unable to see them in a local movie house, as Bigger Thomas did, they find them in *Hollywood-Cinéma*, "six years old now, it was the only book that there had ever been in the family" (*UB*, 137). Like *Black Boy*'s hero, they also dream of finding freedom in the city. Suzanne, for instance, passes most of her time waiting by a nearby bridge, sure that one day "a man would stop, perhaps, why not? Because he had would have seen her near the bridge. She would perhaps please him and he would offer to take her to the city. . . . Joseph was also waiting for a car to stop in front of the bungalow. That one would be driven by a woman with platinum blonde hair, smoking English cigarettes, and wearing make-up" (21-2).

Suzanne's waiting is the first textual instance of durassian *attente*. As such, it forcefully undermines the notion that if this passive practice proves anything, it is that to Duras, as to patriarchs, passivity is of a piece with female biology. Rather than ground Suzanne's *attente* in her female gender, Duras roots it in the material conditions of her existence. Isolated on the Kam Plain, she is imprisoned in a "prison-world" (67). Moreover, consistent with her claim to capture imprisoned women at the moment they begin to stir, Duras places Suzanne's *attente* by one of the most politically charged positions in this highly political novel: the Kam Bridge.

The Kam Bridge is an integral component in the roadway system Duras uses to graphically represent the structures and relations of colonial rule. In accordance with *Un Barrage*'s general flow from isolated to contextualized image, she lays out only one road in Part I—the Kam Plain's single trail— and then returns, in Part II, to fill in that initial sketch with a detailed exposition of city streets. It takes but a brief look at the Kam Trail to get a sense of the way in which Duras uses the roads themselves to figure the divisive structures of colonial rule and the traffic on them to figure its unequal and oppressive relations. As it traverses the entire narrow Kam Plain lengthwise (33), the Kam Trail divides the native peasants on the mountain side from the *colon* mother's family to the seaside. It was built "in principle to drain off the future riches of the plain all the way to Ram" (33), but since the plain proved so poor that it had no other riches "than its infants with their pink mouths always open in hunger" (33), it serves only urban *colon* hunters who come to the forest to kill animals and return with their bodies to the city.

An inbetween place in the rural road system, the Kam Bridge is the site of multiple articulations and junctures. It runs directly over the stream in which Joseph swims with native children and where, the reader is encouraged to surmise, at least some colonial differences dissolve. Sitting there, watching them, *en attente,* Suzanne effectuates political articulations of her own: recording in her mind the image of these children playing together, she projects this image of egalitarian interaction into 1950 France, giving the lie to colonial ideology. Indeed if we are to believe Bourdieu, by introducing their private experiences into French public discourse, she establishes them as *legitimate.*

"Private" experiences undergo nothing less than a *change of state* when they recognize themselves in the *public objectivity* of an already constituted discourse, the objective sign of their right to be spoken and to be spoken publicly: "Words wreak havoc," says Sartre, "when they find a name for what had up to then been lived namelessly." Because any language that can command attention is an "authorized language," invested with the authority of a group, the things it designates are not simply expressed but also authorized and legitimated. This is true not only of establishment language but also of the heretical discourses which draw their legitimacy and authority from the very groups over which they exert their power and which they literally produce by expressing them: they derive their power from their capacity to *objectify* unformulated experiences, to make them public—a step on the road to officialization and legitimation—and, when the occasion arises, to manifest and reinforce their concordance (*Outline of a Theory,* 170-1).

As it joins Duras's continental readers with Indochina, Suzanne's *attente* by the bridge marks the crossroads between two political stages in her life. As she watches the swimmers before her, she looks constantly to either side, studying the road leading to the village of Ram in one direction and to an unnamed colonial city in the other. Transparent political signifiers, Ram and the city represent alternative ways in which Suzanne might assume her position in respect to the image of the swimmers before her. Ram embodies the solution the mother, like Mlle Barbet before her, had chosen: working within the colonial system. Its only business is a bar-canteen whose proprietor works so clearly in its interests that the colonial government had given him a Legion of Honor medal (41). Unnamed, the colonial city marks the site of still unknown and ever unforeseeable new perspectives and different solutions. Not surprisingly, Suzanne experiences three of the major events in her political bildung and procures the rationale and funds for the fourth as she sits, *en attente,* next to, or very close by, the Kam Bridge. Less expected, perhaps, is the fact that if all four of those scenes find theoretical bearings in Lacan, they draw their literary inspiration from Wright.

In "Long Black Song," which was available in French a year before Duras began *Un Barrage,* Richard Wright wanted to make an implied comment on white racist society. To that end, he recalls, he "conceiv[ed] of a simple peasant woman, whose outlook upon life was influenced by natural things, and contrast[ed] her with a white salesman selling phonographs and records" (Fabre, "Introduction," 257). In the resulting story, Wright's heroine sleeps with that white traveling salesman, he leaves her a phonograph in return, her husband finds out and shoots the white man, and he is burned to death by white men in his turn. In *Un Barrage,* Duras borrows from this scenario to compose the first of four scenes in which her heroine must define her place as a woman under patriarchal capitalism. More precisely, Suzanne's dilemma is how to define herself in relation to what Sartre called the gaze *[le regard]* of the other. For weeks, her rich but weak suitor M. Jo had been gazing at her lustfully, boring her to tears. Then one day he comes to the bathroom door and asks to be the first man to see her naked. Reading his request in terms of free unimpeded circulation of the sort Duras and her friends at the rue Saint-Benoît valued, Suzanne considers opening the door on the grounds that this body "was not made to be hidden but, to the contrary, to be seen and make its way in the world" (*UB*, 73). Shifting Wright's motif, the phonograph, to the instant of her heroine's decision, Duras transfers it from the realm of the gift to that of exchange so as to reveal the relations of power at work on this scene. Suzanne's decision is not only to be or not to be seen, but how to define herself in relation to the patriarchal capitalist gaze that defines women's bodies as objects of exchange? Driving home the fact that to acquiesce to his demand would mean dancing to his tune henceforth, Duras identifies the phonograph in question as a model that was actually being promoted in late 1940s French newspapers: if Suzanne will let him see her entirely naked, M. Jo says, he will give her "the most recent model of THE VOICE OF HER/HIS MASTER and records to boot" (72). And "so it was," Duras writes, "that just at the moment when she was going to open the door to give herself to the world see *[se donner à voir]*, the world prostituted her" (73).

Both Suzanne's act and Duras's conclusion find their full meaning in the context of what Duras and her friends at the rue Saint-Benoît conceived of as the writer's role in the revolution. As Italian Communist and writer Elio Vittorini phrased it: "The writer does not write to make beauty, but to make truth. I believe that all philosophy must be completed. It does not ever express the entire truth of an epoch. Together, rational forces and poetic forces produce works that express the truth of that epoch. As Eluard said, it is the writer who gives that truth to be seen *[la donne à voir]*" ("Une interview," 1). In her heroine's decision, Duras's reader is thus invited to see both one truth of her postwar epoch—that under patriarchy women are, as Lévi-Strauss was then showing, objects of exchange—and one truth of Duras's scriptural practice: that in the service of the revolution, it was making that truth visible; giving it to be seen.

Shaped by lacanian theory, Suzanne's second defining scene occurs by the Kam Bridge. There, M. Jo ups the ante by offering her the choice of three diamond rings in exchange for eight days with him in the city. Putting a diamond on her finger, Suzanne recalls her childhood riches: "Her eyes did not leave the diamond. She smiled at it. When she was a little girl and her father was still alive, she had had two children's rings, one set with a sapphire, the other with a fine pearl" (126). Recalling how she had lost those rings, "the mother had sold them" (126), she imagines that by putting her body into circulation like diamonds are, she could regain what she had lost: "But then her imagination lost its way.... It was a reality apart, the diamond; its importance was neither in its brilliance nor in its beauty but in its price, in its possibilities, unimaginable to her until then, of exchange" (126).[5] Like *La Douleur's* epiphany at Gare d'Orsay, Suzanne's encounter with the diamond marks an irremediable break: the diamond is, as she says, "an intermediary between the past and the future. It was a key that opened the future and sealed the past definitively" (126).

By the time M. Jo brings the diamond to the bridge, Suzanne's presence there is so closely associated with watching the swimmers as to make his arrival resonate as a violent intrusion into her line of sight; a slicing through of her fascination. That he brings with him three huge diamonds—cutting tools par excellence—merely strengthens that sense of severance. M. Jo, Lacan might suggest, functions as the bearer of symbolic power, who, intruding into the Imaginary scene where the child stands bound up in its fascination with its *imago*, triangulates and thus breaks the fixation. In Lacan, such triangulation would allow the child (Suzanne, for instance) to define herself in relation to existing power, which the triangulator seems to symbolize, and to emerge into the Symbolic Order. In this case, however, M. Jo's attemped triangulation ends in spectacular failure, leaving Suzanne not in the Symbolic Order at all, but merely transfixed again—this time by the diamond ring. This failure is directly related to the gap between M. Jo and the power he purports to symbolize. A weak and stupid man, he is incapable of masking the fact that his power is not coextensive with his being: in fact, he carries the symbols of his power around in a most artificial and appended fashion, as the diamonds in his coatpockets; or as, in the apt title of King Missile's 1992 song, a "detachable penis."[6] Crucially, the breach between the power he wields and M. Jo's person is so wide that it permits Suzanne's mother to stage a coup: relocating her daughter to the bungalow, she takes over as triangulating instance in her subject definition.

Replacing M. Jo's symbolic power with physical force, the mother beats Suzanne. Seconding her fists with a barrage of words, she performs a massive historical contextualization. Inserting both the diamond-*imago* and Suzanne into their historical contexts, she establishes them as bloodied products of oppression. Speaking as she beats of "the seawalls, the bank, her illness, the roof, the piano lessons, the cadastral agents, her old age, her fatigue, her death" (136), she inserts Suzanne and her beating into the history of her own oppression. As the beating continues, her narrative reinserts the diamond-*imago* into its place of provenance in the racist colonial order—"the bloodied hands of a black man [who] extracted [it] from the stony bed of one of those nightmarish rivers of the Congo's Katanga mining region" (140). Informed of their histories in the patriarchal colonial order, Suzanne sees her future in the diamond-*imago* differently: in a system where circulation benefits men like her father and M. Jo, she and the diamond, bloodied bodies extracted from bloodied bodies, merely circulate in a closed circuit of exchange, between and within the "inhuman and concupiscent hands of [their] jailers" (140).

Demonstrating that the participants in *Un Barrage*'s maternal beating scene can be understood only in relation to their contexts, Duras encourages us to contextualize the scene itself. Modeled on wrightean precedent, it takes its bearings from his beating scenes, which occur, as do all of his crucial scenes, in one of two registers: that of the definition of the African American subject as enslaved or that of the enslaved subject's attempt to define itself in more liberated terms. In Wright, the beating is applied either by representatives of the status quo or by the family. In "Fire and Clouds," the beating concerns the black male subject's relation to U.S. white racist power structures: beaten by white men, Reverend Taylor must define himself either in relation to those hegemonic structures or to the African American community. In *Black Boy,* a maternal beating works though the relation of Wright's autobiographical self to his family and community. *Black Boy* opens, we recall, as four-year old Richard sets his house afire, hides in fear beneath it, is found by his father and beaten unconscious by his mother. To Hakutani, Wright's maternal beatings demonstrate the devastating effects of oppression in the absence of tenderness in the U.S. black Southern family (125). To Gilroy, they mobilize a form specific to the African American community in the United States, where violence historically mediates racial difference and maintains the boundary between the white and black experience. In his view, white racist violence against blacks was internalized and reproduced within the black community, where it came to shape all aspects of social life, including its most intimate relations. Gilroy concurs with Ralph Ellison's view that Wright links the reproduction of violence in the community to culturally specific nurturing practices that are themselves the legacy of white racial terror on the institution of the black family in the South:

> One of the Southern Negro family's methods of protecting the child is the severe beating—a homeopathic dose of the violence generated by black white relationships. Such beatings as Wright's were administered for the child's own good; a good which the child resisted, thus giving family relationships an undercurrent of fear and hostility, which differs qualitatively from that found in patriarchal middle class families, because here the severe beating is administered by the mother, leaving the child no parental sanctuary. He must ever embrace violence along with maternal tenderness, or reject, in his helpless way, the mother (Gilroy, 174-5; Ellison, *Shadow,* 85-6).

Duras's citation of Wright's beating scenes thus confronts us with an issue of interpretation: in whose service does the mother beat Suzanne? Is her beating designed to force her to assume the subjugated subject position within the status quo or to help her define herself in more liberated terms? Suggesting that it has its place in the latter project, Suzanne's beating yields knowledge crucial to her liberation: by obtaining the diamond ring without sleeping with M. Jo, she had liberated it and permitted it to "begin its career, henceforth freed and fecund" (*UB*, 140; 112). Defining herself in relation to that *imago*—the diamond ring as liberated by her act, but also herself in/as the diamond-*imago* liberating herself—Suzanne finally begins to find a political voice.

Insisting her presence with unprecedented force and resolve into her family's now thoroughly revolting "we," Suzanne ends Part I of *Un Barrage* by giving birth to the voice that will become revolutionary in Part II. But as Part I closes, their "we" remains rebellious and reactionary; convinced by liberal promises. Rather than overthrowing existing relations of power, it can merely imagine reversing existing hierarchies and taking its oppressor's place. As Joseph affirms a hackneyed *vouloir, c'est pouvoir*—"If we want to be, we can be as rich as the others, shit, all we have to do is want it, and we're rich" (164)—and the mother a vengeful "we'll run them down on the roads," Suzanne adds her voice to theirs only to give voice to her emotional disconnect: "And then, we'll not give a damn about crushing them. We'll show them everything we have, but we won't give them one little thing" (164). Fortunately, in liberating the diamond, Suzanne provided herself with a means of freeing herself from this reactionary position. The diamond provides her family with a reason for going to the city: selling the diamond and getting rich, they believe, they will find freedom. If this goal is shown to be illusory, their displacement proves productive: it allows Suzanne to escape the immobility and incarceration of the plain.

No more than Richard Wright does Duras depict the city in terms of deliverance from prejudice or exclusion. Instead, like him, she portrays it in ambivalent and contradictory terms: when Suzanne leaves for the city, she embarks, just as *Black Boy*'s hero does, on a lonely, isolating, and alienating experience. But if in the move from the rural to urban setting, she merely exchanges the Lords of the Lands for the Bosses of the Buildings, as Hakutani has it of Wright's heroes (109), her move also provides her, too, with potential avenues of transcendence. Like young Richard's flight to the Northern city, Suzanne's trip to the colonial city marks her commitment to knowing a world that has as yet no meaning to her, other than that of being "outside and beyond" (Stepto, "Literacy," 82). But where Wright's heroes work in the city to attain knowledge through literacy, Suzanne uses means that are consistent with the conditions of her own oppression. In accordance with later feminist accounts of women's sexual alienation and with her own understanding of post-Revolutionary rational thought, Duras depicts her heroine as divided from her emotions; not yet in touch with sexuality. As she had said earlier, in an emphatically negative personal register, "Me, if I marry him, it will be without any feelings for him'" (95); "Me, I don't want to be in anybody's arms" (101); "Me, I do without love" (95). But if this voice, which first emerges as Suzanne's, is to become revolutionary, then she must find, beginning with her city sojourn, a means to transcend the divisions of rational thought and reconnect with the second and nonrational mode of consciousness—sexuality and emotion, but also laughter, music, and song (chapter 4).

Duras's Colonial City

Turning the page between *Un Barrage*'s Kam Plain and the colonial city is a real trip: gone are the vague landscapes, epic portraits, and hazy dreams; gone, too, the vague accusations attributing the mother's situation to bad luck, land, water, sea, and shit. In their places stand a remarkably clear-sighted, concrete narrator whose detailed structural diagram of the city fills in the image of colonialism evoked in *Un Barrage*'s opening tableau with real material and socioeconomic detail.

Built by "the mother-country" (170), this city is the model of "all colonial cities" (167). Like them, it is structured on colonial divisions: "there were two cities in this city; the white and the other" (167). Below the white district, "native faubourgs" (171) assume, geographically, the posture Wright followed Nietzsche in calling the "frog's perspective"—the "angle of vision held by oppressed people . . . an outlook of people looking upward from below" (Foreword, 11-4). Rising above them, the white district, Eden, assumes the colonialist posture that Marie Louise Pratt termed "promontory." In the heart of this Eden district stands the financial heartland, Mecca, where "one found not official power, the Palace of the Governors, but deep power, the priests of this Mecca, the financiers" (167). Decades before postcolonial studies, Duras portrays the Eden district as the place where whiteness is constructed and colonial divisions are installed:

> The white districts of all the colonial cities in the world were always of an impeccable cleanliness in those years. That was true not only of the cities: the whites too were clean. As soon as they arrived, they learned to take a bath every day, as one has little children do, and to dress themselves in the colonial uniform, the suits of white, color of immunity and innocence. With that, the first step had been taken. The distance augmented in the same proportion, the initial difference being multiplied, white by white, between them and the others, who washed themselves with rain from heaven and the muddy waters of the streams and rivers (167-8).

Reworking the figure of the colony as zoo she had constructed in "Le Boa," Duras reverses the role attributions in the original scene by Wright: black prisoners reminded his young hero of zebras in a zoo; in *Un Barrage*, Eden district whites assume an analogous role: "Watered several times a day, green, flowering, these streets were as well kept as the paths of an immense zoo where rare species of whites watched over themselves" (168). Describing Eden in the same terms she had used for the boa, she tears off colonialism's majestic mask to reveal it as narcissistic, self-referential, self-serving: "The glistening of the cars, the store windows, the watered asphalt, the brilliant whiteness of the clothes, the shimmering freshness of the flowerbeds made the upper district a magic brothel *[bordel]* where the [white] race could give itself, in undiluted peace, the sacred spectacle of its own presence" (169).

With this colonial structure in place, *Un Barrage* begins to contextualize the mother's Kam Plain narrative of colonialism. On the plain, native children appear to die and be replenished in equal proportions. In the city, the native zone's progressive dimunition is revealed as the sine qua non of colonial success: "The incredible success of the colonial institution was demonstrated by the development of the native zone and its constantly growing retreat" (170). On the Plain, Suzanne had seen the image of colonial wealth coming from bloodied native hands. In the city, that image is translated into Indochina terms; filled in and inserted into the chronology of colonial rule's demise:

> It was the *grande époque*. Hundreds of thousands of native workers bled the trees of hundreds of thousands of hectares of red earth, bled themselves opening the trees that grew in an earth that had by chance been called red before becoming the possession of several hundred white planters of colossal fortune. Latex flowed. Blood, too. But the latex alone was precious and collected, and collected, paid. The blood was squandered. One still avoided imagining that one day a great number of them [native people] would come to demand the price of all that blood (169).

Turning then to Suzanne, Duras positions her precisely where, by virtue of her life history to date, she should assume her subject position. True to her family's borderzone socioeconomic and cultural places, she stays at the Hôtel Central, located between the elite white Eden and the native part of town, where Indochina's *indigènes coloniaux* (17)—its "poor white trash"— were relegated. Here as on the Kam Plain, Suzanne sits between *imago* alternatives. In contrast to their rural counterparts, her urban *imagoes* transparently reveal the positions they offer as figures of western patriarchy's traditional feminine roles—the Virgin, figured by Suzanne's mother, and the Whore, by the hotel manager, Madame Marthe. With strikingly similar socioeconomic positions, the mother and Madame Marthe differ, like the roles they represent, in their relation to sexuality. Where her mother believed that by denying her own sexuality she could save Suzanne, Madame Marthe used her sexuality "to preserve her [daughter Carmen] from a fate like her own" (172). Indeed "during her twenty years as a whore, she had saved the money to buy enough stock in the Association of Colonial Hotels to assure them the management of this hotel" (172)

With Suzanne in the role of the Virgin's daughter, Madame Marthe's 35 year-old daughter, Carmen, stands as her patriarchal inverse: she is, in

Duras's phrase, "a true whore's daughter" (174). From her initial urban position, Suzanne can see that Carmen and her mother both have restricted movement. However, in the same way that her mother's inability to see colonial structures had caused her to misplace blame for her own and native suffering, Suzanne's failure to see patriarchal structures causes her to misinterpret these women's constricted movement as resulting from their own ontological flaws. Had Carmen had a face to go with her beautiful legs, she believes, "one would long ago have witnessed the delectable spectacle of seeing her installed in the upper district and covered in gold by some bank director or rich northern planter" (173). Not having that face, Carmen is trapped walking back and forth in the corridor joining the hotel terrace and dining room. And had the diamond that had promised to make them rich not had "a serious flaw, a carbon spark [un crapaud], that greatly diminished its value" (177), her mother would not have had to walk up and down city streets day after day, vainly trying to procure full price for it anyway. But if the mother's efforts are as futile as they seem, her absence proves useful: thanks to it, Carmen can slip into the space of Suzanne's subject formation and try her hand at inflecting it.

Introducing sexuality into that scene, Carmen informs Suzanne that freedom and dignity can be won using other "weapons than those [the mother] thought good" (183). Dressing and coifing Suzanne, she advises her to go for a walk in the city, "but not to let herself be had" (184) by the first man who comes her way. Suzanne then leaves to wander white city streets, never having imagined that "there would be a day in her life that would be as important as this one, when, for the first time, alone and seventeen, she would go out to discover the great colonial city" (185). On that red letter day, as she walks chic streets, Suzanne acts out a vision she had seen back by the bridge: the vision of herself circulating unimpeded, with its hints of the unimaginable and seemingly infinite possibilities of her circulation. In the process, she comes to see what her Kam Plain isolation prevented her from seeing: that circulation takes place not in a neutral space where it might be free, but in a specific sociocultural and economic context with equally specific relations of power.

Walking City Streets

Walking Eden streets, Suzanne encounters the gaze, which Sartre was exploring in relation to subject formation in such 1940s works as *L'Etre et le Néant* and *Réflexions sur la question juive*. As she begins her trek up this district's streets, a barrage of elite gazes bears down on her: "They looked at her. They turned to look, they smiled"; "They turned to look. They smiled. As they turned around, they smiled"; "They still noticed her" (185-6). Linked to the differences between Suzanne and the elite girls around her, their mocking gazes "other" her: "no young white girl of her age ever walked alone in the streets of the Haut-Quartier"; "even the [white] women were rarely alone"; "the girls you met there passed in groups, dressed in sports clothes. Some, tennis rackets under their arms" (185). When Suzanne returns their gaze, however, she sees in these women the same apparent ontological perfection, elegance, and majesty that Duras's young heroine had seen in the boa and that Lol V. Stein would find in Anne-Marie Stretter: "She found that all of these women were beautiful and that their summer elegance was an insult to everything that was not them . . . they walked like queens, spoke, laughed, made gestures in absolute accordance with the general movement, which was one of an extraordinary ease at living" (186).

Submitting to this regard, Suzanne defines herself in its terms: "It came insensibly, from the moment she entered the avenue . . . it had become more pronounced, increasing until it became, as she reached the center of the Haut-Quartier, an impardonable reality: she was ridiculous and everyone saw it"; "The more they looked at her, the more she persuaded herself that she was scandalous, an object of complete ugliness and stupidity" (186). Conceding her ontological inferiority—"She herself, head to foot, was contemptible"(187)—filled with hatred of her mother and herself, and looking ever more like the Beggarwoman, she "walked over to the edge of the sidewalk, by the gutter, into which she "would have wished to fall dead and glide away" (187). Leaving the streets for the shelter of the Eden Cinema, Suzanne leaves knowing things about the relation of class, gender, and mobility that her mother's and Carmen's discourses of equal rights and opportunities had not allowed her to see: "It was not given to everyone to walk in these streets, on these sidewalks, among these lords and children of kings. Not everyone commands the same faculties of movement" (186).

Eden Cinema

On the Plain, Suzanne had imagined that "going to the cinema every evening was, along with circulating in an automobile, one of the forms that human happiness could take" (122). When she arrived in town, Carmen had told her that the greatest value of the movies "was that they aroused desire in girls and boys and made them eager to flee their families" (199). As it turns out, the Eden Cinema is where Suzanne's countryside dreams are unmasked as ideological illusion.

Suzanne enters the Eden Cinema as an "oasis, the dark room of the afternoon, the night of solitary people, an artificial and democratic night, the great egalitarian night of the cinema, more real than the real night, more ravishing, more consoling than all of the real nights, the chosen night, open to all, offered to all" (188). A beautiful woman dressed in courtly attire passes on the screen; "men went crazy for her, fell in her wake" (188). When she meets her love in Venice, the public looks on transfixed: "Gigantic communion of the audience and the screen. You would want to be in their place. Oh! how you would want it! Their bodies entwined" (189). Having been informed of unequal class and gender relations, Suzanne sees through this image. Past the end of the film, she sees, behind its ideological narrative of reciprocal love, the actual gender relations it hides, relations that are not only violent and unequal, but cannibalistic:

> Their mouths approach one another with the slowness of a nightmare. Once they are close enough to touch, their bodies are cut off. Then, in their decapitated heads, you see what you wouldn't know how to see, their lips face-to-face, open halfway, open still more, their jaws fall apart like in death and in a brusque and fatal relaxation of their heads, their lips join like octopuses, crush each other, try in the deliriousness of the starving, to eat, to make each other disappear in a reciprocal absorption (189).

In sex as on the streets, Suzanne realizes, equality is an "impossible and absurd ideal to which the structure of the organs clearly does not lend itself" (189). As surely as the boa ate the chick, as regret devoured Mlle Barbet, as the cadastral agents consumed her mother's money and health, and as surely as the city diamond dealers will eat Suzanne's mother alive, so too will this beautiful filmic courtesan be consumed. Ignorant victims of patriarchy, this woman is, like her mother, a "kind of old whore without knowing it" (193). Freeing Suzanne from that role, this knowledge liberates her from Joseph's tutelage as well. As she exits Eden Cinema, she defines herself in more liberated terms by affirming her resolve to move from now on exclusively according to her own desire: "*I* don't give a damn where *I* go . . . *I'll* go where *I* want! (192; my emphasis).

Going where she wishes, Suzanne moves to a place where another Duras heroine will soon follow—to a bench in a square (see *Le Square*). In a sequence of events that begins there, she completes the final self-positionings leading up to her emergence as a subject. An apparently static site, the bench is in fact traversed by radical reversal: it is, after all, a position defined by one who knows that diamonds can be flawed, that the apex of colonial respectability is a whorehouse, that the cinema's artificial night is truer than "real" nights on city streets, that mothers are whores. In such a world,

Carmen's "lies," as Suzanne calls them, ring surprisingly true, particularly her assertion that "whores . . . are the most honest and least bastardly [*salaud*] thing in this colossal colonial brothel" (198). Aligning her voice with Carmen's overtly self-directed sexuality and just as overtly deceitful discursive practices, Suzanne proclaims, in an emphatic subjective "I," her intention to become a fully sexual feminine subject: "*I* think *I* want to grow up to be like Carmen. . . . Like Carmen only better . . . *I* warn you, *I'm* a Carmen type" (211-2; my emphases).

Bricolage, Negativity, Refusal

In a masterful scene of bricolage, Suzanne appropriates patriarchy's tools to liberate herself from its incarceration. Running into M. Jo on her way back to the movies, she takes him along to help, unawares, in her liberation. In the Eden Cinema, she contextualizes and disempowers his male gaze: "She had already been looked at [*Il lui été déjà arrivé d'être regardée*] like this by men she passed in the Haut-Quartier on her way to the movies" (223). Exiting the Eden Cinema, she returns with him to the scene of her Eden and Mecca street humiliation. Rather than walk those streets, she now cruises them in his Morris Léon Bollé. Imbued with the attributes of Duras's early figure for colonialism, the boa, this limousine steps out fully into that role. If in Duras's established symbolics, Suzanne should figure the unsuspecting chick, unlike her predecessors, this chick enters the boa's mouth informed of patriarchy's cannibalistic dynamics; indeed, she enters it a *self-cognizant* whore and a liar to boot. And that knowledge, as the old adage has it, will set her free. Rather than being subsumed into the boa, she will use the boa to empower herself. Moving along Eden streets, she will transmute colonialism's one-way transports into the medium of her liberation: *negativity*. Fluid, in movement, exceeding colonial categories, the Morris Léon Bollé transports Suzanne across categorical boundaries, permitting her to combine their elements and define herself as feminine and empowered.

Stimulating M. Jo's desire, Suzanne becomes so "drunk on the city" (226) as to imagine her way past the cityscape before her. Watching the film at the Eden, she had seen past its ideology to the relations of power it hides; watching the city, she sees the end of those relations without seeing, for as much, what might rise up in their wake: "The car rolled, the sole reality, glorious, and in its wake the entire city fell back, crumbled away, brilliant" (226). As the limousine soars high above the city, M. Jo touches Suzanne's breasts and tells her, "You have beautiful breasts" (226). Like

"Le Boa's" heroine before her, she stares at her breasts, the free-floating sexual appendages and alter egos in which she can and does define herself as a fully sexual female subject: "Above the terrifying city, Suzanne saw her breasts, saw the erection of her breasts higher than everything standing in that city, over which they would prevail" (226). Allowing his desire to reach its apex, she bolts from the limousine "without a look *[un regard]* for M. Jo" (227). Proclaiming her staunch refusal and thus asserting her sexual self-determination, she affirms: *'I* can't. It's no use. With you, *I* never could" (228), she defines herself as, in the rue Saint-Benoît's terms, a revolutionary subject of the radical refusal. Refusing what Orlando Patterson calls the oppressed subject's social death, she silences M. Jo's privileged voice: "He did not reply. Thus it was that M. Jo disappeared from Suzanne's life" (228).

Multiplicity, Non-Rationality, Revolution

If Suzanne's voice is to achieve revolutionary stature, it must exceed her individual instance to achieve collective form. As her family leaves the city to return home, Suzanne's mother paves the way for that transition by handing narrative control to her daughter; "I don't have the strength to begin all over again" [242]. In turn, Suzanne opens up *Un Barrage*'s narrative "place" to other victims of patriarchal colonialism. As they emerge through her place, their voices render *Un Barrage*'s narrative voice multiple and heterogeneous. As they enter into dialogue, they reverse colonialism's cannibalistic relations and undermine the ideological narrative articulated in the first part of *Un Barrage*. In the course of Part I, that narrative was produced by a pastiche process that cannibalized native voices and stories; in Part II, as each oppressed voice rises up to tell its tale, those voices work together to progressively "eat holes" in it.

First comes the *caporal*. Employed gratis by the mother, the *caporal* helped build the Kam Trail. His story presents readers with scenes of native prisoners and workers chained together like the black prisoners in Wright's chain gang, overseen by indigenous militiamen as Antelme showed concentration camp internees also were, working 16-hour days, malnourished, beaten, buried alive. Translating the *caporal*'s Vietnamese words into French—"The corporal said he had been beaten as much as a man could be without dying" (246)—Suzanne corroborates his account: "The corporal had, indeed, been so beaten that the skin of his legs was blue and thin as the thinnest cloth" (248). She records the oppression of native worker wives;

the *caporal*'s in particular—"During this time, like all the recruits' wives, the caporal's wife gave birth to children one after the other and they were always the products of the militiamen" (246). And she introduces into her text his wife's indirect speech, informing us that "what she did know was that she had not ceased to be pregnant by the militiamen and that it was the corporal who had got up at night to dig the little graves for the dead children" (246). Inserting her story into an international frame, Suzanne links high infant mortality in Indochina to that in other colonized regions—Africa, South America, Manchuria, and Mississippi, the home state Wright had textualized in *Black Boy*:

> [The children] did not stop playing except to go die. Of destitution. Everywhere, and in all times. . . . No doubt children died everywhere of it. In the entire world, in the same manner. In the Mississippi. In the Amazon. In the cadaverous villages of Manchuria. In the Sudan. On the Kam Plain, too. And everywhere like here, of misery. Of the mangoes of misery. Of the rice of misery. Of the milk of misery, of the too thin milk of their miserable mothers (330).

As these voices leech away the mother's ideological narrative, Part II's multiple and heterogeneous narrative voice reveals the real causes and agents of native children's massive demise. It shows that rather than an immutable Human Condition or green mangoes, colonial rule kills the children by creating the shortage of food that forces them to take to the Kam Trail, where *colon* motorists run them down. As this narrative voice informs continental readers, "when a driver ran over one he stopped, paid a tribute to the parents, and left. Most often he left without paying anything, the parents being far away" (331). And if the *colons* are dissatisfied with this situation, it reveals, that is solely because "the children interfered with the circulation of their automobiles, damaged the bridges, tore up the roadways, and created even problems of conscience" (332).

To introduce the mother's firsthand testimonial, Duras has her autobiographical stand-in perform "true theater": standing by the Kam Bridge, she reads a testimonial letter the mother wrote but did not send to cadastral agents:

> I also know that all the knowledge I have of your villainy and the villainy of your colleagues, of those who preceded you and of those who will follow you, of the government itself . . . would be of no use to me if I were the only one to have it. For the knowledge one man has of the crimes of a hundred others is of no use to him. That's something it took me a long time to learn, but I know it now for the rest of my life. And so there are now hundreds on the plain who

share my knowledge, who know what you are, and perhaps two hundred who
know you as I know you, in detail, in your methods, your ways of doing
things. I'm the one who explained to them, at length and patiently, what you
are, and who fervently keeps alive in them the hatred of your kind (292-3).

In Suzanne's mind, the mother's letter calls up a memory: two years earlier,
in the time of "Joseph's springtime" (310), he had become a completely
different person. That day, a cadastral inspector had come to the bungalow,
certain that the dams had failed and ready to repossess their land. Standing
tall and bare-chested, Joseph had lied: "Our dikes held up. . . . We have a
terrific harvest, you never saw anything like it in your life" (310). Confronted with the image of a lower-class *colon* refusing to submit to a class
superior, the mother had broken free of rational strictures, burst out
laughing, assumed a Zolaesque posture and screamed, "Bastards! . . .
Dogs! . . . Thieves! . . . Assassins!" (314). Increasing his threats, the cadastral
agent had reminded them that their fates were in his hands. Making it clear
that the inverse applied, Joseph had picked up his gun, aimed it at the
cadastral agent, kept it there a while, raised it toward the sky, and fired. As
he did, what Mascolo terms the second and nonrational mode of consciousness erupted onto the scene: while the agent ran as fast as he could toward
his car, Joseph, then the mother and Suzanne burst out laughing.

Finally, with this image of the nonrational mode's revolutionary potential in her mind, as her mother lies dying and *Un Barrage* nears its close,
Suzanne brings laughter, music, and joy to what she senses will be, like her
rendez-vous with the diamond and her city-street walk, "an act of great
importance, perhaps the most important in her life thus far" (320). Three
weeks later, to the notes of her own favorite tune, "Ramona," she goes off to
the fields with the neighbor boy, Agosti. Later on, corroborating the
revolutionary gains made in their intimate relations, Agosti had taken "his
handkerchief from his pocket and wiped off the blood that ran down his/
her *[ses]* thighs. Before leaving, he had put its bloody corner into his mouth,
without disgust, and, with his saliva, again wiped the spots of dried blood"
(343). Coming past the end of their sexual relations, Agosti's gesture
rewrites the image Suzanne had seen past the end of the film at the Eden
Cinema: where that filmic image had revealed and reinforced hierarchical
divisions, his gesture signals their creation of a proto-revolutionary mini-
collective. Formed materially by the comingling of their bodily fluids
(saliva, blood), that community is signaled grammatically by Suzanne and
Agosti's ephemeral coincidence in the space of a sole pronoun—*ses* (in the
original French, the citation above reads: "Il avait sorti son mouchoir de la
poche et il avait essuyé le sang qui avait coulé le long de *ses* cuisses" [343]).
No longer identifiable as being *either* "his" *or* "hers," this pronoun an-

nounces Suzanne's and Agosti's creation of something new: *both* him *and* her commingled to form one single community (like Antelme's one human race) built on difference and love. Seeing that image, Suzanne gains knowledge crucial to the revolution: "That in love [or sex] differences could abolish themselves to such an extent, she would never forget" (343).[7]

After the mother dies and Suzanne and Joseph prepare to leave, the revolution seems close at hand. Speaking to native peasant neighbors gathered around the bungalow, Joseph adopts his mother's pedagogical tone and sounds quite the revolutionary leader:

> I'm leaving you everything . . . especially the guns. . . . If you do it, do it well. You must take their corpses into the forest, way beyond the last village, you know it well, in the second clearing. In two days time, there will be nothing left of them. Burn their clothes in the brush fires you light at night, but be careful about the shoes, buttons. Bury the ashes afterwards. Drown their car, far off, in the stream. Have buffaloes drag it on the shore, put huge rocks on the seats, and throw it into the stream where you dug the ditch when we wanted to make the seawalls *[barrages]* and in two hours time, it will be sunk out of sight. Above all, don't get caught. See that none of you confess. Or if you do, all of you confess. Together. If you are a thousand to have done it together, they can do nothing to you (362-3).

As Joseph speaks, his earlier words to Suzanne seem to resonate on that revolutionary air: "I thought about the Kam agents. I told myself that one day I must get to know those agents from very close up. That I must not be satisfied to know them as I knew them on the plain, through their dirty tricks *[saloperies]*, but that I must get into their schemes, know their filthiness *[saloperies]* without suffering from it and keep my meanness all the better to kill them" (275). Floating there, his earlier words hark up Suzanne's own: "Thinking [Joseph's words] over, she perceived with emotion that she felt capable, herself, of conducting her life as Joseph said she must. She saw then that what she admired in Joseph was also in her" (285). As Suzanne and Joseph prepare to leave the plain and their voices die down, young peasant children's birdlike voices rise up in *Un Barrage*'s final phrase. Innocent, collective, and revolutionary, they take over the text, opening it onto a space of hope and rebirth: "But the children had left at the same time as the sun. You could hear their sweet babbling voices coming out of the cabins" (365; 288 mod.).

In this concluding line, the voice that had begun to emerge in *Un Barrage*'s opening tableau assumes collective and revolutionary dimensions. Fittingly, this revolutionary voice rises up within a transparent citation of the famous opening phrase of Marx and Engels' *Manifesto of the Communist Party*, a phrase that was, like both Duras's dead horse and French colonial

rule in Indochina, centenarian in 1950: "A spectre is haunting Europe—
the spectre of Communism" (31). Closing *Un Barrage* with the native
children's voices, Duras presents them as the fulfillment of Marx's, Engels',
and her tableau's promises. By 1950, the spectre the fathers of Marxism had
seen haunting Europe in the mid-nineteenth century had moved close
enough to be audible. As she places her revolutionary hope in native
children, Duras concludes her novel by reaffirming the place of her politics
and of her writing as alongside not only Marx and Engels, but Wright as
well, who was developing, in the period of *Un Barrage*'s writing, the
"somewhat confused beginnings" of a view he would hold fully in the
1950s; she, for the rest of her life: "The salvation of humanity could come
only from the Third World" (Fabre, *Unfinished Quest*, 316).

Chapter 6

Diaspora and Cultural Displacement: Linda Lê and Tran Anh Hung

C'est toujours une histoire de viande.

—*Vinh L.*

So severe was *Un Barrage*'s critical reception and so unequal the balance of power between Duras and her critics that it was a full quarter century before she returned to her Indochina tale. As discussed in chapter 1, Geneviève Serreau had tried twice in the fifties to bring *Un Barrage* to the stage: in 1955 she had failed for lack of financing; in 1959 her producers had elided her left-political preface and the public had largely refused to attend the play because of its firm anticolonial stance. By 1977 both Duras's power and France's social fabric had changed. Consecrated by Lacan in 1965, she reached the intellectual heights thanks to neo-lacanian feminist interest in her work. Under the pressures of rising postcolonial immigration, including that which followed the 1975 communist takeover of Saigon, French society was much more diversified. Buoyed by both changes, Duras transformed her Indochina story for the theater in *Eden Cinéma*[1] and aligned herself with her Asian borderzone *errante*, the Beggarwoman. If *Eden Cinéma* put Duras's *Indochina* once again squarely before the French public, seven years later *L'Amant* placed it at the French cultural center stage, and that novel's success had a significant hand in shaping the contours of *Indochina*'s mid-1980s to early 1990s French cultural *renouveau*. In 1988 one young artist issued from the 1975 immigration, writer Linda Lê, textualized the problematic this saturation of French cultural space with Duras's *Indochina* created for Vietnamese diasporic artists. In this, the

second phrase of her second novel, Lê both responded, whether consciously or not, to Duras's hegemonic instance and defined her own project,
in this novel at least, as discovering a way to avoid that positioning: "I was
walking for hours, not knowing where to go or how to flee this Beggar who
was following my steps" (*Fuir,* 7). On Bourdieu's logic, we know, there is
no escape: all players seeking to enter a field of struggle are constrained to
respond to its hegemonic instance, if only to contest it. Thus, in so far as
creative artists of the Vietnamese diaspora either want or need to engage
textually in French in France with their native land, they must respond to
Duras's *Indochina.* As they respond to it, Lê and filmmaker Tran Anh
Hung, to name only the best-known artists of that diaspora, are now
formulating the third-order response to Jean-Paul Sartre and his notion of
intellectual engagement which, as we know, ruled the French intellectual
and literary field from the center at the mid-century.

As seen earlier, Richard Wright's first-order response to Sartre displaced literary engagement from the privileged place of the "objective"
witness bearer to the subjective place of one black man under U.S. white
racism. With his response, literary engagement widened its theoretical
bases to include psychoanalysis and broadened its purchase to become
antiracist as well as marxist and antibourgeois. In their turns, Beauvoir,
Duras, and Fanon formulated second-order responses to Sartre and his
hegemonic notion of engagement by further dragging and extending
Wright's displacement of intellectual engagement in their respective autobiographical directions. As Beauvoir displaced the "place" from which
engagement was articulated toward her place as a bourgeois woman under
western patriarchy, literary engagement further widened its purview to
include feminism. As Fanon extended it toward his place as a French-
educated bourgeois professional black man under western racist colonialism, engagement broadened the scope of its antiracism to the diasporic and
colonial arenas. Between Beauvoir's 1949 response and Fanon's of 1952,
Un Barrage dragged the place of intellectual engagement toward Duras's
place as a borderzone colonial "white trash" female. Psychically, Duras's
response was arguably more threatening to the French cultural subject in its
colonial configuration than either Beauvoir's or Fanon's for one primary
reason: it focused intellectual engagement on that subject's deep structuring and generative instance—*Indochina.* In her response to Sartre and
Wright, Duras shifted the "place" from which that instance was represented away from the place of the white male subject it subtends and
guarantees toward the *(créole)* borders separating it from that which it
excludes as "object" and "other" and whose abiding exclusion alone permits
it to survive as "subject" and "the same."

Constrained by the dynamics of field competition to respond to the hegemonic instance in the field of Indochina representation, hence to Duras, Linda Lê and Tran Ang Hung drag intellectual engagement toward their own "places" vis-à-vis French culture, while continuing to engage with that same representation, *Indochina*. The question of whether or not their work could or does further destabilize the psychic structures of the French colonial subject—a question independent of any alleged intention to destabilize or any desire to represent Indochina per se at all—must be addressed, first of all, to their respective complex and contradictory social, economic, and cultural places. In theory, their work would appear to promise to perform a perspectival gestalt similar to that *Un Barrage* attempts to perform—namely, the promise to make the French colonial subject see Indochina from the profoundly destabilizing and arguably fatal place of its "other." Whether or not it actually does perform such as gestalt depends, of course, on the exact parameters of the "place" from which each one represents Indochina.

Although they are cultural borderzoners like Duras, Lê and Tran are positioned quite differently that she is in the borders. Born in early 1960s Vietnam, they both moved to France after the communists took control of Saigon in 1975, with the third-wave of Vietnamese immigration. In contrast to the preceding waves, theirs was neither small nor invisible: only 7,000 Vietnamese immigrated to France in 1962; by 1982, 35,000 would (Bousquet, 88). Where the smaller earlier waves managed to isolate themselves from the French, theirs became part of the perceived "immigrant problem." By 1984 anthropologist Gisèle L. Bousquet found that "most of the Parisians I met during my year of fieldwork complained to me about what they called the 'Vietnamese invasion' and their 'taking over' of native districts" (88). Marginalized by the French, these often bourgeois elite South Vietnamese immigrants were marginalized by Paris's established Vietnamese community as well:

> The increasing number of refugees who arrived in France after 1975 does not participate in the already established Vietnamese community's social life. Leaders of Vietnamese anti-Communist political organizations have constantly warned the refugees that the established community is controlled by a communist organization affiliated with the Vietnamese Communist Party. These leaders of anti-Communist organizations promote the polarization of the community into political and social divisions (90).

Adolescents at the time of their immigrations, Tran and Lê completed their secondary educations in France: she then pursued French literature to the doctoral level; he, cinematography at the Ecole Lumière. Interviewed on Bernard Rapp's literary program, *Caractères*, at the time of *Les Evangiles du crime*, Lê further explained, "In Vietnam I completed my studies in French, with the result that I already felt like a foreigner in my own country. I have very little familiarity with Vietnamese culture, I know very little about it. I know French culture better." Formed on social, educational, and cultural borders, Lê and Tran take their places in the borderzone group of which Pham Quynh insists: "We think . . . in cross-breed/hybrid *[en métis]*" (Yeager, 90).[2]

Thus on the level of culture, Lê's and Tran's third-order responses retain Duras's and Fanon's displacement of the Sartrean field in the direction of French colonial cultural borderzones; in the arena of Indochina's borders, they displace her white *créole* place toward their Vietnamese *créole* positions. On the socioeconomic level, their responses also shift Duras's displacement of Sartrean engagement from his bourgeois place to her lower-class position. Issued from the former South Vietnamese bourgeois elite, they do not return the place of intellectual engagement to its 1940s Sartrean French bourgeois position. Rather, they drag it toward a place that is structurally similar to but disjunctive from Duras's own. As discussed in chapter 3, in French colonial Indochina, Duras's place at the bottom of the *colon* socioeconomic hierarchies was the closest to the native hierarchies: in relation to the French colonial elite, Duras was in the poor white-trash position; in relation to the Vietnamese, she was nonetheless in the place of the colonizer. Tran's and Lê's places are inverse to hers: in relation to the Vietnamese masses, they were in the bourgeois elite; in relation to the French, they were nonetheless in the place of the colonized. Like the place toward which Duras displaced the field in her second-order response, their places were thus ambiguous. The difference between their places and hers is that where her mother's lower-class place was scheduled for abjection from the French colonial order, their South Vietnamese elite forebears were being educated for enhanced "assimilation."

I began this book by claiming that Duras managed to funnel the voices of cultural difference into French culture because of her positional ambiguity and by showing that that same ambiguity permitted conservative critics to elide those voices and her revolutionary textual politics. Lê and Tran not only have similar ambiguities: they also began responding to her Indochina in a late 1980s-1990s period characterized both by the reemergence of a conservative political agenda Alice Jardine links directly to the 1950s and by the French colonial nostalgia films Norindr brought to our attention. The following pages explore the creative work of Lê and Tran in their responses to Duras's *Indochina*, with one eye to the ways in which conservative pressures shape or contain them and the other to the ways in which they escape that containment to disturb and displace her hegemonic Indochina and the (still colonial) psychic structures it subtends. On the broadest level, they are concerned with the relation between representation, cultural displacement, and social change. What is the relation between the displacement of persons, their creative work's displacement of their new culture's imaginary and representational repertories, and any possible reconfiguration of that same culture's imaginary structures? If Norindr has it right and the French colonial representation of Indochina was internalized to form the generative and deep structuring instance of the French colonial subject, *phantasmatic Indochina*, does it follow that modifying that representation works to modify, in analogous or unforeseen ways, that subject's psychic structures? Does modifying Indochina, one of the fundamental cultural images in which the French community "imagines" itself, in Anderson's term, modify that community's self-imagining? Or in Pierre Nora's, does transforming one of France's principal *lieux de mémoire* also modify the nation's self-definition? Finally what does it mean, where social change is concerned, that the counter-representation of Indochina Duras deployed against the French colonial ideological image in the political spirit of Ho Chi Minh is today being responded to by descendants of their former South Vietnamese bourgeois opponents? As discussed in chapter 4, Mascolo held that to be a revolutionary, the intellectual must work in the private sphere, become a proletarian of the spirit, and create new values for the revolution. If this is the case, what new values do Tran and Lê create for the new transnational or transmodern era that critics including Jardine see looming on the horizon?

Linda Lê's House of Blue

It would be grossly inaccurate to portray Linda Lê's scriptural project as political or as an attempt to represent Vietnam. As Sharon Lim-Hing has argued, it is rather involved with issues related "to the family and the self against a backdrop of failure, suicide and psychic torture" (116). To realize this project, however, the conditions of Lê's life history require her to engage textually with her native Vietnam, and this engagement constrains her to respond at least partially and inadvertently to Duras. Inadvertent though her response might be, Lê's writing resonates strongly and broadly with Duras's. This is not surprising: she situates her textual universe within the same imaginary and literary geographical frame, France-Southeast Asia, and saturates it with trademark Duras figures, topoi, and scenes—dysfunctional families, beggars, wandering, incest, homoeroticism, madness, criminals, watercrossings portrayed as decisive to a character's bildung, politically significant dinners recalling the stunning bourgeois circulation of a succulent but slowing sliding salmon in the 1958 *Moderato Cantabile*. Each "cited" element marks a place in Duras's Indochina upon which Lê brings to bear the pressures of her own historical moment, cultural background, and social place. Her treatment of two such key places—*la chambre noire* (the black room) and *la maison bleue* (the blue house)—provide an initial sense of the transformations she effectuates and the direction in which her response to Duras "drags" the contours of her predecessor's hegemonic Indochina.

Generally, Lê retains a given Duras signifier and attaches to it additional signifieds that challenge or contradict Duras's own. In Duras, for instance, *la chambre noire* is a site of mystery and creation; the internal place from which her writing emerges, as if dictated by a power external, superior, and/or unknown to her. Lê does not buy the mystery. She associates *la chambre noire* with a young Vietnamese girl who ate human flesh with her fellow boat person, Vinh L. repressed that memory, and comes to Vinh L. for help in recalling it. In his narrative of their encounter, Vinh L. casts the girl's *chambre noire* as the psychic place of her cannibalistic act's repression: "In discreet steps, by crude allusions, I forced 'Baby vulture' to remember her crime; in the instant when she prepared to make the avowal, I provoked amnesia, I helped her to take refuge in the dark room *[la chambre noire]*" ("Vinh L.," 198). Taken as a response to Duras, Lê's point appears clear: Duras's work is cannibalistic; it nourishes itself on the raw literary and imaginary "stuff" of the former French colonial Indochina, just as Vinh L. and Baby Vulture ate Vietnamese flesh. Making this point, Lê gestures toward her own conception of human and scriptural relations as well as her own scriptural project.

Consistent with Mascolo's communist ethics and like Duras, Lê develops an account of human relations based on a fundamental human material need: food. As discussed in chapter 5, Duras 's "Le Boa" concludes that where political and sexual relations are concerned, we have one choice: not merely To be or not to be?, but To be the boa or the chick? To consume an other, transform it into myself and survive, or to be ingested, digested, and transformed into it? Forty years later, Lê's first novel, *Un si tendre vampire* positioned itself vis-à-vis *Un Barrage*'s famous epithet, "colonial vampirism," to elaborate an account of writing as vampirism. Then in 1992, Lê positioned her short story "Vinh L." in relation to a central city name in Duras's Indochina, Vinh Long, in order to categorize all human relations as cannibalistic. Her story's narrator admits to having eaten human flesh in his crossing, refers to one Japanese man as a "devourer" of female flesh, claims families consume their infants, recalls the Vietnamese folktale in which Imperial Queens eat their rivals' children. In response to *Fuir'* s opening

query, "Comment fuir le mendiant [How to flee the Beggar]?," Lê thus
responds with and extends Bourdieu: There is no escape: to survive one
must eat; to ingest is to be contaminated. Or in scriptural terms, all survival
requires response, all response is inclusion, all inclusion is contamination,
all that survives is contaminated. As Vinh L. puts it, "Your books resemble
me: they are patched together bodies [corps rapiécés]" (191).

If all writing is plagiarism—"the form in which civilization accepted
cannibalism" ("Vinh L.," 176)—it is also, as Geneviève Idt's account of
Sartre's writing as "unmarked pastiche" demonstrates (chapter 1), the
guarantor of apparent cultural homogeneity. Vinh L.: "I chewed culture
without swallowing *[mâchouillé]*, regurgitated and then chewed thoughts
again, but if I could, like all authors, pass my crime through the grinder of
words, after a few dozen pages, nothing would remain of it. The hard ball
that weighs on my belly, I am going to introduce it into the grinder of
literature and nothing will come out but a rush of words" (225). A writer of
the diaspora, Lê stresses not only the "ingestion" of the cultural "other," but
especially, as Duras had, its residue. As Vinh L. put its, "the man that I had
killed, devoured, ruminated, belonged to me from the inside. But me, too, I
belonged to him. I was no longer but an envelope, he was squatting *[il
squattait]* in my entrails" (191). Lê thereby captures her project's intersection with the transformative revolutionary dialectics achieved by Duras's
heroine, *Un Barrage*'s Suzanne, in the belly of the boa (Chapter 5). Suzanne
positioned herself within the symbol of power (M. Jo's Morris Léon
Bollée) and, therein, on the site of her mother's abjection. Assuming the
full power of both places (sexual and abject), she managed the transubstan-
tiation of the limousine into negativity and defined herself as a fully sexual
feminine, and by that token, revolutionary subject. Now, Lê positions her
writing vis-à-vis Duras's as the young immigrant population in Leïla
Sebbar's *Shérazade*[3] situates itself vis-à-vis Paris's buildings: they squat the
Buildings of the Bosses (to recall Hakutani's term); she squats Duras's
Indochina Lê would thus mime, albeit in a different register, the coup
succeeded by *Un Barrage*'s Suzanne: she would transform the hegemonic
discursive construct Indochina from the inside and according to her
own aims.

In 1997 Lê took on Duras's *maison bleue* (blue house) and raised the
issue of property rights: Whose house is "Indochina"? In Duras, *la maison
bleue* is the house of the Chinese lover's father and his son after him; the
textual and imaginary site where memory, fantasy, and desire connect
Duras and her French readers to the former colonial Indochina. Appropriating the *maison bleue*, Lê transforms it into the Vietnamese home of the
Vietnamese father of the eponymous diasporic heroines in *Les Trois
Parques*. As she does, she moves the blue house from *Indochina* to Vietnam;

from the register of erotic and exotic colonial desire to the family drama. With her recoding of the *chambre noire*, Lê's *maison bleue* put into French cultural circulation "doubles" of Duras's topoi, whose meanings they challenge, contradict, and subvert. Henceforth Duras's father's house, Indochina, cohabitates French cultural space with Lê's father's house, Vietnam. But the 1997 emergence of Lê's *maison bleue* had been a decade in the making. Since 1987 she had been wrestling with Duras's Indochina, bringing the pressures of her "place" to bear on its elements. One can recapture the larger lines of this prior textual engagement in her turn of the decade, 1988-1992, treatment of Duras's Vinh Long and Beggarwoman. Key in Duras's Indochina, they were crucial to Lê's challenge.

If Duras's late 1970s merge with the Beggarwoman showed how liberating rising immigration could be for a former French *colon créole* in Paris, in *Fuir*, Lê transforms Duras's Beggarwoman to show how difficult it made life there for the immigrants themselves. Her Beggar is a Japanese man living "demi-fou" and homeless in Paris; her transformation of Duras's second wandering figure (her various textual stand-ins) is a North Vietnamese bourgeois professional working a white collar position at the Parisian embassy and living in a suburban apartment with his wife, a South Vietnamese doctor's daughter. In *Un Barrage,* an elite French colonial gaze bears down on Duras's young heroine as she walks the colonial city streets, enforcing existing hierarchies, shaping her sense of identity, transforming her wandering, or *errance,* into flight (chapter 5). In *Fuir,* Lê registers the increased French anti-Asian racism of the 1980s, a decade often referred to as the "decade of the beur" (Rosello, 1999) by depicting the French racist gaze bearing down on her wanderers. As French children ridicule them, they learn that not all races are free to walk Paris's streets, or—reading through Duras's prior conclusion—to navigate its social or economic systems. When a French barman rejects the Vietnamese hero's attempt to distinguish himself from the Beggarman—"Eh! Yellows among themselves! good-for-nothings between themselves!" (*Fuir,* 11)—he defines himself in terms consistent with the analyses of racism and its effects on subject definition elaborated in Sartre's *Réflexion sur la question juive* and developed in the direction of class and gender in *Un Barrage* and of colonial racism in Fanon's *Peau noire, masques blancs.* Conceding what looks to him like his own ontological inferiority, as *Un Barrage'* s Suzanne had before him, he affirms: "After all, I was nothing, nothing but an exiled guy with brown skin, tinted with a fine layer of dust" (13).

Like Duras, however, Lê also portrays the gaze as providing its object with the means to undermine the gazer. By identifying the ethnicities of the two men lumped together by the racist gaze as Japanese and Vietnamese, she invites readers to turn the gaze around and ironize on (their own)

French stupidity: Could they not distinguish a Japanese from a Vietnamese man? Were they unable to distinguish a vagrant from the nation that had taken Indochina from France during World War II from a bourgeois native of France's model colony? Crucially, the racist gaze bearing down on them creates between the Japanese and Vietnamese men that which might not have arisen without it: the space of dialogue. With Mascolo, Duras considered dialogue the sole place from which real (revolutionary) thought might arise. Consistently, from the dialogistic space conjoining Lê's Asian heroes rises up the Vietnamese man's representation of Vietnam. Rather than idealize his native land, this man depicts his local North Vietnamese peasant society and his mother in particular as subjected to superstitions. He shows the gaze serving the same normative function in North Vietnam as Duras had showed it serving in Indochina: it had been directed on him and on the tree that had been planted, as per village tradition, at his birth. When his tree was perceived as deformed, he was judged abnormal—"the decomposing state of my tree ruined my reputation in villagers' eyes" (18). Disowned by his parents, he was sent away to live in exile as his Aunt's son; "Exiled," he thus insists: "I was already in my country" (15).

The figure of the Aunt in *Fuir* is one of Linda Lê's most important responses to Duras's Indochina. Emerging in the course of the Vietnamese man's dialogue with the Japanese Beggar, it emerges as a memory of his adolescence. Both that memory and the conditions of its emergence directly parallel those of the French woman's dialogue with her Japanese lover in *Hiroshima mon amour*, and that dialogue's production of the heroine's memory of her adolescent experience as a German soldier's lover and then a *tondeuse* (shaved woman) in postwar Nevers. In *Fuir*, Lê transforms this story to conform to the peasant traditions of North Vietnam. Married at 15 to a rich impotent old man, the Aunt is discovered three weeks later by her husband with a soldier of unspecified origins. Her husband's family whips her, shaves her head, and repudiates her; her family sends her to another village to live, as Duras's *tondeuse* before her, alone, isolated, and outcast. With these tales, both Duras and Lê tell of bordercrossing and its sanctions. *Hiroshima mon amour*'s Nazi-French couple is, like its Japanese-French couple, a displaced figuring of *L'Amant*'s Chinese lover-*colon* girl couple: all worry through cultural bordercrossing in situations where bordercrossing is marked as political collaboration. Introducing Vietnam into the circuit of nations in which bordercrossing is heavily sanctioned, Lê works against the idyllic "othering," as a noncontradictory or homogeneous space, of her native land.

In Lê as in Duras there springs forth, from the status quo's exclusionary othering, the transgressive practice of *errance*. Leaving the North, Lê's

Vietnamese peasant's route South parallels that taken, a bit to the West, by Duras's Laotian Beggarwoman: he travels from his village to Ho Chi Minh City; she, from Savannakhet to Calcutta. Subsequently, he, too, leaves Vietnam for Paris, where, we understand, he narrates his Vietnamese childhood alongside Duras/the Beggarwoman. As he tells it, his life in Cochin China resonates with and ironizes on Duras's (mythologizing) narrative of her childhood there. He led an "drifter's existence *[existence à la dérive]*" (108) in the South, his brother-in-law lusted after him, and he composed a mythic version of his life story for self-serving reasons— "Whores, errance, all that was part of the myth I had created for my personal use" (107). Becoming more radically aimless than Durassian *errance,* his wandering recalls Agnès Varda's 1985 *Sans toit ni loi:* indeed, composing a self-profile similar to that of Varda's Sandrine Bonnaire character, Lê's Vietnamese man recalls: "I tried in vain scratching the earth beneath my feet, I didn't find a bone to chew. Nothing of my own: not homeland nor family. Orphaned by the fickleness of fate, exiled by cowardliness, married by chance, made cuckold like all the world. I was a bohemian who didn't understand anything about the poetry of wandering *[errance]*" (148-9).

In 1992 Lê responded to Duras on the site of Vinh Long, which had entered French cultural discourse aligned with Duras in 1977, when *Les Lieux de Marguerite Duras* printed the first photographs of her Indochina childhood, including one of her family in a horse-drawn carriage driven by a native man, riding along an avenue in this city, which was, to them, Indochina's most beautiful. As suggested by the reaction of the narrator in Duras's *L'Amant de la Chine du Nord* to the news of the Chinese lover's death—"For a year I regained the age of the Mekong crossing on the ferry from Vinh Long" (12)—Vinh Long went on to occupy a central place in the durassian imaginary, where it functions as a site of encounter and of departure. In Ving Long, Duras's heroine stand-in has her defining encounter with Anne-Marie Stretter (Duras and Porte, 61); "between Vinh Long and Sadec" (*A*, 17), she takes the ferry across the Mekong to her equally crucial encounter with the Chinese lover. Associated with Stretter, who "slides into" (Duras and Porte, 73) Duras's condensed figures for French colonialism per se—Calcutta, misery, and hunger— Vinh Long bodies forth French colonialism. The place where her Mekong crossing begins, it also figures the beginning place for the transgressive practices that promise to bring down colonial rule—*errance,* desire, and prostitution (73-4). Consistent with Marx's belief that bourgeois capitalism contains within itself the seeds of its own destruction, Duras's Vinh Long thus figures, at one and the same time, French bourgeois capitalist colonialism and the internally derived (indigenous) tools that will bring it down.

In 1992, then, Lê brought the pressures of the fall of Saigon and the "boat person" exodus to bear on Duras's Vinh Long. Under these pressures, the *errance* Duras associates with Vinh Long is transformed into flight, the city becomes person, and that person, Vinh L. bodies forth South Vietnam's displacement to France. Lê's depiction of this displacement, its events, and their consequences takes its place within Duras, Antelme, and Mascolo's intellectual lineage (Chapter 4). Indeed, Vinh L.'s boat-person experience closely recalls Antelme's experience as a Nazi-camp internee: both were limit situations taking them to the most extreme point of real material need, from both proceeds epiphany, and from both epiphanies comes the possibility of revolutionary change.

As Vinh L.'s physical displacement from Vietnam to France erases the geographical distance separating the colonial categories (métropole and colony), he comes to murder a man and eat his flesh. If Antelme's experience permits his thought to escape the categories of rational thought and perceive Nazis and non-Nazis as members of one human race, Vinh L.'s permits his thought to escape French colonial categories and perceive the cannibal and the writer—French colonialism's emblematic "savage" and "civilized" human forms—as two faces of one human dynamic. In Mascolo, only the full satisfaction of all material needs could raise revolutionary practices to the revolutionary plane of desire. Taking the desire that shapes the colonial subject and its ingestive relation to its "other" to its logical end, Vinh L.'s experience proves so satisfying that it results in his complete loss of desire—"Eating human flesh once, one sole time, I procured such a penetrating pleasure that it emasculated me" (195). In *Le Ravissement de Lol. V. Stein*, Duras uses punctuation to arrest the melodic flow of "Lola Valérie Stein" and create the staccato "Lol V. Stein," registering this heroine's alienation, under bourgeois patriarchy, from the nonrational mode of thought, its attendant music, desire, and revolutionary promises. Lê borrows Duras's means, truncating the name of Duras's own most beautiful city of *errance* and revolutionary promise, Vinh Long, to register her character Vinh L.'s desirelessness. But if Lol V. Stein wandered city streets in an attempt to discover her desire, Vinh L. will write in an attempt to rediscover his. If writing in French permits him to "copy men of letters," it does not permit him to represent his dead Vietnamese father. Representing him would require engaging not with the former colonizer's desire, but with the corporeality and materiality of Vietnamese culture:

I believe I have very good dispositions to become a man of letters.

I have always lived in abstraction and, even faced with misfortune, I have found no other defense than to take refuge in abstraction. I realized that today, while wishing, as I read a letter from my mother, to imagine my father dead. I tried, but in vain, because truly, I didn't ever see my father alive (225).

The story ends with Vinh L's decision to return to the mother(land). As Lê narrates it, his return represents a step back to the "before" of his present subject position, to a presubjective, preoedipal space in which he might manage to redefine himself in relation not to a colonial *imago,* but to an imago proffered by his motherlands, his personal and culture origins, their musics and rhythms.

Tran Anh Hung:
Journeys Home and the Transnational Market

The year after Vinh L. decided to return to the mother(land), Tran Anh Hung brought the mother(land) to the French screen. The third internationally-marketed French produced film on the former French colonial Indochina in as many years, his *Scent of Green Papaya* (original Vietnamese title, *Mui Du Du Xanh*) completed a de facto trio whose languages of expression reflect the western imperialist engagements there—Annaud's 1991 English language *The Lover,* Wargnier's 1992 French *Indochine,* and Tran's 1993 Vietnamese representation. Between them, these films mark the major axes of the 1991-1993 cinematic subfield whose players competed for the right to define the legitimate discourse of "Indochina." Written, directed, and produced by newcomers to their fields, *The Scent of Green Papaya* was the fledgling player in this subfield. Of its competitors, *Indochine* amassed the greatest sum of official cinema field capital.[4] Balked by some in France for linguistic treachery and feebly recognized by juries, *The Lover's* reprise of Duras's Indochina story suggests that it would nonetheless have had greatest resonance in the popular cultural domain, where Norindr has the colonial ideological *Indochina* deployed from the late nineteenth-century and where my research shows Duras placing one foot of her mid-twentieth-century borderzone (literary and popular) counter-representation to it.

Duras's aim in *Un Barrage* was to unmask French colonial ideology and reveal conditions of oppression in Indochina. As he describes it, Tran Anh Hung's aim in *The Scent of Green Papaya* was to reverse the workings of ideology in colonial nostalgia films such as *The Lover* and *Indochine* by representing Vietnam's Vietnamese population: "The humanity of the Vietnamese people is not visible," he explained, "What I wanted to do specifically was to show the humanity of a country" ("Portraying"). In *Un Barrage* Duras responds to the colonial ideological representation of Indochina from her place as a borderzone and bordercrossing lower-class *colon* girl after the Holocaust and during the Indochina War. Recalled later as having been "outside" of the native population, that place shaped an absence in her creative work that Duras would only represent, to my knowledge, in these previously cited words to Gauthier: "I remember a grace, a nearly collective grace, you see, circulating, of these girls who were . . . made of a sort of receptivity to nature. They spoke little, they amused themselves among themselves, and they received the rain, the heat, the fruits they ate, the baths in rivers, you see, a receptivity that was apparently very, very elementary" (Duras and Gauthier, 143, ellipses in original).

Positioning his response to Duras vis-à-vis her Asian girl scene, Tran Anh Hung elaborates it from his place as a bordercrossing Vietnamese man of the post-French colonial rule, predominately bourgeois 1975 diaspora. Picking one girl out of her rural peasant group and naming her Mui ("scent"), he makes her heroine of a tale set in the 1950s, but which rewrites *Un Barrage*'s *colon* girl's trip to the *grande époque* colonial city. Tran presents Mui's story in two slices of life—one 1951; the other 1961. In 1951 we meet ten-year-old Mui as she arrives at the end of a two-hour walk from her rural peasant home to become a servant for a wealthy bourgeois merchant family in Saigon. If in Duras's colonial city, the *colon* girl meets the French colonial elite's "othering" gaze, in Tran's 1951 Saigon, Mui is met by the welcoming gaze of this family's Vietnamese bourgeois mother. And if, in response to the "othering" gaze, Duras's *colon* girl discovers both the existence of social and gender inequalities and the transgressive practices that might bring them down (*errance,* desire, female sexuality), in response to this integrating gaze, Mui learns how to prepare Vietnamese food (culture) and, more generally, to be a Vietnamese woman. By 1961 Mui is working for this family's elder son, who breaks with a westernized Asian fiancée for this emblematic traditional Vietnamese woman, who finishes the film pregnant by him.

As Bourdieu's work shows, competition in the literary field is partly shaped by pressures in the ambient social field. Consistently, *The Scent of Green Papaya* was partly shaped by the social pressures of 1990s France, which, in Alice Jardine's view, were directly linked to the conservative 1950s social pressures that shaped Duras's critical reception (chapter 1). In the United States, Jardine perceives "flashes" of the First American Fifties (1945-1955) "resurfacing—politically, culturally, and psychologically—in the 1990s" ("Flashes," 109). Concurring with Ellen Messer-Davidow, she believes these flashes reflect direct ideological and institutional connections

between the 1950s Old Right and the 1990s New Right. As we have seen,
Jardine describes the First American Fifties as a period of "almost frantic
domestic containment of women, homosexuals, and racial and ethnic
minorities" (108) and the apparently spontaneous separation of intellectual
work from left-wing politics. This McCarthy period established the terms
of the battle that was still being waged four decades later in the 1990-1992
Political Correctness Campaign. More organized and technologically
sophisticated than its 1950s forebear, the PC Campaign aimed "to test
historical, print-based and newer electronic forms of intellectual surveil-
lance for broader introduction into the 1990s marketplace" (111). By at
least mid-1991, the PC Campaign was helping to shape the French social
field in which *The Scent of Green Papaya* was being composed. There, its
antileftist politics were often explicitly acknowledged by stressing the
linguistic connection between "Le P(olitically) C(orrect)" and "Le P(arti)
C(ommuniste)" (122), thus alluding to the broader spectrum of leftist
positions the campaign sought to discredit and rout out. As if to reveal this
1950-1990 connection, the pressures of the 1990s French social field
shaped the displacement of Tran Anh Hung's memories of 1962-1975
Vietnam back one decade (to before his birth) to compose *The Scent of
Green Papaya'* s representation of 1951-1961 Vietnam. Thus, his film
assumes its place among the 1950s "flashes" in early 1990s France.

Bearing down on Duras's writing through the literary-critical comprador
class, conservative 1950s pressures worked to contain her political and
cultural threats and resolidify, in its firm prewar configuration, the psychic
structures of a French colonial subject disrupted by the European war
traumas and faced with the Indochina conflict and the threat of broader
colonial wars. Marking their debt to the discourse of French colonial
propaganda, her critics countered her threats with its strategies—silence,
saturation, and displacement. They silenced her cultural and historical
narratives by displacing attention onto the icon *Duras*. They saturated
French literary critical discourse on her subject with *Duras,* which functioned *both* as a site of transmogrification in which Duras's political and
cultural differences were assimilated into modernizing French culture and
made productive *and* as a cultural nodal point where the French community's self-imaging "morphed" into cultural, symbolic, and financial capital.
One of three models of the French woman writer proposed by *Time* in
1953, *Duras* staked its market niche in that issue's pages: it would provide
images of La Belle Colonie and its model native population. By 1958 *Duras*
entered the international culture market with René Clément's film, *Un
Barrage contre le Pacifique* and began to deliver those scenes in moving
images. That same year, which was midway between the 1954 Dien Bien
Phu battle that ended colonial Indochina and the 1962 Evian Accords that

ended the French Empire—*Duras* offered, to a French colonial subject soon to be in lack of the real material, social, and geographical grounds in relation to which it might continue to sustain itself, *her* "Spectacular" terrain.

But as we also recall, maintaining the French colonial subject had never been the endgame: that had always been to shape that subject's desire to changing social, economic, and political needs. In the early decades of Empire, the goal was to maintain popular electoral support of colonial policy; by the late 1930s, it was also to elicit support of Mandel's native troop project. The 1950s brought a transition: the end of Empire, hence of the need of popular support, and the beginning of France's modern consumer capitalist era, hence the need for increased consumption. Past the end of the colonial rule era, French culture would continue to take neocolonial profits in at least two ways. It would retain the erotic-exotic charge associated with the former Empire within the French cultural niche on the international market, both as such (that is, as French colonial scenes), but especially in a semirepressed form reminiscent of that used in the construction of *Duras,* which would imbue French scenes and vedettes with the exotic and erotic allure once reserved for the former colonial object. In both cases, postcolonial era desires would be cathected onto consumer objects marked "colonial." Indeed, it was to this desire to consume things colonial that Duras made her own 1980s appeal—implicitly in composing *L'Amant;* self-avowedly in selling its film rights—in order to turn the profit that would provide her son a decent inheritance.

For all of these efforts, by the time *The Scent of Green Papaya* was being composed, the French colonial subject was in trouble. Under the combined weight of the 1980s World War II disclosures and rising immigrant demands, it could no longer prevent itself from returning, over and again, to the grounds of Dien Bien Phu, where its psychically crucial colony, Indochina, had been lost. By 1992 multiple television documentaries and films on its subject had appeared—Pierre Schoendoerffer's *Dien Bien Phu,* Patrick Jeudy's *Récits d'Indochine: Chronique des journées de la bataille de Dien Bien Phu,* and Yves Rémy and Ada Rémy's *La Mémoire et l'oubli.* Impelled toward an encounter with the bloodied colonial grounds from which *phantasmatic Indochina* had been designed to protect it 120 years earlier, that subject could but turn itself backward, go retrograde, in an attempt to safeguard its psychic structures by engaging its desire nostalgically with *grande époque* Indochina in, for instance, *The Lover* and *Indochine.*

If it was shaped in part by the pressures of the 1990-1992 French social field, *The Scent of Green Papaya* was shaped by multiple eras and transformations. The 1950s that flashed into the early nineties and accounted for some of their pressures housed two parallel transformations—from the colonial to the postcolonial rule era; from the premodern to the modern consumer capitalist era. Added to this were the 1990-1992 "endings of at least this phase of the postmodern era" (Jardine, "Flash," 109) and the preintimations of the new era toward which they will lead, which Jardine envisages as "something more 'transmodern'" (109). As one might expect, *The Scent of Green Papaya* also (partly) responds to the early 1990s threat to the French colonial subject in multiple registers. It responds to the "resurfacing 1950s" threat, Dien Bien Phu, with the means of the 1950s— the counterimage. Moreover, as a counterimage, it was produced in the same way 1950s Duras criticism created *Duras:* by disengaging, in an apparently spontaneous fashion, from the social history, especially left-wing oppositional, of that era. As he began *The Scent of Green Papaya,* Tran recalled, he believed that he could not make his film without talking "about the war." In the course of its development, he came to believe that "all that had nothing to do with the poem I wished to create"; or, alternately, that "I was just not capable of having such external historical details enter into the poetic whole of my effort" ("Portraying").

In fact, the history Tran does not represent is not that of the 1960s Vietnam War, but rather, consistent with his memories' displacement to the 1950s, the communist and feminist opposition of that decade. From 1954, the Diem government's failure to achieve any semblance of democracy combined with its violent attempt to rout out Communists in the countryside turned the Saigon region rural peasantry increasingly toward Communism. By 1960, the Communists were embarked on a "full-fledged insurrection supported by the peasants in the Mekong Delta and coastal provinces northeast of Saigon and of the ethnic minority tribes in the highlands of central Vietnam" (Buttinger, *VPH,* 460). In the same period, Madame Nhu, wife of one of Vietnam's most powerful political figures, was making what one historian calls "a great show of militant feminism" (447). In the 1950s, she created a Women's Solidarity Movement and a young women's paramilitary corps, and was instrumental to the passage of the 1958 Family Code and the 1962 Law for the Protection of Morality. If she may not have been widely liked or managed to improve women's position (447), Mme Nhu did put feminism before the public eye and disturb the tranquillity of Vietnamese men: "With a stroke of the pen, Mme. Nhu outlawed divorce, dancing, beauty contests, gambling, fortune-telling, cockfighting, prostitution, and a hundred other things dear to the hearts of Vietnamese men" (Browne, 196).

Having coalesced thanks to the elision (jettisoning) of this historical and social opposition, *The Scent of Green Papaya*'s Vietnam shares many characteristics with the French colonial representation of Indochina. Focused on women, it presents a feminized Asia (recalling Sarraut's regular reference to Indochina as France's *fille d'Asie*), which it aligns, as colonial thought does, with nature (Tran in fact provided all of his actors with animal models to help them capture their characters). It represents Vietnam as a "harmonious whole" or "poem" and the Vietnamese "soul" ("Portraying"), as timeless, ahistorical, and permanent in the face of historical change. To wit, its final phrase: "However the cherry trees change, they keep the shape of the cherry tree." Its sustained linguistic silences, rhythmic slowness, and female focus recall Duras's films on women and women's spaces (most notably *Nathalie Granger)*; indeed, they almost make *The Scent of Green Papaya* read as a reprise, from the ashes, of *India Song* and its emblematic object of French colonial desire, Anne-Marie Stretter.

But, the product of changing times, *The Scent of Green Papaya* rewrites the French colonial image of Indochina as France's model colony in 1950s modern-era bourgeois consumer capitalist terms. It presents Vietnam as Kristin Ross contends capitalist modernization presents itself: "Capitalist modernization presents itself as timeless because it dissolves beginning and end, in the historical sense, into an ongoing, naturalized process . . . whose uninterrupted rhythm is provided by a regular and unchanging social world devoid of class conflict" (10). The *Scent of Green Papaya* elides the unevenness of those left behind by "ingesting" the story of Mui, not as the de facto adopted bourgeois daughter, but as the little daughter of Saigon region, probably Communist peasants forced to leave her family and serve the urban bourgeoisie. Its "Vietnamese humanity" is a modern bourgeois capitalist family; its modern Vietnamese woman is contained, apparently per choice, to domestic spaces. In the larger context of French colonial discourse on Indochina, *The Scent of Green Papaya*'s representation of women reads as both a perfect realization and a modern era rewrite of early twentieth-century French colonial educational plans for "the native woman." As we have seen, French administrators held native woman's alleged penchant for wandering, *errance,* responsible for her failure to realize her reproductive potential. Rather than remain in rural areas and reproduce, they believed, she wandered from rural areas to colonial cities, where she squandered her reproductive sexuality in prostitution and lacemakings. Consistent with the 1950s modern era's diminished need of peasants and increased need of urban labor, *The Scent of Green Papaya*'s heroine walks from the countryside to the city, stepping out, as she does, of ongoing Vietnamese peasant history and into the privatized domestic space of modern bourgeois capitalism. Arriving at age ten, she learns precisely those skills colonial educators counseled for native females in Indochina from that same age—cooking, dishwashing, clothes washing, and, more generally, domestic and maternal skills. And rather than arrive in the city only to waste her sexuality non-reproductively, Mui ends up reproducing (for) the bourgeoisie.

The Scent of Green Papaya is set in the period when, Ross believes, France's experience revealed modernization as a *"means* of social and especially racial differentiation" (11). In the 1950s, the French separated, both within and without France, from the (former) colonized. This was the era of the "great cordoning off of the immigrants," who were removed to the banlieues in a "massive reworking of the social boundaries of Paris and the other large French cities" (11). This separation of the French from the former colonized peoples coincided with the process Ross terms, with Edgar Morin and others, "privatization," and describes in terms of the withdrawal of the French to within the nation, the home, and the automobile, the emergence of a broad privatized, depoliticized national middle class, and the replacement of class-based identities by a "national subjectivity" (11-2). Transplanting this dynamic from 1950s France to 1950s Vietnam, *The Scent of Green Papaya* narrates the ingestion of the Vietnamese peasantry and the concomitant emergence of a Vietnamese national subject. Because it emerged in 1993, at the end of at least a certain postmodern phase, *The Scent of Green Papaya* verily begs us to recall Ross's warning: "once modernization has run its course, then one is, quite simply, either French or not, modern or not; exclusion becomes racial or national in nature" (Jardine, "Flash," 12). But 1993 France was also on the threshold of what Jardine terms a "transmodern era" and suspected would be character-ized by "a more global, polycentric, particularized, informational network of cultures in which geopolitical determinants give way progressively to more techno-symbolic configurations" ("Flash," 109). By then, the form of the French (colonial) subject had already changed: it was no longer either the subject of the image, which images and counter-images worked to disrupt or strengthen, or the subject "of consensus," which one endeavored to change by persuasion, as Duras had in *L'Empire Français* and *Un Barrage*. A subject of the flash, of access, and of the remote, it protects itself "whenever and wherever" it feels threatened by "hit[ting] the remote control fast" (109). Just as this subject emerged, so too did *The Scent of Green Papaya*. What then can this film tell us about the new transnational age? About the (desired) function of representations of the former Indo-china in that age?

A film about the preparation and eating of traditional Vietnamese food, *The Scent of Green Papaya* suggests that in the new era, the (French) colonial subject will endeavor to ward off threats to its integrity by eating them. This film takes its place within a larger series of turn-of-the-decade western representations of (cannibalistic) consumption. That series in-cludes, in addition to Lê's *Fuir*, films such as Gabriel Axel's 1987 *Babette's*

Feast, Bob Balaban's 1988 *Parents,* Peter Greenaway's 1989 *The Cook, the Thief, His Wife and Her Lover,* Jean-Pierre Jeunet's 1991 *Delicatessen,* and Henry Jaglom's 1992 *Eating.* These films rework for a new era the problematics Duras addressed as early as 1958 in *Moderato Cantabile,* whose salmon dinner scene both revealed the ingestive logics of the post-Revolutionary bourgeoisie, especially but not only in its 1950s modern consumer capitalist form, and appropriated that logic in the service its own critique and rejection by vomiting of that same bourgeoisie and its culture. In contrast to *Moderato Cantabile,* the late 1980s-early 1990s representations of consumption reflect an apparently growing desire on the part of the West to consume the former colonial other by consuming its cuisine; by eating, in this case, "Vietnamese." That is, they appear to be shaped by the same desire shaping the burgeoning of ethnic restaurants in western cities, which have begun to give rise to luxurious chain restaurants whose Vietnamese cooks, receptionists, and wait staffs guarantee cultural authenticity. If *The Scent of Green Papaya'* s footage on Mui's apprenticeship in traditional Vietnamese food preparation reads to the diasporic audience as scenes from a childhood kitchen and homeland, to western eyes, it reads as the schooling of a new cook for the kitchens of the emerging transnational era. Dixit one western critic, in words worthy of fine wine: "Delicately flavored as much by the inherent appeal of its classic Cinderella-like story as by its pictorial beauty, 'The Scent of Green Papaya' is a lovely experience in the dreamily exotic" (Stack, C14).

As we saw in chapter 1, Geneviève Idt casts Sartre's corpus as unmarked pastiche: consuming works from other cultures, ingesting them into his thought and work, he enriched French intellectual production. Duras, increasingly, and Lê, especially, write against the Sartrean pastiche; explicitly marking, even parading, their cultural borrowings. From the postwar, Duras molded her French language writing around syntactical traces of her early Vietnamese fluency and punctuated them with the gaps and silences that Kristeva's work permits us to perceive as rhythmic traces of an Indochina-formed semiotic. Increasingly in France's diversifying social and cultural fabrics, she also introduced foreign names and phrases in, for instance, *La Pluie d'été.* Lê's writing parades its other cultural stuff more boldly still. "Vinh L." is riddled with loosely attributed citations—from an Italian writer we are encouraged to identify as Pasolini, an unnamed Czech writer, a Danish prince, an American author, a Viennese painter, an Austrian writer, a "Czech transnihilist" (192-223). In this context, *The Scent of Green Papaya* appears as one of these other cultural borrowings, detached and circulating independently in the French and international cultural fields, marked as (racially and nationally) "other," cathecting spectator desire onto a vast array of exotic images, ethnic food, and other exotic consumer objects of desire. Its circulation recalls Ellen Messer-Davidow's view that the immediate goal of the 1990-1992 PC Campaign was to transform "the higher-education system into a free-market economy" (Jardine, "Flash," 113). Indeed, *The Scent of Green Papaya* appears to take its place in an emerging international free-market economy in exotic images suited to provide a threatened French colonial subject replete with cash and armed with a remote with the plethora of images its survival (and expansion) requires.

From the 1930s to the 1950s, as we have seen, French colonial propaganda blocked threats to the French colonial subject using the three-pronged approach we know well: silence, saturate, and displace (chapter 1). In the 1930s, procolonial efforts silenced the German threat by displacing popular attention onto fabricated sex scandals and saturating French culture with idyllic images of the colonies. In the late 1940s and 1950s, they silenced the Indochina war and Ho Chi Minh's nationalist position by displacing French cultural attention onto an alleged U.S. threat and saturating the mass circulating press with lofty reiterations of the *mission civilisatrice*. In the early 1990s French culture was saturated with images of Indochina/Vietnam, which displaced consumer attention onto an infinite array of other consumer objects. The question, then, must be: What threat to the French colonial subject does this saturation and displacement attempt to silence? Clearly it can no longer be construed as Dien Bien Phu alone, for that was the threat posed to the older colonial subjective form. What threat to the French colonial subject in its emerging "transmodern" configuration does this 1990s saturation and displacement work to silence? At this juncture, the answer would appear clear: immigrant-related unrest in the French social field—legal or illegal, lower class, homeless, in the streets and in your face, disruptive, violent, demanding; immigrants begging on streets and demonstrating in churches, the attendant blood and forced repatriations.

Toward Starvation

But *The Scent of Green Papaya* was only the first full-length film by Tran Anh Hung and producer Christophe Rossignon. In the course of its production, their inexperience and lack of capital (financial and symbolic) twice prevented them from engaging directly with Vietnam: Tran's attempt to work through wartime memories was precluded by temporal displacement; the entire film crew was physically displaced from Vietnam. One interviewer calls Rossignon's "producing debut . . . a major wakeup call. With Tran Anh Hung and his crew already installed and working in Vietnam on critically acclaimed 'The Scent of Green Papaya,' Rossignon stopped the shoot and ordered everyone back to Paris . . . 'That was my first lesson as a producer,' Rossignon recalls. 'You have to be prepared to assume your responsibilities even when the risks are frightening'" (Williams). Forced into the posture of the weaker player, Rossignon found himself, like *Moderato Cantabile*'s heroine before him, with one sole response: as Williams puts it, he lost "his lunch in the gents on the flight back to France." Made with the symbolic capital accruing to the well-prized *The Scent of Green Papaya*, Rossignon and Tran's second joint project, *Cyclo*, appeared in 1995 alongside the also Rossignon-produced *La Haine* by Mathieu Kassovitz. If *The Scent of Green Papaya* suggests the use to which the French colonial subject would put the creative products of artists from its former colonies, *Cyclo*, like *La Haine*, shows some of the ways in which those artists might attempt to resist that containment and subvert the French colonial subject of the transmodern (Jardine) and transnational era.

Approached as a narrative, *Cyclo* appears to validate the lessons laid down in early nineteenth-century French colonial education textbooks for native students in Indochina. It reads as a cautionary demonstration of the threats of native woman's wandering, of her ignorance concerning proper childbirth techniques, of urban corruption, prostitution, and evil modern transports. It figures France's abiding presence in culturally valuable forms—a *chanteuse*, for instance, and the pure bottled waters of Evian (the Evian Accords). It tells of an orphaned boy who makes his living driving the cyclo his father left him, his beautiful sister, and their struggle to survive in Ho Chi Minh City slums with a younger sister and grandfather. It takes them from innocence to a world of crime and corruption (drugs, prostitution, murder) linked to U.S. and international capitalism by the constant transfer and counting of dollar bills. In the end, it returns them to the protective confines and lifestyle figured by the French-designed cyclo and nature-lined urban streets, suggesting their voluntary reintegration into the traditional Vietnamese life represented in the colonial textbooks, duly updated for the urban age.

But there are, as Tran Anh Hung said to Jean-Marie Dinh, "several levels of reading in a film. What it recounts, what it talks about, what it says." Of the three, he continued, "narration interests me the least"; "I am attached to style." Unlike Duras, who believes that intellectual work and creative processes and products have their part in the overall work of the revolution, Tran told Dinh that he has "no faith in the capacity of a work to change the course of things." Clearly, it would be overstating or even misstating Tran's position to attribute to him or his filmic project explicit or radical political aims; yet *Cyclo* does perform, wittingly or not, some work that Duras considered revolutionary. Moreover, the work it accomplishes is directly linked to Tran's conception of the cinema, which intersects with her own understanding of it in crucial areas. As seen in chapter 2, Duras hated the capitalist cinema she called "obese," typed as Hollywoodian, and rejected as reinforcing the sheeplike structures of the existing—"incarcerated" (to recall Wright's term) or "imprisoned" (her own)—subject. In contrast, she believed in writing, theater, and documentary film as means of putting the subject at risk and on the route to revolutionary social change. Tran defines his creative project very similarly, both in contrast to American cinema and in terms of putting the actually existing subject at risk. As he says to Dinh, "I have another idea of the cinema. It tells me that somewhere, a film should permit spectators to be reborn." In the same way that Duras aims, in Elio Vittorini's phrase, to *donner à voir;* to give truths of her epoch "to be seen," Tran affirmed to Dinh that he seeks neither to preach nor to denounce, but rather "to show."

In making *Cyclo,* Tran told Henri Behar, he sought "to show the Vietnam I see. With the contamination which comes from the conscience of war." To that end, *Cyclo* takes on Duras's "Indochina," as it had been moved in the colonial nostalgia direction by Annaud's *The Lover.* Tran "replaced" Annaud's actors, Tony Leung and the English Jane March with a Chinese actor whose name is a near homonym, Tony Leung (II), and a Vietnamese actress, Nguyen Nhu Cuyhn. Displacing his hero from the slightly older and better known Annaud actor (Tony Leung Kai Fai) to the younger Tony Leung Chiu Wai, who is called Tony Leung (II), to mark the difference, he establishes his film's displacement of *The Lover* as generational. Called "the poet," Tran's hero is, like his Chinese lover forebears, a sensitive and chain-smoking guy. But where Tony Leung played a dutiful Chinese son, Tony Leung (II)'s poet rebels against his father and sells his soul to a crime ring headed by the Boss Lady in Cho-Lon. In contrast to Annaud's wealthy, chic, and impeccably dressed Chinese lover cruising *grande époque* Saigon in a Morris Léon Bollée, Tran's poet walks (and wanders) the back streets of Ho Chi Minh City disheveled in a crumpled suit. Like his Chinese lover forebear, he has an affair in Cho-Lon; not with a nubile young *colon* maid in a luxury bachelor flat paid for by his father, however, but at her place with a Boss Lady amply experienced and well past the prime.

Like Duras's wandering Beggarwoman, the Boss Lady, too, got pregnant as an adolescent, left home, had a child. Now, she sits in her Cho-Lon living room singing lullabies that resonate with the (Laotian) chants sung by the Beggarwoman in Duras's *India Song.* Shown in these moments, her pose aligns her with the figure Lynn Higgins finds undergirding Duras's fantasmatic on the pain of war: the *mater dolorosa.* Higgins: "All the personifications of waiting, mourning, and lamentation figure through their disfiguring tears what I take to be the underlying matrix-narrative of Duras's representations of the pain of war: the *mater dolorosa*" (178). As Higgins recalls, the *mater dolorosa* emerged during the European plague of the Middle Ages and expressed, as Marina Warner contends, that period's unimaginable mass suffering. It became dogma in 1950, after the European mid-twentieth-century collective horror.

But if Tran's displacement of this European figure to Vietnam registers the parallel displacement of the European horrors, *Cyclo* discourages spectators from making a hard link between the chaotic and violent situation in contemporary Saigon and the former French colonial rule. Aligning the signifier "French" with regularly appearing bottles of Evian served in chic restaurants, in fact, it aligns France with the peace accords. This association suggests that those Accords *cleansed* France's historical part in Saigon's actual situation, a connotation that is reinforced by the visual alignment of the Evian water bottles with the pure waters in which the cyclo driver's virgin sister incessantly rinses her long hair. This association further suggests that the French legacy in Southeast Asia is not to be found in Vietnam's present violence and chaos, but rather in its enduring marks of high culture and civilization (the cafés, the *chanteuse*, for instance). In sharp contrast, *Cyclo* does directly link contemporary Vietnam's violence, corruption, and crime to constantly circulating U. S. greenbacks, thus underscoring the roles of the American/Vietnam War and U.S.-lead western capitalist imperialism.

Although *Cyclo* aligns its Boss Lady with Duras's *mater dolorosa* in Indochina, the mother, and reinforces this link by having her mentally handicapped son resonate with the Duras's "little brother," *Cyclo'* s Boss Lady does not simply reiterate the mother in *Un Barrage*. Neither "sheltered from the struggle and fertile experiences of injustice" nor "virginally innocent of all familiarity with the powers of evil" (*UB*, 25), the Boss Lady has sexual experience, street smarts, strength, and commercial skill. If a comparison might be made with *Un Barrage'* s women, she is much more, to recall Suzanne's phrase, Madame Marthe's type—a whore. Living in Cho-Lon, the Chinese section of today's Ho Chi Minh City, she is also the worst nightmare of a French colonial educator such as Poirier (chapter 3)— a commercially savvy native woman aligned not only with freely determined sexuality and reproductive inadequacies, but with the Chinese, as well. Indeed one might, perhaps, go so far as to see in *Cyclo'* s Boss Lady the image of the feminist so stunningly absent from *The Scent of Green Papaya'* s 1950s scene—Madame Nhu.

Be that as it may, incorporating the consistently threatening figure of the Boss Lady into *Cyclo'* s representation of Vietnam forces into the light both the conditions of oppression that its absence from *The Scent of Green Papaya* helped repress and the consequences, where that first film was concerned, of that absence. Tran casts the actress who played Mui in *The Scent of Green Papaya,* (his wife) Tran Nu Yen Khe, as the cyclo driver's sister. Having established her in his first film as the graceful and delicate figure of traditional Vietnam, he now shows her forced into the prequelles of prostitution and then submitted to the acts of violence implied in patriarchal colonial desire for the exotic and erotic colonial object. Handcuffed, beaten, violently raped, she is Vietnam pillaged by an international capital (culture-consuming) machine; she is also Tran Anh Hung's first feature-length representation of Vietnam, *The Scent of Green Papaya,* appropriated by that same "machine" in the service of its own aims.

As we know, Duras placed her revolutionary hopes in women, children, the mad, and (in her now-dated term) the Third World. Least inserted into the structures and categories of post-Revolutionary western bourgeois thought, she believed, they have the best chance of wriggling their thought outside of it; least invested in the bourgeois social order, they are most likely to challenge and change it. With her postwar intellectual cohort and the 1970s neo-lacanians, Duras also placed her revolutionary hopes in Mascolo's second and nonrational mode of consciousness, which registers, for instance, corporeality, touch, silence, rhythm, music, the mother. As if following Duras and Wright, *Cyclo* presents the route from present-day Saigon to a less enslaved future in terms of trauma, epiphany, and *imago* alternatives. Linking the particular experience of an individual character to the general collective experience, it suggests that if a given character succeeds in defining him/herself in more liberated terms, so will Saigon and, through it Vietnam, achieve greater freedom. Like Duras, *Cyclo* identifies the second nonrational mode of knowledge—embodied in this film's poet, women, and children—as the crucial means to articulate the transition between the present and the improved future.

Cyclo first presents its poet as a potential route to the future. In addition to the Boss Lady, the poet has a second lover: the cyclo driver's beautiful sister, whose violent rape presents him with the trauma that permits him to "see" what he had not previously—the fact of her spilt blood, as it were; her oppression. Unable to see, any more that *Un Barrage'* s mother or Joseph could before him, the larger structures and relations of oppression responsible for it, he reacts to his revelation just as, standing on the Kam Plain after his mother's death and before his departure, Joseph had threatened to: in a bloody rooftop scene, he stabs the patriarchal capitalist who raped the cyclo driver's sister, and, then, in an act of bricolage, street style, stuffs the $600 that man had offered him to pay for his "mistake" into his mouth, suffocating him. Beyond its diegetic significance, his act recalls not only the vulgar slogan that has one sticking dollars where one would, but the political adage widely if perhaps inaccurately attributed to Lenin that the capitalist West will end up hanging itself, if given enough cord. But despite its politically provocative symbolics, the poet's act, like the poet himself, remains defined by and thus trapped within existing relations of power.

Ignorant victim—whore, Duras would say—of the existing social order, the poet kills himself by self-immolation. His death combines with a second traumatic event—the accidental death of the Boss Lady's son (who is hit by a speeding truck like the cyclo driver's father before him) to dislodge a second figure from her imprisoned subject position: the Boss Lady. Precipitated into a semiconscious (Wright) or depersonalized (Duras) state, the Boss Lady stands transfixed, staring at her lover's flaming apartment. In this state, she has an epiphanic revelation whose contours are shaped by Duras's emblematic signifier for Indochina—*la maison bleue* (the blue house). As previously noted, Linda Lê would resignify Duras's blue house (the Indochina house of the Chinese lover's father) as the Vietnamese home of the Vietnamese father of the diasporic heroines in her 1997 *Les Trois Parques*. Two years before her, in this 1995 film, Tran became the first artist of the Vietnamese diaspora I know of to appropriate Duras's blue house in the service of his creative project: to show the Vietnam he saw still reeling from the violence of the U.S. Vietnam war, under the pressures of international forces, torn by corruption, drugs, the cult of the dollar, chaotic, confused, contradictory. Tran bodies forth the blue house, Vietnam, as *Cyclo'* s now drunken, drugged, half-crazed cyclo driver who, having been tempted by the street gang, waits, alone, for the fatal punishment of its sadistic "snuffer," Mr. Lullaby. As he waits, the cyclo driver smears himself head to foot in blue paint, transforming himself into the blue house of Vietnam. Against *The Scent of Green Papaya'* s delicious image of Vietnam, this scene of the cyclo-diver-cum-blue-house is nauseating: comprised of lengthy close-ups of the hero coated in blue, it lingers on his face covered in slime, lips squirming with maggots, a live goldfish wriggling in his mouth. This image both campaigns strongly against its own consumption and reveals Vietnam, so tempted by the forces of international capital, as abjected in that new world order.

In the meanwhile, as the Boss Lady stands staring at the flames, images/ *imagoes* pass before her eyes and ours of those killed by capitalist imperialist violence—the cyclo driver's father, her own son, her poet lover. Seeing in these images the epiphanic sight of Vietnam marginalized and oppressed by the order she has heretofore served, the Boss Lady redefines herself in relation to those passing *imagoes,* as an apparently salvational maternal figure. Extending her love for her dead son to the cyclo driver, she saves his life and, with it, that of the "blue house," Vietnam. Quite clearly, more than one troubling question remains, but the most pressing for our present concerns is: For precisely which future does she save them? Or, stated otherwise, does her epiphany transmute the Boss Lady into a truly "self-cognizant whore," to use Duras's term, or does it transform her into a patriarchal and nationalistist figure of a reactionarily defined Vietnamese nation? Does *Cyclo* devolve, through her, into a conservative, gendered, and nationalistic appeal? Or does it open out, through her, onto an unforeseeable but more politically promising future? Does it return to an essential identity? Or does it look toward a transition from its actual chaos and de facto enslavement, in the wrightean sense, to a more liberated, self-defined identity and self-determined future?

Rather than formulate a coherent vision of the future, which neither Duras nor Wright do either, *Cyclo* responds "as if" to this query with a series of fast flashes, rapid punches, and quick connections that proffer only a series of possible *imago*-alternatives of that future and, with it, of the political significance of the Boss Lady. Working as Duras thought true art must, these images put the spectating subject at risk by barraging it with brief and reiterating syntagms, networking, linkages, displacements, and associations. Together they create a sense of chaos, confusion, and contradiction that effectively "gives" certain political and social truths of 1990s Ho Chi Minh City "to be seen." Often, and arguably most often, this finale sequence gestures in the direction of reactionary political solutions. But amidst its confusion, it also manages to insinuate into French cultural space at least one left-wing revolutionary image that mid-twentieth century Vietnamese nationalists had struggled in vain to "give" to the French "to see."

First in *Cyclo'* s finale comes an *imago* suggesting that Vietnam's future depends on women's return to traditional patriarchal feminine roles: the cyclo driver's beautiful sister walks though a park gazing at little children and then joins a mother and her child for lunch, as if bodying forth the new maternal value. Next, to a drum roll, comes what looks like a lengthy class-analysis: the camera pans the urban slums where the heroes live, moves past a statue erected by the French, settles for a while on an international tourist complex reminiscent not only of Norindr's stress on the emerging French "Indochina" tourist industry, but of Duras's Eden districts, where the French colonial elite basked in their grandeur and played tennis, as Tran's tourists are. But what are we invited to suppose this images *means?* That Vietnam's less enslaved future depends on closing off Vietnam's borders, engaging in protectionism, overthrowing the class system, or expelling westerners? Or that its less enslaved future depends on normalizing trade relations with the West?

Leaving these queries unanswered, or, perhaps, responding to them, *Cyclo* next presents an *imago* that casts the route to Vietnam's future as a return to the countryside, or at least nature, and to a traditional pre-western contact Vietnamese lifestyle. In this image, the cyclo driver's family rides together in his cyclo, as it has not since the opening frame, down a tree-lined Ho Chi Minh City street. As they move together toward a renewed family life, the hero's voice utters these phrases in voice-over: "Yesterday the cat came back. We thought he was dead. He's even more handsome than before. So handsome that nobody recognized him. I remember my father right before he died. It was a Sunday, the only day he took a nap at home. The cat was sleeping in the sun, a gash across his face. My father slept." Again, how are we to construe this cat? Is it an image of nature; the alleged natural essence of Vietnam, for instance? Or is it designed to call up images of wild animals, jungles, and guerrilla warfare? Here, as throughout this unrelentingly ambiguous finale sequence, the response is undoubtedly that it points us at one and the same time in the direction of both meanings.

Most importantly to our present concerns, the cyclo-driver's words refer us back to the March 1953 *Time* magazine, in which Duras's photo illustrates a review of the English translation of *Un Barrage* (chapter 1). That review itself was sandwiched between a lengthy retrospective on the just dead Stalin and an update on the McCarthy trials. In the photo, Duras gazes toward far off places, and the furry cat in her arms signals her connection to Indochina's jungles and the exotic scenes her writing would deliver. In the context of the Cold War and the McCarthy trials, Duras's cat marked her former French Communist Party affiliation, her abiding marxist politics, and the threat that, in the increasingly conservative 1950s, her work might be read as socialist realism and rejected. But if in 1953 Duras's cat could still mark, despite her former PCF ties, Indochina's exotic and erotic jungles, in 1954 the French would lose that colony to the Communists and from 1961, its jungles would increasingly be aligned with the guerrilla tactics deployed by Ho Chi Minh's Vietminh and the napalm the U.S. military used in an attempt to burn them out.[5]

No sooner does the cyclo driver note the cat's return, than this *imago* alternative springs forth: a modern classroom in Vietnam in which Viet-namese children in western-style shirts and red cravats sing and play musical instruments. This classroom *imago* calls to mind the idealized native-girls'-school classroom described by the early twentieth-century Colonial Ministry's attaché Poirier (see chapter 3). As it does, it encourages us to read the closing shots of the cyclo driver's family riding in the cyclo along tree-lined streets as a sign of their effective voluntary reintegration into the vision of traditional Vietnamese life presented in French colonial education textbooks. This reading would have been recognizable as such to some in mid-1990s France even without prior knowledge of early twentieth-century French colonial educational discourse, for it had appeared in at least one of that decade's military propaganda films, Stéphane Deplus's 1984 *Indochine*.[6] At the same time, however, *Cyclo*'s classroom scene also calls to mind the native children's voices rising up at the end of Duras's *Un Barrage*, an even more likely connection to have been made by mid-1990s spectators in France, where the novel had been re-issued in paperback and was being widely read for the first time since 1950. Like the native children's voices that rise up at the end of *Un Barrage*, *Cyclo*'s children appear to sing in a tomorrow they will help realize. Finally, *Cyclo*'s classroom scene resembles a third and markedly more threatening revolutionary image: the photographic image of the revolutionary vision of Vietnam that brought French colonial Indochina down. Wielding strong enough French cultural imaginary resonance to have been chosen, as if inadvertently, by *Le Petit Robert II* to illustrate its entry for Vietnam, that image is titled, by the dictionary itself, "Viêt-nam: Hô Chi Minh in the company of Vietnamese children" (see Figure 10).

Four decades after Ho Chi Minh came to France to negotiate, was displaced to Biarritz and then to Fontainebleau, tried but failed to get his views to mid-century French readers, a film written and directed by an artist of the South Vietnamese immigration "flashes" Ho's 1950s revolutionary visage into the beginnings of the new transmodern (Jardine), transnational era. In the process, it retroactively resignifies, in accordance with the psychic process Freud terms "nachträglickeit" (chapter 1), the durassian cat as having been, all along, the Cold War visage of the anticolonial nationalist and Communist threat to French colonial rule. Finally, as Ho's image flashes into French spectators' minds and *Cyclo*'s final credits roll, the Boss Lady's voice rises up in song. Two decades earlier, the Beggarwoman's voice had opened *India Song*, a film performing the end of the French colonial era. Now, the Boss Lady's voice rises up to end this film of new beginnings. Duras would have qualified the maternal words she sings as being of the political nature of what Dionys Mascolo called the radical refusal. She may not know what she *wants*, but she clearly knows what she does not want, and that she refuses absolutely: "If I, the Heron, die by boiling, May it be in clear water, To ease my children's sufferings. Bom has a fan made of palm leaves The rich man says, I'll trade you Three cows and nine buffalo I don't want your buffalo I'll give you a pond of fish I don't want your fish I'll give you a raft of precious wood I don't want your wood, I'll give you a bird. . . . " Trailing into ellipses, the

Figure 10. Ho Chi Minh surrounded by Vietnamese children, *Le Petit Robert*, 1988. Courtesy Keystone Pressedienst.

Boss Lady's song joins the native children's voices that closed *Un Barrage* in 1950 and those that close *Cyclo* at the end of the millennium. If at the mid-century, Ho Chi Minh's voice was silenced to ensure a western capitalist victory and *Un Barrage*'s native children's voices, to strengthen French national culture, *Cyclo*'s fin-de-millennium, transnational era native children, the Boss Lady's words proclaim, will refuse to be ingested/consumed. Rather than regurgitate the bourgeoisie as Duras's heroines did, they will attempt to deprive the colonial subject of its object, withdraw its nourishment, starve it to death. Ironically, then, this Vietnamese diasporic response to the repressed anticolonial "calls" in Duras articulates a third-order response to Sartre that lends credence, where the French colonial subject is concerned, to his suspicion that scarcity would be the most pressing concern of the next century.

But in addition to the flourishing ethnic restaurants, that subject's intent to continue consuming is marked in our contemporary era by visual signs

Figure 11. Linda Lê in *Vogue Paris*, March 1999. Kate Barry / Courtesy *Vogue Paris*.

reminiscent of those found in the 1950s reception of, for instance, Duras, and at the beginning of this study in the pages of *Time* magazine. Where those mass circulating images of its desire figured French female writers promising exotic scenes, those circulating today feature, for instance, the exotic and erotic image of writer Linda Lê, resembling, especially in the shots where her hair is thrown sleeking over one shoulder, the female lead in Tran Anh Hung's *The Scent of Green Papaya* and *Cyclo* who cannot stop rinsing and re-rinsing her luxurious hair (see Figure 11).[7] One might almost suspect that, on the imaginary level, the French colonial subject is finishing the century in Paris by succeeding in the coup it plotted at the beginning of the century in Indochina where, one fine day, ministerial attaché M. Poirier's gaze had lingered longingly on the faces of young native girls in the new native schools, penetrated clothing of western design, caressed their little girl faces, necks, nails, moved down to their bare feet, risen to pass through their unoiled hair and over betel-free teeth, and wondered: "In what French village primary school could we/would we have found as much?" (267).

Notes

CHAPTER 1

1. See especially, Bourdieu, "Champ du pouvoir," "Champ intellectuel," *In Other Words, Outline of a Theory of Practice,* and *Rules of Art.*
2. As Sorum uses these terms, "anticolonialism" means opposition to the exploitation of the colonies for the sole benefit of the métropole and the insistence that the colonies must be administered in the interests of its native peoples. It thus corresponds to the positions of Camus and *Combat,* for instance. In contrast, "anti-imperialism" signifies opposition to colonialism per se, the belief that colonialism is illegitimate, and that the colonies must be granted independence (15-6). Duras appears to have been anti-imperialist by 1950, when *Un Barrage contre le Pacifique* appeared, or three years before *Les Temps modernes* took its stanch anti-imperialist position under the leadership of Francis Jeanson. As mine does not purport to be a detailed and close comparative analysis of the various positions against French colonial rule taken by individual intellectuals, journals, and critics, I have used the terms "anticolonial" and "anti-imperialist" interchangeably.
3. Consistently, Toril Moi finds "striking" parallels between *The Second Sex* and *Black Skin, White Masks:* just as Beauvoir combines Lacan with Sartre to construct a complex theory of female alienation under patriarchy, she notes, so does Fanon combine them to theorize black alienation in a white racist society (*Simone,* 204).
4. Sarraut's 1917 Code of Public Instruction restructured public education in Indochina in accordance with the aims of French colonial propaganda. Four years later, Sarraut had initiated the "propagandizing" of metropolitan public instruction by making colonial documentation available to public educators. Public education in France had ignored the Empire before the war; now, Education Minister Léon Berard asked public school teachers to "give [students] as rich an image as possible of their country, of the mother country and her distant daughters" (August, 188; Programmes et Instructions, 15), and Colonial Minister André Hess more explicitly explained: "What is requested of you is to develop [in students] a colonial mentality" (August, 120). This trend continued to increase until the eve of the war. In 1927 the *baccalauréat* exam included, for the first time, a question on colonial geography. By 20 September 1938 the growing prominence of Empire in all

aspects of French national life was reflected in Minister of Education Jean Zay's modification of the primary program in geography. At the urging of procolonialists, Zay insisted the geography syllabus be revised to devote all of the attention to Overseas France that it required (122). For his part, Colonial Minister Mandel established a directorate to disseminate colonial propaganda to students and announced a *Journée scolaire de la France d'outre-mer* entirely devoted to the Empire. As August notes, these efforts were part of the imperial studies movement that "integrated imperial history and geography into the general program of all state-aided schools" (123).

5. Adler has Duras working there from 9 June 1938 (130); Vircondelet from September (*MD*, 126).

6. In the 1920s some colonial governments directly subsidized some French newspapers. In 1928 the Colonial Ministry's Service intercolonial d'information et de documentation, in which Duras would work in the 1930s, assumed that task. Ministerial subsidies depended on a newspaper's editorial policy, propaganda efficacy, and circulation. The subsidized press included *Le Temps*, the most influential newspaper in government and intellectual circles and hence the best paid, *Paris-Soir*, *Le Petit Parisien*, the radical-left *L'Œuvre*, the radical *La République*, the liberal republican *Journal des débats*, the sports and financial *Paris-Midi*, the catholic *La Croix*, *La journée industrielle*, and *L'Europe nouvelle*. The socialist *Le Populaire* and the communist *L'Humanité* received no funds (August, 90-1). Although direct subsidies were no longer paid in the 1930s, the mass media was still for the buying: as Weber notes, those who paid had their issues widely and favorably covered (129-30).

7. Both France's need of the colonies and its perception of threats to them increased dramatically in the interwar years. Its need of the colonies increased due to its high World War I casualties, the Depression's disastrous effect on its foreign trade, the rising Nazi threat, and the government missteps that resulted in its draft contingents and armaments being, by the 1938 Munich Accords, at "their hollow worst" (Weber, 177). The threats France perceived to its Empire included the Bolshevik Revolution and the Third International, which "proclaimed the solidarity of workers from the colonizing nations with those of colonized countries" as well as the right of each and every nation to self-determination (Thành Khoî Lê, 103). French procolonialists were also anxious about Wilson's Fourteen Points on self-determination and sovereign rights, the League of Nations, Germany's colonialist movement, and, from 1934 on, Italy's Radio Bari (August, 56-61). As they saw it, Communist discourse threatened to reveal the conditions of their oppression to both colonized and French working classes, Wilson's Fourteen Points threatened to reveal the contradiction in post-Revolutionary French liberal thought, and Radio Bari and the German colonial movement raised fears that France's "civilizing mission" would lead instead to miscegenation and France's own "decivilization."

8. Weber cites Jules Sauerwein's *Trente ans à la une*, which attributes these words to an American attaché.

9. Weber associates this accusation with the competitive and political threats posed by the prodigious textual production of Jews in France in the 1930s. From 1933 to 1939, French and exiled Jews published a yearly average of 40 books and 200 articles, most of which were oriented to the socialist or communist left (104).

10. They peaked in May 1931 and remained intense for the next several years. In 1933-1935 (as in 1929-1931), they decreased by 50 percent, pointing to the continuing need for the sustained propaganda efforts of which Duras was part (August, 152).

11. This is Sorum's term for the militant group of people of higher income, education, and social status, including important business and administrative people, who tended to be the strongest supporters of Empire. He believes this procolonial elite may have imposed its imperialist policy on the French political leadership (7-11). In that case, Duras's 1930s propaganda work would have helped shape this elite and, through it, the colonial policies she opposed after the war.

12. The problem of insufficient and inaccurate information on this colony would not be remedied until at least mid-1952, when the first book-length studies of the Indochina war, those by Devillers and Mus, appeared (Sorum, 56).

13. "Qu'est-ce que la littérature" was published in installments in *Les Temps modernes* from February to July 1947; *Black Boy*, from January to June 1947. The March installment of Sartre's essay consecrates *Black Boy* as the emblematic instance of engaged literature, which that same installment theorizes.

14. Ross identifies the emergence from 1950 to the mid-1960s "of what might be termed a comprador class serving the interests of the state: financiers, developers, speculators, and high administrative functionaries. Modernization brought into being a whole new range of middlemen and go-betweens, new social types that dominated and profited from the transformations wrought by the state" (8).

15. For a compelling analysis of the political implications of space- and place-based identities, see Dirlik.

16. Boschetti locates Jean-Henri Roy in the journal's inner circle, but emphasizes that he handled only literary "criticism and reviews—a function which fills much space but has no influence whatsoever" (173; 268n2).

17. For images of Duras posing à la Sagan, look, for instance, at the photograph taken by Robert Doisneau and published in *Nouvelles littéraires* on 18 June 1959. For much more masculine Duras à la Sartre see, for instance, the series of uncredited images illustrating her 1963 interview with Pierre Hahn.

18. This description was provided by a single March Book-of-the-Month Club News page distributed to libraries, so that they could affix it to the novel's first page, as Northwestern University Library did. Readers were thus encouraged to read Ward's narrative through this description.

19. Magny's article stands out as particularly sensitive to Duras's historical, political, and scriptural concerns. It reads *Le Square* as marxist revolutionary and gender transgressive and stresses that, by situating her anticapitalist

critique on the level of language, she establishes language as a means and site of both repression and potential social change. In the 1990s Duras described *Le Square* in terms that are consistent with Magny's: she insisted that this play incorporates a "trace of dialectic" and "a kind of theory of needs from Marx" (Jardine and Menke, 78) and described it as "completely political. . . . It shows two dialectics confronting each other: the dialectic of courage—marxist . . . .and the dialectic of cowardice" (Preface, 5).

20. For the intersection of her thought with Debord's on this subject, see his *Debord contre le cinema*.

21. Contrary to Clément's claim that she was moved by his film, Adler insists that Duras "did not ever like René Clément's film." He had evacuated the violence, "recuperated" her life and her mother's, constructed a happy ending, "led spectators to understand that after the mother's death the son was going to accept white colon society by building a barrage himself" (336).

22. Karen Pinkus, private conversation with author, March 1999.

23. One barometer of the power of such conservative readings is our received understanding of Duras's reasons for leaving Gallimard to publish *Moderato Cantabile* with Editions de Minuit. Critics widely contend that her decision was based on her desire to align her work with experimental fiction, for which Minuit was known. This interpretation fails to take into account the fact that at the time Minuit was also considered the premier house of antigaullist and anticolonialist texts. As a result, critics neglect the most proximate explanation for her 1958 decision—Mascolo's move from Gallimard to Minuit one year earlier to publish his critique of French intellectual isolation from extrahexagonal revolutionary struggles, *Lettre polonaise sur la misère intellectuelle en France*.

CHAPTER 2

1. For Duras on this declaration, also known as the *Déclaration des 121,* see Duras, "Ecrit pour tous les temps."

2. Duras said she found a draft of a text named "Théodora" in the same blue armoires where she found the notebooks containing *La Douleur*. In a short text by that name forming part of *Yann Andrea Steiner* (26-33), Théodora is linked to survivors (she stayed in the hotel housing returnees), to Duras (the hotel seems to be the one she stayed in during Robert Antelme's post-camp convalescence, as textualized in *La Douleur),* to gender instability and homoeroticism (the narrator caresses her body, shifts gender pronouns), and/or to an intimate encounter with one's alienated self.

3. See also Marini's reading of the Beggarwoman as the "la femme de Calcutta" (180).

4. The third book was Montrelay's, which, while also written for a psychoanalytic audience, was not promoted as a counter-discourse to the patriarchal status quo or marketed to the feminist audience as forcefully as Marini's.

Symptomatically, Minuit published Montrelay in its *Critique* collection; Marini in the *Autrement dites* collection. Despite its merits, Montrelay's book did not mark a new or defining moment in the struggle to define Duras.

5. Rare before the seventeenth century, the use of the term "territoires" rose alongside the nation-state; both were well-established by the mid-eighteenth century. A *territoire* is defined as "an expanse of earth's surface on which a human group lives; especially, a national political collectivity" *(Petit Robert I*, 1950).

6. Irigaray was born in 1930 in Belgium, Kristeva on 24 June 1941 in Silven, Bulgaria (*Contemporary Authors*, s.v. Luce Irigaray and Julia Kristeva), and Cixous in Oran, Algeria on 5 June 1937 (*Contemporary Authors*, New Revisions, s.v. Hélène Cixous).

7. The original French used here, Marini's "ça va (n')à quête," plays on the name of the Beggarwoman's home town, Savannahket.

8. The relation between Duras's textual stand-in, "la petite blanche," and the Chinese lover situated the girl on the grounds of miscegenation. For a female, this was the most threatening and "abjected" of places in the colonial order. In the period of their alleged encounter, French colonial pressures were bearing down energetically on those specific grounds (see, for instance, Stoler). The relations between the girl and the lover also establish her as a collaborator with the French colonialists' historic competitors for Indochina, the Chinese. In *L'Amant*, Duras shows herself in bed not merely with a man of a different race, but with a Chinese man. Alain Robbe-Grillet and Adler both note the surprising appearance of Ramon Fernandez, a Gallimard reader, Nazi collaborator, and Duras's friend, and his wife Betty in *L'Amant*, a text that otherwise concerns Duras's Indochina years. In fact, first titled *L'Amant: histoire de Betty Fernandez*, early versions of the novel began in the salon of Marie-Claude Carpenter in winter 1942. As its original title implies, *L'Amant* establishes a relation of analogy between Duras and the Fernandezes (indeed, it suggests Betty Fernandez as a figure of Duras); they slept with the Germans; she, with the Chinese (lover). By underscoring the parallels in their respective collaborations, Duras puts into practice what *La Douleur* presents as the only possible response to World War II: rather than "othering" (Nazi crimes or Nazi collaborators, as the purges Sartre led did) all of us, as members of one sole human race, must work to assume our responsibility (for them).

9. See for instance Bergain's fake interview in which Duras is offered the position of Minister of Culture in a new socialist administration.

10. One might wonder whether Duras wrote *L'Amant* to procure the Goncourt, one of four French literary prizes said to "brin[g] glory and fortune to their beneficiaries" (Erval, 1295). The Goncourt had eluded her since 1950, when she lost to Paul Colin. French academician Emile Henriot registers the importance of this prize to a literary career at the mid-century when he opens his December 1950 newspaper column with the tale of one publisher's November meeting with a provincial bookshop owner, who placed his order thus: "If Mr.*** wins the Goncourt, send me a hundred copies of his novel. If

he does not, I don't want any." As for whether one could prejudge (and attempt to construct) a prize winner or not, Erval notes: "It would not be difficult to name several novels that appeared during the fall 'custom-made' and which 'normally' should have been among the prize-winning novels" (1298). For an interesting presentation of the 1950s prix Goncourt as a social rather than literary phenomenon, see Bourin.

11. On 1 April 1942, Vichy decreed the formation of a Commission de Contrôle du Papier, which it presented as an attempt to "ward off the threat that German censorship would be extended" by engaging in preemptive French self-regulation. The Commission read texts, decided their political appropriateness, literary merits, and the quantity of paper, if any, that would be allotted to their publication. Duras served as Commission secretary (Fouché, 15).

12. Oddly, the two copies of *Le Point* that I consulted had different paginations, both of which I include.

13. In response to criticisms such as the one Rey Chow levies against *Hiroshima mon amour*, it is worth noting, once again, the need to read literary and filmic artists and their works in relation to all of their multiple and complex historical, social, and cultural contexts. Duras's screenplay for this film is most fully and productively read not only in relation to white people or Western colonialism and its well-known objectification of their racial, cultural, and colonial "others" (see, for instance, Niranjana), but also in the context of Duras's hatred of cinema as one of the Western bourgeois capitalist and colonialist society of the spectacle's prime ideological means, on one hand, and her relative valorization of documentary film, on the other. Different than what one might have expected, her actual valuation should at least encourage us to question the view that she simply dismisses to the textual background and objectifies the Japanese people in *Hiroshima mon amour*'s documentary footage, as, for instance, Annaud does the Vietnamese populations in *The Lover*. *Hiroshima mon amour* should also be considered in relation to Duras's constant wrestling, from 1945 on, with what for her was a major political problem: the chasm bracketing off the intimate and quotidian life from the political sphere of the collective and world historical (chapters 4 and 5).

Chapter 3

1. On French women's social status in twentieth-century France, see Delphy.

2. Throughout this discussion, my use of Kristeva's psychoanalytic understanding of the terms "abject" and "abjection" takes account of Judith Butler's critique of Kristeva in *Gender Trouble* and combines Kristeva's understanding with Butler's social rewriting of the term. Together, their notions of "abjection" permit me to "map" between Duras's complex social background and its psychic consequences. Butler defines the abject, we recall, as "those 'unlivable' and 'uninhabitable' zones of social life which are nevertheless

densely populated by those who do not enjoy the status of the subject, but whose living under the sign of the 'unlivable' is required to circumscribe the domain of the subject" (*Bodies That Matter*, 3).

3. Historians disagree as to the intended function of the Franco-Vietnamese schools. Some believe Sarraut's altruistic discourse expressed a genuine desire to provide native students with a modern education; others, like Léon and Kelly, portray his promises as manipulative ideological rhetoric. Views in these debates tend to be decided on the grounds of intent. In response to Kelly's indictment of these schools, for instance, McConnell contends that the documents do not convince him the French had a "grand design for obscurantism" in the native schools, or that "their purpose . . . was the consciously obscurantist one of keeping the Vietnamese ignorant of the modern world"(14-5). My own primary concern is not with conscious colonialist intentions but rather with unconscious desires, the fantasies and projects they shaped, and the ways in which those projects shaped, in this case, individual and collective student psychés in the schools for native and French students in Indochina.

4. On Sarraut's opposition to spreading modern knowledge too quickly in the native community, see McConnell.

5. The first labor strikes against taylorism took place from 1910 to 1912 (Boyer, 45). In the U.S., a House Committee on Labor was charged, circa 1911, with investigating taylorism's "treatment of the 'human factor.'" Thompson provides a useful list of the terms of the debate at that time: "Discussion is usually based on the truisms that system cannot take the place of honesty and intelligence, that specialization can be carried too far, that driving is an undesirable feature of factory management, that the workmen should not be made into automata, that they should not be set working against each other's interests, that attention should not be centered exclusively upon men above the average of ability, that the factors of habit and prejudice should not be ignored, that no solution of economic problems is complete which ignores the problem of distribution, and that the desires and aspirations of the men toward self-government and democracy must be recognized. Most of these points are mentioned in the Report of the House Committee on Labor" (40). Despite the fact that the American Federation of Labor convinced Congress to outlaw taylorism in all public workplaces from 1912 to 1915, Daniel Nelson contends that those years saw a veritable "race to efficiency" in U.S. industry (83-5).

6. This was in keeping with Taylor himself, who often hinted that his organizational methods might be productively applied to social ends.

7. Among bibliographical sources on the subject suggested at the time were chapter 14 of Gilbreth (1909), Emerson (nd), and Blackford and Newcomb (1914).

8. For a compelling broader analysis of gender-specific cultural pressures in early twentieth-century French colonial Indochina, see Stoler.

9. Identical Vietnamese male and female educations were suggested only in economics, where it was argued that "girls' education should not differ . . .

from that of boys, since they are called to the same transactions" (Poirier, 269). However, the perceived Chinese Threat regularly caused this equality to modulate into a female advantage in statements such as "she alone will permit the annamite *[sic]* race to defend itself against the Chinese economic invasion" (269).

10. My emphasis. This classroom scene recalls the faux harem postcards by French photographers of the nineteenth and early twentieth centuries analyzed by Alloula. On his findings, the French male colonial visual domination of North African women begins with groups of veiled exotic women and culminates in individual nudes (prostitutes) in (staged) harem interiors. In contrast, in the literature on female education in Indochina, the male colonial gaze's conquest of native women begins with the isolated Vietnamese woman, who is seen as "nearly mistress of herself and easily accessible to the stranger" (Poirier, 266) and culminates in images such as Poirier's mastered, westernized Asian school girls. This discrepancy appears consistent with that between the French perception of the North African and Vietnamese populations.

11. Clearly, this group of native girls can be taken to figure a fully feminized, mastered, and taylorized Indochina; a textual realization of colonial stereotypes of Indochina's native people as model *colonisés* and of Indochina itself as the model colony.

12. Osborne cites Fournier (1937) as a textualization of this general colon fear of the Vietnamese as potential francocides.

13. After World War I, French colonial officials were therefore required to keep close track of the Vietnamese workers and soldiers who had returned from service in France. The French colonial fear recalls the fear of white Americans after World War II that African-American soldiers may have been contaminated by the lack of apparent anti-Black racism in Paris or by Communism. For more on the U.S. case, see Stovall.

CHAPTER 4

1. Similarly Mascolo: "From the end of the war, I was scandalized that I had not tried to scream out when I found myself next to people wearing the yellow star in the metro. I had allowed it, in sum, in my stupidity, my insensibility, I had admitted it like one admits frequenting the invalids, accident victims, like one admits a misfortune" ("Itinéraire," 36).

2. On the jacketback of Edgar Morin's *Autocritique,* the 1959 editor explains: "All attempt to become conscious calls for a psychoanalytic return to oneself, an 'auto-critique,' that is, a certain share of autobiography."

3. To reconceive language as negativity, Kristeva looks to previous thinkers on this subject. Beginning with Hegel, she finds an account of negativity as that which is heterogeneous to the categories of thought and logic. She considers his account insufficient, however, because it fails to think negativity outside

the bounds of thought, a failure that causes it to erase negativity altogether. In search of a materialist extension of negativity, Kristeva turns to Lenin, where she finds negativity construed as the objective law of the natural and social worlds. She does not espouse Lenin's position fully either, however, for failing to retain the negativity Hegel located within thought, she believes, he ends up subjecting the subject "as a unit, to the social and natural processes" (*Revolution,* 113). Finally, Kristeva finds in Freud's account of negativity "the very movement of heterogeneous matter, inseparable from its differentiation's symbolic function" (113). Without forgetting Hegel or Lenin, she elaborates with Freud her conception of language as the concrete form of negativity (heterogeneity) and the freedom of the subject.

4. One gain in Kristeva's semiotic over its Freudian unconscious and Lacanian imaginary forebears is that she dissociates it from the metaphysical and the natural and associates it instead with the historical, social, and cultural. In contrast, early theorists often linked the unconscious to the "id," a notion Groddeck developed in response to patients' sense of acting on impulses beyond their control: "'It shot through me,'" people say; 'there was something in me at that moment that was stronger than me' *[C'était plus fort que moi].*" Groddeck took these statements as evidence that "what we call our ego behaves essentially passively in life"; that "we are 'lived' by unknown and uncontrollable forces"; that "man is animated by the Unknown, that there is within him an 'Es,' an 'It', some wondrous force which directs both what he himself does, and what happens to him. The affirmation 'I live' is only conditionally correct, it expresses a small and superficial part of the fundamental principle, 'Man is lived by the It.'" Freud's 1920-23 revision to the psychic topographies developed the "id" in an inverse direction. Using the term as he believed Nietzsche also had to signify "whatever in our nature is impersonal and, so to speak, subject to the natural law," he defined the id as the "great reservoir" of instinctual energy and libido. At that time, Freud reduced the separation of the instinctual/biological and the psychic: where boundaries had separated the "id" from the psychic, he stressed "the continuity in the evolution from biological need to the id, and from the id to the ego as well as the super-ego." On this view, "The ego is not sharply separated from the id; its lower portion merges with it," "the super-ego is not a completely autonomous agency"; it "merges with the id," and "the id is 'open at its end to somatic influences.'" Freud understood the ego defenses to be engaged against that great instinctual reservoir, as if safeguarding human development from the merely instinctual (all citations, LaPlanche and Pontalis, 197-9).

5. For an insightful discussion of Duras's use of light, see Hill.

CHAPTER 5

1. Wright spent "hour upon hour trying to master the craft of fiction, experimenting with words, with sentences, with scenes; and with the help of

other novels or prefaces after he had found grammar books and style manuals quite useless, he tried patiently to make his writing jell, harden, and coalesce into a meaningful whole" (Fabre, "Beyond," 48-9). Similarly, Mascolo recalls Duras working "for at least twelve or fifteen years, in the greatest anguish before the act of writing, with an extraordinary scrupulousness [*scrupule*]. During all of these years of writing unsure of itself, from this lack of assurance, she ended up finding a style, a language of her own" (*IP*, 39). Thus it may well have been for her as Houston A. Baker, Jr., has it for Wright, that the "fight for survival in early life [may have] contributed to the success of [her] early works."

2. As has been noted by Ki Chung Kim and others, James Baldwin perceived the fact that Wright did not develop a positive notion of what humans might or ought to be as a failure and a weakness, rather than as a political necessity and revolutionary ethical value, as Duras, Mascolo, and the others at the rue Saint-Benoît would have construed it.

3. Keenly interested in psychoanalysis, Wright took part in psychiatrist Frederic Wertham's study on writers and free association in spring 1946. Together, they opened a free juvenile psychiatric clinic, the Lafargue Clinic, in Harlem (Fabre, *Unfinished*, 292). For more on the founding of the Lafargue Clinic, see (Wright, "Psychiatry"; Wertham).

4. It works, then, as Camus's anticolonialist position (in Sorum's definition) insisted that it must not (chapter 1, n2).

5. Suzanne's temptation to go the city with M. Jo in exchange for the diamond (and, we understand, her sexual favors) recalls Zora Neale Hurston's *Jonah's Gourd Vine*, which Duras could have read in French by fall 1944. Although Hurston's Mehaley loves an already married man, she settles for a second man, Pomp, because he promises to take her far away from their poor U. S. South countryside in exchange for her thus prostituted future.

6. I am indebted to Peter Van Rossum for bringing this song to my attention.

7. This *Un Barrage* scene shocked male readers from 1950 to at least the early 1970s. Where Cismaru, for instance, claimed that her "shocking" and "even more shocking" (42) *political* narratives "detract from the central plot and distract the reader" (43), he was outraged by the gender politics in this scene of sexual initiation. Reading it as "a self-debasing display of [Agosti's] belief in a personal unworthiness to possess such a beautiful girl as Suzanne" (45), he rushed to his fellow man's defense: "It is not in the robust, self-assured, girl-chaser character that [Agosti] has to consider himself inferior to or undeserving of any girl's favor" (45). In her English translation, Briffault resolves Duras's ambiguity in a way that works as surely, if more subtly, to safeguard Agosti's male pride. Indeed, she removes both the ambiguity and revolutionary promise from Duras's phrase, "il avait essuyé le sang qui avait coulé le long de *ses* cuisses" (343) by translating it as "[he had] wiped the blood that ran down *his* thighs" (270; my emphases).

CHAPTER 6

1. For my reading of *Eden Cinéma*, see Winston.
2. See also Ollier's groundbreaking work on Linda Lê, which played a crucial part in the development of my own thinking about her work and its relation to Duras.
3. Sebbar's title suggests its own self-positioning vis-à-vis Duras, whose well-known collection *Les Yeux verts* appeared two years earlier.
4. In 1992 *Indochine* won the National Board of Review Award for the Best Foreign Language Film. In 1993 Catherine Deneuve was nominated for an Academy Award as Best Actress and *Indochine* won the Oscar for the Best Foreign film (France). In 1993 it was nominated for a César in the category of Best Director. That same year, it won Césars for Best Actress, Cinematography, Production Design, Sound, Supporting Actor. In 1993 it also won the Golden Globe for Best Foreign Language Film and the Goya Award for Best European Film. In 1994 it won the U.S. Political Film Society award in the category "democracy" and was nominated for the award in the category "human rights." *The Lover* fared much less well. It was nominated for an Oscar for best cinematography in 1993; it won a César for best musical score. *The Scent of Green Papaya* won the Camera d'or at Cannes in 1993, a 1994 César for the Best New Director of a Feature Film. Submitted by Vietnam for the Academy Award in Best Foreign Film, it received the nomination but did not win.
5. As it is internalized in Duras's subsequent corpus, the cat provides one trace of her competitive constraint to respond to the hegemonic terms of her own critical corpus. The cat would reappear in her work, most notably in the late 1970s Aurélia Steiner stories, where it stands starving and meowing in the park outside the room in which one narrator writes. At a time when Duras was making her angriest public statements against the mindless "autisms" of organized (rationalized) thought and politics, including the PCF, her narrator showed herself to be of no mind to nourish the cat.
6. Funded by the French Service d'information et de relations publiques des armées, this propaganda film is available in English under the title *Prelude to Vietnam*. The early to mid-1980s rise in conservative representations of the French and U. S. Vietnam Wars helped pave the way for the later 1980s-early 1990s rise of feature films of colonial nostalgia. In the U.S. in 1983-1984, a battle broke out between left-wing and right-wing representations of Vietnam on public television airways. It began when war correspondent Stanley Karnow served as chief corespondent for a multiseries reconsideration of the U. S. Vietnam War and its legacy on PBS, titled *Vietnam: a Television History.* In 1984-1985 Accuracy in Media, Inc. produced and W. E. Crane directed a conservative counter-representation to Karnow's series, television's *Vietnam*, which, narrated by Charlton Heston, included two parts—"The Real Story" (1984) and "The Impact of Media" (1985). In its marketing summary, this series presents itself as "a two-part documentary in

which military experts, scholars, journalists, and Vietnamese exiles present evidence of errors in the documentary *Vietnam: a Television History* and explore the influence of the American news media on public opinion and official policy during the Vietnam War." Such 1980s-early 1990s conservative documentary films worked as the colonial nostalgia films also did, to shore up the psychic structures of the Western (and French) colonial subject. Documentary films worked to persuade that subject on the conscious level; nostalgia films worked in the unconscious or imaginary register to solidify it.

7. For a photograph showing Lê with her hair arranged over one shoulder, see the table of contents page of *Paris Vogue* 795 (March 1999).

Works Cited

Adler, Laure. *Marguerite Duras.* Paris: Gallimard, 1998.

Ageron, Charles-Robert. *France coloniale ou parti colonial?* Paris: Presses Universitaires de France, 1978.

Alloula, Malek. *The colonial harem.* Translated by Myrna Godzich and Wald Godzich. Minneapolis: University of Minnesota Press, 1986. Originally published as *Le Harem colonial: images d'un sous-érotisme.* France: Garance, 1981.

Alphant, Marianne. "Duras à l'état sauvage." Review of *L'Amant,* by Marguerite Duras. *Libération,* 4 September 1984.

Althusser, Louis. "Ideology and Ideological State Apparatuses (Notes Toward an Investigation)." In *Lenin and Philosophy and Other Essays.* New York: Monthly Review Press, 1971.

Anderson, Benedict. *Imagined Communities: Reflections on the Origin and Spread of Nationalism.* London: Verso, 1983.

Andrea, Yann. *Cet amour-là.* Paris: Pauvret, 1999.

Andrew, Dudley. "René Clément." In *International Dictionary of Films and Filmmakers-2; Directors,* edited by Laurie Collier Hillstrom. 3rd ed. Detroit: St. James, 1997, 172-74.

Anglemont, Edouard d'. Review of *Indiana,* by George Sand. *La France littéraire* 4 (November 1832): 457. Cited in Naomi Schor, Introduction to *Indiana,* by George Sand. Translated by Sylvia Raphael. Oxford: Oxford University Press, 1994.

Annaud, Jean-Jacques. *L'Amant.* Illustré par les photos de Benoît Barbier. Paris: Grasset, 1992.

Annaud, Jean-Jacques. "L'Amant." Interview with Pierre Billard. *Le Point* 1008 (11 January 1992): 50-55 (60-65).

Antelme, Monique. "Jorge Semprun n'a pas dit la vérité." *Le Monde,* 8 July 1998, 11.

Antelme, Robert. *The Human Race.* Translated by Jeffrey Haight and Annie Mahler. Malboro, Vermont: Marlboro Press, 1992. Reprint, with foreward by Edgar Morin. Evanston: Marlboro/Northwestern University Press, 1998. Originally published as *L'Espèce humaine.* Paris: La Cité Universelle, 1947; Reprint, Paris: Editions Gallimard, 1957, 1990.

Anzaldúa, Gloria. *Borderlands/La Frontera: The New Mestiza.* San Francisco: Aunt Lute Books, 1987.

"A propos de la conference de Hot Springs." *Le Monde,* 1 February 1945.

Argenlieu, Georges-Thierry d'. "L'Amiral d'Argenlieu inspecte la région de Mytho." *Le Monde,* last ed., 13-14 January 1946, 2.

Armand, Alain, Carpanin Marimoutou and Monique Severin, eds. *Figures de la littérature réunionnaise contemporaine.* Réunion: Comité de la culture de l'éducation et de l'environnement, 1988.

Armel, Aliette. *Marguerite Duras et l'autobiographie.* Paris: Le Castor Astral, 1990.

Aron, Robert, and Arnaud Dandieu. *Le cancer américain.* Paris: Rieter, 1931.

Assouline, P. *Albert Londres, vie et mort d'un grand reporter, 1884-1932.* Paris: France Loisirs, 1989.

———. *Gaston Gallimard: un demi-siècle d'édition française.* Paris: Balland, 1984.

———. *Homme de l'art: D.-H. Kahnweiler (1884-1979).* Paris: Balland, 1988.

———. *Monsieur Dassault.* Paris: Balland, 1983.

———. "La Vraie Vie de Marguerite Duras." *Lire* 193 (October 1991): 49-59.

Astre, Georges-Albert. "Un grand romancier noir: Richard Wright." Review of *Native Son,* by Richard Wright. *Fraternité* (10 October 1946): 3.

August, Thomas. *The Selling of the Empire: British and French Imperialist Propaganda, 1890-1940.* Westport, Conn.: Greenwood Press, 1985.

Bain, Chester Arthur. "The History of Viet-nam from the French Penetration to 1939 (Parts I-III)." Ph.D. diss., American University, 1956.

Baker, Jr., Houston A. "Racial Wisdom and Richard Wright's *Native Son.*"In *Long Black Song: essays in Black American literature and culture,* edited by Houston A. Baker, Jr. Charlottesville: University of Virginia Press, 1972.

Bauër, Gérard. "Un littérature noire: Richard Wright et René Maran." *Paris-Presse.* 10-11 August 1947.

Beauvoir, Simone de. *Les Mandarins.* Paris: Editions Gallimard, 1954.

———. *Lettres à Nelson Algren (1947-1966).* Paris: Editions Gallimard, 1977.

———. *The Second Sex.* Translated by H. M. Parshley. New York: Knopf, 1953. Reprint, New York: Vintage Books, 1989. Originally published as *Le Deuxième Sexe.* Paris: Editions Gallimard, 1949.

Bergain, Michel. "Duras, de gauche complètement." *Globe,* 13 January 1987.

Blackford, Katherine M. H., and Mr. Arthur Newcomb. *The Job, the Man, the Boss.* New York: Doubleday, Page and Co., 1914.

Blanchot, Maurice. Review of *Le Square,* by Marguerite Duras. *Nouvelle Revue Française* 39 (1 March 1946): 492-503.

———. "The Painfulness of Dialogue." In *The Siren's Song: Selected Essays,* edited by Gabriel Josipovici, translated by Sacha Rabinovitch, 199-206. Brighton, Sussex: Harvester Press, 1982.

Boschetti, Anna. *The Intellectual Enterprise: Sartre and Les Temps Modernes.* Translated by Richard C. McClearly. Evanston: Northwestern University Press, 1988. Originally published as *L'impresa intelletuale (Sartre e Les Temps Modernes).* Edizioni Dedalo, 1985.

Bourdieu, Pierre. "Champ du pouvoir, champ intellectuel et habitus de classe." *Scolies. Cahiers de recherches de l'Ecole normale supérieure* 1 (1971): 7-26.

———. "Champ intellectuel et projet créateur." *Les Temps modernes* 246 (November 1966): 865-906.

————. *In Other Words: Essays Toward a Reflexive Sociology.* Translated by Matthew Adamson. Stanford: Stanford University Press, 1990.

————. *Outline of a Theory of Practice.* Translated by Richard Nice. Cambridge: Cambridge University Press, 1977. Originally published as *Esquisse d'une théorie de la pratique.* Genève: Droz, 1972.

————. *The Rules of Art: genesis and structure of the literary field.* Translated by Susan Emanuel. Cambridge: Polity Press, 1996. Originally published as *Les Règles de l'art: genèse et structure du champ littéraire.* Paris: Editions du Seuil, 1992.

————. Sociology in Question. Translated by Richard Nice. London: Sage, 1993. Originally published as *Questions de sociologie.* Paris: Editions de Minuit, 1984.

————. *The Political Ontology of Martin Heidegger.* Translated by Peter Collier. Oxford: Polity, 1991. Originally published as *L'Ontologie politique de Martin Heidegger.* Paris: Editions de Minuit, 1988.

Bourdieu, Pierre, and Jean-Claude Passeron. *The Inheritors: French Students and Their Relation to Culture.* Translated by Richard Nice. Chicago: University of Chicago Press, 1979. Originally published as *Les Héritiers: Les étudiants et la culture.* Paris: Editions de Minuit, 1964.

Bourin, André. "Panorama des Prix Goncourt." *Les Lettres nouvelles* (19 November 1959): 2-3.

Bousquet, Gisèle L. *Behind the Bamboo Hedge: The Impact of Homeland Politics in the Parisian Vietnamese Community.* Ann Arbor: University of Michigan Press, 1991.

Boyer, Robert. "Le taylorisme hier: présentation." In *Le Taylorisme: actes du Colloque international sur le taylorisme,* edited by Maurice de Montmollin and Olivier Pastré. Paris: Editions La Découverte, 1984.

Brauër, Gérald. "Auteurs noirs: Richard Wright and René Maran." *Paris Press,* 10-11 August 1947.

Brison, Danièle. "Duras, l'écrivain du silence." *Dernières Nouvelles d'Alsace,* 13 November 1984.

————. "La bonne nouvelle." *Dernières Nouvelles d'Alsace,* 13 November 1984.

Browne, Malcolm. *The New Face of War.* Indianapolis: Bobbs-Merrill, 1965.

Bulletin de l'Enseignement de l'Afrique Occidentale Française, 1933, no. 82.

Bulletin Officiel de l'Expédition de Cochinchine, part 3, 1862.

Butler, Judith. *Bodies That Matter: On the Discursive Limits of Sex.* New York: Routledge, 1993.

————. *Gender Trouble: Feminism and the Subversion of Identity.* New York: Routledge, 1990.

Buttinger, Joseph. *Vietnam: A Dragon Embattled.* Vol. 1. New York: Praeger, 1967.

————. *Vietnam: A Political History.* New York: Praeger, 1968.

Camus, Albert. *L'Etranger.* Paris: Gallimard, 1946. Reprint, Folio, 1957.

Carlton, Frank T. "Scientific Management and the Wage Earner." In *Scientific management; a collection of the more significant articles describing the Taylor system of management,* edited by Clarence Bertrand Thompson, 720-733. Cambridge: Harvard University Press, 1914. Originally published as preface to *Principes d'organisation scientifique des usines.* Paris: H. Dunod et E. Pinat, 1912.

"Ceci n'est pas une émeute." *Les Temps modernes* 77 (March 1952): 1537-1543.

Chow, Rey. "Is 'Woman' a Woman, a Man, or What?: The Unstable Status of Woman in Contemporary Cultural Criticism." *differences* 11.3 (1999/2000): 137-168.

"Chronologie des relations franco-vietnamiennes, 1945-1953." *Les Temps modernes* 93-94 (August-September 1953): 463-472.

Cismaru, Alfred. *Marguerite Duras.* New York: Twayne, 1971.

Cisneros, Sandra. *The House on Mango Street.* New York: Vintage, 1989.

Cixous, Hélène. "Sorties." In Cixous, Hélène and Catherine Clément. *La Jeune Née.* Paris: Union Générale d'Editions, 1975.

Clark, Sue Ainslee, and Edith Wyatt, *Scientific Management as Applied to Women's Work: Chapter VII in Making Both Ends Meet.* New York: The Macmillan Co., 1911. Reprinted in *Scientific management; a collection of the more significant articles describing the Taylor system of management,* edited by Clarence Bertrand Thompson, 807-834. Cambridge, Harvard University Press, 1914. Originally published as preface to *Principes d'organisation scientifique des usines.* Paris: H. Dunod et E. Pinat, 1912.

Clement, René. *France-Observateur,* 8 May 1958.

Cohen, Margaret. "Women and fiction in the nineteenth century." In *The Cambridge Companion to the French Novel: from 1800 to the present,* edited by Timothy Unwin, 54-72. Cambridge: Cambridge University Press, 1997.

Coindreau, Maurice-Edgar. *Aperçus de littérature américaine.* Paris: Editions Gallimard, 1946.

Colette. *Gigi.* Paris: J. Ferenczi & fils, 1945.

———. *Mitsou, ou, Comment l'esprit vient aux filles.* Paris: A. Fayard, 1929.

Colin, Paul. *Les Jeux Sauvages.* Paris: Editions Gallimard, 1950.

Copjec, Joan. *'India Song/Son nom de Venise dans Calcutta désert:'* The Compulsion to Repeat." In *Feminism and Film Theory,* edited by Constance Penley, 229-43. New York: Routledge, 1989.

Crowther, Bosley. Review of *Gervaise,* by René Clément. *New York Times,* 12 November 1957. Reprinted in *New York Times Film Reviews.* Vol. 3. New York: The New York Times and Arno Press, 1970, 3021-3022.

Cuisinier, Jeanne. "Détails." *Les Temps modernes* 18 (March 1947): 1115-1132.

Dannaud, Jean-Pierre. "Service Inutile." *Les Temps modernes* 18 (March 1947): 1095-1114.

De Gaulle, Charles. "Une déclaration du Général de Gaulle au sujet du projet de Constitution." *Le Monde,* 29 August 1946, 3.

Debord, Guy. *Guy Debord contre le cinéma.* Aarhus: Institut Scandinave de vandalisme comparé, 1964.

———. *La Société du Spectacle.* Paris: Bruchet/Chastel, 1967.

Delphy, Christine. *Close to Home: A Materialist Analysis of Women's Oppression.* Translated by Diana Leonard. Amherst: University of Massachusetts Press, 1984.

Devillers, Philippe. *Histoire du Viêt-Nam de 1940 à 1952.* Paris: Editions du Seuil, 1953.

Dirlik, Arif. "Place-Based Imagination: Globalism and the Politics of Place," Unpublished ms., n. d.

Drake, St. Clair, and Horace R. Clayton. "Black Metropolis." Translated by Catherine Le Guet. *Les Temps modernes* 11-12 (August-September 1946): 523-542.

Duhamel, Georges. *America the Menace; scenes from the life of the future.* Translated by Charles Miner Thompson. Boston: Houghton Mifflin, 1931. Reprint, New York: Arno Press, 1974. Originally published as *Scenes de la vie future: 30 bois originaux de Guy Dollian.* Paris, A. Fayard & Cie: 1934.

Duras, Claire de Durfort, duchesse de. *Ourika.* Paris: Chez Ladvocat, 1824.

Duras, Marguerite. *Abahn Sabana David.* Paris: Editions Gallimard, 1970.

———. *Agatha.* Paris: Editions de Minuit, 1981.

———. "Assassins de Budapest." *Le 14 Juillet* 1, 14 July 1958. Reprint, *Outside,* 88-91; *Le 14 Juillet,* facsimile reprint, edited by Daniel Dobbels, Francis Marmande, and Michel Surya. Paris: Lignes, 1990.

———. *Aurélia Steiner, Aurélia Steiner, Aurélia Steiner.* In *Le Navire night,* 115-136, 137-166, 167-200. Paris: Mercure de France, 1979.

———. *A Ernesto.* Boissy St Léger: François Ruy-Vidal et Harlin Quist, 1971.

———. *Un Barrage contre le Pacifique.* Paris: Editions Gallimard, 1950. Reprint, Folio 1991.

———. "Le Boa." *Les Temps modernes* 25 (October 1947): 613-622. Reprinted in *Des Journées dans les Arbres.* Paris: Editions Gallimard, 1954.

———. "Bon Plaisir de Marguerite Duras." Radio program produced by Marianne Alphant, with Denis Roche, Jean Daniel, Gérard Desarthe, Nicole Hiss and Catherine Sellers. France-Culture, 10 October 1984.

———. "Le Bureau de poste de la rue Dupin." Interview with François Mitterrand by Marguerite Duras, *L'Autre Journal* 1, 26 February-4 March 1986, 31-40.

———. '*Le Camion:* La dame des Yvelines." Interview by Dominique Noguez, produced by Jérôme Beaujour and Jean Mascolo. In *Marguerite Duras: Œuvres cinématographiques.* 43-52. Paris: Ministère des relations extérieures; Bureau d'animation culturelle, 1984. Videotape, Vidéothèque de Paris, Forum des Halles. Texts reprint, under the title *La Couleur des Mots: Entretiens avec Dominique Noguez autour de huit films.* Paris: Editions Benoît Jacob, 2001.

———. *Césarée.* In *Le Navire night,* 7-91. Paris: Mercure de France, 1979.

———. "Confucius et l'humanisme chinois." *France-Observateur,* 13 March 1958.

———. *Détuire, dit-elle.* Paris: Editions de Minuit, 1969.

———. "Duras dans le parc à amants." Interview by Marianne Alphant, *Libération,* 13 June 1991, 26-27.

———. "Ecrit pour tous les temps, tous les carêmes." *L'Autre Journal* 9, November 1985.

———. *L'Eden cinéma.* Paris: Mercure de France, 1977.

———. *Emily L.* Paris: Editions de Minuit, 1987.

———. "Les Feuilles." *Confluences* 5, no 8 (October 1945): 819-832.

———. "Les Fleurs de l'Algérien." *France-Observateur,* 20 September 1957.

———. *L'Homme atlantique.* Paris: Editions de Minuit, 1982.

———. *L'Homme assis dans le couloir.* Revised, Paris: Editions de Minuit, 1980.

———. "L'Homme nu de la Bastille." *L'Autre Journal* 4, April 1985.

———. "Ils n'ont pas trouvé de raison de me le refuser." Interview by Marianne Alphant. *Libération*, 13 November 1984.

———. *Les Impudents*. Paris: Plon, 1943. Reissued Paris: Gallimard, 1992.

———. "L'Inconnue de la rue Catinat." Interview with Herve Le Masson. *Le Nouvel Observateur* (28 September 1984): 92-93.

———. *India Song*. Paris: Editions Gallimard, 1973.

———. *'India Song:* La couleur des mots." Interview by Dominique Noguez, produced by Jérôme Beaujour and Jean Mascolo. In *Marguerite Duras: Oeuvres cinématographiques*, 21-31. Paris: Ministère des relations extérieures; Bureau d'animation culturelle, 1984. Videotape, Vidéothèque de Paris, Forum des Halles. Texts reprint, under the title *La Couleur des Mots: Entretiens avec Dominique Noguez; Autour de Huit Films*. Paris: Editions Benoît Jacob, 2001.

———. Interview by Bernard Pivot. *Apostrophes*, 28 September 1984.

———. Interview by Bernard Rapp. *Caractères*, 5 July 1991.

———. "An Interview with Marguerite Duras." Interview by Susan Husserl-Kapit. *Signs* 1 (1975): 423-34.

———. "Je suis pour les femmes de plus en plus." Interview by Jean-Claude Lamy, *France-Soir*, 20 June 1991.

———. "La Lecture dans le train." *L'Autre Journal* 9, November 1985.

———. *The Lover*. Translated by Barbara Bray. New York: Harper & Row, 1986. Reprint, New York: HarperCollins, 1992. Originally published as *L'Amant*. Paris: Editions de Minuit, 1984.

———. "Madame Dodin." In *Des Journées dans les Arbres*. Paris: Editions Gallimard, 1954.

———. "Les mains négatives." In *Le Navire night*, 106-114. Paris: Mercure de France, 1979.

———. *La Maladie de la mort*. Paris: Editions de Minuit, 1982.

———. "Marguerite Duras: Les hommes de 1963 ne sont pas assez féminins." Interview by Pierre Hahn. *Paris-Théâtre* 198 (1963): 32-37.

———. "Marguerite Duras." Interview by Alice Jardine. Translated by Katherine Ann Jensen. In *Shifting Scenes: Interviews on Women, Writings, and Politics in Post-68 France*, edited by Alice J. Jardine and Anne M. Menke, 71-78. New York: Columbia University Press, 1991.

———. "Marguerite Duras: Non je ne suis pas la femme d'Hiroshima." Interview by André Bourin. *Les Nouvelles littéraires* (18 June 1959). Reprint in *Les Nouvelles littéraires* (5 January 1976).

———. *Marguerite Duras à Montréal*. Edited by Suzanne Lamy and André Roy. Montréal: Editions Spirale, 1981.

———. "Marguerite retrouvée." Interview by Frédérique Lebellay. *Nouvel Observateur* (24-30 May 1990): 59-63.

———. *Le Marin de Gibraltar*. Paris: Editions Gallimard, 1952.

———. "Mes amours, c'est à moi." Interview by Pierre Assouline. *Lire* 193 (October 1991): 58-59.

———. *Moderato cantabile*. Paris: Editions de Minuit, 1958.

———. *Le Navire Night*. Paris: Mercure de France, 1979.

———. *Nathalie Granger*. Paris: Editions Gallimard, 1973.

———. "*Nathalie Granger:* La classe de la violence." Interview by Dominique Noguez, produced by Jérôme Beaujour and Jean Mascolo. In *Marguerite Duras: Oeuvres cinématographiques.* 11-20. Paris: Ministère des relations extérieures; Bureau d'animation culturelle, 1984. Videotape, Vidéothèque de Paris, Forum des Halles. Texts reprint, under the title *La Couleur des Mots: Entretiens avec Dominique Noguez; Autour de Huit Films.* Paris: Editions Benoît Jacob, 2001.

———. *The North China Lover.* Translated by Leigh Hafrey. New York: New Press, 1992. Originally published as *L'Amant de la Chine du Nord.* Paris: Editions Gallimard, 1991.

———. *Outside, papiers d'un jour.* Paris: Albin Michel, 1981. Reissued, Paris: P.O.L., 1984.

———. "La Perte de la vérité." *L'Autre Journal* 8, October 1985.

———. *Petits Chevaux de Tarquinia.* Paris: Editions Gallimard, 1953.

———. *La Pluie d'été.* Paris: P.O.L., 1990.

———. "'Poubelle' et 'la Planche' vont mourir." *France-Observateur,* 27 March 1958.

———. "Pourquoi le 14 Juillet?" *France-Observateur,* 24 July 1958.

———. Preface to *Le Square.* Paris: Editions Gallimard, 1995.

———. "La Princesse Palatine à Versailles. Portrait d'une famille royale." *L'Autre Journal* 10, December 1985.

———. *The Ravishing of Lol Stein.* Translated by Richard Seaver. New York: Grove, 1966. Reprint, New York: Pantheon, 1986. Originally published as *Le Ravissement de Lol V. Stein.* Paris: Gallimard, 1964.

———. "La Reine des Nègres vous parle des blancs." Interview with Sarah Maldoror. *France-Observateur,* 20 February 1958.

———. "Des samourai d'un type nouveau." *France-Observateur,* 27 February 1958.

———. "*Son nom de Venise:* Le cimetière anglais." Interview by Dominique Noguez, produced by Jérôme Beaujour and Jean Mascolo. In *Marguerite Duras: Oeuvres cinématographiques.* 33-41. Paris: Ministère des relations extérieures; Bureau d'animation culturelle, 1984. Texts reprint, under the title *La Couleur des Mots: Entretiens avec Dominique Noguez; Autour de Huit Films.* Paris: Editions Benoît Jacob, 2001.

———. *Le Square.* Paris: Editions Gallimard, 1955. Revised 1990.

———. "Sublime, forcément sublime Christine V." *Liberation,* 17 July 1985.

———. "Un train de mille cadavres qui nous arrive du Pakistan." *France-Observateur,* 6 February 1958. Reprint in *Outside, 195-197.* Paris: P.O.L., 1984.

———. "Usine." Conversation with Leslie Kaplan, *L'Autre Journal* 5, May 1985.

———. *La Vie tranquille.* Paris: Editions Gallimard, 1944. Revised, 1972. Reprint, Folio, 1988.

———. "Vous faites une différence entre mes livres et mes films?" Interview by Jean-Michel Frodon and Danièle Heymann. *Le Monde,* 13 June 1991.

———. *The War: A Memoir.* Translated by Barbara Bray. New York: New Press, 1986. Originally published as *La Douleur.* Paris: P.O.L., 1985.

———. *Yann Andrea Steiner.* Paris: P.O.L., 1992.

———. "Les Yeux verts." *Les Cahiers du cinéma.* Special Issue 312-313 (June 1980). Reissued, augmented, as *Les Yeux verts.* Paris: Cahiers du Cinéma, 1980 and 1987.

Duras, Marguerite [Marguerite Donnadieu], and Philippe Roques. *L'Empire français*. Paris: Editions Gallimard, 1940.

Duras, Marguerite, and Michelle Porte. *Les Lieux de Marguerite Duras*. Paris: Editions de Minuit, 1977.

Duras, Marguerite, and Xavière Gauthier. *Woman to Woman*. Translated by Katharine A. Jensen. Lincoln: University of Nebraska Press, 1987. Originally published as *Les Parleuses*. Paris: Editions de Minuit, 1974.

Ellison, Ralph. *Shadow and Act*. New York: Random House, 1964.

Emerson, Harrington. *The Scientific Selection of Employees*. New York: The Emerson Company, n. d.

"*Un Enfant du pays* par Richard Wright." Bourges *Le Berri républicain*. 25 July 1947.

"*Un Enfant du pays* par Richard Wright." *L'Avenir du Cannes et du Sud-Est*. 22-23 June 1947.

Ernaux, Annie. *Cleaned Out*. Translated by Carol Sanders. Elmwood, Illinois: Dalkey Archive Press, 1990. Originally published as *Les Armoires vides*. Paris: Editions Gallimard, 1974.

Erval, François. "Défense des prix littéraires." *Les Temps modernes* 98 (January 1954): 1295-1300.

Escoube, Lucienne. "Aucun film n'a jamais dépeint la vie des noirs dans les villes américaines', nous dit le romancier Richard Wright." *L'Ecran français* (19 November 1946): 12.

Fabre, Michel. "Beyond Naturalism?" In *Richard Wright*, edited by Harold Bloom. New York: Chelsea House Publishers, 1987.

———. Introduction to "Long Black Song." In *Richard Wright Reader*, edited by Fabre, Michel, and Ellen Wright. New York: Harper and Row, 1978. Reprint, New York: Da Capo Press, 1997.

———. *The French Critical Reception of African-American Literature: From the Beginnings to 1970*. Westport, Conn.: Greenwood Press, 1995.

———. *The Unfinished Quest of Richard Wright*. Translated by Isabel Barzun. New York: William Morrow and Company, 1973.

Fanon, Franz. *Black Skin, White Masks*. Translated by Charles Lam Markman. New York: Grove Press, 1968. Originally published as *Peau noire, masques blancs*. Paris: Editions du Seuil, 1952.

"The Foreman's Place in Scientific Management." In *Scientific management; a collection of the more significant articles describing the Taylor system of management*, edited by Clarence Bertrand Thompson, 395-404. Cambridge: Harvard University Press, 1914. Originally published as preface to *Principes d'organisation scientifique des usines*. Paris: H. Dunod et E. Pinat, 1912.

Foucault, Michel. *Surveiller et punir: naissance de la prison*. Paris: Gallimard, 1975.

Foucault, Michel, and Hélène Cixous. "A Propos de Marguerite Duras." *Cahier Renaud-Barrault* 89 (1975): 8-22.

Fouché, Pascal. *L'Edition française sous l'Occupation, 1940-1944*. Paris: Bibliothèque de la littérature française contemporaine de l'Université de Paris VII, 1987.

Fournier, Christiane. *Hanoi, escale du coeur*. Hanoi: Editions Nam-Ky, 1937.

Frankenberg, Ruth. *The Social Construction of Whiteness: White Women, Race Matters*. Minneapolis: University of Minnesota Press, 1993.

"French Without Tears." Review of *The Little Madeleine,* by Madeleine Henry. *Time* (9 February 1953): 102.

Gates, Henry Louis, Jr., and K. A. Appiah, eds. *Richard Wright: Critical Perspectives Past and Present.* New York: Amistad, 1993.

Gide, André. *Voyage in Congo.* Translated by Dorothy Bussy. New York: Penguin, 1986. Originally published as *Voyage au Congo.* Paris: Editions Gallimard NRF, 1927.

Gilbreth, Frank B[unker]. *Motion Study.* New York: Van Nostrand Co., 1911.

———. *Bricklaying System.* New York: M. C. Clark Publishing Co., 1909. Reprint, Easton, Penn.: Hive Publishing Co., 1974.

Gilroy, Paul. "Without the Consolation of Tears: Richard Wright, France, and the Ambivalence of Community." In *The Black Atlantic: Modernity and Double Consciousness.* Cambridge, Mass: Harvard University Press, 1993.

Girard, René. "Pride and Passion in the Contemporary Novel." *Yale French Studies* 24 (Summer 1959): 3-10.

Girardet, Raoul. *l'Idée coloniale en France de 1871 à 1962.* Paris: La Table Ronde, 1972.

Gordey, Michel. "Une Interview de l'écrivain Richard Wright: L'Amérique n'est pas le nouveau monde." *Les Lettres françaises* (10 January 1947): 1, 7.

Graef, Ortwin de. *Serenity in Crisis: A Preface to Paul De Man, 1939-1960.* Lincoln: University of Nebraska Press, 1993.

Gramsci, Antonio. *Selections from the Prison Notebooks.* Edited and Translated by Quintin Hoare and Geoffrey Nowell Smith. New York: International Publishers, 1971.

Greenberg, Clement. "L'Art américain au XXe siècle."*Les Temps modernes* 11-12 (August-September 1946): 340-352.

Guicharnaud, Jacques. "Woman's Fate: Marguerite Duras." Translated by June Beckleman. *Yale French Studies* 27 (Spring-Summer 1961): 106-113.

Hakutani, Yoshinobu. *Richard Wright and Racial Discourse.* Columbia: University of Missouri Press, 1996.

Hardy, George. *Une conquête morale: l'enseignement en A. O. F..* Vol. 11. Paris: A. Colin, 1917.

Hare, David. "Comics." Translated by Catherine Le Guet. *Les Temps modernes* 11-12 (August-September 1946): 353-361.

Harper, Michael. *Afterword: A film.* In *Debridement.* Garden City, New Jersey: Doubleday, 1973.

Hemery, Daniel. "Aux origines des guerres d'indépendance vietnamiennes: pouvoir colonial et phénomène communiste en Indochine avant la Second Guerre mondiale." *Le mouvement social* 101 (October-December 1977): 3-35.

Henrey, Mrs. Robert [Madeline] [Robert Henrey, pseud.]. *A Century Between.* New York: Longman, Green and Co., 1937.

———. [Robert Henrey, pseud.]. *The Foolish Decade.* London: Dent, 1945.

———. *The Little Madeleine.* London: Dent, 1951. Reprint in U.S., as *The Little Madeleine: the autobiography of a little girl in Montmartre.* New York: Dutton, 1953.

———. *Madeleine Grown Up: The Autobiography of a French Girl.* New York: Dutton, 1952.

────. *Madeleine Young Wife: the autobiography of a French girl.* New York: Dutton, 1954.

────. *Milou's Daughter, Madeleine: a sentimental journey to the south of France.* New York: Dutton, 1955.

──── [Robert Henrey, pseud.], trans. *Letters from Paris, 1870-1875.* London: J. M. Dent and Sons, Ltd., 1942.

Henriot, Emile. "La Vie littéraire." *Le Monde,* 20 December 1950, 7.

Heymann, Daniel, and Michel Frodon. "L'Amour du travail." *Le Monde,* 23 January 1992, 31.

Higgins, Lynn. *New Novel, New Wave, New Politics.* Lincoln: University of Nebraska Press, 1996.

Hill, Leslie. *Marguerite Duras: Apocalyptic Desires.* New York: Routledge, 1993.

Hoog, Armand. "The Itinerary of Marguerite Duras: (Or, From the Dangers of the American Novel to the Perils of the Abstract Novel, Without Mishap)." Translated by Gaston Hill. *Yale French Studies* 24 (Summer 1959): 68-73.

Hurston, Nora Zeale [Zora Neale]. "La calebasse de Jonas." Translated by Marcel Duhamel. *L'Arbalète.* Vol. 9. (Fall 1944). Excerpts originally published in *Jonah's Gourd Vine.* Philadelphia: J. P. Lippincott, 1934.

Huyssen, Andreas. *After the Great Divide: Modernism, Mass Culture. Postmodernism.* Bloomington: Indiana University Press, 1986.

"Indochine S. O. S." *Les Temps modernes* 18 (March 1947): 1039-1052.

"Indochine: L'oeuvre de M. Sarraut." *L'Asie française* 172 (January-April 1918): 38-41.

Iommi-Amunategni, Jean-Paul. "La Place de L'Amant." *Le Matin des Livres,* 13 November 1984, 25.

Irigaray, Luce. *Ce Sexe qui n'en est pas un.* Paris: Editions de Minuit, 1977.

────. *Speculum de l'autre femme.* Paris: Editions de Minuit, 1974.

────. "Women on the Market." In *This Sex Which is Not One.* Ithaca: Cornell University Press, 1977.

JanMohamed, Abdul. "Rehistoricizing Wright: The Psychopolitical Function of Death in *Uncle Tom's Children.*" In *Richard Wright,* edited by Harold Bloom. New York: Chelsea House Publishers, 1987.

Jardine, Alice, and Anne M. Menke. "Exploding the Issue: "French" "Women" "Writers" and "The Canon"? *Yale French Studies* 75 (1988).

Jardine, Alice. "Flash Back, Flash Forward: The Fifties, The Nineties, and the Transformed Politics of Remote Control." In *Secret Agents: The Rosenberg Case, McCarthyism, and Fifties America,* edited by Marjorie Garber and Rebecca L. Walkowitz, 107-123. New York: Routledge, 1995.

Kanapa, Jean. "Petit anthologie des revues américaines." *Poésie 47* 41 (November 1947): 115-133.

────. "Un 'nouveau' revisionnisme à l'usage des intellectuels." *L'Humanité,* 22 February 1954, 2.

Kaplan, Alice Yeager. *Reproductions of Banality: fascism, literature and French intellectual life.* Minneapolis: University of Minnesota Press, 1986.

Kelly, Gail Paradise. *Franco-Vietnamese Schools, 1918-1938: regional development and implications for national integration.* Ph.D. diss. Madison: University of

Wisconsin-Madison, Center for Southeast Asian Studies, Occasional Paper 6 (April 1982).

———. "Colonial Schools in Vietnam: Policy and Practice." In *Education and Colonialism*, edited by Kelly, Gail P., and Philip G. Altbach, 96-121. New York: Longman, 1978.

Kristeva, Julia. *Powers of Horror: An Essay on Abjection*. Translated by Leon Roudiez. New York: Columbia University Press, 1982. Originally published as *Pouvoirs de l'horreur essai sur l'abjection*. Paris: Editions du Seuil, 1980.

———. *Revolution in Poetic Language*. Translated by Margaret Waller. New York: Columbia University Press, 1984. Originally published as *La Révolution du langage poetique*. Paris: Editions du Seuil, 1974.

———. "La Maladie de la douleur: Duras." In *Soleil noir: Mélancholie et dépression*. Paris: Gallimard, 1987. Translated by Katharine A. Jensen under the title "The Pain of Sorrow in the Modern World: The Works of Marguerite Duras," in *PMLA* 102 (March 1984): 138-52.

Lacan, Jacques. "Hommage fait à Marguerite Duras, du *Ravissement de Lol V. Stein*." *Cahiers de la Compagnie Madeleine Renaud–Jean-Louis Barrault* 52 (December 1965): 7-15.

———"The Mirror Stage as Formative of the Function of the I as Revealed in Psychoanalytic Theory." 1936. In *Ecrits*. Paris: Editions du Seuil, 1966.

"Lady with a Lance." Review of *The Second Sex*, by Simone de Beauvoir. *Time*, 23 February 1953, 110.

Lange, Monique. "Marguerite Duras: *Un barrage contre le Pacifique*." Review of *Un Barrage contre le Pacifique*, by Marguerite Duras. *L'Observateur* 12, 29 June 1950, 19.

Laplace, Yves. "Le Goncourt du silence." *24 heures*, 13 Novembre 1984.

LaPlanche, Jean, and J.-B. Pontalis. *The Language of Psycho-Analysis*. Translated by Donald Nicholson-Smith. New York: W. W. Norton, 1973. Originally published as *Vocabulaire de la psychanalyse*. Paris: Presses Universitaires de France, 1967.

Le, Huu Khoa. *Les Vietnamiens en France: la dialectique de l'insertion-identité*. Ph.D. diss., University of Nice, 1983.

Lê, Linda. *Les Evangiles du crimes*. Paris: Julliard, 1992.

———. *Fuir*. Paris: La Table Ronde, 1988.

———. Interview by Bernard Rapp. *Caractères*. France 2, 24 April 1992.

———. *Un si tendre vampire*. Paris: La Table Ronde, 1987.

———. *Les Trois Parques*. Paris: Christian Bourgois, 1997.

———. "Vinh L." In *Les Evangiles du crime*. Paris: Julliard, 1992.

Lê, Thành Khoî. *Histoire de l'Asie du sud-est*. Paris: Presses Universitaires de France, 1959.

Lebovics, Herman. *True France: The Wars Over Cultural Identity, 1900-1945*. Ithaca: Cornell University Press, 1992.

Le Chatelier, Henri. "Preface to the French edition." In *Scientific management; a collection of the more significant articles describing the Taylor system of management*, edited by Clarence Bertrand Thompson, 842-859. Originally published as preface to *Principes d'organisation scientifique des usines*. Paris: H. Dunod et E. Pinat, 1912.

Lefebvre, Henri. *The Production of Space*. Translated by Donald Nicholson-Smith. Oxford: Basil Blackwell, Ltd., 1991.

Lefort, Claude. "Les pays coloniaux: analyse structurelle et stratégie révolutionnaire." *Les Temps modernes* 18 (March 1947): 1068-1094.

Léon, Antoine. *Colonisation, Enseignement et Education: Etude historique et comparative*. Paris: L'Harmattan, 1991.

Lévi-Strauss, Claude. *Les Structures élémentaires de la parenté*. Paris: Presses Universitaires de France, 1949.

―――"The Structural Study of Myth." 1955. Translated by Claire Jacobson and Brooke Grundfest Schoepf. In *Structural Anthropology*. New York: Basic Books, 1963. Originally published as *Anthropologie structurale*. Paris: Plon, 1958.

Lim-Hing, Sharon Julie. *Vietnamese novels in French: rewriting self, gender and nation*. Ph.D. diss., Harvard, 1993.

Lowe, Lisa. *Critical Terrains: French and British Orientalisms*. Ithaca: Cornell University Press, 1991.

Luccioni, Gennie [Lemoine-Luccioni, Eugène]. "Marguerite Duras et le 'roman abstrait.'" *Esprit* (July-August 1958): 73-76.

―――. *Partage des femmes*. Paris: Editions du Seuil, 1976.

―――. Review of *Le Square*. *Esprit* 234 (January 1956): 148-150.

Magny, Olivier de. Review of *Le Square*, by Marguerite Duras. *Les Lettres Nouvelles* (November 1956): 653-55.

Mallet-Joris, Françoise. *Le Rempart des béguines*. Paris: Julliard, 1951.

Malraux, André. *The Royal Way*. Translated by S. Gilbert. New York: Vintage, 1955. Originally published as *La Voie royale*. Paris: Editions Bernard Grasset, 1930.

Maran, René. *Bataouala*. Paris: Editions Albin Michel, 1921.

Marcus, Greil. *Lipstick Traces: a secret history of the twentieth-century*. Cambridge: Harvard University Press, 1989.

Marini, Marcelle. *Territoires du féminin: avec Marguerite Duras*. Paris: Minuit, 1977.

Marx, Karl, and Frederick Engels. *Manifesto of the Communist Party*. Peking: Foreign Language Press, 1975.

Mascolo, Dionys. *Autour d'un effort de mémoire: Sur une lettre de Robert Antelme*. Paris: Maurice Nadeau, 1987.

―――. "Autour de la rue Saint-Benoît: An Interview with Dionys Mascolo." Interview with Author. *Contemporary French Culture* 18, 2 (1994): 188-207.

―――. *Le Communisme: Révolution et communication, ou la dialectique des valeurs et des besoins*. Paris: Gallimard, 1953.

―――. *Lettre polonaise sur la misère intellectuelle en France*. Paris: Editions de Minuit, 1957.

―――. "Un itinéraire politique." Interview by Aliette Armel. *Magazine littéraire* 278, June 1990, 36-40.

―――, ed. [Jean Gratien, *pseud.*]. *Oeuvres choisies de Saint-Just*. Paris: Editions de la Cité universelle, 1946.

Mascolo, Dionys, Jean-Paul Sartre and Bernard Pingaud. *Du rôle de l'intellectuel dans le mouvement révolutionnaire selon Jean-Paul Sartre, Bernard Pingaud, Dionys Mascolo.* Paris: Eric Losfeld, 1971.

Masson, André. *The Transformation of Hanoi, 1873-1888.* Translated by Jack A. Yeager. Edited by Daniel F. Doeppers. Madison: University of Wisconsin-Madison, Center for Southeast Asian Studies, Occasional Paper, 8 (1983).

McConnell, Scott. *Leftward Journey: The Education of Vietnamese Students in France 1919-1939.* New Brunswick and Oxford: Transaction Publishers, 1989.

McCumber, John. *Time in the Ditch: American Philosophy and the McCarthy Era.* Evanston: Northwestern University Press, 2000.

Mehlman, Jeffrey. "Deconstruction, Literature, History: The Case of *L'Arrêt de mort.*" In *Proceedings of the Northeastern University Center for Literary Studies,* edited by Herbert L. Sussman. 2 (1984): 33-53.

Memmi, Albert. *Portrait du colonisé précédé du Portrait du colonisateur.* Corrêa: Buchet/Chastel, 1957.

Merceron, Jacques. "Richard Wright rencontre à Paris le premier metteur en scène qui s'intéresse à son oeuvre." *Libération,* 18 December 1946.

Messer-Davidow, Ellen. "Manufacturing the Attack on Liberalized Higher Education." *Social Text* 36 (1993).

Moi, Toril. "Appropriating Bourdieu: Feminist Theory and Pierre Bourdieu's Sociology of Culture." *New Literary History* 1991. Reprint in Moi, *What is a Woman?* Oxford: Oxford University Press, 1999.

———. *Simone de Beauvoir: The Making of an Intellectual Woman.* Oxford: Basil Blackwell, 1994.

———. *What is Woman? and other essays.* Oxford: Oxford University Press, 1999.

Molbert, Suzanne. "Noirs et blancs." *L'Arche* 23 (9 February 1947): 146-47.

Montesquieu, Charles de Secondat. *De l'esprit des loix.* 1748. Paris: Garnier-Flammarion, 1998

Montrelay, Michèle. *L'ombre et le nom: sur la féminité.* Paris: Editions de Minuit, 1977.

Morand, Paul. *Champions du monde, roman. Bois originaux en couleurs de Robert Lemercier.* Paris: J. Ferenczi, 1932.

Morin, Edgar. *Autocritique.* Paris: Julliard, 1959.

Moutet, Aimée. "La première guerre mondiale et le taylorisme." In *Le Taylorisme: actes du colloque international sur le taylorisme,* edited by Montmollin, Maurice de, and Olivier Pastré, 67-81. Paris: Editions La Découverte, 1984.

Mowrey, Peter C. *Award-Winning Films.* Jefferson, N. C.: McFarland, 1994.

Mus, Paul. *Viêt-Nam, sociologie d'une guerre.* Paris: Editions du Seuil, 1952.

N.... "Regard sur notre action politique en Indochine." *Les Temps modernes* 18 (March 1947): 1133-1149.

Nadeau, Maurice. "L'Art de ne rien conclure." *France-Observateur,* 6 March 1958, 104.

———. Review of *Un Barrage Contre le Pacifique,* by Marguerite Duras. *Combat,* 22 June 1950.

Nason, Richard W. Review of *This Angry Age,* Columbia/De Laurentiis film, dir. René Clément. *New York Times,* 26 June 1958. Reprint in *The New York Times*

Film Reviews. Vol. 3. New York: New York Times and Arno Press, 1970: 3065-3066.

Nelson, Daniel. "Le taylorisme dans l'industrie américaine, 1900-1930." In *Le Taylorisme: actes du colloque international sur le taylorisme,* edited by Montmollin, Maurice de., and Olivier Pastré, 51-66. Paris: Editions La Découverte, 1984.

Niranjana, Tejaswini. *Siting Translation.* Berkeley: University of California Press, 1992.

Noiriel, Gérard. *The French Melting Pot: Immigration, Citizenship, and National Identity.* Translated by Geoffroy de Laforcade. Minneapolis: University of Minnesota Press, 1996. Originally published as *Le Creuset français: histoire de l'immigration xix-xx siècles.* Paris: Editions du Seuil, 1988.

Nora, Pierre. *Les Lieux de mémoire.* Paris: Editions Gallimard, 1984-1991.

Norindr, Panivong. *Phastasmatic Indochina: French Colonial Ideology in Architecture, Film, and Literature.* Durham: Duke University Press, 1996.

Nourissier, François. "Complainte soixante-huitarde." *Le Figaro,* 24 January 1976.

———. "'L'Amant,' de Marguerite Duras." *Le Figaro Magazine,* 20 October 1984.

O'Brien, Tim. *The Things They Carried.* New York: Houghton Mifflin, 1990.

Ollier, Leakthina Chau-Pech. "Consuming Culture: Linda Lê's Autofiction." In *Of Vietnam: Identities in Dialogue,* edited by Jane Bradley Winston and Leakthina Chau-Pech Ollier. New York: Palgrave, forthcoming.

———. "Quand les métèques se mettent à écrire." Paper presented at the 1998 International Narrative Conference, Evanston, Ill., 2 April 1998.

Osborne, Milton. *Fear and Fascination in the Tropics: A Reader's Guide to French Fiction of Indochina.* Madison: University of Wisconsin-Madison, Center for Southeast Asian Studies, Occasional Paper 11, 1986.

———. "From Conviction to Anxiety: Reassessing the French Self-Image in Viet-nam." Flinders University Asian Studies Lecture 7, delivered 15 June 1976 at School of Social Sciences, The Flinders University of South Australia.

———. *The French Presence in Cochinchina and Cambodia: Rule and Response 1859-1905.* Ithaca: Cornell University Press, 1969.

Oulmont, Charles. "La vie étrangère en France: un Américain découvre l'Ancien Monde." *Le Spectateur,* 2 July 1946.

"Outdoor Snake Pit." Review of *The Seawall,* by Marguerite Duras. *Time,* 16 March 1953, 118-120.

Pastré, Olivier. "Attention: un taylorism peut en cacher un autre." In *Le Taylorisme: actes du colloque international sur le taylorisme,* edited by Montmollin, Maurice de, and Olivier Pastré. Paris: Editions La Découverte, 1984.

Paulino-Neto, Brigitte. "Inconvenante Linda Lê." *Paris Vogue* 795 (March 1999): 220-222, 269.

Peyre, Henri. "Contemporary Feminine Literature in France." *Yale French Studies* 27 (1961): 47-65.

Pham Van Ky, "L'Ogre qui dévore les villes." *Les Temps modernes* 14 (November 1946): 238-252.

Picon, Gaëtan. "Les Romans de Marguerite Duras." *Mercure de France* (June 1958): 309-314.

Piel, Jean. "Un vrai roman." *Critique* (December 1950): 270.

Pinkus, Karen. Private conversation with author, March 1999.

Poirier, M. "La politique d'éducation en Indochine: l'éducation de la femme annamite." *L'Asie française* 143 (February 1913): 265-270.

Pratt, Mary Louise. *Imperial Eyes: Travel Writing and Transculturation.* London: Routledge, 1992.

Prêtre, M. "L'enseignement indigène." *L'Asie française* (August 1912): 311-343.

Prévost, l'Abbe de. *Manon Lescaut: Histoire du chevalier des Grieux et de Manon Lescaut.* 1731. Reprint, Paris: Gallimard, 1972.

Proctor, Robert N. "Censorship of American Uranium Mine Eppidemiology in the 1950s." In *Secret Agents: The Rosenberg Case, McCarthyism, and Fifties America,* edited by Marjorie Garber and Rebecca L. Walkowitz, 58-75. New York: Routledge, 1995.

Programmes et Instructions de l'enseignement primaire. Paris, 1948.

Renan, Ernest. *Qu'est-ce qu'une nation?* In *Œuvres complètes,* 1, 887-906. Paris: Calmann-Lévy, 1947-1961.

Riding, Alan. "Like Acting and Love, Honor Suits Jeanne Moreau." *New York Times,* 13 January 2001.

Rimbaud, Patrick [Marguerite Duraille, pseud]. *Virginie Q.* Paris: Ballard, 1988.

Rochefort, Christiane. *Le Repos du guerrier.* Paris: Grasset, 1958.

Rolland, Jacques-Francis. Interview with author, 17 October 1991.

Rosaldo, Renato. *Culture and Truth: the remaking of social analysis.* Boston: Beacon Press, 1989.

Rosello, Mireille. "Discussions." In *Postcolonialisme & Autobiographie,* edited by Alfred Hornung and Ernstpeter Ruhe, series vol. 20. Amsterdam: Rodopi, 1998.

————. *Infiltrating Culture: power and identity in contemporary women's writing.* Manchester U. K.: Manchester University Press, 1996.

Ross, Kristin. *Fast Cars, Clean Bodies: Decolonization and the Reordering of French Culture.* Cambridge, Mass: MIT Press, 1995.

Rossignon, Christophe. "Interview with Christophe Rossignon." Interview by Michael Williams. *Variety* 371, 1 (11 May 1998): C24.

Rousseau, Jean-Jacques. *Du Contrat social ou, principes du droit politique.* 1755. Reprint, Paris: Serpent à plumes, 1998.

Rousseaux, André. "Richard Wright et la terreur noire." *Le Figaro littéraire,* 17 January 1948, 2.

Roy, Claude. "Le barrage des pacifiques." Review of *Un Barrage contre le Pacifique,* by Marguerite Duras. *Les Lettres Françaises* 318 (29 June 1950): 3.

————. "Sur Genet et Duras." *La Nouvelle Revue Française* 104 (August 1961): 311-314.

————. *Nous.* Paris: Editions Gallimard. Reprint, Folio, 1972.

————. "Pourquoi me tuez-vous?" *Europe,* 31 July 1948, 99-105.

Roy, Jean-Henri. "Un barrage contre le Pacifique." Review of *Un Barrage contre Le Pacifique,* by Marguerite Duras. *Les Temps Modernes* 58 (August 1950): 375-376.

————. "Correspondance." *Les Temps modernes* (March 1947): 1150-1152.

Sagan, Françoise. *Bonjour Tristesse.* Paris: Julliard, 1954.

Said, Edward. *Orientalism.* New York: Pantheon, 1978.

Salève, Robert. Review of *Un Barrage Contre le Pacifique*, by Marguerite Duras. *France-Observateur*, June 1950.

Sand, George. *Indiana*. 1832. Translated by Sylvia Raphael. Oxford: Oxford University Press, 1994.

Sarkozy, Nicolas. *Georges Mandel: Le moine de la politique*. Paris: Grasset et Fasquelle, 1994.

Sarraut, Albert. "La Propagande doît renaître dans l'instant même ou meurt l'Exposition." *Le Monde Colonial Illustré* 101 (1 January 1932): 4.

Sartre, Jean-Paul. *L'Etre et le Neant: essai d'ontologie phénoménologique*. Paris: Editions Gallimard, 1943.

———. "La littérature, cette liberté." *Les Lettres françaises* 15 (1944): 8.

———. *Les Mains sales*. Paris: Editions Gallimard, 1948.

———. *Les Mots*. Paris: Georges Braziller, 1964.

———. "Qu'est-ce que la littérature." *Les Temps modernes* 17 (February 1947): 769-805; 18 (March 1947): 961-988; 19 (April 1947): 1194-1218; 20 (May 1947): 1410-1429; 21 (June 1947): 1605-1641; (July 1947): 75-114.

———. *Réflexions sur la question juive*. Paris: P. Morihien, 1946.

Schor, Naomi. Introduction to *Indiana*, by George Sand. Translated by Sylvia Raphael. Oxford: Oxford University Press, 1994.

Schrecker, Ellen. *No Ivory Tower*. New York: Oxford University Press, 1986.

Sebbar, Leïla. *Shérazade: 17 ans, brune, frisée, les yeux verts*. Paris: Editions Stock, 1982.

Selous, Trista. *The Other Woman: feminism and femininity in the work of Marguerite Duras*. New Haven: Yale University Press, 1988.

Senghor, Léopold Sédar. Introduction to "Trois poètes négro-américains: Countee Cullen, Jean Toomer, Langston Hughes." *Poésie 45* 23 (February 1945): 32-33.

Serreau, Geneviève. "L'Adaptation de *Un barrage contre le Pacifique*." *Les Cahiers Renaud-Barrault* 52 (December 1965): 40-44.

Serreau, Geneviève. *Un Barrage contre le Pacifique*. Théâtre-Club, 6 January 1960.

Sherwood, John M. *Georges Mandel and the Third Republic*. Stanford: Stanford University Press, 1970.

Sorum, Paul Clay. *Intellectuals and Decolonization in France*. Chapel Hill: University of North Carolina Press, 1977.

Stack, Peter. "Scent of Green Papaya Wafts Over Romantic Saigon of '50s." *San Francisco Chronicle*, 25 March 1994.

Stepto, Robert B. "Literacy and Ascent: Black Boy." In *Richard Wright*. edited by Harold Bloom, 75-107. New York: Chelsea House Publishers, 1987.

———. "I Thought I Knew These People: Wright and the Afro-American Tradition." In *Richard Wright*, edited by Harold Bloom, 57-74. New York: Chelsea House Publishers, 1987.

Stoler, Ann Laura. "Carnal Knowledge and Imperial Power." Leonardo, Michaela di, and Robert N. Lancaster. *The Gender/Sexuality Reader*. New York: Routledge, 1997.

Stovall, Tyler. *Paris Noir: African Americans in the City of Light*. Boston: Houghton Mifflin, 1996

Tate, D. J. M. *The Western Impact: Economic and Social Change.* Vol. 2. *The Making of Modern South-East Asia.* Kuala Lumpur: Oxford University Press, 1979.

Les Temps Modernes Editorial Board. "Et Bourreaux, et Victimes." *Les Temps modernes* 15 (December 1946).

———. "La Mort a une couleur." *Les Temps modernes* 11-12 (August-September 1946): 575-576.

Thaddeus, Janice. "The Metamorphosis of Black Boy." In *Richard Wright: Critical Perspectives Past and Present,* edited by Henry Louis Gates, Jr. and K. A. Appiah. New York: Amistad, 1993.

Thiébaut, Marcel. "Parmi les livres." *La Revue de Paris* 54 (October 1947): 162-163.

Thompson, Clarence Bertrand. "The Literature of Scientific Management." In *Scientific management: a collection of the more significant articles describing the Taylor system of management,* edited by Clarence Bertrand Thompson, 3-48.

———. ed. *Scientific management: a collection of the more significant articles describing the Taylor system of management.* Cambridge: Harvard University Press, 1914.

"Tout Paris le dit." *Une Semaine dans le monde,* 4 January 1947.

Tran Anh Hung. "Portraying the rhythm of the Vietnamese soul; an interview with Tran Anh Hung." Interview by Alice Cross. *Cineaste* 20, 3 (Summer 1993): 35-37.

———. "The Cyclo Press Conference." Interview by Henri Behar, Film Scouts Interviews, Webcast Multimedia, Inc. (10 October 1995).

———. "Cyclo dans l'oeil du cyclone." Interview by Jean-Marie Dinh. *La Lettre d'Hermès,* 12, n. d.

Tran Duc Thao. "Sur l'Indochine." *Les Temps modernes* 5 (February 1946): 878-900.

———. "Les relations franco-vietnamiens. *Les Temps modernes* 18 (March 1947): 1053-67.

Truffault, François. "Notre techniramage." *Cahiers du Cinéma* 14, 84 (June 1958): 52-55.

Turim, Maureen. *Flashbacks in Film: Memory and History.* New York: Routledge, 1989.

Vian, Boris. "Norman Corwin." *Les Temps modernes* 11-12 (August-September 1946): 362-368.

Vircondelet, Alain. *Duras: Biographie.* Paris: Editions François Bourin, 1991.

———. *Marguerite à Duras.* Paris: Edition ˙1, 1998.

———. "Les Pistes brouillées." Interview by Pierre Assouline. *Lire* 193 (October 1991): 52.

Vittorini, Elio. *Uomini e no.* Milano: Bompiani, 1945.

———. "Une interview d'Elio Vittorini." By Dionys Mascolo [pseud., Jean Gratien] and Edgar Morin. *Les Lettres françaises* 27 June 1947. 1, 7.

Waller, Margaret. "Richard Wright." *New Letters* 38 (Winter 1971): 198.

Ward, Mary Jane. *The Snake Pit.* New York: Random House, 1946.

Warner, Marina. *Alone of All Her Sex: The Myth and Cult of the Virgin Mary.* New York: Knopf, 1976.

Weber, Eugen. *The Hollow Years: France in the 1930s.* New York: Norton, 1994.

Werth, Alexander. *France 1940-1955.* London: R. Hale, 1956.

Wertham, Frederic. "An Unconscious Determinant in *Native Son.*" *Journal of Clinical Psychopathology* 6 (July 1944): 111-115.

Williams, Michael. "Christophe Rosignon." Variety 371: 1 (11 May 1998), C24.

Winston, Jane. "Marguerite Duras: Marxism, Feminism, Writing." *Theatre Journal* 47 (1995): 345-365.

Wittig, Monique. "The Point of View: Universal or Particular?" *Feminist Issues* (Fall 1983): 63-69.

Wright, Gordon. "The Resurgence of the Right in France." *Yale French Studies* 15 (Winter 1954-1955): 3-11.

Wright, Richard. "Big Boy Leaves Home." Translated by Marcel Duhamel under the title, "Le Départ de 'Big Boy.'" *L'Arbalète* 9 (Fall 1944).

———. *Black Boy.* Translated by Marcel Duhamel as "Jeunesse noire." Parts 1-6, *Les Temps modernes* 16 (January 1947): 578-609; 17 (February 1947): 806-845; 18 (March 1947): 988-1031; 19 (April 1947): 1219-1275; 20 (May 1947): 1430-1472; 21 (June 1947): 1642-1678. Originally published as *Black Boy.* New York: Harper and Brothers, 1945. Reissued as *Jeunesse noire.* Paris: Editions Gallimard, 1947.

———. "Débuts à Chicago." Translated by J.-B. Pontalis. *Les Temps modernes* 11-12 (August-September 1946): 464-497.

———. "Fire and Clouds." Translated by Marcel Duhamel under the title, "Le Feu dans la nuée." Parts 1 and 2, *Les Temps modernes* 1 (October 1945): 22-47; 2 (October 1945): 291-391. Originally published as "Fire and Clouds," in *Uncle Tom's Children.* New York: Harper and Row, 1938.

———. Foreword. *Pan-Africanism or Communism,* by George Padmore, London: Dobs, 1956.

———. "Long Black Song." In *Richard Wright Reader,* edited by Ellen Wright and Michel Fabre, 257-286. New York: Harper and Row, 1978.

———. *Native Son.* New York: Harper and Brothers, 1940. Translated by Hélène Bokanowski and Marcel Duhamel under the title, *Un enfant du pays.* Paris: Albin Michel, 1947.

———. "Psychiatry Comes to Harlem." *Free World,* 12 (September 1946), 49-51. Reprinted, "Psychiatry Goes to Harlem," *Twice A Year* 14-15 (1946-1947): 349-354.

———. *The Outsider.* New York: Harper and Brothers, 1953.

———. *Uncle Tom's Children.* New York: Harper and Row, 1938. Translated by Marcel Duhamel under the title *Les Enfants de l'oncle Tom.* Paris: Albin Michel, 1946.

———. *White Man, Listen!* Garden City, New Jersey: Anchor Books and Doubleday, 1964.

Wylie, Philip. "Mom." Translated by Catherine Le Guet. *Les Temps modernes* 11-12 (August-September 1946): 319-339.

Yeager, Jack. *The Vietnamese Novel in French: A Literary Response to Colonialism.* Hanover: University Press of New England, 1987.

Zola, Emile. *Thérèse Raquin.* 1880. Reprint, Paris: Gallimard, 1994.

FILMS CITED

Allegret, Marc. *Please! Mr. Balzac.* Raymond Eger. 1957.

Annaud, Jean-Jacques. *The Bear*. Claude Berri for Renn Productions. 93 min. 1988.

———. *Black and White in Color*. Reggancs, S.F.P., Artco Film Productions with the Société Ivorienne de Production. 92 min. 1987.

———. *The Lover*. Claude Berri for Renn, Burrill, and Films A2. 115 min. 1992.

———. *The Name of the Rose*. Neue Constantin Film Produktion. 129 min. 1987.

Axel, Gabriel. *Babette's Feast*. A. S. Panorama Film International. 102 min. 1987.

Balaban, Bob. *Parents*. Parents Production-Vestron Pictures. Great American Films Limited partnership. 82 min. 1988

Preminger, Otto. *Bonjour Tristesse*. Columbia Pictures Corp., Wheel Production. 93 min. 1953.

Carné, Marcel. *The Adulteress*. Paris Film Productions, Lux Compagnie Cinematographique de France. 106 min. 1958.

Clément, René. *Au-dela des grilles (The Walls of Malapaga)*. Francinex, Italia Production Film. 90 min. 1948.

———. *Gervaise*. Agnès Delahalie Productions, Compagnie Industrielle et Commerciale, Silver Films. 114 min. 1957.

———. *Jeux interdits*. Silver Films, Mondex Films. 90 min. 1951.

———. *La Bataille du rail*. Coopérative Générale du Cinéma Français. 2379 meters. 1945.

———. *Les Maudits*. Speva Films. 105 min. 1946.

———. *Un Barrage contre le Pacifique* (also called *La Diga sul Pacifico*, *The Seawall*, and *This Angry Age*). Dino de Laurentiis, Columbia. 104 min. 1957; release 1958.

Decoin, M. *Folies Bergères*. Productions Jacques Roitfeld. 90 min. 1958.

Deplus, Stéphane. *Indochine: Prelude to Vietnam*. Le Service d'information et de relations publiques des armées, 56 min., 1984.

Duvivier, M. *Le Temps des assassins (Deadlier Than The Male)*. CICC (Films Borderie), S. N. Pathé Cinema, Films G. Agiman. 1957.

Duras, Marguerite. *Agatha, et les lectures illimitées*. Productions Berthemont, 1979.

———. *Aurélia Steiner*, dit Aurélia Melbourne. Films du Losange, Paris Audiovisuel. 30 min. 1979.

———. *Aurélia Steiner*, dit Aurélia Vancouver. Films du Losange, Paris Audiovisuel. 40 min. 1979.

———. *Césarée*. Films du Losange, Paris Audiovisuel. 11 min. 1979.

———. *Le Camion*. Cinéma 9, Auditel. 80 min. 1977.

———. *Les Enfants*. With Jean Mascolo and Jean-Marc Turine, 1985.

———. *L'Homme atlantique*, Berthemont, I.N.A., Des femmes filment. 42 min. 1981.

———. *India Song*. Sunchild Productions, Films Armorial, S. Damiani, A. Valio Cavaglioni. 120 min. 1975.

———. *Les mains négatives*. Films du Losange, Paris Audiovisuel. 16 min. 1979.

———. *Son nom de Venise dans Calcutta désert*, Benoît-Jacob, Cinéma 9. 118 min. 1976.

Gaspard-Huit. *The Bride Is Much Too Beautiful*. Production Générale de Films, Société nouvelle, Pathé Cinéma. 92 min. 1958.

———. *Maid in Paris*. Yvon Guezel, Continental Distributing. 1957.

————. *Paris Holiday.* Tolda Productions. 101 min. 1958.

Greenaway, Peter. *The Cook, the Thief, His Wife and Her Lover.* Allarts Enterprises, Erato Films, Films Inc. 124 min. 1989.

Hall, Stuart. "Race: The Floating Signifier." Edited, introduced, produced, and directed by Sut Jhally. 85 min. Northhampton, Mass: Media Education Foundation, 1996. Videocassette.

Jaglom, Henry. *Eating.* Judith Wolinsky. 110 min. 1990.

Jeudy, Patrick. *Récits d'Indochine: Chronique des journées de la bataille de Dien Bien Phu.* Text by Frédéric Mitterrand. In series *Destins,* Télévision 5. 52 min. 1987-1989.

Jeunet, Jean-Pierre. *Delicatessen.* Constellation Productions, Union Générale Cinématographique, Hachette Première et Cie. 96 min. 1991.

Kassovitz, Mathieu. *La Haine.* Lazennac, Le Studio Canal+, La Sept Cinéma. 95 min. 1996.

Lacombe, Georges. *The Light Across the Street.* United. 1957.

Lynch, David. *Dune.* Dino de Laurentiis, Universal. 137 min. 1967.

Minelli, Vincente. *Gigi.* Arthur Freed Productions/MGM. 117 min. 1957.

Oswald, Gerd. *Screaming Mimi.* Sage Productions, Columbia Pictures Corporation. 79 min. 1958.

Passolini, Pier Paulo. *Oedipus Rex.* Arco Film and Somafis. 2859 meters. 1967.

Rémy, Yves, and Ada Rémy. *La Mémoire et l'oubli.* 60 min. 1992.

Schoendoerffer, Pierre. *Dien Bien Phu.* 140 min. 1992.

Tran Anh Hung. *Cyclo (Xich lo).* Lazennec, Association rélative à la télévision Européenne, Canal Plus, SFP Cinéma, Lumière, Sept Cinéma, Salon Films (H. K.) Ltd., Giai Phong Film Studio. 120 min. 1995.

————. *Scent of Green Papaya.* Lazennac, SFP Cinéma, Sept Cinéma. 104 min. 1993.

Vadim, Roger. *And God Created Woman [Et Dieu créa la femme].* Iéna, U. C. I. L., Cocinor. 2509 min. 1956; U.S. release 1957.

————. *No Sun in Venice.* 1958.

Varda, Agnès. *Sans toit ni loi.* Ciné Tamris Films. 105 min. 1985.

Verneuil, Henri. *Lover's Nest.* Jacques Gauthier. 1957.

Wargnier, Régis. *Indochine.* Générale d'Images, BAC Films, Orly Film, Ciné Cinq, Paradis Film. 156 min. 1992.

Index

Books without an author's name are by Marguerite Duras. Within entries, Duras's name is abbreviated to MD. Entries under individual author's names have been reduced in favor of keyword organization to enhance clarity.

Abahn Sabana David, 66
abject (the), 97, 161, 165; abjection, 186; 218-19 n2; abject, defined, 117-19; desire, abjected, 139-40; Mandel, George, as, 17; and negativity, 148-49; place, the mother's (MD) as, 117-20. *See also Cyclo*
Adler, Laure, 41, 47
African American literary tradition: autobiography and bildungsroman, 157; and French literary tradition, shaping of, postwar; in *Les Temps modernes*, 24. *See also* Wright, Richard; Hurston, Zora Neale
"Afterward: A Film" (Harper), 158
Algren, Nelson, 33, 82
Alloula, Malek, 220
Althusser, Louis, 140, 158
Amant de la Chine du Nord, L', 76-77, 86-87
Amant, L' (Annaud), 86-88
Amant, L', 4, 70, 83, 149; capitalizing on, 71-73; collaboration and, 217 n8; ideology, colonial, and, 72; imaginary, colonial, and 71-72; prix Goncourt, 70-73. *See also Duras* (representation)
ambiguities: cultural, recoded as racial, 88; place, cultural, 186; of place, the mother's (MD), 119; positional (MD), 186; racial (MD), 6, 33, 55, 82. *See also* displacement
Anderson, Benedict, 3, 11, 187
Annaud, Jean-Jacques, 4, 76, 83-90
Antelme, Robert, 5, 29, 123, 147, 178

anticolonialism *v.* anti-imperialism, 213 n2
anxieties and fears: of infiltration and contamination, 100, 117; of contamination, comp to. U.S., 220 n12; French, of threats, perceived, to Empire, 214 n7; of U. S., 16-17, 22-24, 215 n9 ; *colon,* of Vietnamese, 220 n12
Anzaldúa, Gloria, 94, 96
Argenlieu, Georges-Thierry d', 22, 24
Aron, Raymond, 16
assimilation. *See also* women writers
Assomoir, L' (Zola), 44
Assouline, Pierre, 78-83
attente (waiting), 27-28, 135, 138, 147, 165-67
August, Thomas J., 15
autocritique, 133, 135, 220 n2
Aymé, Marcel, 18

Baker, Jr., Houston A., 222 n1
Baldwin, James, 222 n2
Barrage contre le Pacifique, 4, 12, 63, 76, 127, 160-82; aim, revolutionary, 162; and *Black Boy*, 160, 165; beating scenes, and Wright, 163, 169-70; Bible, the, and, 161; Camus and, 160; circulation, 167-68; consciousness, second mode, and revolution, 180-81; context, cultural, 30; dialectics, revolutionary, 189; ethics, communist, and, 149; gaze, 167; *Indiana* and, 161-62; laundering of, 31, 34; liberation, urban, treatment of, 158, 171; Malraux and, 160; mass media and ideology, treatment of, 158, 175-77; narrative voice, as response to *Les Temps modernes*, 27-28; *Native Son* and, 158; reception, 1950s French, 30-36; refusal, subject of, 178; review, *Time* magazine, 36-40; revolution and, 29; *(se) donner à voir*, and Vittorini, 168; tale, the mother's, 163-65; voice, narrative, 160; whiteness, construction

of, 172; world-hole, as. 162. *See also* cinema scenes; Hurston, Zora Neale

Barrage contre le Pacifique (Serreau), 41, 51, 59

Barrage contre le Pacifique (This Angry Age; La Diga sul Pacifico; The Seawall) (Clément), 44-48, 58, 83, 69, 71-72, 196; ambiguities (MD), displacement of, 46; competitive strategy, as, 45; MD novel, displacement of, 46; *Duras,* displacement, cultural, by, 49-50; reaction to, 49; *Duras,* resignification of, 46; *Duras,* replacement of, 47-48, 50; *Indochina,* displacement of, 46-47; reception, French, 44, 45, 47; reception, U. S., 44, 46; textual politics, *v.* MD's, 46-47.

Bataille du rail, La (Clément), 44

Bataille, Georges, 131, 139

battles, representational, 21-23; press, effect on, 23-24; 1980s *Duras,* 73-74; 1990s *Duras,* 76-92

Baudrillard, Jean, 48

Beauvoir, Simone de, 1-2, 12, 33-34, 37-38, 40, 56, 82, 184

Beggarwoman (character), 175; as *créole,* 63; and *Cyclo,* 205; and *la dame du Camion,* 69; and *Le Juif,* 69; marginalized, figure of, 69; and MD, 65, 69; *métisse,* as, 64; neolacanian feminism, 62; nomadism of, 62; pressures, immigration, and, 63; transformation, diasporic, of (Lê), 190; *Un Barrage,* 190; "Woman," 67. *See also errance;* Le Juif

Bérard, Léon, 213 n4

Berri, Claude, 83

Bert, Paul, 101

Bidault, Georges, 24

Black Boy (Wright), 5, 15, 26, 28, 162, 171, 179, 215 n13

Blanchot, Maurice, 19, 41, 71, 73, 76, 78

Blum, Léon, 17

"Boa, Le," 40, and Wright, 157-60

Bonjour Tristesse (Sagan), 36

bordercrossing: and anticolonial sentiment, 100; and anxieties, *colon,* 100-1; cultural, and collaboration, 191; geographical, and competitiveness (MD), 14-15; geographical, and education (Sarraut), 14, 101, 103; racial (Wright), 25; sanctions, 191. *See also* displacement

borderlands. *See* borderzone(s)

borderzone(s), 173; Anzaldúa on, 94; difficulties of, 96; place, women's

under patriarchy, 173; Rosaldo on, 94. *See also* ambiguity; displacement; marketing, consumer cultural; place, cultural; Rue Saint-Benoît, groupe de la; individual headings

Boschetti, Anna, 27, 215 n16

Bourdet, Claude, 32

Bourdieu, 6, 10, 14, 166, 184, 189

Bousquet, Gisèle L., 185

Butler, Judith, 218

Caldwell, Erskine, 32-33, 37, 55

call and response. *See* field, competitive

Camion, Le, 4, 69, 144

Camus, Albert, 160, 213 n2

Cancer américain, Le (Aron and Dandieu), 16-17

cannibalism: in "Le Boa," 135; cannibal, and writer, 193; culture, consuming, 197; eating the other, films on, 200-1; ethics, communist, 189, 193; in *Moderato cantabile,* 201; pastiche (Sartre), and, 189; relations, colonial, as (Lê), 188-90; relations, colonial, 178; relations, gender, as (MD), 176; relations, patriarchal, as (MD), 177; writing as, 188-89

Ce Sexe qui n'en est pas un (Irigaray), 67

censorship. *See* containment *under* critical practice; battles, representational; *Duras* (representation); *Wright* (representation)

Cet Amour-là (Andrea), 91

Cet Amour-là (Dyan), 91

Champions du monde (Morand), 16

Chow, Rey, 218 n13

cinema scenes: *attente,* 135; *Black Boy,* 158; consciousness, two modes, 136; *Cyclo,* 209-211; depersonalization, 136; "Fire and Clouds," 158-59; *métissage,* and, in *India Song,* 64; mirror scenes, MD, 135-38; mirror stage, Wright, 158-59; mythic original, in *La Douleur,* 145-46; *Native Son.* 158; *Son nom de Venise,* broken mirrors in, 65; subject, subversion of, 136-37; translation, revolutionary, in *Lol V. Stein,* 139-44; *Un Barrage,* 163, 175-78; "Long Black Song," 167

Cismaru, Albert, 222 n7

Cisneros, Sandra, 94

Cixous, Hélène, 59, 64, 68, 124, 137

Clement, René, 44, 58, 69, 71-72, 76, 83, 88, 196

Code of Public Instruction (Sarraut), 101, 109

Cohen, Margaret, 53
collaboration. *See L'Amant*
colon, defined, 95
colonial nostalgia. *See* nostalgia, colonial
colonialism, French; support, popular, of, 30; *v.* other colonies, 21-22
Commission de Contrôle de Paper, 218 n11
Comité des intellectuels contre la poursuite de la guerre en Algérie, 48
committed writing. *See* engaged literature *(littérature engagée)*
Communauté inavouable, La (Blanchot), 71
Communisme, Le (Mascolo), 5, 127. *See also* ethics, communist
compradorization: defined, 215 n14; practice, critical, as, 30
Contrat Social (Rousseau), 99
counterimage. *See* representations.
créole(s); 63-64, 82, 137, 150, 161-62, 184; in Sand, 63-64; MD as, 69, 82.
critical practice, 30, 33-35; anxieties, 55; containment and, 9-10, 12 (MD); extra-French cultural meanings, silencing of, 93; gendered, 222 n7; laundering, 22, 31, 72, 88; sexuality, treatment of, and colonial anxieties, 55; race, and political silencing, 25-27; strategies, 196; virilization, textual, and political silencing, 34-35, 60-1, 74-75, 80; feminization, textual, and political silencing 56-57, 60-68, 79-82. *See also* cannibalism; compradorization; *Duras* (representation); *Wright (representation)*
Cyclo (Tran Anh Hung), 202-12; ambiguities in, 208-9; French colonial legacy, treatment of, 205; imago alternatives and subject, of flash, 208; and *Indochina,* 204; and MD, 206-7; and Mascolo, 206-7, 210; and textbooks, colonial, 203, 210; and *Time,* 209; and true art (MD), 208; and *Un Barrage,* 206-8; and U.S., 205; Vietnam, as abjected, 207; and Wright, 206-7

Dandieu, Arnaud, 16
"Débuts à Chicago" (Wright), 29
De Gaulle, Charles, 22, 50, 53, 149
de Man, Paul, 78
Debord, Guy, 13, 48, 158
Déclaration sur le droit à l'insoumission, La, 56-57
Deplus, Stéphane, 210, 223-4 n6
Derrida, Jacques, 124
Des journées entières dans les arbres, 40

dialogue. *See* ethics, communist; Lê, Linda
diaspora, Francophone Vietnamese, 5; and *Indochina,* 183-84; engaged literature, displacement of, 183-85; immigrations, 185; marginalization, 185. *See* individual headings
Dien Bien Phu. *See* subject (the)
Dirlik, Arif, 215 n15
displacement, 4; ambiguities, colonial, to European (MD), 35; ambiguities, cultural, to sexual, (MD), 35; binaries and borders (Rue Saint-Benoit), 150; colonial categories, 193; colonial propaganda, 16-17; 22; colonial-era and MD, 4; cultural, 187; *Duras,* in creation of, 13; engaged literature, of (Wright), 12, 24-26; Francophone cultural, 5; French popular attention (Tran), 202; French popular attention, of *(Wright),* 26; French-Vietnamese negotiations, of, 24; Ho Chi Minh, of, 24; intertextuality and, 7; literary engagement, of, 184, MD's literary lineage, 60; memories, of (Tran), 196; of perception of MD, 30-6; origins of writing and politics (MD), 72; psychic (MD), 4; *Un Barrage's* cultural borders 55. *See also* ambiguities; critical practice; French colonial propaganda; shift, Francophone cultural; *Duras* (representation)
Doisneau, Robert, 215 n17
Dong Kinh Free School, 100-1
doubling. *See Indochina* (representation)
Douleur, La, 5, 58, 144-150, 168
Du côté de chez Swann (Proust), 35
Duhamel, Georges, 16
Duras (representation), 3, 25; ambiguity, 11; anxieties, colonial, repression of, 55-57; borders (MD), 67; connections, diasporic, silencing of, 12; conservative victory, 88; construction of, 9-10, 31-36, 54; containment and success, tool of, 4; containment, writers, women, 56; difference, silencing of, 11; displacement, colonial issues, 55; efficacy, 10, 13; efficacy, neocolonial, 197; emblematic feminine writer, function of, 56; eroticization of, 55-56; exclusions, 5, 12; feminine desire, 67; feminine sentimental, and political silencing, 79-81; forgetting, French cultural, of *Un Barrage,* 71; French colonial propaganda, 13; French cultural advantage of, 68; history of, 196-97; as ideological, 5; imagining,

cultural, and capitalist productivity, 11-12; and intertexts, silencing of, 60; Lacan's, 59-60; market appeal, 68; neocolonial, comp. to 1950s, 67; neolacanian sentimental, 66-68; nostalgia, colonial, 50, 72; object of desire, 67; product, dialectical, 4, 7, 10; social exclusions, 2-3; social sentimental, 54, 56; structure of, 11, 80-81; subfield, 10-11; tool of containment, 9; traits, 11; U. S. introduction, 53; *v.* MD, 56; veiling and deceit, 82-83; women writers, silencing of, 13. *See also* critical practice; place, cultural; battles, representational

Duras, Claire de Durfort, duchesse de, 64

Duras, Marguerite: aims, political and scriptural, 1; on bourgeois women, 62, 138-39; capital, symbolic, 59, 76; children and revolution, 73-74; cinema and social change, 77, 204; cinema, 49; collective intellectual work, 7; communism, 75-76, 78; critical history, 2-3; despair, political, 78; ethics, communist, and, 132-35; film, documentary, 48-49; genius, competitive, 27; Kristeva, and, 133-35; laughter, song, music, 62-63; place of writing and politics, 124-25; politics, 1930s, 17; position, political, 213 n2; Spectacle, 77; spring 1945 and, 124; subject, cartesian, and, 124; textual politics, 215-6 n19; textual project and *créole* (MD), 137; on theater, 48; true art, 77, 179; on writing, as autocritique, 133, on writing and politics, 75; on writing as translation, 77, 136; 135; writing, and revolution, 1; writing, and self-definition, 137; cultural background: "outside," 97-98; anorexia, cultural, 97; borderzones, removal from, 96; culture, Vietnamese, 96; education reforms 111; educational shaping of, 107-8, educational shaping, traces of, 108-9; identity, French cultural, 96-97; mother, 96; narrative of, 96; nomadism, 95; psychic position, 97; Sartre's, 95; social position, 94-95; student strikes, disconnect from, 120-23. *See also* education, French colonial (Indochina)

Duras: biographie (Vircondelet), 76, 78

Dyan, Josée, 91

Eden Cinéma, L', 69

education, French colonial (Indochina), 101-12; communication, native-*colon,* 111; Franco-Vietnamese schools, 101, 219 n3; native male, "feminization" of, 111; placing, 106-7, 109-12; planning, 101-9; political weapon, 101; propagandizing of, 13-14; *quoc ngu,* 99-100, 113; relation, imagined, to Indochina, 121-22; resistance, peasant, 108; stereotypes in, 107; taylorization, 101-9; textbooks, citation, anticolonial, of, 50; weapon, political, as, 101. *See also* Duras, Marguerite; education, native women

education, French: propagandizing of, 13-4, 213 n4; women, 1930s, 14

education, native women, 112-16, 219-20 n9; Chinese threat and, 113-14, 220 n9 ; Confucian moral code and, 113-14; discourse of, 112-13; male colonial gaze and, 115-16; place, mother's, in (MD), 116-120; placing, as, 113; silencing of, 112; struggle over, 112; substitution, logic of, 115-16;women, *colon,* role in, 115-16.

education, pre-French colonial, 98-100

elites, procolonial, 22, 215 n11

Ellison, Ralph, 170

Eluard, Paul, 168

Empire français, L' (Duras and Roques), 15, 17-18, 78, 200

engaged literature *(littérature engagée),* 20, 27-28; and female writer, 34; first-order response, 12, 25, 184; second-order responses 12, 27, 184; third-order response, 184-86. *See also* displacement; individual headings

Engels, Friedrich, 181-82

epiphanies. *See* Rue Saint-Benoît, groupe de la; World War II

errance, 139, 199; and Beggarwoman, 114; and cinema scenes (MD), 136; as *créolité,* 64; and *la dame du Camion,* 114; and epiphany, political, 175; and gaze, the, 174-75; and negativity, 141; transformation, postcolonial era, of 190, 193; and "woman," native, colonial image of, 114. *See also* othering

Espèce humaine, L', 29, 127

Esprit des lois (Montesquieu), 99

ethics, communist, 5, 128-32; and Debord, 130; dialogue and communication, 7, 125-30; difference, 132; grounding of, 129; and Kristeva, 131; language, use of, *v.* Sartre's, 129;

negativity, 131; post-structuralist thought, 124; power, 131; rational thought, 131, refusal, radical, 131, 178; revolution, 129-30, 131-32; sovereignty (Bataille), 131-32; subject of, and Lacan, 128; theory, as oppressive, 128-29; thought, inclusionary, 6; tragic, 132; utopia, 131, 142; on value, materialist, *v.* idealism, 148; weakness, human, 132. *See also* Rue Saint-Benoît, groupe de la; Mascolo, Dionys; Duras, Marguerite
Etre et le Néant, L' (Sartre), 174-75
exile, 88, 191

Fanon, Franz,184
feminist challenge, containment of. *See* writers, women
"Feuilles, Les," 55
field, competitive, 223 n5; call and response, and 9-10; critical practice and, 10; dynamics of, 10; literary, and pressures, social, 197; response, requisite, 10, 184-85; sites of response, 10
films, 1950s French, 45
"Fire and Clouds," (Wright), 170
First American Fifties, 3, 195
Fontainebleau, 17, 24
forgetting. See *Duras* (representation)
French colonial propaganda: defined, 15; discursive techniques of, 16; MD, 13-14; popular colonial desire, 14-16; prewar, 17; print press, effect on, 22-24; producer of (MD), 15; writing style (MD), 13, 15-16. *See also Duras* (representation); *Wright* (representation); *Indochina* (representation); *Proust* (representation)
Freud, Sigmund, 17-18, 221 n3-4
Fuir (Lê), 184, 188, 190-92; Beggarwoman, transformation of, 190-92; gaze, French racist, in 190-91; *Hiroshima mon amour* and, 191

Gallimard, Claude, 44
Gallimard, Gaston, 44
gaze, the, 143, 177; colonial elite, 195; male colonial, and women, Vietnamese, 220 n11; *v.* North African, 220 n10; racist French, 190-91; subversion, diasporic, of, 190-91. See also *Barrage contre le Pacifique;* education, French colonial (Indochina); *errance*

gender: equality, as impossible ideal (MD), 176. *See also* critical practice; *Duras* representation); Sand, George
general and particular (MD), 85, 131-35, 145, 162, 218 n13
Gervaise (Clément), 44-45
Gilroy, Paul, 170
Girard, René, 54
Graef, Ortwin de, 78
Gramsci, Antonio, 12
Guichardnaud, Jacques, 31, 53-54, 56, 59

habitus, 14, 156
Hahn, Pierre, 215 n17
Hakutani, Yoshinobu, 169, 171, 189
Hall, Peter, 60
Hall, Stuart, 33
Harper, Michael, 158
haunting. *See* World War II
Hegel, G. W. F., 220-1 n3
Henry, Madeleine ([Mrs.] Robert Henrey), 36-37, 40
Heptaméron, L' (de Navarre), 60
Hess, André, 213 n4
Heston, Charlton, 223 n6
Higgins, Lynn, 204
Hill, Leslie, 221 n5
Hiroshima mon amour (Renais), 85, 218 n13
Ho Chi Minh, 21, 24-6, 187, 202, 209-11
Hölderlin, Friedrich, 127
Holocaust. *See* World War II
Hoog, Armand, 53-54, 67
House on Mango Street, The (Cisneros), 94-95
Hugo, Victor, 61
human race, 147
Hurston, Zora Neale, 222 n5
Huyssen, Andreas, 35

icons, 9. *See also* individual headings
identity, shaping of. See place, cultural
ideology: knowledge and ignorance, 1, 8
Idt, Geneviève, 29, 57, 189, 201
Imagined Communities (Anderson), 3
imago (the). *See* cinema scenes
immigration, postcolonial: interest, intellectual, 66; and "place," stress on, 66; pressures of, 183; and subject, colonial, 197. *See also* diaspora, Francophone Vietnamese
imperial studies movement, 214 n4
India Song, 4, 60-65; and desire, colonial nostalgic, 61; and desire, object of, 64; and *Duras,* 61; ideology, French

colonial, and, 61-62; *Indiana* and, 60-66; rememoration, Proustian, and, 60; self-positioning in, 60.

Indiana (Sand), 60-65

Indochina (representation): Annaud and, 85-86; Clément's *Duras* and, 46; displacement, diasporic, of, 190; education, colonial, discourse of, 220 n11; MD and, 6, 70, 183; in MD, 6; nostalgia, colonial, and *Duras*, 57; *phantasmatic Indochina*, 4-5, 13, 25, 46-47, 106, 137, 187, 194, 197; doubling, diasporic, of, 189-90, 207; rewriting, consumer capitalist (Tran), 199; squatting of (Lê), 189; subject, colonial, contested, 189; subject, French colonial, 4, 6, 46; taylorism and, 106, 109

Indochina, French colonial: demographics, 95-96; divisions, colonial, in, 98, 117; misinformation on, 22, 215 n12; racism, anti-Chinese, in, 113-14; strikes, student-peasant, 118-19

Indochine (Prelude to Vietnam) (Deplus), 210, 221-22 n6

Indochine (Wargnier), 194, 197, 223 n4

interpellation, 146, 149, 158

intertextuality, 7

Irigaray, Luce, 66, 68, 74, 87, 124

irrational (the). *See under* consciousness, second mode

JanMohammed, Abdul, 157-58

Jardine, Alice, 3, 37, 74, 186-87, 195

Jeanson, Francis, 213

Jeux interdits (Clément), 44

Jew (the), in MD, 69, 146. *See also* Beggarwoman; nomadism; Mandel, Georges

Julliard, René, 35

Kaplan, Alice Yeager, 78

Karnow, Stanley, 223 n6

Kim, Ki Chung, 222 n2

King Missile, 169

Kristeva, 68, 124; abject, 97, 117-20; and ethics, communist, 131, 150; MD, 136; semiotic, 201, 221 n4; subject-in-process, 141; thetic, 19

Lacan, Jacques, 1, 31, 50, 59, 66-67, 87, 135, 167-68

laughter. *See under* consciousness, second mode

laundering. *See* critical practice

Le 14 Juillet, 50

Le Chatelier, Henri, 102-4

Lê, Linda, 183-94, 211; contamination and survival, 188-89; *Indochina, transformation of*, 187-94; *Indochina, squatting*, 189; place, cultural, on, 186; representations, French, of, 212. *See also* creative works, individual headings

Lemoine-Luccioni, Gennie (Gennie Luccioni), 31, 50-51, 59, 79

Lenin, V. I., 221 n3

Lévi-Strauss, Claude, 168

Lieux de Marguerite Duras, Les (Duras and Porte), 66, 69, 71, 192

Lieux de memoire, Les (Nora), 3-4, 66, 187

Lim-Hing, Sharon, 187

Lionnet, Françoise, 6

Litvak, Anatole, 39

Lover, The (Annaud), 4, 76, 83-91, 194, 197, 204, 218 n13, 223 n4

"Madame Dodin," 40

madness. *See under* consciousness, second mode

Magny, Olivier de, 31, 41, 215-16 n19

Mallet-Joris, Françoise, 36, 56

Malraux, André, 5, 83, 160

Mandel, Georges, 15, 17-18, 146, 197, 214 n4

Mangano, Silvana, 45-46, 50, 58

Manifesto of the Communist Party (Marx and Engels), 181-82

Manon Lescault, 141-42

marginalization. *See* place, cultural

Marimoutou, Jean-Claude Carpanin, 61

Marin de Gibraltar, Le, 40

Marini, Marcelle, 31, 66, 150, 216-17 n4

marketing: cultural, 71; domestic, borderzone (MD), 35-36; international (Beauvoir), 37-38, 40; international (Henrey), 36-37, 40; international, borderzone (MD), 39-40

Marx, Karl, 1, 10, 181-82

Mascolo, Dionys, 5, 19-20, 41, 50, 53, 123, 144, 147-49, 187, 210

mater dolorosa, 205

Maudits, Les (Clément), 44

Mauriac, François, 28

Mehlman, Jeffrey, 78

Memmi, Albert, 103

memory (cultural): forgetting and national historical narrative, 3; MD on, 68-69, 136, 141; and social change, 142

Menke, Anne M., 74

métissage, 6, 88, 97; cultural, recoded as racial, 88; and marketability, 88;

thinking in, 186; writing as (MD), 75. *See also* cinema scenes; Beggarwoman mimicry, 74, 87
mirror stage. *See under* cinema scenes
mission civilisatrice (civilizing mission), 22, 160-61, 202, 214 n7
Moderato cantabile, 97
Moi, Toril, 212 n3
Montesquieu, Charles de Secondat, 99-100
Montrelay, Michèle, 216-17 n4
Morand, Paul, 16
Moreau, Jeanne, 87-88, 91
Morin, Edgar, 20, 30, 34, 123, 200
Mouvement National des Prisionners de Guerre (et des Deportées), 145
music. *See under* consciousness, second mode

nachträglickeit (deferred signification), 17-18, 155, 210. *See also* place, cultural
Nadeau, Maurice, 31-32
Nathalie Granger, 199
Native Son (Wright), 157-58, 165; and Althusser, 158; and Debord, 158; mass media and racist ideology, treatment of, 158
Navarre, Marguerite de, 60
negativity, 177; Kristeva, 133-34; Lenin, 134; language as, 220-21 n3; Rue Saint-Benoît, 133-34. *See also* abject; *errance;* ethics, communist
neo-lacanian theorists, 50. *See also* individual headings
newspapers, French: subsidized, 214 n6
Nhu, Mme., 198
Nietzsche, Friedrich, 48, 131, 172
Niranjana, Tejaswini, 218 n13
Noguez, Dominique, 7, 66
nomadism, 62, 69, 95
Nora, Pierre, 3, 11, 66, 187
Nordinr, Panivong, 4, 13, 25, 47, 85, 137, 186-87, 194, 208-9
nostalgia, colonial: Annaud, 83; films of, 197, 223-4 n6. *See also Duras* (representation); *Indochina* (representation)*; India Song*
novels, colonial, 16, 215 n10

Ollier, Leakthina Chau-Pech, 223 n2
oppression, French colonial: *le juif* (MD) and, 155; nazism (MD) and, 154-55; textualization of (MD), 166-70; 172-73; and writing (MD), 155
Orientalism (Said), 66

Osborne, Milton, 117
othering, 175; and *errance,* 192; MD, 65, 217 n8, 218 n13; refusal of (Lê), 191. *See also* ethics, communist
Ourika (de Duras), 64

Partage des femmes (Lemoine-Luccioni), 50
Passeron, Jean-Claude, 14
pastiche, writing as: and homogeneity, cultural, 189; *Pluie d'été,* 201; Sartre and, 29, 57, 189, 201; *Scent of Green Papaya,* 201-2; "Vinh L.," 201; writing against, 201
Patterson, Orlando, 178
Paul et Virginie (Saint-Pierre), 65
Peau noire, masques blancs (Black Skin, White Masks), 12
Petits Chevaux de Tarquinia, 40
Peyre, Henri, 53-54, 56
Pham Quynh, 185
Pham Van Ky, 23, 29
Phan Boi Chau, 100
Picon, Gaëtan, 9-10
Piel, Jean, 35, 56, 67
Pinkus, Karen, 216 n22
place, cultural: Beauvoir, 2; borderzone (Lê), 6, 185-86; borderzone (MD), 97-98; borderzone (Tran Anh Hung), 185-86; deferred revision of (MD), 18; domestic *(Duras),* 13; Fanon's, 12; in Francophone shift (MD) 5-6, 12, 30; in Francophone shift (Sartre), 29-30; in Francophone shift (Wright), 5, 24-25; literary and cultural, *India Song,* 65; Mandel's, resignification of, 17; market, international *(Duras),* 11; MD's, 2, 4, 9, 19, 27, 120-23, 144, 184, 186; MD, resignification of, 155; memory, 66; nazism and colonialism (MD), 65; of colonial subject, 111, 172; "outside" (MD), 94, 122; "outside" (Wright), 156; postwar France (Wright) 25-26; postwar, Rue Saint-Benoît, 137; Sartre, 6; Spectacle *(Duras's),* 13; subaltern challenge (Wright), 13; Wright, 5-6. *See also* education, French colonial; marketing, consumer cultural;
placing. *See* critical practice; education, French colonial
plagiarism. *See* cannibalism
Poirier, M., 165, 205, 210
Porte, Michelle, 31, 66
position, cultural. *See* place, cultural
Pouvoirs de l'horreur (Kristeva), 97
Pratt, Mary Louise, 111, 172

Presley, Elvis, 4
privatization. *See Scent of Green Papaga*
Prix Goncourt, 217-18 n10
Proctor, Robert N., 1, 5, 8
propaganda, French colonial. *See* French
    colonial propaganda
Proust (representation), 54-55, 79
Proust, Marcel, 35, 37, 54
pulp fiction, 1950s, 35-6

race. *See Wright* (representation); critical
    practice
Ravissement de Lol V. Stein, Le, 4-5,
    57-58, 62, 120; depersonalization in,
    138-39, 141, 143, 146-47; doubling,
    and displacement, 57; ethics,
    communist, and, 137-44; object, of
    desire, colonial, and, 58; passing,
    cultural, and, 58; revolution in, 143-44;
    translation, failure of, 142; word-hole,
    the, and 58
Réflexions sur la question juive (Sartre), 174
Rempart des béguines, Le (Mal-
    let-Joris), 36, 56
Renais, Alain, 85
Repos du guerrier, Le (Rochefort), 56
representations: battles, 1990s *Duras*,
    76-77; consumer capitalism and, 197;
    counterimages (1950s), 37; desire,
    colonial, shaping of, 197; historical
    memory and identity, 3-4; *Scent of
    Green Papaya* as, 198; "woman," 2. *See
    also* battles, representational; critical
    practice; French colonial propaganda;
    World War II
Reproductions of Banality (Kaplan), 78
response, sites of. *See* field, competitive
Révolution du langage poétique, La
    (Kristeva), 131; and ethics, commu-
    nist, 133-34
Rimbaud, Patrick, 74
Rochefort, Christiane, 56
Rolland, Jacques-Francis, 18
Roques, Philippe, 15, 17-8
Rosaldo, Renato, 94, 96
Rosello, Mireille, 100
Ross, Kristin, 200
Rossignon, Christophe, 202-3
Rousseau, André, 25
Rousseau, Jean-Jacques, 99-100
Roy, Claude, 19, 25, 31-3, 82
Roy, Jean-Henri, 31-4, 55, 88, 215 n16
Rue Saint-Benoît, groupe de la, 3;
    borderzone(s), logic of, 127; camps, as
    limit situations, 126; clear language,
    145; communism of thought, 127;

depersonalization, 125-27; epiphany,
    149; human race, 125, 127;
    judiazation, 127; modes of thinking,
    126; PCF opposition, cultural, 128;
    primal scene, mythic, 125-28; progress,
    myth of, 127; project, revolutionary,
    137; subject, putting at risk, 126; *v.*
    Enlightenment (rational) thought
    126-27. *See also* ethics, communist

Sagan, Françoise, 36
Said, Edward, 66
Saint-Pierre, Bernadin de, 65
Sand, George, 4, 60-61
Sans toit ni loi (Varda), 192
Sarraut, Albert, 13, 101-7; rhetoric of,
    taylorist discourse, 104-5
Sarraute, Nathalie, 56-57, 68
Sartre, Jean-Paul, 20, 25, 27-29, 55, 95
saturation. *See* critical practice; French
    colonial propaganda
Scènes de la vie future (Duhamel), 16
Scent of Green Papaya (Mui Du Du Xanh)
    (Tran), 194-202, 223 n4; 1990s
    shaping of, 195-98; and desire,
    consumer, 202; and *Duras*, 198; and
    India Song, 199; and *Indochina*, 198;
    and modernization, social and racial
    differentiation in, 200; and silencing,
    198-99; and *Un Barrage*, 194-95;
    women, images of, and education,
    colonial, 199-200
Schor, Naomi, 61-62
Schrecker, Ellen, 3
Schuster, Jean, 50
scientific management. *See* taylorism
Sebbar, Leïla, 198, 223 n3
Second Sex, The (Le Deuxième Sexe), 2, 12,
    34, 37, 56; *Black Skins, White Masks*
    and, 213 n3
Selous, Trista, 2
semiotic. *See* Kristeva, Julia
Senghor, Léopold Sédar, 25
sentimental fiction, 35, 53-54
Serreau, Geneviève, 31, 41, 51, 59, 183
Service intercolonial d'information et de
    documentation, 214 n6
sexuality, feminine, discourse of, and
    repression of colonial anxieties, 55-57.
    See also critical practice; displacement;
    Duras (representation)
Seyrig, Delphine, 61
Shérazade (Sebbar), 189
shift, Francophone cultural, 4: and
    immigration, 12. *See also* displacement;
    place, cultural

Si tendre vampire, Un (Lê), 188
silencing. *See* critical practice; French colonial propaganda
simulacrum, 48. *See also The Lover* (Annaud), *L'Amant (*Annaud), Moreau, Jeanne
Snake Pit, The (Litvak), 39
Snake Pit, The (Ward), 37-39
Sociology in Question (Bourdieu), 10
Son Nom de Venise dans Calcutta désert, 4, 65-66, 144
"Sorties" (Cixous), 64
sovereignty, 139, 143. *See also* ethics, communist
Spectacle (the), 9, 13, 48, 158
Speculum de l'autre femme (Irigaray), 66
Square, Le, 40-41
Stoler, Ann Laura, 217 n8, 219 n8
Stovall, Tyler, 220 n12
style, search for, 221-22 n1
subaltern challenge, 12. *See also* engaged literature
subject (the): *Black Boy,* 158; cartesian, 1; cartesian, failure of, 124; challenge to (MD), 30; contradictions in, 19; destabilization of, 19, 29; Dien Bien Phu, postcolonial era threat of, 198; disruption of (MD), 27; Existentialist, 157; "Fire and Clouds," 157; of flash, transmodern-era, 200-1; French colonial, 13, 64; French colonial, and the abject, 118-19; French colonial; in trouble, 197; imprisoned (MD), 204, 207; *Native Son* and, 158; psychoanalytic (in Wright), 157; scholarly interest in, 66; subject, enslaved (Wright), 157-58, 169-70, 204, 207; refusal, radical, of, 178; subject-in-process, 141; subversion of, 203. *See also* cinema scenes; place, cultural

taylorism, 101-9; colonial extension of, 101-2; categories, colonial, redefinition of, 101-3; strikes against, 219 n5; war effort and, 103; discourse of, 104; phrenology and 106-7. *See also* education, French colonial; Le Chatelier, Henri; Sarraut, Albert
Television's Vietnam (Accuracy in the Media), 223 n6
Territoire du féminin avec Marguerite Duras (Marini), 66, 71
Third World, 183

Tran Anh Hung, 6, 184, 194-211; creative work, and social change, 204; refusal, radical, 211
Tran Duc Thao, 23, 28, 29, 122
Trois Parques, Les (Lê), 189-91, 207; blue house (MD), transformation of, 189-90; and *Indochina,* diasporic double of, 189, 207
Truffault, François, 44-5, 47

Uomini e no (Vittorini), 127

vampirism, colonial (MD), 189. *See also* cannibalism; plagiarism
Van Rossum, Peter, 222 n6
Varda, Agnès, 192
Vice-consul, Le, 60
Vietnam: a Television History (Karnow), 223 n6
Vietnamese culture and writing: competency, French *colon,* 95, 117; language and style (MD), 75, 82, 201
Vietnamese nationalists, 20-21; in *Les Temps modernes,* 23-24; *See also* World War II; Ho Chi Minh
"Vinh L." (Lê), 188-94; cannibalism, 188; chambre noire (MD), transformation of, 188; ethics, communist, and, 193; Vinh Long (MD), transformation of, 189, 192-3; *errance,* 193-94
Vircondelet, Alain, 11, 31, 51, 76, 78, 88; on MD, 79; symbolic capital, 78-9; and *Proust,* 79-83
Virginie Q. (Rimbaud), 74
Vitez, Antoine, 75-76
Vittorini, Elio, 127, 147, 168, 204

Walls of Malapaga (Au-delà des grilles) (Clément), 44
Ward, Mary Jane, 37
Warner, Marina, 205
Weber, Eugen, 14
women and transcendence: MD *v.* Beauvoir, 159, 178-79
women writers, borderzone: assimilation of, 56, 68; feminism, containment of, and, 56; French colonial exotic and, 57; French culture niche, and, 57; "French" "feminists," 68; MD, 34, 56, 72; Sarraute, 56; Yourcenar, 56
women, Vietnamese. *See* education, colonial; native girls'
Woolf, Virginia, 56
World War II—(Occupation, French discourse of): and nationalists,

Vietnamese, 20-21; response, Vietnamese, 21-22;--(spring 1945 disclosures): epiphanies, 19; haunting or obsession, 19, 127; and intellectual politics, 19-20; and intellectual work, redefinition of 20; and intellectuals, postwar, 18-19; interpretation of, 20; and writing (MD), 19; photos, and psychic displacement, 5. *See also* Ho Chi Minh; Vietnamese nationalists; French colonial propaganda; subject; engaged literature; Rue Saint-Benoît, groupe de la

Wright (representation): displacement, French popular attention, 26-27; and ideology, French colonial, 25; race, foregrounding, and silencing, politics, 5, 25-27; and *Les Temps modernes,* 26-27

Wright, Richard, 5-6, 12, 24-27, 29, 172, 178-79, 183, 184; American Communist Party, opposition, cultural, 156; communication, 156; community in, 156; ethics, communist, and, 222 n2; influence, formal on MD, 155; place, French literary, 157; politics, comp. to Rue Saint-Benoît, 156, 157-58; and psychoanalysis, 222 n3; response to (MD), 157-58; revolution, intellectual's role in, 156; writing, as "site of response," 156-55. *See also* cinema scenes; engaged literature; place, cultural; *Wright* (representation)

Yourcenar, Marguerite, 56-57, 68

Zay, Jean, 17, 213-14 n4
Zola, Emile, 44, 61